Spotted Lily

Also by Anna Tambour

Monterra's Deliciosa & Other Tales &

www.annatambour.net

Spotted Lily

ANNA TAMBOUR

prime

SPOTTED LILY

Copyright © 2005 by Anna Tambour

Cover Art:
The Artist by Norman Lindsay (Australian) c.1921,
copyright © Lin Bloomfield
Stomates on scouring rush, electron microscope view,
copyright © Dennis Kunkel Microscopy, Inc.
Book Design: Anna Tambour

All rights reserved. No part of this publication may be reproduced or transmitted in any form or by any means, electronic or mechanical, including photocopy, recording, or any information storage and retrieval system now known or invented, without permission in writing from the publisher, except by a reviewer who wishes to quote brief passages in connection with a review written for inclusion in a magazine, newspaper, broadcast, etc.

Published by Prime Books
www.primebooks.net

ISBN: 0-8095-4482-2 (HB)

ISBN: 0-8095-4483-0 (PB)

Cover and Text:
JAJ Graphics Pty Ltd
Sydney Australia

To Keith Brooke

I

'How many angels can dance on the head of a pin?' I asked.

'Six, I think. But, really, dear, this is not my field.'

'And I read somewhere that you turn us into sort of butterflies, and keep us in lacquered boxes with airholes, for transport.'

'I couldn't possibly comment on that.'

The Devil and I were sitting in my room, getting to know each other. He'd just been accepted in our sharehouse, 'Kitty is thirty-five dollars a week, no coffee or coffee substitutes or power drinks included' for the room next to mine, which was convenient for both of us.

It was Pledge Week, and we had to make the most of our time, but to do that, we had to get to know each other a little better.

I changed the subject.

'Why do you have Pledge Week?'

He examined the pressed tin ceiling, seeming to be considering whether he should answer. When I had almost forgotten my question, he answered. 'We have to. We lose too many to heaven these days.'

I knew I had to learn fast, but if he didn't start to make sense, this was not going to work. 'Come again?'

He cocked an eyebrow at me, then scratched himself behind somewhere and examined his nails. I tried not to look at his hands. As he wasn't forthcoming, I tried again. 'Isn't forever forever?'

'Ah . . . Yes, it is, in hell as it is on earth. But you make the rules, not we. And when you change your minds, you do manage to make an ado for us.'

'Like what? Please don't speak in riddles.'

'A regular omnium-gatherum of disorder, don't you know?'

I obviously didn't.

'A tumult, bother, hubbub, farrago of disorder. A regular huggermugger of change that we could well do without.'

I still didn't understand his words in this context, and with some of them, in any context. *What the hell* sprang to mind, but the words that came out were, 'Could you give me an example?'

He sighed.

'And could you please try to speak in more accessible language. We *are* in twenty-first century Australia here. You do keep up, don't you? You must have *some* Australians there.'

He bowed, a trifle condescendingly. 'I will try. Eh, you know, don't you read the papers? Don't you see what you're doing to us? It messes our morale something awful, you know.'

Although the 'Eh' was New Zealand, and he was trying a leeetle too hard, I couldn't quibble with his delivery. However, I was no closer to understanding. I think he must have thought me frustratingly dense, because his brows beetled, and I felt a prickle of sweat chill my back. He waved his hand, and in it appeared an *International Herald Tribune*. 'Look at this article,' he commanded, and threw the paper into my lap. It was singed but readable, and two days old.

I had no idea which article, so began to read down the first page, with rising panic.

'Oh dear. I do so apologize,' he said, in either an apologetic or a patronizing tone. It was so hard to read him. He grabbed the paper and opened it up, folded it neatly, and handed it back. 'Read that,' he pointed, 'and *do* try to think. Think about the after-effects.'

I *hate* it when someone talks to me like that. But I read.

> **ANGLONG VENG, Cambodia** In a case of Disneyland meets the killing fields, Cambodia's Ministry of Tourism is drawing up grandiose plans to upgrade the final stronghold of the Khmer Rouge into a million-dollar theme park.

I looked up, grinning. 'This is a joke, isn't it?'

He scowled, something I do not wish to see again. 'Do I look like a jokester,' he asked rhetorically. 'Read on.'

I did, all of it, including the part that said:

> "Pol Pot was a kind man and the only people killed during the Khmer Rouge time were Vietnamese spies," said Kim Syon, director of the Anglong Veng health center and son of a senior Khmer Rouge leader. "In the next 10 years people will begin to see the positive result of what Pol Pot did."

I wanted to wash. 'But this is gross.'

'No, love, it is normal,' the Devil said sadly. 'Do you know how many people we will lose, and do you know what our futures markets are saying about the new arrivals whom we had banked on for the next few years?'

Whom now. Was he having me on? Was the 'on' itself, the dangling preposition—snide? And... and *futures markets*. Wait a bloody minute. I thought of something Dad said whenever he met someone he thought was serving him potato skin and calling it bangers and mash: 'There's something crook in Muswellbrook.' I felt in this conversation with the Devil, like I was standing in Muswellbrook's main street as the main attraction—the town fool. It was about time I assert myself.

'You're shitting me,' I told him. 'Why are you trying to take advantage of my gullibility?'

His eyelashes fluttered. 'Oh dearie me. You asked, and I'm telling you how it is. I never lie.'

I shot him a look that would pierce most people of my acquaintance.

He looked blandly back. However, he *seemed* truthful.

But first, I had to take care of something that was making this getting-to-know all the harder. 'Would it be possible if you don't call me "dear" or "love"? In my culture, it *is* kind of a put-down.'

He might have been miffed, for he said, 'Miss Pendergast—'

We could not go on like this. 'Excuse me, but "Miss" isn't something I've been called since I was fifteen, by anyone with whom I wish to associate.'

He looked uncomfortable, and his brows began to move.

'My friends call me Angela,' I added quickly, and then wondered if that would offend. 'Would you mind calling me Angela? Or if you prefer, any other name would be fine. Like maybe Imelda. Someone you know.'

'Imelda?'

She was the only one who came to mind. Perhaps not dead yet.

I was wracking my brains when he coughed. I looked at his face and he smiled. 'Angela has a certain ring to it. Look, Angela. Think of Jefferson. Do you know Thomas Jefferson?'

'Yeah. Great American forefather. I don't imagine you would know him.'

He scratched somewhere I don't want to know again, this time with a smug grin. 'You obviously don't keep up. He's in our place now. Something to do with his love life.'

'You mean . . .'

'You decide, we abide, my, er . . . Angela. And we must keep abiding, which means that our populations are forever moving back and forth . . . and even disappearing and appearing again.'

'What do you mean?'

'Caligula? You *do* know of him?'

'I saw the movie.'

'Before the movie.'

I don't like to be reminded of what I don't know, but thought it best not to obfuscate. 'No.'

'You don't have to feel defensive. Caligula was a wonderful . . . what would you say . . . resident, for centuries, and then faded away. He's only recently come back to us. And with your attention span these days, it could be that we only have the pleasure of his company for one or two of your years.'

'Unless "Caligula" is re-released,' I mumbled, thinking.

'Come again?'

'Skip it,' I said, still thinking.

Suddenly a sharp tang of stink stung my eyes and jammed its choking fumes down my windpipe.

'I do demand respect,' he said.

'Sorry,' I mouthed. And I was. It was impossible to breathe.

He waved his hand and the worst evaporated.

'Sorry,' I repeated, to clear the air completely. 'I think I'm beginning to understand. 'But don't you gain from heaven, too?'

'Yes. Like I said, we've got Jefferson now, and the markets say we'll have Ghandi soon. You know Ghandi?' he added somewhat condescendingly.

'Yes,' I said, somewhat hurt.

'Well, it *is* hard to tell, you know.'

'The markets?' I had to ask.

I was secretly (though I couldn't let it show) happy that he looked at last, confused. 'Don't you know markets?' he asked. 'Futures trading? I thought you were all obsessed with it nowadays.'

'Not *all* of us,' I had to remind him. And all of a sudden I realized that for all his ultra-cool appearance, he was remarkably ignorant. Very gently and respectfully I asked, 'You don't know much about us, do you?'

'What do you mean?' he answered, and I was happy to smell that he wasn't offended.

'Well, here we are in a share house, and maybe you need some background on your housemates. Kate, remember—the one who chaired the interview today. She teaches ethnic studies at Sydney Uni, but she also inherited this house which was an investment from her North Shore parents who didn't think enough of her to leave it to her unmortgaged. So then there's us tenants who are also her housemates. Jason, who is going to bug you to death on your implants. Did you see his bifurcated tongue? It's very like yours.'

'I didn't notice. I was looking at his tattoos.'

'They're only part of his performance. He is a work in progress.'

The Devil yawned.

I tried not to gag. 'Do you mind if I light a cone?'

'What do you mean?'

'Incense. I like to burn incense. Little cones of scented natural dried stuff.'

He waved his hand graciously. 'Be my guest.'

I was crawling over to the little table with its celadon saucer and collection of Celestial Sky, thinking I should possibly change brand names tomorrow, when he grabbed my arm with a grip you might expect the Devil to have.

I thought I was about to die.

'It's not garlic, is it?'

'Never,' I managed to smile.

'I do apologize,' he said after a final little squeeze. I felt like a fruit. 'Did I hurt you?' he asked solicitously.

'Only a bit,' I lied. 'But what do you care?'

He shrugged, the same shrug as the bank manager gave me in some little French coastal town when he refused to cash my travellers cheque because my signature on it didn't exactly match the one on my passport.

'That reminds me,' I said (though it hadn't—I just needed to change the subject) as the scent of, I think it was called 'Bavaghindra' filled the room. 'Why do you have Pledge Week?'

'You aren't very perspicacious,' he observed. 'Pledge Week,' he said slowly as if I were a child, 'is necessary because, outside of our permanent population of futures markets operators, Pledge Week provides the only new source of once acquired, stable and permanent population that we have.'

The fingers of fate frolicked upon my back in a most disconcerting manner. I shrugged, which not only made me feel great and I hope, annoyed him in the same can't-admit-it way as his shrug did to me, but I think established my position far closer to the peer level necessary to our smooth working relationship.

He must have thought I still did not understand. 'When you come with me—'

'My coming is forever.'

We looked into each other's eyes for so long that I wondered whether it was a blink contest. Eventually I had to blink. 'That is correct,' he said. 'When you come with me, your coming is forever.' And his face changed from its solemnity, to one of Christmas cheer.

The actual elements of his smile, when I could steel myself to really look, were rather heart-flutteringly beautiful, and not at all like Jason's barracuda-shaped mouth of crooked, filed teeth. The smile of the Devil was broad, and his teeth looked good enough to be capped.

— 2 —

I WAS JUST THINKING I had enough mental meat to chew on for the moment when the Devil asked, 'Why did you Pledge?'

'Don't you know our motivations?'

The Devil was still sitting on my bed on the floor. He picked up a corner of my bedspread and leaned over to smell the sheets. I don't know why, but this embarrassed me. The laundromat was four blocks away, and since I didn't have anyone I was sleeping with at the moment, I hadn't bothered stuffing them into my backpack for a rather long time. He sniffed deeply. 'I am not the Omniscient, you know,' he said, smoothing the bedspread back into place.

I didn't ask about the Omniscient. This was already almost too much for one day.

He crossed his legs and rocked back. He had already looked pretty amazingly hung in those tight jeans—the major reason that Andrew had voted for him in the house meeting—but now he looked oddly enough, double hung.

I couldn't help asking, 'Do you have a tail?'

'Of course.' He adjusted his crotch and then scratched it, looking for all the world, just very very male-modellish. 'But I asked you,' he said. 'Why did you call?'

Now he had me confused. 'I didn't call. What call?'

'When you wrote to your Julie "I just want fame. Only that, and I wouldn't mind it in a week, and at this point I don't give a shit what I write."'

I could feel a flush climbing my face. 'You have read my emails?'

'We only read mail when it relates to us.'

'But I never mentioned you at all.'

'But you did,' he said, reminding me for a moment of Miss Waldenmere in first form.

'But please, I don't mean to be rude, but I did not.'

The left side of the Devil's lip rose as if caught by a fishhook. 'Angela, my dear—'

I hoped my anger was not showing, but Jeesus, I yearned to pound him into fishpaste.

'Angela,' he sighed, in a maddening display of put-upon tolerance. 'Your undertext *reeked* of the appeal for me to save you.'

The books piled all over the floor did not help me one bit. I glanced at the top one on the nearest pile: *The Bestseller*. It leered at me.

'And when I arrived this morning, what did you do?' he needled, in a maddening tone of reason.

I thought back. Sunday morning. The day of the interviews for the new housemate. There had been a number of calls already, and we knew that the kitchen would be full. So tedious, but if I didn't attend, I wouldn't have a vote, and then I could get a housemate-from-hell on the other side of the wall. So I had groaned and crawled out of bed. I had then thought of the other duty of my day: to produce something. Anything. And that made me look forward to the house meeting, in preference.

I remembered what I did next. Check my email, in which there was a letter from Julie telling me about how she has this new idea for a screen play and how she is going to begin writing it. And then I remembered my reply to Julie. And then I remembered smelling a smell that made me check the extension cord, and then I remembered finding it just fine, but still there was that smell, and then I saw this person in the corner.

'I remember,' I said to him.

I remembered more.

'What the fuck are you doing in my room!' I hissed at the person, not wanting to yell in case he was a sleep-deprived spunky-looking overnighter of Simone's who had just strayed to the wrong room from the loo downstairs. Simone always liked exhibitionists, and this one looked just her type. Very sexy, but in a narcissistic way. A great head of hair, but I do remember thinking that if he really wanted the horns to show, he should shave himself bald, though maybe he thought that was common. I was just thinking of telling him to get out and back to Simone's bed, when he spoke.

'Are you interested in developing your true potential?' I remember him—the Devil—asking, and then I remember to my shame, that I answered 'yes', though upon reflection, this is the worst come-on line I have ever heard.

I was mind meandering when the Devil dragged me back to the here-and-now. 'When I explained to you who I was, you didn't fidget or scream, or run out of the room, or jump out of the window, did you?'

I thought back. 'I guess not.'

'Have you thought about why?'

I was thinking, when he interrupted. 'I'll tell you why,' he said, cracking his knuckles one by one. 'You—and I mean all of you—never truly think of the future. Only of what you want now... and you think the future can, I think your phrase is, "go to the Devil", but again, you don't mean it.'

'Don't mean it?'

'You don't think it will come. Not when it is what you don't want. At least when it relates to yourself.'

I thought about my credit card.

'Then you've answered your own query,' I observed, as he hadn't repeated his question about my motivation for wanting him, or not being frightened about doing a deal with him when it came right down to the deal itself.

He bent and eased the laces on his thick black boots. 'You were very creative,' he said 'about getting me into the house.'

'What? The Australian War Memorial communications officer who is on stress leave, with your lifestyle-discrimination case pending in the Federal Court?'

'Yes, that. I could never have thought of that.'

Perhaps he was flattering me. Perhaps not. 'You need to know cultural stuff, to be able to have the right cover.'

'So true,' he crooned, and I wasn't sure why. 'And the name.'

'Your name?'

'Yes.'

I was unaccountably pleased. 'You like it?'

'Quite.'

'Brett Hartshorn does kind of roll off the tongue,' I admit that I bragged. 'And with respect, your ideas...' and then I ran out of words—'sucked' seemed suddenly, ineloquent.

But there was one question that had to be answered before we could really establish a working relationship. 'Why are you here for the week?'

He opened his bootlaces even more, and sighed. 'Quite frankly,' he said, 'a holiday.'

This was something I had never read about. 'The Devil... you... take holidays?'

'I need to keep in touch.'

'Don't you know what's going on all the time?'

'Do you?'

'Of course not.'

'The deuce you say!' he grinned, and his chin bristled with five-o'clock shadow. 'Well, I don't either. You must stop thinking of me as omniscient.' A thought seemed to strike him. 'Think of me as a construct. Does that help?'

He even pronounced it as CON-struct. For one wonderful and awful moment, I thought: are all the philosophy professors dead? But anyway, this was getting too deep for me. He was incontrovertibly the Devil, and he was sitting on my bed, the only soft sitting place in my room, and I was cross-legged on the floor a metre away. I had more questions. But first: 'Uh, I don't know how to put this, but what do I call you?'

Now he was confused. 'Can't you guess?'

I hadn't a clue. So many names came to mind. Mister Devil (sounding like a drink), Beelzebub, the Evil One, the Tempter, the Prince of Darkness, His Satanic Majesty, plain old Satan.

But none of them seemed right. Besides, they were all hard on my tongue. For comfort, I would have preferred what he would have been called where I grew up, if he'd rolled into town: Beez, Evo, Maj, or even Horny. And then there were the other names that were just part of Bunwup's Saturday night crowd: Ugly (handsomest bloke in town), Boozer (the parson who came to the pub and drank orange squash), and of course, the ever common Blue, for redheads.

The Devil interrupted this train of going-nowhere thought. 'I was always partial to "The Angel of the Bottomless Pit", he said. 'Until you called me Brett.'

He smiled that wide smile of his.

'So, Brett,' I continued, rather inordinately pleased. 'Why do you come up here — or is it down?'

'It's more like over, he said, stretching himself full length on the bed. 'I like to get a feel for things during Pledge Week, and then we always have our pledgers chaperoned by someone, as it were, throughout the week.'

'Why?'

He plumped my pillow and shoved it under his head. 'Trust. And getting the job done.'

This was confusing all over again. I remembered all the instances I'd read about the time being up and the person being dragged off to hell, or shoved in the Devil's collecting box and stuffed in his pocket. 'I thought a deal is a deal with you.'

'It is,' he said, 'but we've got competition. You must know of our competition? And besides, you . . .' And here he bowed and waved his hand in a gallant swashbuckle of a flourish. 'I don't mean to impute— but you in a more generic sense—don't always play straight. We prefer not to let you go once you've signed.'

That made sense. Once, in response to a radio station's pledge drive that had some story that made me cry, I rang the station and pledged. This reminded me.

'And besides,' he said. 'About that award-winning best-seller that you're going to write, that's going to win you fame . . .'

'Yes?' Suddenly I felt all over again that thrill of signing the contract, only hours ago.

'Who's going to write it?'

I panicked as the whole vision fractured. 'Me?'

His raised his eyebrows so high, his horns moved. 'Not a word, my silly worrier,' he said, and I know I should never use the word *soothingly*, but he did say it that way.

I was trying to figure out how he was going to coerce anyone really good to write it when he pointed to his chest. And then he smiled not only soothingly, but rather egotistically. I didn't care. After five years of everyone asking *When is it coming out?* I was off the hook. I could just go to work and come home, and in a short time, only a hell's week, the book would be done and I would be . . .

The room swam with the smell of success, mixed with Celestial Sky.

I felt alive of an aliveness that I had never felt. In one week (I hadn't asked about the details of what this meant exactly, or read the contract that closely, as it had seemed rude at the time), anyway, it was hard to put all these thoughts in coherent order (which had always been one of my problems)—there would be me, the finally-famous writer of some book (unnamed as of yet). My whole body thrilled (I could *feel* somewhere—probably my intestines—effervesce with joy). The book—my book that had eluded me for bloody *years*—this book that I'd talked about writing for *years* but never specified, would finally be written, holdable, read by others, translated, quoted, and plagiarized— and would be ghost-written by the Devil himself, 'Brett Hartshorn', the best words of fiction I ever thought up.

3

I woke in a panic—the contract.

It was on some sort of parchment—signed in my blood. When I had asked for a copy for myself, he told me there were no duplication services in hell, nor carbon paper, and that if I were unhappy, I could tell him then and there and he would rip it up and return 'from whence I came' immediately. He held the document with his hands poised to rip it from end to end.

'Yea or nay,' he demanded.

I assumed there was no cooling-off period.

His hands moved in opposite directions, stretching the parchment.

'Yea!'

But now, I remembered—how long would I have to enjoy my success? I hadn't looked.

The big luminous hand on my watch pointed to 2, and somewhere near my desk, paper rustled and then fell silent as a Sydney cockroach the size of a Medjoul date flew from it, to land on my pillow with a thud.

Launching myself out of bed, I threw the pillow at a wall, pulled on pants and shirt and socks, and left my room. I tapped on his door just loud enough for him to hear if he were awake.

'Yes,' he answered immediately.

'It's Angela here. Could I please come in?'

'By all means.'

I entered, and this was the first time I had been in the room since Callum, the previous housemate, had lived here. Outside of a table and chair and a mattress without sheets, there was nothing else besides the Devil himself and—by the head end of his mattress, a black bag that looked like what doctors must have once carried, and a small round-topped trunk that was either black or very old, either metal or wood or some kind of skin, and if it had handles, I surely couldn't see them, but various wing-like projections stuck out all over it.

He was lying on the bed with his hands behind his head.

'Oh!'

'Do I offend you?' he asked.

I thought about this. 'Nah. I wasn't prepared, is all.'

He spread his knees and smiled. 'I don't carry jahmies.'

'Not many people wear them nowadays,' I said, pulling over the chair.

He rolled over on his side and began playing with his tail. Was this a technique? If so, I was having none of it.

'Can I please look at the contract?' I said ever so coolly.

'Do you like my tail?' he asked, finding my eyes and I admit, holding them in his gaze.

'Very, but is it possible for me to just look at the contract?'

'I'm glad. No, actually. It is against the rules.'

Oh, so this is how it was to be. I needed to clutch something, so wrapped my arms around my waist and tore my eyes away from his.

Trying to gaze out the window, I asked, 'Don't you make the rules?'

'I am merely the administrator,' he said smoothly, running his tail back and forth over his lips.

The hair on the end moved and shone like a shampoo ad's. It was silky and black and long and as beautiful as our cattle's tails back at Wooronga Station. I used to love combing Boofhead's before a show. But never before had my whole life been at stake.

'I have to know,' I said—quite firmly—'just how long I have.'

He sighed. 'You never think it's long enough.'

'But how long? I don't remember seeing.'

'It didn't say.'

'What?!'

He sat up. 'Be reasonable, and look at it from our point of view, Angela.'

My molars squeaked from clenching. 'Alright,' I said, opening my mouth and taking a yogic breath. 'Please go on.'

'Thank you,' he said. 'When you are unhappy, you don't care how long you have to live. You often want to end it then and there. But when you are happy, you want to cheat death.'

'So?'

'So the contract you signed said that your book will be a success. That you will achieve fame. Isn't that what you asked for?'

That was exactly what I had asked for.

'And with that, isn't time timeless?'

'I don't know what you mean.'

'You will, if I remember the words of one of your poets, "not go gently".

You will, in fact, want to weasel out of our deal when you think your time is drawing nigh. So we don't put the time down any more, as it is an insoluble dispute in which we find no benefit in taking part.'

The window had no curtain, and the streetlight at the corner lit the room with a greenish glow. The Devil's eyes glowed a contrasting red. I was sitting in an operating room in which my future was on the table — stripped, vulnerable, and waiting for the scalpel.

'I tell you what,' the Devil said. 'I will do something for you that I just don't do. Do you want to reconsider? I will let you out of the contract if you say no now.'

He smiled, showing his molars. 'No hard feelings.'

The patient breathed, innocent of the sharp knives poised. I thought of the state of this patient just a day ago. I thought of the prognosis — thought *honestly* of the prognosis before the Devil dropped into my room.

There really wasn't much to think about.

'Thank you, Brett,' I remember saying. 'No thank you. I don't need to reconsider.' And I think I might have added, 'Operate.'

Anyway, I got up and shuffled off to bed. I don't know what the Devil did for the rest of the night, but I slept until ten.

4

The Higher Light Books, Music & Crystals opened at ten, and I was supposed to open it. Except I was one minute out of bed, having slept through my alarm.

The responsible side of me panicked reflexively, but the logical side of me said I had time to sleep for another few hours. The Light was always dead before noon. And I had no worries that Leonie Bowes, the owner, would know. She was in Chicago now and for another six months at least, learning how to be a franchiser.

I found something almost clean to wear, ran my fingers through my hair and my hand over my face, digging sleepy out. My mouth tasted like sewage but coffee would fix that, and I'd get it next door to the Light.

I ran down the stairs and halfway down, stopped. How could everything be so normal? Why hadn't I thought first of *him*? Wasn't I supposed to wake thinking *Was it all a dream?*

Voices from the kitchen said it hadn't been. I heard the word 'Brett' in two keys, along with some edgy laughter. I had to see.

He was standing at the kitchen counter, pouring soy milk into a bowl of Weet-Bix. At one side of him was Andrew, who took the carton from his fingers and put it into the fridge. At the other side was Simone, holding in her outstretched arms, like an offering, a bundle of cloth.

'Brett' turned to the kitchen table and saw me. 'What a welcome,' he said in a way that I'm sure was a smirk, though they just sidled closer to him. 'Simone's loaned me a set of sheets, and Andrew's let me share his soy milk this morning.'

'Brill,' I found myself saying. The sheets were black satin, but of course. Simone chose her look and her sheets to suit her man. She even had one set that must have been made by Brooks Brothers, a look doomed to failure in this sharehouse setting.

'I've gotta go,' I announced. 'Brett' flashed me an evil grin and a dismissive wave, so I had no choice. Simone and Andrew were preoccupied.

* * *

The day was uneventful, which meant maddeningly frustrating. I had tedious hours to fret over what he was doing.

A flock of customers came at fifteen minutes to closing time. I let them pick up and put down and take to the counter a large pile of things they wanted to buy. At 6:10, the assortment of things they had accumulated was gone over yet again in a group discussion. One of the flock made a disparaging remark about one book in the pile, and without further discussion, they all streamed out the door.

After closing for the night, I rushed home, a five-minute walk.

The only sound in the house was the tinkle of the fridge's faulty defroster.

So I had a shower, made a cup of coffee, and took it to my room. I would have checked my email, but now I didn't feel comfortable doing that. Anything I'd write would be a lie.

I tried to read, but couldn't, so I gave in and checked my email. Julie had written.

> anj!
> i've begun my screenplay! it is absoluto fabuloso. i've set it in a city so it could be shot anywhere. i sent a letter to the film board to find out about financing. but enough about that detail especially as anyone with half a brain can suck out the economics. it would be such a good deal for fox here or in hollywood whether they can get tax thingies or not. with me starring and directing they would save wads. I am, for the moment, unknown. but thinking pragmatically, I might just have to settle for selling the script. getting ahead of myself hahaha. the real thing is: I'm writing. how are you doing?
>
> luv ya,
> jules

I wrote:

> Congratulations! Ditto with my book (begun...fabuloso)
> Angela

And I sent it. For a moment I worried over whether I should have put 'luv' or 'love', but only for a moment. Julie liked my reserve. She called it my distinguishing characteristic.

A low level of frizzle began to irritate my stomach, my body's signal of an impending attack of almost unbearable happiness. I vaulted myself out of the chair and began to twirl Sufi-style, arms out, face radiant. The face was right, but I didn't have a skirt, and felt the need for long hair. A pile of books splayed across the floor, ending the dance, and I was dizzy anyway. The frizzle was still there. What would fame feel like? I had a sniff of my armpits and thought about the Devil as publicist. What image would he want for me? Would he be my stylist or would he contract out? Maybe, to be prepared, I should buy a pair of stilettos and practise walking.

My journal caught my eye. I picked it up with both hands and nuzzled it. The cover was Italian leather, tanned with mountain chestnuts. The volume was thick and heavy, filled with linen-rag paper from a 600-year-old water-powered paper mill in Florence.

There was no entry for yesterday.

It had been neglected for a day — and such a day! There was *so* much to write.

The Waterman was out of ink. The wide-nibbed Lamy felt argumentative. The Sheaffer, though a present from Mum, felt right. I opened the journal and wrote:

The Devil

and stopped. I had to come to a decision about this. I couldn't think of him as the Devil, and call him 'Brett'. Besides, he looked like a Brett.

Carefully, I crosshatched over *The Devil* and crosshatched the other way, adding new furbishments till I paused to examine my work. It looked like a dog's dinner. If I had thought I would put ink on a page in such a way, I would have bought a ring binder.

The journal sat mutely in my lap till I had to respond. I opened to a random page, and began reading.

> Got my locks off today. Inspired! They suggested a post-dread I hadn't seen before It has a name: 'peekaboo' because your scalp glows through. Hair colour: a yellowy-green-natural-nylon. I could hardly stop gaping into every window as I walked home, to see my head.

Mail today from Paris Review, Atlantic, N Yorker. Paris Rev's was so small that maybe they have $$ problems. Atlantic's was I assume a rejection but there wasn't anything in the envelope. N Yorker's came in an email, and although it was a rejection, it was the reason I spent two days' pay to get a new look. They almost took my story! These are their exact words: 'We're sorry to say that this manuscript is not right for us, in spite of its evident merit.'

Staring sightless for what must have been a minute, I reached my psyche out towards that particular moment, to experience again that thrilling squiggle in my innard being that happened when I first read 'evident merit', but nothing happened. So I read on.

Felt good enough to ring Mum. Yesterday Dad's best dog disappeared. Dad spent all night looking and found him this morning. Snakebite. Dad had to do the dog in with the back of a shovel. Worst part was, when Dad swung Bonzer saw.

Dad asked for the phone, and it was He was only a pup when you left (pause) but already showing promise. Paaause. Mum took over (better for us) and it was all How soon is your book coming out??? I said I got my hair dressed then it was all Them Washing my hair and Massaging my scalp etc and it put her right for a while. But then it was Tell me More. I don't know which I hate more. Making up shit, or having to pry her off. Angus cut his thumb half off bunghole-crutching a stroppy old ewe, but he'll live. He was so mad he chewed the top of her ear clear off. Only halfway goodoh part of the conversation, as we all could laugh a bit then, even Dad, Nothing ever changes. Stoicism, girl, stoicism!

But calloo callay! Even that didn't manage to wreck my day.

Tonight I went to a YWAE evening (haven't a clue what it stands for) at the old Arts School in Plunkett Street. Gordon told me about it.

Fiona Ransomme spoke (Gordon's heard of her) on How to Get Over the Thousand Word Mark. Awesomely fantabulous, but she had to leave right after her talk. Gordon and I were so hyped we went to Nostramamma's. In our mutual debrief, we realized that, illuminated by Ransomme, our problem is: we get bored with our characters too fast. I finally had to burst out my good news about just WHY I had celebrated today. So I told Gordon about the New Yorker being a fan of my work, and that it is just a matter of me warping my style to suit their taste. He got a funny look on his face. Gordon jealous??? He asked what their letter said exactly. I could only remember the 'evident merit'. I got one of those last week, he said. Has he been improving himself behind my back? He then asked Do I think they all WANT our flash fiction? A funny question, considering we both seem to be almost THERE. But maybe he lied about his success.

It made me think of our goal again, and our focus. I rebalanced us with this reminder. Seriously, Gordon, I said, These magazine are only stepping stones. Our books are our real goal.

I don't know how he's going on his now. He said he's in the grip of writer's block.

He had some NY'rs with him from the library, so we wrapped up the evening reading stories from them, howling ourselves hoarse they were so boring.

A line and arrow lead to a margin note. I turned the book sideways.

TRY-ON NUMBER 5: Gordon asked again if he could sleep with me. I again rejected him with gentle élan. He asked if I had saved my hair. My hair! I think if I had said yes, he would have asked for a dread as a fetish. Eeew!

The day's log hadn't ended, though the snake of the margin note ended with the book in the right position to continue reading.

SELF-ASSIGNMENT FOR TOMORROW: Explore the Name Issue. Is my name inhibiting someone who loves my work, but is put off by my name? And would it be the Angela part or Pendergast? Should I be a female? male? Or should I be a neuter (A.J. Pendergast—Gordon says this means female in hiding)
Till tomorrow!

My left foot tingled, half asleep. I closed the diary and closed my eyes, distancing myself from the mesmerization of the Story of My Life.

Reading it now had been like finding out that someone had watched me as I squeezed a pimple on the tip of my nose (leaving a blotch and gaping pore) and then subsequently performed a double-jointed strip routine in front of a mirror, with snakes.

Thinking of anyone reading this, my scalp crawled.

Of the piles of books all over the table and floor, the journal pile was the tallest. I had kept a journal since the first year of my escape from the bush. The journals chronicled with religious devotion, my undergraduate and graduate years at Sydney Uni (BA, Masters in English), my year backpacking, my few years at the Commonwealth Bank, Bettawong Branch (only a block away from my present employment) until I was retrenched, then a variety of jobs in the neighbourhood—cafes, mailbox droppings, and the present fill-in position at the Higher Light—every single day, every plan, dream, success, every bedding, longing, thought, every soggy wad of rumination, up until the day before yesterday.

I knew without having to read further, that I was bored with the main character. Bored, but embarrassed to tears.

The problem now was not easy. The journals could not just be dumped into the household rubbish. They were, for the most part, 'recyclable cardboard paper mix'. Cardboard and paper had to be sorted, tied, and neatly placed in specially marked recycled-plastic CARDBOARD and PAPER open-topped trays, and then stuck out on the kerb on the night of the second Tuesday and the second Wednesday of the month, for 4:30 am pickup.

I could not take the risk of these labelled journal covers (meticulously labelled) and naked pages being exposed to the perusal of a whole inner-city's worth of passers-by, not to mention the gold strike this would be to my housemates. Besides, the size of the PAPER tray barely accommodated the house's discards without all the additional material that I needed to secrete between the pages of media dross. Getting rid of the journals by secreting them bit by bit would take twenty years.

Dropping the journals into bins around the city was out of the question. Too many people excavated, looking for food or opportunities. So I stripped the sheets from my bed and threw one on the floor, gathered up the pile of books in their variegated covers and shapes, laid them sideways on the sheet like bricks, pulled up the edges, tied them together, and dragged the lot into the corner, kicking the dirty clothes pile away first. Then I draped the other sheet over the bundle so that it fell over the mass with a suitable nonchalance, and dumped the rest of the laundry over it all.

Stepping back to examine my handiwork, I was satisfied. Now my room looked neater, one pile of books gone. The dirty clothes corner was still the dirty clothes corner, merely making a statement that I had become a shopper. And as far as my sheets went, I sighed.

5

A COUGH GRABBED my hair, I could swear, down to the down on my labial lips. How long had *he* been watching?

I spun on my sock-clad heels, the better to berate him. 'There *is* a door,' I noted.

He was leaning against the door jamb. 'I *did* knock,' he said dryly, and I felt my chest break out in a hot blush, rising quickly to my neck.

My shoes needed putting on, which took a while. He watched.

I grabbed my bag. 'Hafta go shopping. Wanna come?'

Growing up in a place where water is the gift of that miser, life, and dust is the daily ration, my mum's philosophy became my own. Why worry about the colour of your sheets if you are supposed to be sleeping? And if there's enough light to see their hue, what are you doing in bed? And if they smell natural, shouldn't everything?

I have always hated choosing things I don't care about, and sheets fall into that category. So whenever I had to, I bought a set of hospital-grade whites, and wore them till they would come out from a wash as laundry lint. The journal crisis had precipitated the present need to buy earlier than my wont.

And yet again, I wished they sold these in 'dust'. Or, in inner-city Sydney, 'grime' would have been the right colour.

By the time we caught the bus, there was only an hour of downtown late-night shopping left.

I had only asked Brett along because the words spewed out of my mouth. Now I regretted the decision. He wasn't Gordon. The guy sitting in the seat behind me in the standing-room-only 431 Bettawong Point to City was the Prince of Darkness, only a.k.a.'d 'Brett' at his amusement, and he was bound to do . . . what? I could not face the thought, so decided that the only way to deal with it, was not to.

But he accompanied me in my grim mission to find, buy, get out, like a labrador on a lead — quiet, compliant, observant, dull.

'Have you eaten?' I asked when we were on the bus home, my sheets the only purchase.

His answer was a cross between 'uehh' and a groan. I looked him in the face for the first time since morning. The skin on his cheeks glowed with a celadon translucence, the sheen of a cold sweat—like the underbelly of a tree frog.

'You're sick!' I told him, as if he didn't know. 'Do you get car sick?' I asked. Did he know what car sickness was? When precisely *was* his last holiday?

'Uarghh,' he said, and put his head between his knees.

'Burp,' I instructed. 'All the bus drivers are the same. Start, jerk, stop. Want to walk?'

He wagged his head, which I took for 'Yes'.

We got out at the next stop. The air was typical for November—warm and sticky as an armpit, and thick with inner-city early-summer fug: two-thirds emissions and one-third frangipani and jasmine flowers. We were a half-hour stroll from home, slightly less to my neighbourhood haunts.

'What kind of food do you eat?' I asked, as we stopped at a light. It hadn't occurred to me that he *would* eat, until I saw him with the bowl of Weet-Bix and soy milk (though, upon reflection, I could imagine them being served in hell).

'I'm not hungry,' he said.

The light was stuck, so we ran across—or rather, I ran, he plodded, and a cabbie nearly hit him.

He barely made it up the kerb, and leaned right over. I thought he was going to sprawl. Instead, he let me lead him to the nearest closed shop, where we sat on its windowsill.

He looked pitiful. 'What's wrong,' I asked. 'You can tell me.'

'I ate what I was given this morning,' he said, his head hanging. 'But your kitchen doesn't agree with me. And neither do any of the eating establishments in your neighbourhood.'

Insufferable snob!

If I were a dog, my ruff would have stood. 'I live,' I informed him, 'and you are holidaying, in Bettawong! Sydney's intellectual cum artistic cum . . . and I quote, best eats Mecca.'

My lips had drawn back, tasting blood and flesh and fight, when I came to my senses.

'What do you require?' I asked with a solicitude I felt not an iota.

'No garlic?' he asked in a voice so soft.

A host of black-and-white movies swarmed my brain, all streaked by lightning and scented by the reek of antiseptic garlic purifying the world of fiends. 'I thought garlic was an old wives tale.'

He laughed. It was a low laugh sounding like distant thunder, so it was probably coincidence that I heard glass shattering somewhere near.

He put his hand on my shoulder and turned himself so that we faced each other squarely. 'Angela,' he said. 'One old wife is worth a thousand preachers in the harm old wives have done to me. And garlic *does* hurt.'

We left our windowsill perch and walked together in silence.

I observed him out of the corner of my eye. He still looked ghastly, but over the worst of his attack. Had he eaten any garlic? Was it just the smell? How did the house affect him? Was he around during lunch? Or did Victor, Kate's dog, whose favourite place was under the kitchen table, breathe on him?

But the Devil wasn't born yesterday, nor was he fiendish in only one part of the world. History and garlic were intertwined. Something didn't add up, but I didn't have the time to learn math now.

Question: Thinking preventatively, should I put a garlic clove in my bag, wrapped, for my protection? Would it?

Answer: Deal with the present, who walks beside you.

I ran my mind over Bettawong's eating establishments with a new criticality. Although they were almost the main business on the street, I could not think of a single one that wouldn't smell of garlic—from Rigamoto FX, all the way to the old Chinese take-away frequented by pensioners and public housing types, to ... crikey. The only place I could think of that maybe wouldn't have garlic was Nippon, across the street from the Higher Light, but it was always closed.

'I could use *something* to eat,' he mumbled beside me. 'I haven't eaten since morning.'

I glanced at him and tripped on a crack. His walk was almost sprightly, the tree-frog sheen gone. We were by now at the edge of Bettawong, in front of The Last, an ex-cafe that was between tenants. It inspired me.

'What you need is a restorative coffee and cake,' I said. 'But this one's expensive. Do you have money?'

I dug into my bag and began to fumble things around.

He put his hand on mine. 'I have.'

I nodded, being in the middle of a gulp of salivation.

Three minutes later, we were sitting at a table for two in The Troppo.

The Troppo's parties—tremendously dear (like everything at the Troppo)—with Chinese finger pulls and magic stone rings, and rattles—parties only for adults—Troppo's was not McDonald's—were what made The Troppo. And I'd heard that if you came just for coffee and cake and paid only a dollar extra, you'd get a little paper parasol stuck jauntily in your slice of cake.

I hoped Brett would shout me for the parasol, too.

We were lucky there was an empty table. It was almost ten o'clock. Come ten thirty, every table would be taken and no one would leave until kick-out time at half-past midnight. Brett looked introspectively quiet, which suited me down to the ground. He was hardly chit-chat capable.

I was blissfully daydreaming when he startled me by asking when someone would come and take our order. I checked my watch. We'd been here only twenty minutes.

'I don't know,' I answered, a tad annoyed, but I looked around to see who was working tonight. A girl with harlequin glasses that she was taking off and fondling, and putting on again. Did they have prescription lenses or plain glass? I watched for a while, deciding 'plain glass'. She was standing by the cash register. I thought of trying to attract her attention, but that seemed so *American*.

She'd come. They all did eventually.

A flicker of flame caught my eye, and I turned my head.

Brett was playing with himself. He had one elbow resting on the table, his arm raised so that his hand was in front of his face. His hand was clenched with his thumb up, and it was flaming like a candle-wick.

Before I could even . . . *anything*, he blew it out.

Then he stuck his thumb underneath his fisted fingers again, and flicked it out Zippo-lighter style. It lit instantly. He quenched it, and lit again. Then he repeated the performance. And repeated it yet again.

'Stop that,' I whispered. 'What are you trying to do?'

'Get some—'

I deliberately turned my back to him, distancing myself in the eyes of everyone in the place. I heard snatches of conversation—'like him *trés much*', 'she can't smell the ferret, but the whole bloody flat stinks of its fucking pee', 'those little red peppercorns'. And by the cash register, those harlequin glasses were being taken off and put back on again. I smiled to myself, feeling a surge of national pride. Brett was looking weird amongst a typically tolerant group of Australians, which meant that he was playing to a totally inattentive house.

A roar at my back got all our attention. Brett's thumb now threw up a bonfire reaching almost to the ceiling.

That finally got a response. The harlequin glasses dropped to the floor, and I heard the lovely sound of crunching underfoot as their owner rushed to our table.

She leaned toward Brett, breathing down his chest.

'I'm only studying,' she panted. 'But that's the best act I've ever seen. Have I heard of you?'

'I dare say,' Brett said, quenching his thumb with a panache that was sickening to watch. I had never come close to that level of self-assurance.

'My dear Angela,' he drawled, 'Would you be so kind as to order for us both.'

The coffee came, and then the cake, with parasols.

He stuck his finger in his coffee, tasted it, and made a face. He stuck two fingers in his cake (*Over-the-Troppo: Troppo's own Devil's food cake Topped with Chocolate-covered Cherries, Filled with Hazelnut Cointreau Cream, and all Surrounded by a Lake of Raspberry Couli*) and held his fingers upright, splayed their widest. Then he tasted tentatively, each finger—one from the base up, the other from tip to base—at the same time, running the tips of his forked tongue up and down, down and up those fingers, and licking carefully around, sometimes having his tongue tips meet like mating snakes.

He was doing it on purpose.

'Eat,' he said.

'I'm not hungry,' I answered.

She was standing behind my chair like a waiter in a European restaurant. I could feel her there.

'Eat,' he commanded, and handed me my fork, never taking his eyes from his fingers.

I began to eat, choking back tears.

The coffee was lukewarm.

The finger and tongue performance ended. (I have excellent peripheral vision.)

Then the next performance began.

He removed the parasol from his cake and placed it by his plate. Then he *played* with his cake, using the long nail on his left little finger. I hadn't noticed this nail before, but it was the length of a hatpin.

Every time I stopped eating, he stopped playing, and repeated his command.

When he finally finished moving his food around, he stuck the parasol into it rakishly and sat back to admire his work. I was by this time finished with my cake, having pushed down the last of it.

The mess on his plate was nothing less than something murdered for pleasure.

He was not Gordon. Not at all.

He got up and walked out of Troppo's. I followed him out.

He was going in the wrong direction. Anyway, I needed to stop him. 'There wasn't any garlic,' I laughed (poorly).

'That's true,' he said, slowing down. 'But I'm not a sweet tooth. And I like my hot drinks hot.'

'We have to go back,' I told him gently. 'Home is the other way. And besides . . .' I had to add, hoping he wouldn't be angry, especially as it complicated matters because he hadn't paid the bill, which had never come. 'I forgot my sheets at Troppo's.'

'You don't have to worry about them,' he said, stretching his lips in a rictus of a smile.

He was trying. I felt enormously relieved.

And that was so nice of him to remember the sheets, but where were they? He wasn't carrying anything that I could see.

'You're not going back,' he explained, and began to walk again, away from home.

'What?'

'I can't live there,' he said.

I grabbed his arm. 'But I do.' I could hear my voice shaking. 'We can move if you like. I'll give notice and we can look next week.'

He peeled my hand from his arm, gently but firmly. 'No, my dear,' he said, and began walking again.

His stride was so long that my side cramped.

'But . . . all my stuff is there!'

He didn't deign to answer.

There was a time when I was in a cathedral in Spain where the bannerless staircase corkscrewed up to a murk of infinity — and halfway up, I glanced down, towards blackness. I slid down the wall to grasp the stone step and the wall behind — unable to move, too frightened to cry. The next tourists found me, clogging the way. They tried to reason, but I was beyond that. As I heard their steps echo ever more faintly downwards, every muscle in my body locked except my sphincter, which relaxed so completely that half my insides, it seemed, ran down the stairs. Eventually an ambulance crew followed my trail up the stairs and rescued me, as I feigned unconsciousness.

No kind tourists would find me now. No ambulance crew would save me. I forced myself to assess my situation coolly, and was glad that I was able to — that I had matured since the staircase incident.

I'd signed the contract, but the Devil hadn't provided anything. I could break it off, and this Devil business would be just like the staircase incident, just like other times when my body cruelly let me down, just like the journals, just like the book — something to forget and get beyond.

He was five long strides ahead when I stopped. Turning, I strode back over my own footsteps, my mood instantly lightening. Within a block, a wild regret even made me giggle. Those beaut horns and tail — such a waste on *him*.

As I walked, the air smelt less polluted, more frangipani'd, and my thoughts felt cleared of muck. Tomorrow I would wake and go to work, and tomorrow night, maybe think about saying *yes* to Gordon.

6

'You can't,' I heard him say.

He was stalking—too far back for me to hit him, just close enough to speak in a conversational tone.

'They're no good to you,' he said, as I went into The Troppo.

My sheets were gone. Some bastard had nicked them!

The dunny was out back, so that's where I went, passing it and the chaos of rubbish, to open the back gate.

Lost him!

I walked the back alleys knowing that he would look for me at home, and then, not finding me, leave to hunt elsewhere.

By 3 am, I missed bed so much, I decided it was safe to return.

On the corner of my street, the same obnoxious but comforting streetlight shone. I slid the key in the door and the key turned smoothly, and I shoved the door and it opened. Nothing jumped out at me in the hall. No fiends lurked in my room.

I threw myself on the bare mattress without even taking off my shoes, to sleep the sleep of forgetfulness.

He climbed the stairs on all four feet, his tail slashing against the railing. At the top of the stairs, he stood, six feet tall, and his forefeet became hands, and he pulled a handkerchief out of his jeans and wiped it against the wall, and the pea-green paint blistered and gasped. He waved his cloth, and flames galloped across the wall, galloped toward my room.

I woke to the sound of breaking glass. Rough hands grabbed me, knocking the wind out of my solar plexus as they flung me over a shoulder, like a sack of wheat. I was handed out of my window, to be loaded onto another shoulder and carried down a ladder.

A stretcher, noise. Flashing red lights. Suck, suck, suuuuck. My lungs finally pull in air, my mouth tastes the acrid bite of wet ash. City ash—eucalypt, plastics, electric wires. An oxygen mask grips my face, and I shove it away. Professional words urge me down, and hands shove me flat onto the hard stretcher mat. Medics slide my stretcher into an ambulance faster than a sheep into a race, but I'm no sheep.

'Hey!' I crack my skull rolling off the stretcher, but I have to be fast.

They're closing the doors already, ready to drive off. Not soon enough to keep me in.

They're not insulted when I hit out, resisting their assistance. I'm just a situation that fixed itself. They walk toward the fire truck. I feel bad momentarily that I didn't thank them.

A cacophony of noise, lights, confusion, purpose.

Firemen aim hoses. Fierce water shoots, thudding into the house. One hose is firing into my bedroom window.

I recognize some of the people in the crowd, but not many. None are my housemates.

'I told you,' *he* says, into the back of my neck.

He sounds gentle, but his next words chill. 'Where do you want to go from here?'

I didn't dignify him with an answer.

'Come,' he says, and I let him lead me towards the crowd's back, and away.

'You didn't have to burn it.'

My teeth felt furred, my stomach contorted, I ached too much for *this* to be the dream.

We were sitting on the grass under a giant fig tree at the bay end of Bettawong Street. The sound of water lapping against the wharf was so pleasant, it was obscene.

I turned to *him* and didn't care what he did to me. 'Why did you!'

I didn't ask. I screamed. It didn't matter to me whether he would be angry—what my goddamn *punishment* would be. I didn't care about anything but screaming and crying and screaming some more.

So far, he hadn't answered. He had led us to this place and forced me to sit, to 'calm' me, he said. My head throbbed, and I wanted to hit something.

Now, I was too tired to do anything more than sit and try not to think of the present, the past, the future.

'You did it, Angela,' he said into the void.

I swung around but didn't say anything, as I needed to hear him say something I could understand, maybe for the pleasure of hating him.

'You didn't listen to me,' he said. 'You thought you could walk away.'

'But,'

'But nothing, Angela. The contract gave me a hell's week.'

He took my hands in his. I pulled away, and his hands tightened around mine like a Chinese finger pull—but this was no party favour. His grip only lessened when I stopped pulling away, but left a bruise of a promise that made my veins pulse with pain as blood flowed again. I lowered my eyes to the ants at the grass near my crotch, for lack of knowing where to look.

'Angela...' He cupped my jaw in his hand and tilted my head so that my eyes had to meet his. 'It isn't even a hell's hour yet.'

Fainting has never been part of my repertoire, but I wished I could then. As it was, all I could do was sit. Sit and think. Above us, fruit bats screeched in the fig tree, leather wings breaking figs from their stems as the bats squabbled. All around us, plops of ping-pong-ball fruits punctuated the gentler slaps of water against the harbour wall metres away.

All that stuff I'd read at the Higher Light suddenly became useful, as it helped me now to realize that things were possibly all arranging themselves for the best. But I could mull this later. Now was the time to say something. 'Did anyone get hurt?'

'Do you want?'

'Of course not!'

'Angela,' he said, a warning note in his voice. 'Tell the truth.'

I had to establish equilibrium again, so I asked a question. 'What did you do with Simone? And Andrew, for that matter?'

'You mean?'

'You know!' I hated his coy act. 'Did you let them ravish you? And how did you hide your, uh, tail?'

He seemed surprised at the questions, but answered. 'No to both, though they fought over me at breakfast.'

I was intrigued in spite of myself. 'How did you get rid of them... or did you?'

'I did try to fend them off permanently, but,' and here he sighed theatrically, 'but I fear that I only whetted their appetites.'

He was such a ham I couldn't help grinning, something that made me almost more angry at myself than him.

'What story did you tell them?'

'Do you really want to know? Oh, only that I had fallen in love with you.'

He pulled a used tampon out of his breast pocket, dangling it between us like a warm dead rat.

I yanked away from him and smashed my skull against the tree's trunk. 'Where did you get that thing?'

His right eyebrow circumflexed. 'Don't you recognize it?'

'Mine?'

He ran it back and forth under his nose, like a Corona, and stuck it in his mouth and sucked.

I wanted to throw up.

'They had the same reaction,' he said.

'You . . . ?'

'Your essence, carried with me.'

Would they tell everyone they know? Wouldn't I? Could I stop them?

He broke into my panic. 'I asked you a question.'

'What?'

'They died in the fire,' he announced, casual as *it rained yesterday*.

'No!'

'Not yet, but they will have. Now make up your mind.'

'I don't want them to die! Of course not. I'm not a horrible person. But why did you have to ruin my life? I can't live in the neighbourhood now. Everyone here will know by tomorrow.'

He just sat there looking at me, his expression as animated as a dead shark.

Simone and Andrew's fate rested in the balance. And not just theirs. My head itched as my heart and my brain fought against each other. Even though this was his holiday, it was my life. It was important that I teach him compassion, even though my housemates were nothing to me — and in Simone's case, less than nothing.

'Well?' he asked.

'You haven't harmed Simone or Andrew, have you?' I answered, clutching his knee. 'Or Jason, or any of them?'

'Tsk, tsk,' he clucked. 'Now that I know your wishes, though I am not completely convinced . . . no.'

'And the house?'

'A total loss, sorry to say.'

'Not so bad,' I said without thinking.

'Eh?'

'Insurance,' I explained. And then I felt remorse for people I didn't even know, and with the way my life was going, I was sure I would never know. I felt for the future of people wanting insurance. The more accidents, the more rates go up. Insurance companies must follow the rules of profit. No one I knew now would understand me in this silly remorse, but I learnt it at the bank, and it stuck.

But enough pity for them. I felt for my bag and something to blow my nose on. 'My stuff!'

I had to ask, hating having to. 'Where'd you put my stuff?'

He shook his head, and offered his hand. 'Ready, Angela?'

. . . everything . . .? everything!

He stood and adjusted his crotch with an impatient jerk.

There was one thing left. 'The store. My job. I have responsibilities.'

'Sorry,' he said. That tone, I recognized. The same gentle élan I'd used on Gordon.

7

Brett gave me five minutes to think of a 'comfortable lodging with service to my desire, or I will choose for both of us'.

I assumed he meant super-fancy room service, and I only vaguely knew how room service works. As to the place . . . But those years of browsing style magazines in Bettawong's coffee shops came in useful now as I remembered an intriguingly exclusive little hotel.

The Restonia, I recollected, didn't 'do bookings'. Its clients were 'friends' who 'come for stays'. The write-up had reeled off a list of rumoured friends—movie and music names I instantly forgot—and their memorable reasons for choosing the Restonia: its 'discretion' and its claim to service 'every desire'. The rumour of its secret vehicular access had been mentioned, and tantalizingly unconfirmed.

I had never progressed beyond youth hostel, so I didn't know how we would go getting in, assuming the Restonia wasn't full of friends. I looked like I had slept in my clothes, but everyone does when they arrive fresh from overseas in our arse-end continent. Brett looked fab, but I didn't know if an establishment this exclusive could deal with people without credit cards. Then I thought it was probably the only hotel I could think of, that would possibly be used to accommodating a man with wads of cash in his pants, and no memory of where he put his wallet.

In the pale light of dawn, I led off on our trek, walking towards the centre of town, and then veering off. The air was fresh, and there was almost no traffic. Brett walked beside me, and when I found an all-night city petrol station and went in for directions, he accompanied me, standing beside me as I asked to use their phone book, then handing me the petrol-smelling street directory they handed him when I asked if they had one. Our destination was only three blocks away, though these grease-heads had never heard of it.

When we finally arrived, I almost missed it.

The Restonia was a confusingly small, unremarkable upended shoebox packed between two defunct old clothing factories in a quiet street. Beside the solid front door, a small brass plaque saying only 'The Restonia' was screwed to the smut-dusted stone above a brass buzzer. It was 6:30 am. I pressed the buzzer and there was a thirty-second delay. Then, fast as a footfall brings red ant soldiers from their nest, the door opened and three men swarmed, closely followed by another with a polka-dot bowtie and patent leather slip-ons—the manager, who introduced himself to Brett as Justin Abernathy and presented his staff, all dressed to casual perfection: Jim, Kevin, and Ferdinand.

Manager and staff were smooth as couli and possessed of intimidating levels of personal hygiene. They 'on behalf of the Restonia' embraced Brett's friendship almost immediately. A friend had been forced to cancel, as it were, only hours ago, due to his tragically awkward death. Oh, everyone would read about it soon enough.

And how long was 'sir' thinking of staying? (and I had thought entertainment industry types were casual).

'A week, or I don't know. I don't want to be pushed,' Brett answered peremptorily, which elicited a Pavlovian grovel response.

'And how would sir like to pay?' Bow Tie delicately broached.

And now, the bugger! I was holding my breath when Brett pulls out of somewhere on his person, a string of credit cards longer than a tapeworm, all naturally Mr Brett Hartshorn's.

I didn't catch his home address, but did see him sign the 'friendship book'. His signature was partly what I expected—jagged, thick, black. Well, this was a no-brainer. I know my graphology: 'Disturbed'.

What I did *not* expect were those forward and backward slants. They said, and loudly: 'I am Conflicted!'

I wandered away so he wouldn't notice my noticing anything odd, but my sensitivity was misplaced. No one saw me looking at his signature, because no one noticed me at all. I followed them all to his suite, and walked in like self-propelling baggage.

The Restonia 'might do', he announced after our breakfast things were removed. I had ordered for both of us by just picking up the phone. ('There is no menu as such, Madam. What is your desire?')

For me: Alhambra Bakery's fruit toast, macadamia butter, grilled fresh figs with double cream, a large pot of medium strong coffee (not bitter), and a bowl of demerara sugar and a jug of cream, not milk, and a chocolate-covered dried plum.

And for Mr Hartshorn (this was harder because I needed to put his desires into what I judged to be the proper culinary context—and he was no help there, his order to me being unusually crude and to-the-point—but I must have translated right): Heart tartare au Jus Masai, no dipping sauce, and hold the toast.

Now breakfast being over, I had time to soak thoroughly in my disappointment at our thousands-of-dollars-a-night luxury accommodation. We had eaten Eastern-style in this room—ironically, our 'lounge'—seating mats and a low table having been brought in specifically for the purpose, and removed.

The furnishings: mirrored walls, a tall pile of rubber-covered exercise mats, a gym (the whole gym, I think) taking about half the space of the enormous room, and in one corner a luxuriously appointed shrine to Ganesha, the elephant god.

Our bedrooms maintained the same motif of health, spiritualism, and pain. Their bathrooms were stark, and dedicated to extreme internal hygiene.

The water room, if one could call it that, had the redeeming quality of being the exact opposite in tone, though eminently functional. As large as our lounge, it was Egyptian deco style with Roman sybaritic requirements, updated for the twenty-first century. The water-use choices alone would have boggled me if I weren't already lost in the range of personal toys and odd beautification equipages. One hose ending in a long needle was typically mysterious. Liposuction touch-ups?

Brett hadn't commented one way or the other on the suite, other than glancing at the most evil-looking parts of the gym with a bit of a double-take.

I, on the other hand, told myself *I should have told you so*. I'd jumped from my own level of accommodation experience and expertise—'bring your own sleeping sack, and don't put your bare feet on the floor in the shower'—to this.

I should have known that at this level of friendship, there would be room enough for a Sufi celebration, but no welcome: chocolate waiting on my pillow (the cruellest blow), nor electric jug, tea and coffee in instant sachets, two cups and saucers and spoons, (one for night and the other for morning), nor jug of water from the tap and a carton of milk in a little fridge that would live near the bed, humming all night with a comforting *brrr*. And no shortbread biscuits in cellophane wrapping, nor little old TV. Here, there was not even a clock-radio. Maybe room service sang.

And my bed! At Kate's, my bed was a thick crumpet of a single mattress that she would have picked up at an op shop, and it lived on the floor. But now I missed it.

This mattress was also plonked on the floor or as close as dammit, and was a prison-bed-size rice cracker. The pillow, only one, was—yes, I picked it up to check—crunchily macrobiotic. I *hate* millet hulls! The bedclothes ensemble: sheets, pillowcase, and a penitential blanket, all in classic basic grime.

Continuing on. My bedside table: a slab of glass floating upon an egg of granite. No drawers filled with brochures for Olde Sydney, Harbour ferry rides, strip shows and escort agencies, sheepskin products, crumpled bus tickets, complimentary condoms.

Continuing on. A wall-length inbuilt wardrobe that didn't even offer me a forgotten shoe, nose ring, pair of handcuffs. Not even a used Cherry Ripe wrapper that I could smell for comfort.

That was my bedroom. Brett's was even worse. Only a rice cracker on the floor and a sword on the wall.

The Devil however, was happy.

Thus began the new chapter of my life.

8

As I said, Brett was happy. As soon as breakfast was over, he seated himself on the pile of futon mats.

Up there, he withdrew mentally from me, but I was stuck below, cross-legged on the floor. Finally, I interrupted with a polite 'Excuse me.'

He needed to get to work, he said. What did I want?

I had several needs, but one most urgent. My persona.

Simone and Andrew, and by now, half of Bettawong, would have heard of the adventure of my used tampon. I could not afford my fame to be compromised by that, nor any other incident (incidents that I did not feel the need to explore, especially with present company).

He had a hard time understanding, and actually, didn't. But he did finally accept what he called my 'sensitivity' to the fact that he had ruined my life, and that in doing so, I could not possibly become famous as 'Angela Pendergast'.

'Pity,' he commented. 'Angela appealed to me.'

But my persona and my fame were linked so much that he allowed his work to be interrupted, to sort this out.

We focused, therefore, on me, cheering me up immensely. I, Angela Pendergast, needed a name by which my book would be by-lined, but that was not enough. I needed a whole new identity, as I could not afford the by-line to be just an author pseudonym. I needed a whole new persona, with appropriate documentation (something that seemed to be another speciality of Brett's).

Therefore—and this was when things began to be fun—'Angela dear, who would you like to be?'

My past explorations for a name were useless now, as they had revolved around Angela Pendergast. Therefore I started afresh, bringing up first, the female/male androgyne thing—and I could *not* come to a resolution.

Then Brett suggested a lateral approach. 'What is this bestseller to be?'

'What? I thought we were speaking of my name.'

'What do you call . . .?' He scratched the place between his horns, always the itchiest. 'You know, like fairy tales, Volkswagen repair manuals, airport books, Marlowe or Shakespeare, Mills & Boon?'

He'd been studying, perhaps too hard, though I guessed what he was getting at.

'Genre?'

'Yes!' His hand whacked the rubber mat so hard that for a moment, I expected clouds of dust to fly. 'Now, what genre do you want your book to be?'

A good question. Very professional. He suddenly gave me confidence.

I told him of the state of the book trade at the moment, and the gossip I had heard as to the near future. Then I reminded him of the specific part of our contract that I knew I had specified and signed to have: *fame, that lasts*. Which meant that we had to look at things not only from the short-term view, but from the historical perspective.

Eventually, we settled on the book's description. I could not find pen or paper anywhere, so we both swore to memorize these words:

> The book, title unspecified, embraces the human condition, its ups and its downs, incorporating adventure, mystery, and romance, in proportions being 2, 1, 4. Length, medium thick.

Perfect! So with Brett's problem out of the way—what he was to write—we were free to return to my name—who I was to be.

There were so many names to choose from that suited the description of an author of the specified book, that I had to run off and have a meditational shower in the water room. It was a long one, as there were so many bottles and jars to open and sample—a long table was as full of them as the rest of the suite was empty of every other article of comfort and joy. I would have saved all the bottles—real crystal, I think—but I didn't even have a bag to put them in.

When I returned, Brett was still in the same place on top of the mat pile in the lounge.

I began with the more impressive names I had thought up: Iolanthe, Fitzwillia, Cerise. Going on to the classic: Juliette, Ophelia, Scarlett. Then onwards to the tragic: Norma, Bonny, and so on. Then: people whose names I wished I had picked before they got to them first.

The mat pile rocked precariously as Brett sat up from a slouch, exhaling 'Hmm.'

I was grateful that he didn't add a comment. None of the names sounded as good as they had when jets of water pulsated over my nipples and the scent of something called 'Figuera by Eugenia Haich' clouded my judgement.

Now, as I uncrossed my legs to find a new uncomfortable position, my brain emptied and my new identity withered and blew away, light as air, bereft of expression, voice, personality.

I looked up to him, and the back of my neck cracked.

'Desirée?' he offered.

Instantly, the whole name blossomed, as the familiar old surname on Mum's side of the family met the romantic and exciting Desirée.

So Desirée Lily I became, and then I ordered lunch.

9

LUNCH WAS divine, which I only expected. Brett had the same as breakfast, though more. For myself, I ordered a salad, 'something simple and fast, with pine nuts, apricots, and lots of cracked Jamaican pepper, and capers and plum vinegar, and rocket of course, and ouzo-splashed grilled baby octopus, to be mixed in a eucalypt bowl unseasoned by garlic.' That and iced lapsang souchong with coconut milk. I didn't bother thinking up dessert, because dessert had been served before lunch, and I had been picking at it ever since. The fabulous meringue of my name. Dessert came 'with the Restonia's compliments' anyway — a huge plate of fresh dates that I devoured to the last sticky one, Brett not wanting any.

Now, lunch removed (service here was instantaneous), I felt confident enough to push for our next meeting of the day.

'I could use a change of clothes,' I said, as soon as Brett was again ensconced on the pile of mats.

(And toothbrushing stuff. And a bag. I felt naked without a bag, though I had nothing to put in it, and really, no need to have a bag since I never needed a pen or paper again. But I still needed something to clean my teeth, a change of clothes [wouldn't be difficult to shop for, or expensive to get — just another pair of jeans, a couple T-shirts, socks, undies, all in basic black] — and that bag that I needed just *because*, even if it would only hold as much as the Queen's.) But I felt uncomfortable discussing all this with him.

'Could I please have some money? Then I'll take off so you can get to work.'

He drew himself up so high on his mountain that he suddenly looked fairytale royal. He needed something fanciful to complement his majesty. He needed a . . . a hookah! I began to smile.

'A *change of clothes*,' he repeated — so critically, so harshly that spit flew with the 'clothes'. 'And what *else*?'

And just when I thought we were getting along. 'Only pants and a shirt and some cottontails. Nothing different to what I've got on now. And a toothbrush and paste.' I left off the bag, as the look on his face took the saliva right out of my mouth.

'That's *all*, eh?'

I regret to say, I burst into tears.

'Desirée,' he growled with severity—but thankfully, not rage. 'You propose that I spend my money on purchasing just what you need to look the same as you look now, and then you'll come back and brush your teeth, *while I work?*'

I hadn't proposed anything. But at the moment, my sole possessions were my glorious future and the clothes on my back—and the clothes reeked like a hot, post-Christmas rubbish bin, down to the rotting prawn shells.

My teeth chattered, but for my self-esteem I had to answer. 'I haven't *proposed* anything,' I insisted. 'Can't you see I have some simple needs?' I heard the wheedle in my voice, but couldn't stop it.

'I expect no less from you than I do from myself!'

All became clear. This was jail. He was my master. The book was my punishment. And he was a liar. 'But you said you'd write it!'

'Desirée!'

What had once been food leapt from my throat, spattering the bottom of his futon mountain. An insufficiently masticated arm of baby octopus hung from a corner of grey rubber. Before I could breath properly, another convulsive spasm added more mess to the lake on the shiny parquet. Then I retched bile. My teeth had felt velvety before. Now, in the interstices of my top front teeth, shreds of vomit hung.

I ran out of the room and brought back towels, but he stopped me with his hand held up. 'Leave it!'

My body shook, but I stood to attention with the towels hanging from my hands, because I didn't know what else to do. I was too scared, too heartbroken, to think.

'Now now,' he said. 'My dear Desirée.'

He threw down a handkerchief. It landed in the puddle, so he pulled out another that he knotted first, and I caught it.

'Ta,' I said, wiping my face and throwing it back, where it disappeared.

'May I call you Desirée?' he continued, with a token of a smile. 'Good. Now look at yourself.'

That was easy. The walls were full of me.

'Do you see a Desirée?'

And *then*, all became clear.

And when I bent to clean up the mess, he stopped me. 'Would Desirée do that?' And then he added, 'Or would Desirée—'

'Just call room service.'

Of one thing, I was sure. The staff at the Restonia had cleaned up messes far worse than mine.

I didn't get a salary with my new job, but I did get a credit card in my name (Desirée Lily)— with a 'Ms'. Brett was learning! I had to order up a pen and paper to design my signature so I could perform my first task, signing my card—tremendous fun.

My credit limit was 'Whatever makes Desirée Desirée', and when I added 'and then some', Brett nodded approvingly.

This first day was going to be terribly rushed, with now only two hours to closing time, and me being so inexperienced. The only two things I'd ever really shopped for were fancy fountain pens and paper, my only other lash-outs being cake in coffee shops. Those style and fashion magazines I was so addicted to flipping through were nothing I had regarded with any more attention to detail than the clothes in paintings hung in an art museum.

I needed to organize my thoughts before barging out of the Restonia the way I usually barged out of everywhere—without a plan—so I tried lying on my bed, to think. And that re-prioritized my first decision. Instead of leaving the Restonia to rush downtown, I pushed the button in my bedroom wall, for room service.

'Madam' (I wasn't sure about this, but this was their term of address, so I let it be) required: 'A king-size super-comfortable bed with full thickness mattress and box springs, high enough off the floor so I can stand a pair of knee-high boots underneath. And a little fridge stocked with a carton of milk. And a plug-in jug, and a few sachets of instant coffee, and some teabags, and sachets of sugar, and a packet of Tim Tam chocolate biscuits in the fridge, and a chocolate mint on my pillow. And all to be arranged by my bedtime tonight... No, a little earlier than that. Ten o'clock would be acceptable, if that's okay with you.'

A moment after I punched off, Justin Abernathy knocked, asking for Mr Hartshorn. They had a whispered consultation in the lounge, ending with the manager bowing and scraping himself out the suite door.

Then it was time for me to leave. I popped my head into the lounge, asking Brett if everything was alright. From his eyrie, he waved me away in a friendly but I-just-want-to-be-left-alone-to-work manner.

My credit card in my pocket, I was already on my way out when something grabbed my eye, and I grappled it.

Downstairs in the ultra-nondescript lobby, 'Dump this,' I said to the assembled staff, handing to Jim with a difficulty that was repugnantly familiar to me, the massively tricky flowerpiece of calla lilies wrapped in a coil of barbed wire—our sole flower arrangement, which had sat on a cut-glass 'table' in our suite's entrance hall.

'A dozen red roses in a crystal vase,' I ordered, 'for the Hartshorn suite. Oh, and white ones for my room . . . that smell, not just for looks. And a proper table in the hall.' And I added, though I didn't know if they'd revile me for saying it, 'please'.

Then I sailed out the door like I'd done it before, trailing the smells of exotic unguents—and for the last time in my life, my dirty laundry.

One hour left to closing. No time to figure out buses, and I couldn't see a taxi so I jogged downtown, prioritizing like blazes as I rushed. My mouth tasted unbearable, so I ran past the last-forty-five-minutes' crowd into Soul's Chemists first, found toothpaste and a toothbrush and a bag of their strongest mints, ripping it open to crunch some as I shoved myself into the check-out queue. When everything was bagged and I handed over my card, it was knocked back as 'under the purchase limit', so I excused myself to the people in the queue as I eased through them to the perfume display, grabbed the biggest box, and inserted myself back at the check-out counter. Though I had rushed, my assistance didn't make the check-out girl happy, but the new total meant my transaction sailed through. She sourly repacked my purchases and I rushed out of the store, stopping for a moment to open the bag, remove the perfume, and lob it in a rubbish bin—an early Chrissie present to some homeless person.

My mouth tasted so much better, but I only had thirty minutes left. I had never shopped for a new persona before, but the jog down here shook valuable cells in my brain, stimulating me marvellously. Remembering in detail what magazines had advised was impossible, but details never matter. My brain whirled through thousands of pictures and millions of words. As I jogged, the clutter cleared, and one over-riding Instruction emerged, as clear as One Commandment: *Accessorize!* And then my brainstorm whirled some more as the one accessory that had to be *so very* Desirée Lily materialized in my mind's eye. Jewels!

Luckily, only steps from the rubbish bin, Proud's Jewellers twinkled. I weaved through the crowd to its long front window, shuffled between window-shopping nuisances, and then rushed inside. Within three minutes, I could see that none of Proud's jewellery was *jewels*.

Emeralds and rubies and violet and yellow stones (zircons? amethysts?)—anyway, stones of wine-gum colour and size, in a choker collar. At least, that had been my vision, not that I was stuck on that model exactly. But Proud's, though busy as a hive, was disappointingly plebeian. Now there was no time left to find another jewellers, so I had to leave jewels for tomorrow. At the moment, I only had enough time to buy clean clothes.

Around the corner was where I bought my clothes when I had to. The women who wore lipstick where I grew up thought of this as Mecca. I came here when I had first arrived and needed clothes, and it was where I still bought them, whenever I had to. Dependable as Monday, the staff were wrinklies uniformed as mourners, the look never changed, and the vast halls either echoed, or on pension days, filled with muted clucks and the swishes of support-hosed legs against pleated wool skirts.

I brushed past the doorman, to be hit with a dizziness attack. The displays were unrecognisable. The vast hall was still mostly empty of shoppers, but one flaunted a bare midriff. I rode the escalator up, only to be let down again. The whole store reeled crazily in an attempt to go 'youth'. Musical chairs had been played with the stock. The only good thing was that it hadn't worked in terms of bringing in trade. I would have gone elsewhere if I'd known where, but I didn't. Even if I had known, there wasn't time.

I didn't bother looking for underwear. It was hard enough to find where they'd moved the department with the jeans and T's. Dangerously close to kick-out time, I found it, now nefariously musicked to confuse, and fashionably jumbled. Salesgirls aspiring to be chicks hung around the place like cheap perfume. One came up to me and asked me what I wanted. Coward that I was, I answered. 'Black jeans and T. One each.'

'One more purchase, Pam,' she announced as she walked away from me, the bitch! I waited by the till as she rummaged through the mess piled on two tables. She was efficient, though, as in less than two minutes she returned with clothes over her arm, and threw them on the counter, flashing their blackness at me as she unclipped the tags and shoved them in a bag while Pam punched stock codes into the register, and the both of them planned the night they were going to have, beginning in a few minutes—the only acknowledgement of me being a 'sign here please' from Pam, and from her salesgirl accomplice, the final flick-off—a smile as painted on as an Indian statue and the odd command, 'Enjoy your things,' both tossed so casually that if they'd been spit she was directing towards me, they would have hit Pam.

I stabbed them both with my cutting reply, or would have if I could have thought of one. Desirée certainly would—but I slunk out.

It took bloody forever getting home. A taxi would have been a treat, but impossible to flag at rush hour. If there was a technique, I'd have to learn it. But then again, I reckoned that Desirée would have a limo, though upon consideration, that could be worse than a bus if you have to wait for the limo to come when you call...

By the time I got back to the Restonia, I had a dull headache, my socks were sticking to my toes in my hot Docs, and regardless of their orthopaedic pretensions, the arches of my feet sent shooting pains up my leg. Jim opened the door with a smile that looked surprisingly genuine.

I gave him a half-smile, embarrassed about my teeth, and rushed back up to our suite. The entry was bare, its horrid shard-glass table removed, but nothing had been put in its place. *Humph!*

My bedroom door was closed as usual. I opened it to find my every request fulfilled, except for the flowers. And in addition to instant coffee, there was a jar of what smelt like fresh-ground in the fridge, and a little plunger pot on a table—a round table with a white linen tablecloth, embroidered with forget-me-nots! The two cups and saucers matched the tablecloth. I could see through the china! I had forgotten to order a chair, but there one sat—the only one in the suite—comforting as a bap bun. And the bed was so astoundingly luxurious and snowily white (with little sprigs of embroidered white flowers) that I didn't know what to do first. Bathe, change, agonize over tea? or coffee? or change my clothes?

Then my stomach gurgled, and a bubble of bile erupted into my mouth, prioritizing me without my needing to agonize.

I took my purchases to my bathroom, where I brushed my teeth first. Teasing myself by not rushing added immeasurably to the thrill of shedding the old life, putting on the new. But enough of that.

I stripped, kicking my boots out into the bedroom, and dumping my clothes in the trash.

A short shower rid myself completely of the stench of my old clothes, and then I anointed myself with just a little of this, a little of that... But enough of *that*.

I pulled the new clothes out of their bag, stripped them of their tags and stuff and dumped it in the trash (the first time I had ever thrown away pins), tossing the clean clothes onto the surgically spotless bedroom floor. Then it was time to dress, and although I couldn't be Desirée all the way yet, I could imagine the missing accessory already, which put me almost solidly there.

Out in the bedroom, I stepped into the jeans and was pulling them up when I felt resistance at mid-thigh. Glancing back to check what was wrong, I stuck.

The wall behind me was mirrors and my movement drew my eye. Full-length mirrors had not been part of my life. I felt like a butterfly pinned to cardboard, both fixed in my stupid position, and fixed in my gaze. That person was both a stranger and worse—me—the me I had dumped years ago. I had never seen so much of myself before, and at this crucial time in my transformation, I hardly needed memories intruding.

Anyway, I couldn't wear *this*. The bitch had given me the wrong size. These jeans were not shape-camouflage—the *only* style I had worn all my adult life, except for the bank uniform that made me walk with my eyes down—the polyester blouse that gapped just wrongly, and the laugh-at-me black skirt. Ugh! Once retrenched from the bank, I had never needed any other outfit than the one I always wore. Ultra-baggy shirt, ultra-baggy pants, everything in black. I didn't use a belt for the pants, though the waist stuck out behind like an open shopping bag. The shirt covered all.

Gordon once asked me why I wore this—a silly question. I pointed out that everyone in Bettawong wears baggies (who isn't a pensioner or public housing type, or a magistrate or something, but, say, everyone in Nostramamma's), and mostly in black, including Gordon. He dropped the subject.

I had a few boyfriends before I left Wooronga Station, who *said* they liked the way I looked, but once I got to Sydney Uni, the big hurts started coming, without even laughter, and always, it seemed, in tender moments of post-coital intimacy. These comments were so blandly objective, so helpfully accusatory, that I stopped allowing myself to be led into vulnerability, and adopted body camouflage. I was not depressed at the situation. Rather, I was relieved.

And once I knew my writing intentions and the heaviness of the places I was trying to break into, the panache of celibacy gave weight to my gravitas, especially since the body image I ideally needed—it was clear from the black-and-white bio pics—jutting collarbones, jutting hipbones, a hard-edged sharecropper face shadowed by long-fingered, veiny hands—this look was unachievable for me, no matter what I ate. I had hoped that it wouldn't matter, that I could do a Garbo and hide. Be lauded, loved, and celebrated—in absentia.

It was Brett who made me realize that hiding was hopelessly naive. That I couldn't be a name without a face, without a look. I had to be seen, with a look as important as the book, for fame, lasting fame. Not only that, but a look that suits my book, that fits my name, Desirée Lily.

Names came back to me. *Little Bustle*, from my father. *Peaches*, *Rockers* (my brother Angus's abbreviation for Rockmelons), and variations on that theme.

I remembered my other brother Stuart's party trick at shearing time (biggest audience then) of balancing a mug of tea on my bum while I had my hands full and couldn't do a thing. The mug always fell off, but only after teetering for the longest while. If I shook it off, I exacerbated the situation.

Mugs of tea would have been balanced on my chest if the blokes could have gotten away with it. As it was, I developed a powerful set of fists.

My waist only made the situation worse. My hands (small) could almost meet around it, and all my brothers' friends and every station hand grabbed at the waist of the girl with the jokey postcard shape.

All of that I had forgotten, until now—as I shoved the jeans down to my ankles. The T-shirt at my feet was probably just as bad as the jeans—ready to laugh at me if I tried to pull it on, sticking like a rubber band, just above my breasts. My eyes roamed over the disaster in the mirror as my brain raced over my problems. Would my normal uniform, plus the accessory jewels, work? Would my figure be guessed at anyway? Discussed in critical reviews of my work? *Could* I be Desirée Lily?

And then there was a knock on my door, and before I could say 'Just a minute,' the door, as it *would*, flew open.

10

ALTHOUGH I HAVE A painfully good memory, I cannot recall every detail of the next few minutes, though I was conscious through every moment.

My exact words, I don't remember.

My position: *You* try to turn your back, yank stiff, straight jeans up from around your ankles and over an impossible swell of thigh, *and* bend over and cover your body front and back with your arms, all at the same time. You might end as I did, knotted on the floor, a lump forming on your forehead from clonking your head on the hardwood—and your arse, if it is like mine, is pointing (a funny word in my case) high in the air, facing directly towards the doorway. Briefly, I tried to lift the thing that hurt so much that I wished it belonged to someone else—my head—so I could look towards the door, but trying to crane around only made me dizzy. My eyes jammed shut and my forehead kissed the floor again, not gently. Blood that I could hear wooshed between my ears, sounding like milk being shaken into butter in a goatskin, milk with shards of something sharp hitting the back of my eyeballs . . . *woosh, stab, woosh*.

Brett said something. That was his voice, but I couldn't identify words. What I do remember clearly was the voice of Jim, saying 'Excuse me, Miss Lily. I'll just put these here.'

I remember yelling, but not the words. There mightn't have been any words as such.

And I remember being alone in my room, my head impossibly heavy, my thoughts a cloud, and me still folded over on the floor.

I remember the smell of roses, and . . . shit, runny with piss.

I woke in a lake—slicking my arms, kissing my head. Jerking myself upright, I almost fell forward again, but balanced. Yet again in my life, this ingrate that I fed and clothed paid me in humiliation. I wanted, powerfully, to punish it, and I would have. I *would* have, if it wouldn't have hurt me. I tried to get up but my legs were asleep and my feet now woke with needle stabs too painful to touch. Instead, a rivulet ran down the side of my nose which identified, as if I wanted to know the details—flowers, fruit, filth—and my brain paraded Jim saying, 'Excuse me, Miss Lily. I'll just put these here.' In my brain's version, he was full-face centre of the picture, so my mind's eye watched what I know he must have been doing when he said those words. Smirk.

He had to be a champion smirker, for his paid smile was so good. So while I was unable to escape, my brain made me watch Jim enter and say those words, and smirk, and then delicately flare his nostrils and I watched his pupils contract, or would they dilate—I couldn't decide—but the smirk played clearly and with close-ups at least three times before my feet said I could move.

I rolled over in the muck and punched my legs till they obeyed me. Prying the jeans off, I ran with them and the shit-sodden shirt to my shower, where I rammed those taps to maximum downpour, then grabbed bottle after bottle and poured. Anything I could reach I used on me and the mess, stomping on the clothes so hard I could have drawn juice from stones. Eventually, I stopped, but I wasn't finished. My old jeans and shirt, I fished out of the trash and piled on the counter. The sodden lump of new clothes, I threw in the trash.

Using fresh towels and another armful of bottles, I scrubbed the floors, including each of my footsteps, and then pummelled those towels till they were rags and the only smells I could detect on them were dreadfully expensive. And then I stood under another downpour and used everything left on myself—purifying, scraping and polishing till an epidermal layer had whirled down the drain and my skin and hair jangled smells only of bottled scents.

Exhausted, but finished washing, I sniffed . . . roses!

I tried to open my windows to dump those stinkers, but they were hermetically sealed. So I buried vase and all under the sopping clothes disasters, and dressed.

Brett did *not* understand my humiliation.

We were in the lounge, Brett up on his futon mountain, me in the chair that I'd dragged from my room. My hair was still wet. The *eau de homeless person* scent of my old clothes was already overwhelming my washed body. The roses in the entry hall insinuated the lounge's air, but I was too tired to bury them. Besides, I had higher priorities.

Brett did not see that he should have waited for my assent to enter.

I hadn't objected when he first dropped in on me at Kate's place, had I? And he had only bothered to knock here for the show of it, so the Restonia chap could deliver my flowers, which I *had* asked for with some degree of urgency, hadn't I? How was Brett to know I'd be naked?

He was a better self-excuser than I have ever been capable of. His faults he spun to be my shortcomings. 'And once the chap was there, and he'd already gotten an eyeful, what was I to do? Shove him away and compound the problem? Better to let him finish delivering the flowers and leave, and I wager you a tadpole to a muffin, the empty-headed varlet wouldn't have remembered the incident for a moment. Besides,' Brett reminded me . . and on and on he went, in a liturgy of not-to-worry.

If, he assured me, the Restonia lived up to its reputation to fulfil every desire, and if this hostel was of any venerance, the only outré aspect of my activity could be its bad taste—if clichés are judged that harshly. Why, the likes of that young blue-eye must have servanted dining tables in the person of my folded-up body, oh ever so many times, years ago. With candlesticks flaring from . . .!

Oh, Brett could tell me of . . . and he *did*.

So what was I worried about? What was there to be *embarrassed* about? It couldn't be the hired help. And certainly not Old Brett, eh?

Brett just didn't understand me. Actually, he was right about himself. If it had just been Brett at the door, it would have been a temporary shock, but when I thought about it—no more so than my surprise when I entered his room where his nakedness stared at me. And less of a shock than when I thought he'd been reading my journal over my shoulder. My shape, I was sure he didn't notice one way or the other, having seen so many he must have been bored stiff by any of us. And, besides, neither Andrew nor the luscious Simone had gotten a rise out of him. So that left the indescribable—my filthy shame right in front of his eyes—and that didn't bother me when I contextualized it for his culture. The worst part of it, the shit pouring out of my arse and running over the floor, was, when I pictured it from his point of view, just everyday-person stuff. In Art History, I'd seen many pictures of naked people in hell, in all kinds of embarrassing positions, often with things poking up their bums and surrounded by environmental conditions murky in the extreme. Brett couldn't regard filth with the same derisive horror as we. Maybe the gross failure of bodily functions didn't register with him as anything different than, say, a burp after eating. Nature.

But that still left Jim, who had called me then, for the first time, 'Miss Lily', and who I was absolutely positive, would have smirked. And Brett couldn't say for sure that he hadn't, because, although I hadn't actually seen Jim's face, Brett hadn't been looking at him, either.

Brett was blind to the absolute horribleness of this, the intolerableness, the impossibleness of my position, not only now, but in the future.

And the worst part was: Brett didn't see why anyone would want to know what. *What was there precisely*, he asked again and again, *to know?*

His ignorance made me feel silly, and I know it is silly that this snowballed into another feeling, but it did. Because I felt silly, and he didn't understand why, I felt petty to feel silly, and resented feeling petty, and felt angry that I felt petty—a little angry at Brett, which had no adequate outlet, but which made me feel everything all over again, and more so—which made everything so much harder, and impossible to explain.

I didn't get into the issue about my name—that he'd utterly ruined it, and I'd have to pick another—because he genuinely sounded like he was trying to understand. He just couldn't see what there was to be upset about on my part, given that I had forgiven him his honest mistake. Of course he'd take greater precautions in front of others, so as not to compromise my sensibilities, so now let's have a smile, and everything's hunky do?

I just couldn't pretend to be hunky do, whatever that was. Wearily, and tearily, I left him. I had no idea how to deal with tomorrow, but he could order his own dinner, or not, as he chose.

I dragged my chair back to my room, closed the door, took the packet of Tim Tams out of the fridge, climbed into bed, ate the lot—and for afters, cried myself to sleep.

11

Brett woke me with a polite knock at the door.

I didn't bother getting out of bed. 'Come in,' I said, and he instantly appeared just inside without opening the door, as his hands were full.

He carried a breakfast tray adorned with a red rose, and set it on the bed. I threw the rose on the floor and smiled at him. He was trying.

I offered him the foot of my bed to settle on, and he did. I sat up, still in my pongy shirt, and examined my breakfast. It was the same as I'd ordered before. That reminded me. His clothes.

He didn't have BO, his smells being related to his moods and health. His clothes still looked fresh, but I was sure he had no others. Each item fit idiosyncratically, like factory rejects, pulling around the shoulders on the shirt, tight in various places on the jeans, nothing quite symmetrical. I wondered about the state of his socks. He had a habit that I'd noticed, of easing the laces on his boots. A half-memory of something when he was in Kate's house fluttered around my brain.

'What happened to your trunk and bag?'

'They're here,' he said.

I'd expected so.

He watched me eat, and I forbore asking if he'd eaten. Not asking restored a bit of my dignity, and also helped me build up the courage to tell him we couldn't stay here. We'd have to move today. But where?

And now, that perfect name we had made was ruined. I loved the idea of being Desirée Lily, but now she couldn't be.

I was swallowing the last dregs of my procrastination when he announced a 'wonderful surprise'.

'I've taken care of your problem,' he said, 'so we can go to work with no further interruption. And do you want some clothing advice?'

He put the breakfast tray on the floor as I sat up to hear what he had to say. He was so confident, he gave me confidence.

But he wouldn't explain more. 'I've saved the sporting part for you,' he said, as he led me to the lounge, and in there, to the gym.

Jim was stretched there in an extreme athletic position, his arms, legs, head and mouth bound with strips torn from his own clothes.

He opened his eyes. He must have noticed me but he looked at Brett. Big, blue, dilated eyes fringed with curly black lashes. Then he closed his eyes. I thought he might make a noise through his gag, some primal scream, but he made no sound at all.

Brett perched on a part of the gym's extensive anatomy. 'You have the choice,' he said to me. 'Draw and quarter, difficult in this space. Though for you . . .' And he bowed gallantly. 'Or boiling in oil, or impaling, or crucifixion of course, or the old intestine wrap, or a turn of the screw here . . .' And he reached to demonstrate, bringing on another display of eyeball exposure and lash-fluttering, but no noise.

I threw my hand up, which stopped Brett.

'Or,' he continued, 'there's always a simple hanging, though I wouldn't choose hanging as the ceiling here is a trifle inconveniently low.'

He looked to me, but Jim there was quite a gobstopper. I simply couldn't answer. I could only goggle.

'Well then, though we might be troubled afterwards by a gritty residue between the floorboards, you might prefer the currently popular burial in sand with only his head sticking out, and stoning him till he's dead. Or—'

I tore my eyes from Jim, whose eyes were now shut though his eyelashes trembled like leaves under rain. 'You're pathological!' I whispered at Brett with all my might.

He winced, I think.

'Where did you get him?' I asked, not that it mattered.

'Why, you were so upset, I grabbed him before he left, just in case.' And he smiled winningly.

'You mean he was here all along when we were discussing . . .' I couldn't continue. But I had to, so I forced myself. '*Listening* to us?'

'If he could hear through my bedroom door. Is there a problem?'

I sat on an unoccupied limb of the cold chrome body of the gym. 'That was very considerate, Brett.' I leaned closer to Jim. He looked both exhausted and attentive to the drift of our conversation. It annoyed me that during his painful death being discussed and this discussion occurring after his night on a rack, he still controlled himself to a ridiculous degree. Not a quiver of muscle nor a dribble through the anal outlet.

He'd stay right where he was, I decided, until we decided what to do.

'Brett,' I said. 'Let's go to your room.'

His room was as bare as before, except for his bag and trunk at the head of his rice-cracker mattress.

I sat cross-legged at the foot of his bed and he stretched out at the head, leaning back against his trunk.

He waited for me to talk, so I did.

'Thank you, Brett, for thinking of me. No one else has ever been as thoughtful of my feelings. But you can't just kill someone because he's in the wrong place at the wrong time.'

'I don't.' Vertical lines appeared between his brows. 'You do.'

'I don't do anything of the sort!'

'Angela! Desirée. You. You people. You always have.'

He could *infuriate*. 'What are you talking about? Are you *insane*?' Why, indeed, was I asking?

Probably better if I hadn't asked.

'I hate false accusations,' he murmured. The room fogged with that choking smell I had tasted once before.

I struggled to breathe. To understand.

'Justice!' he yelled.

'Gawhhhh.'

'Justice,' he repeated in a conversational timbre, as he waved the fug away. 'Angela,' he said. 'Most of the people you condemn and kill were in the wrong place at the wrong time. And whether I meet them or the others do, or they disappear as if they never were... is all a continuation of the same. The state of being in the wrong place at the wrong time, just like Jim.'

He sensed that I was not with him. 'Do you know anything about the Inquisition?'

I nodded. 'A bit. They killed a lot of people who didn't believe in Jesus, and killed more to make them believe. And there were a lot of people killed for reasons I never got down.' (History 101. I passed, barely.)

'Did the Grand Inquisitor,' he quiz-showed, 'when he died, come to hell or heaven's gate?'

It depended, didn't it, on what people thought of him? Mean old cuss, but then he was the Grand Inquisitor. Did he suffer his fall in respect before, or after death? I didn't know, so couldn't answer.

'And did,' Brett asked, as if I would know 'those judged and convicted by him meet blessed fates or fire and pitch?'

I didn't answer.

'Well, I'll tell you. So much depended on the state of the Grand Inquisitor's dyspepsia, the size of the crowd for an auto-da-fé—'

Like a good primary school teacher, he noticed my confusion. 'The kangaroo court?' he offered, and then went on. 'And then so much depended on whether the fire spluttered out before it reached those sinner's legs writhing at the stake. Or in other condemnations the rope broke, or the axeman missed, or the horse bolted with the damned on her back. Or the mob's wrath outgave... ahhh, revolutions...'

For a minute, he was lost in memories. Then he began all over again. 'Have you ever thought of the witches of Salem?'

'Of course.' I had a good grounding there from the Higher Light, where one shelf was 'Wimmin, Wiccans, and Goddess Worship'. I'd read every book in the shop by my second month there, not that I was into the stuff. It was something to do, and it did make me laugh.

'I'll tell you a bit,' he said, generously, meaning that he didn't think I knew a thing about the witches of Salem, or any other witches. He spoke like he had firsthand knowledge.

'If you had a wart,' he said,' or were uncommonly beautiful, or a widow with property someone else wanted, or liked little kitty cats, or noticed your neighbour doing something he hain't supposed to do, then all it took was a dunking. Dunk and if she drowns, she's innocent. Or was it guilty? Witches in Africa, witches in Europe, witches, witches, witches. Stick her hand in boiling oil, and if she blisters, she's a witch. Light a fire under her, and if it goes out before it reaches her toes, she's a witch. If so, burn her! And to find her in the first place? See that woman walking down the road, leading her pig to market? We're in need of a fine witch. Might as well be she? Or...' And his words ran dry.

We sat for a while. I thought. He looked lost in thought. Maybe he was just waiting.

But that was historical, and we were in Now. 'Justice now,' I pointed out.

'Throw the cards in the air, and they don't come down fair, me pretty!'

And here, he uttered a high, screechy cackle that grabbed the back of my neck in shivers.

He stopped and regarded me with the impersonal affection of a city person to a brown egg. 'I don't mean to scare you, my dear,' he smiled. 'But the way of the world has been that justice comes to those in the wrong place at the wrong time. Always has.'

'But we've progressed!' I protested.

'Hoo hoo!'

'Democracy, and all that.' I was going to lecture him when he interrupted.

'Do you read, child?' he asked, not unkindly, but this tone does make me want to punch someone's lights out.

'Yers.'

'Do you follow the War on Terror?'

'Yes!' But I lied. I'd had enough of it, didn't own a TV or radio, and bad news had cured me of reading the papers.

'Angela?'

'Well, not too much. But you should be much more busy because of it. Especially as the evil is so clear-cut.'

He leaned forward and peered at my face, looking for all the world as if he was searching for blackheads.

'Do you mind?'

'Don't you care what's happening, Angela, in your world?'

He was in some respects, so *other*worldly, and curiously dense. 'Brett,' I told him, keeping my sneer as safe as I could make it, 'You might have power in your place, but a person like me has none whatsoever here.'

He accepted that. However, it didn't deter him. 'Don't you care?'

If he were Gordon, I would have clouted him. 'Care,' I explained patiently, 'is only worthwhile when it's something that does something for you. I don't get off on demos, and . . . but this is beside the point. There is justice, you know. Not perfect, but then nothing is.'

He waved his hand in a swirling motion, and a heavy pile of newspapers fell upon the bed in front of me.

'Read,' he commanded, in a tone that brooked no argument as to the humanly impossible. I scanned as fast as I could. I scanned to the last grubby broadsheet.

'And?' he asked.

'Well...'

'They shoot suspects, don't they?'

'Mm.'

'You're saying they might be just poor bastards guilty as chooks?'

'I hadn't thought to describe them so colourfully.'

And the bombs going off against anyone in their range, condemned by the bomber, terrorist freelance, terrorist state. And a lot more that was the reason I didn't do the news, and wouldn't again. I felt sick.

'And now, it's your justice to keep,' he said, sweeping the papers to the floor. 'What is your sentence?'

I couldn't talk. Politics and history and news and morality bore me *utterly*. That's why I love living for art.

But I couldn't shirk my responsibility in the present situation.

'What will happen to him?' I asked.

Brett sat up, suddenly agitated.

'What do you think will happen to him?' He seemed to want to ask something, but didn't. His face took on a greenish tinge. He was growing ill at an alarming rate.

'Are you...?' This time it couldn't be garlic.

'Nothing.' He waved his hand impatiently, and shot out a question. 'Do you believe in fate?'

'That's a crock,' I laughed.

'Crock? Crocodile?'

'Crock of shit.' I blinked. The expression suddenly sounded crude in his presence. Funny, that. The image of shit in actuality struck me as natural in his context, but the language was crude...

'And... heaven?' he interrupted.

'Never thought of it before you came along,' I answered immediately, and completely fair dinkum, expressing for the first time what I had always felt but never said, even to myself.

He hesitated, but blurted, 'Me?'

'You're here, aren't you? So yes, and I guess that means that heaven must exist, too, but like getting married, I never expected to go there.'

'What did you expect?' He looked enthralled, and terrified.

I'd never thought about it. But now that he asked, 'The worms crawl in. You know the rhyme. You know pinochle?'

'I think so.' I think he didn't, but he didn't want to stop the flow.

And I am also sure that he wanted to ask another question, but couldn't. His sickness seemed to grow, flicker, and then fade away. Maybe it was like, as my gran used to say, when someone walks on your grave.

We eye-balled each other, and he didn't have to tell me that I was procrastinating. I knew.

'Do you think he was a happy person, someone who has friends?' I asked.

His left brow jerked upward, and he nodded his head.

'Then can you kill him in a humane way?'

'If that's what you want?'

'Maybe he'll go to heaven,' I said, though when the word 'heaven' poured from my mouth, it left a saccharine aftertaste. There isn't any heaven, that taste told me—and I couldn't really imagine a believable hell, though the Devil was there in front of me, who could deliver newspapers with a flick of his wrist, and possessed a tail more beautiful than Boofhead's.

He stood up and reached his hand out. 'Proceed?' he asked.

'Yes,' I answered, feeling that it was my responsibility, as a human being.

We walked out together, but Jim must have had a heart attack during our conversation, because his muscles had slackened to their final resting place, and then grown stiff.

12

THE FUNERAL WAS tasteful and small. With the Restonians and Brett and myself, the total number of mourners made less than ten, though many angry tears were shed, especially by Ferdinand. The owner of the Restonia arrived by proxy, in the form of the company lawyer. He sidled up to Brett and tried to engage in small talk, using words like 'cool', meaning, in the lawyer's case, that he had been taking lessons in acting human from his teenage daughter, but they hadn't worked. Brett ignored him, concentrating instead on the rest of the funeral experience.

As it was, the funeral had been necessarily delayed due to all the messy bureaucratic hang-ups caused by Jim's naughty, naughty death.

Mr Hartshorn and Miss Lily forbore the strain with the patience and good-humour always wished for in the upper strata of society, but so rarely demonstrated.

Thus, the Restonia put itself out, slavishly, to fulfil our every whim (and hopefully, avoid any whim we creative artistic types and our lawyers might entertain, of suing the place for gross negligence, illegal entry, mental pain and suffering, and a range of other reasons such as 'outrageous invasion of our peaceful working environment').

One thing is absolutely certain. If it were not for Brett's intervention (at my instigation), Justin Abernathy as well as his aides would have been finding their meals out of gutters. They *knew*, and had known for years, that to Jim, that gym was a nectar-filled flower to a bee. He had been caught on a gym before, and in a very similar position to the one he achieved when he finally had too much fun for one day, and *ruined* ours.

He had been put on probation after 'the DeGraff incident', when the weight of his muscle-bound body tore a chandelier from the ceiling in the DeGraff's suite—an antique Bohemian chandelier they took with them everywhere for luck. It shattered when it fell, and was a source of continuing stress to Blakely White, the toady lawyer, as the DeGraffs mulled over 1) the shock of finding a man half-hung and wholly unconscious, when you get back to your suite from an evening conducting Opera, and 2) an even greater worry—the upward-spiralling value of good-luck lost.

So the entire staff at the Restonia was vociferously grateful to us and eloquently horrified at the shock to our beings upon our discovery, waking fresh from slumbers on a lovely mid-day full of promise—Jim's stiff, room-temperature corpse. Our peace was shattered, our creativity sapped, and our persons inconvenienced by the representatives of and tedious formalities of police and legal procedures.

The Restonia, its owners and its friends we never met wanted to get Jim settled and the past forgotten—or if not forgotten, thoroughly forgiven. So with a maximum of privacy and a minimum of red tape, in a relatively short time, which means *eventually* (or if you are obsessive about minor details, two months—which makes, counting on your fingers, a rancid day in January) the last formalities hanging around Jim's death were put to rest, and Jim was declared Free.

He was taken out of the fridge, suitably packaged, and the funeral, at last, began.

Everyone thanked us for our graciousness, even as the mourners shed their tears of anger at the beautiful, wilful boy, lost too early in life.

Some lovely personal statements were read, the most beautiful, by Ferdinand. Then a person no one knew uttered what I guess was the basic service-providers' minimum: two minutes of vaguely ecumenical words ending with a burst of something vaguely musical, signalling that the funeral directors wanted to be left alone.

We left as Jim's coffin went through the crematory gates to be burned to a pile of ash, bone, and little metal bits.

'Too bad,' Justin said, as he glanced back. 'He would have enjoyed this part.'

'Too right,' sniffed Ferdinand, 'Doesn't seem right.' And he broke into fresh tears. 'Keen as mustard he was, just for a bit of excitement.'

13

Y<small>OU WONDER</small>, do you, about our progress?

It was a busy time. Not only did we cope with all the aforementioned intrusion by red-tapers and the sometimes over-solicitous staff at the Restonia, but Brett and I each had our jobs to do.

I will describe first, how I went.

The problem was, I needed to live up to my name, and I had to learn how. In some ways, it was easy, because the staff at the Restonia, especially Justin, who appointed himself my factotum, sensed my taste for comfort and passion to get rid of the gym (which was taken by the police the next day, anyway) and every bit of the lounge and bedroom taste of the great actor whose death had been prematurely mourned, seeing that he'd turned out to have died, not shockingly inconveniently, but with a level of consideration for others unpractised in his life.

By the end of the first week after Jim's death, the lounge and entrance hall and my room were now harmoniously

1) Carpeted throughout with an under-layer of wall-to-wall sheepskins of my specification, since this was not Justin's expertise: Merino-Corriedale cross, so that I could dig my bare toes into the curls. On top of that, a colourful scattering of Persian prayer rugs, each, as Justin assured me, with a 'name and provenance'.

2) Arted, at least beginning to be. This would be a work in progress. Real art, I specified—nothing Australian. Justin advised me, and in return, I gave him the responsibility of shopping for and buying, the collection. When he realized that his spending limit was unlimited as long as he paid market value, he was discomposed for a day. An extreme reaction, I thought, but he was a sensitive man.

I expected him to bid for a Renoir in an upcoming Impressionists thing Christie's was doing in London, but he refused. They were landscapes, he said, and he wasn't buying for me just so I could have 'names on the walls'. I didn't know what he was thinking, but thought it better to back off and not show the limit of my education. He bought rapidly, but with much angst. Even though it was our money, he didn't like overbidding—a concept I found surreal when the market price for a piece of canvas with a bit of paint would have bought Tasmania, but that is irrelevant. He didn't want to be seen to be an amateur. And he had a definite vision for the Hartshorn-Lily suite. So, on to the collection, as it grew:

An Ingres bath scene, pre-*Playboy*, but the same airbrushed perfection and naked pubes. You could feel the heat of the women in that room.

A life-size sketch by Titian of two crazed men leering at an obese woman. I would have made Justin take it away, but he would have asked me why.

A sooty black and white photo of a woman, taken from the back. Maybe it was raining, for she has grabbed her skirt and the back of it cups her behind, round as a beachball. Heinrich Kuehn did this in nineteen-ten, Justin said, watching me — which put me in a spot. Was he having me on with this Heinrich, and did nineteen-ten have pertinence? Anyway, a photo isn't art unless your whole collection is photos and you have minimalist furniture. Even I knew this. However, there was something about this picture. I found it hard to look away.

He grunted cryptically, and the next day presented me with another photograph. This one wasn't dated, but looked like it was *fin de siecle*, the *siecle* of cinched waists, Pears soap girls, and Dr. Gustav Jaeger's Sanitary Woollen System, wool corsets that had 'all the advantages of girded loins without the disadvantages'. I learnt about him in primary school as one of the heroes of Australia's golden age, and a man who helped to put food on my grandfather's table (more mutton). But about this. He called it *The Pearl Necklace*, and it was by an American, Frank Eugene (lucky I hadn't told Justin 'no Americans' — the thought hadn't occurred to me). The woman in the photo is fondling a pearl necklace. She wears a white dress with a floppy bow at the side, accentuating the smallness of her waist — the centre of the picture.

My favourite, though, almost lost me Justin. I noticed it in a Christie's catalogue that he left with me, his 'mistake' he rued, never repeated. It was a bastard take-off of Fragonard's *Swing* by an apprentice who never amounted to anything. The bastard take-off wasn't how Christie's described the painting, but that and more surprising obscene expressions were what Justin used, his polka-dot bow tie jumping in shock at each new filthy outburst. The catalogue called it *Summer*, but his most polite title for it was 'The Pretender'. I didn't care. I wanted it because it made me laugh. Besides, I didn't know Fragonard from a meat pie, and this was still art. I was forced to put Justin in his place by informing him icily, 'Christie's doesn't sell meat pies.'

He gritted his teeth and obeyed my instructions, buying the thing through a contact because he didn't want to soil his reputation. At least, that's how he put it to me, and more, such as the fact that he paid too much (relishing this detail), telling me that there was stiff competition from an Indonesian noodle manufacturer and a Nevadan brothel chain tycoon. He had to be lying, but I let him spill his spleen. He was such a snob, but we were good for each other.

I made him hang *Summer* in the lounge where Brett and I could look at it and I at least, could laugh. Its carefree country scene was the opposite of real country life. A pink-cheeked lady is high in mid-swing, not on the kind of swing I grew up with (a rope from a gum tree beside what was too often, a dry creek bed) but in the lady's case, a real two-rope swing with a wooden seat, hanging from a leafy oak in an untroubled French countryside, and the breeze and her joy have flipped her skirts up, exposing neatly turned legs and tiny feet clad in blue slippers with small curved heels. Her dress is a frothy white and blue, just like the clouds and sky. Everyone laughs in this work that should have been called *Pastoral Fantasy*, where even the mongrel sheep are adorable.

Then one day Justin brought in a pencil work, 'another Bacchanalia'— every naked bod, male and female, sporting the most ideal dimensions bursting with muscle and health. I was examining the work fresh from Justin's hands. Though only in pencil, the people were so *alive*, when a feature caught my eye. There were gum trees in the scene! Not only that, but . . . 'What's that bloody koala doing there?'

Justin turned to face me with his eyebrows humped in a *who? me?*

'Yes, you,' I said severely.

'What do you think of Rose?'

'I don't have a "Rose" here. There's just this drawing.' I shoved it aside on the chesterfield, and looked around.

Justin explained, 'Rose is the woman in that picture I just gave you.'

I picked it back up and looked. All the women had remarkable similarities.

'Isn't she something!?' he asked.

Justin's taste was showing. I did another take at the paintings on the wall, and back at 'Rose'.

'Rose was his model, Norman Lindsay,' Justin said.

And more, I thought. Unless the artist was chainsawed from the waist down.

Rose was stacked, Rose was firm. Rose was the sort of girl that got tattooed on a million arms.

'My favourite,' he sighed. Yes, he did sigh. 'A tragic life,' he added irrelevantly.

He never elaborated. Was it Rose or Lindsay? I enjoyed the picture, and he bought another—another Rose. Then he bought lots of Lindsays, not all with Rose in them, though it was hard to tell whether the others were camouflage. Some of the subject matter I would have banned as part of my 'Nothing Australian' mandate. I'd been OD'd on Australiana, growing up in it.

But Justin, not knowing that, bought in his Lindsay-buying frenzy, a study of a parrot. If he had told me before I tore off the wrapping, I would have told him that a parrot is something you shoot before it deafens you with its screech, or chews the wood right off your dunny while you're sitting reading your next bumwipe. But Justin didn't get the lecture because Justin didn't know. And I was lucky he didn't. *The Angry Parrot* had me crying, it was so funny. So that was followed with a series of small cartoons on the horrible tortures children put cats to, and the cats' revenge. And then there were dogs bettered by chooks, and the chooks reminded me of our fearsome rooster, Bolt, who my brother Angus always tried to kick.

Justin took me aback with *The Angry Parrot*. Either he had a great, hidden sense of humour, or he was even more clever.

Lindsay was a great success, so I found and gave Justin a thank you. *Marriage*, which had apparently been rejected for publishing, though it was a beautifully rendered scene of love and human beauty, in a kind of dreamtime cloud. Rose was in it, of course.

Oh, he bought more art, and the only choice he made that I didn't care for was a bunch of Indian sculptures. I had been through all that at the Higher Light.

What we learned *not* to do was to buy for Brett's taste, after a disastrous experience.

Justin arrived with a package for Brett one morning just after breakfast. Brett was already in his bedroom, working, but I knocked at his door and explained that Justin had a surprise.

He emerged, preoccupied but smiling in his oddly forbearing way.

Justin unwrapped and held out a heavy framed picture.

Brett blanched and then flinched as if holding back a flood of tears.

His fingers made twiddling motions, which I interpreted as a polite way to say, 'Get this fucker out of my sight.' Then he stumbled to his room, almost coming a cropper on the laces of those clumsy boots. I heard the door close as if he were nursing a hangover—and he didn't emerge till dinner, when he only picked at his food, and had one sip.

Justin sold the picture the next week for a profit, but it was a deflating experience for him because the etching was such a thoughtful choice—a study by Albrecht Dürer for his masterpiece (Art History 201) *Knight, Death, and the Devil*. It was a compliment from Justin that Brett's horns looked so good, that Brett looked such a handsome devil that Justin's only worry was—Brett might have another print from this particular etching series. Justin was only catering to the taste of every artist he had served—the taste to surround themselves with images of themselves in favourite rôles.

Brett confused me, too, with his reaction. When I broached it at dinner, he was still too upset for words. 'Unbearable,' was all he said.

Justin tried next what he described as a 'small, lovely, picture of hell' by the great master of its depiction, Hieronymus Bosch, and that was even worse. Much worse. Brett came out of his room by dinnertime that night and sat with me. He watched me eat and I tried to act cheery and eat nonchalantly—not easy, with that woebegone expression fronting me.

When I was spooning up the last of my passion-fruit fool, he asked 'Do you have nostalgia?'

That took me by surprise. What was there for me to be nostalgic for? 'No,' I said, having nothing else to add.

He shook his head. When I asked what his headshake meant, he said he didn't know he *had* shaken his head.

And next we got to the contentious issue of seating. I ordered comfortable seating, and of course, the removal of the futon mountain. That was a short-lived experiment.

Brett didn't like sofas or chairs, or even the experimental recliner chair I ordered for him. He wanted his futon mountain—and no, its squeaky grey rubber didn't bother him at all. So I had it reinstalled, and he was happy again. He was, however, quite firm about me having my own comfort, so I experimented with a variety of chairs and sofas until Justin commandeered the situation, and produced a monumental leather sofa (he taught me that it was properly, a 'chesterfield') smelling of cinnamon and mushrooms. Justin draped Victorian cashmere shawls over it and piled fat, embroidered cushions against each capacious arm. I didn't object, though it took me a while to figure out how to use them right, and *then* I understood why he was so insistent. They were great under my feet or propping up an elbow or stuffed behind my back when I lay in full recline position, as I learned to do when Justin taught me. I don't know what he grew up with, but I grew up with cracked plastic-leather and rusty chrome kitchen chairs being the seating in the house, the concept of reclining being a deathbed activity, if you are lucky. My life in Sydney had not been one of luxury, either, even when I worked in the bank. Somehow, the money never stretched far enough, and the thought of furnishings had been all so suburban, like having kids and a husband and a car.

Justin considered it his responsibility to extend the powers of my imagination beyond that of just a comfy bed. (I *had* always wanted a comfortable, non-lumpy, non-sagging, very off-the-floor bed, something that I had never had, but had dreamed of ever since reading *The Princess and the Pea*.)

He brought me art books and pointed out important works showing what he called, 'the history of women's recline'. I had taken those few art history classes in uni, of course, and gone to museums in Europe, but I had never *seen*. Justin opened my eyes.

Brett was happier sitting on the floor to eat than he was with a table and chairs. So the table-and-chairs experiment lasted only one meal, replaced by the set-up we had before with the addition for me (Brett declined) of plump cushions. It took another employee to whisk this extra furniture in and out at every meal, but what the hell.

My bedroom took on a level of luxury I could not have imagined, till Justin. He had missed his calling, he said, but my unspoken wishes were his siren song.

Brett wanted nothing of the decorator touch for him. His bedroom requirements were simple. The staff were never to enter, for any reason. And he wanted no redecorating done for him. He had, Justin and I agreed, ascetic taste and pure discipline, as attested to by his rigorous diet.

Speaking of eating, within weeks of our arrival something fishy began cooking in the bowels of the kitchen. It was based on Brett's diet régime—the same meal in three sizes every day, the smallest being breakfast. If you remember, I tried to translate Brett's wishes for that first meal into something a chef could do, but not ever having eaten Steak Tartare, I was wrong with my specifications. Once adjusted to Brett's exacting requirements, the meal for him was: raw heart, chopped roughly, of any beast. No condiments, which meant *nothing* was to be mixed into the mound of meat, or sprinkled upon it. Serve in a bowl, accompanied by a jug of blood, again of any beast—the temperature of meat, liquid, bowl and jug being 37 to 38 degrees centigrade. And nothing else. No little toasts or slices of fragrant warm pumpernickel or coriander leaves or raw eggs, crumbled yolks, caviar. No finely chopped shallot mixed with the meat or even a grind of pepper. Nothing added to the pure food he required for his simple taste. Not even a glass for his drink. Brett liked drinking out of the jug.

Serge Dupuy, the chef of the Restonia, not only made Brett's meals himself, but I knew because of certain hints being dropped—he was planning to copyright Brett's régime as *his*, in a book titled something like *Dupuy's Red Cuisine Path: How to Eat Your Way to Power Muscle*.

Although Serge lacked a sense of honourableness in upholding the client-chef relationship, not to mention copyright and plagiarism (applicable in someone's unique requests in dining?), I enjoyed his creations on my behalf as immensely as he enjoyed making them. I relished our slightly competitive dialogue in the form of me ordering, he cooking, he creating new surprises, me eating them and giving him my judgements.

He was an artist. Sure, he had a sleazy, lazy side—but he was a total *unknown*, without even a line of Woolworths sauces to his name. I looked down on Serge, but did not disparage his wish for fame.

There were only two rules I gave Serge regarding the food he made for me. No meat. Growing up, I had my fill of flesh foods, and swore off meat when I urbanized myself. I didn't hold anything against Brett. He had his needs, but no thank you, for me. The other rule I gave Serge was: no garlic, no matter whether he thought a dish needed just a touch, a little touch, or not. Other than that, the more extravagant the creation, the more wildly creative, exciting and even *decadent* the menu, the better. After all, Desirée Lily would want all that. And I was no longer the girl with the smell of hot mutton fat in her hair, who thought of a cold Tim Tam chocolate biscuit as the height of decadent frivolity.

That leaves the dragon-of-a-problem that *somehow* had to be slayed: my looks.

That day of Jim's death-discovery, events overtook this ultra-priority, but every non-hassled moment I tried to figure out a way to kill this fiend. Jewels had lost their twinkle as the answer. I didn't ask Brett for advice. Although he was blessed with looks, he did nothing with them. Therefore, I expected him to be bloody useless but he must have seen my glumness, for he approached me with an inspiration.

It took me a whole day to summon up my nerve and follow Brett's advice, but I did—calling Justin to an extraordinary tête-à-tête in my bedroom. There I revealed to him with all the dignity that I could, considering the state of my garb, that I was emerging from a chrysalis, but prematurely—my new wings unfolding before the pattern of their colour, pattern, shape, and size was quite determined. I needed a 'determiner' (Brett's suggested word). Justin understood *exactly* what I meant and almost melted with the romance of it all. He immediately suggested Kevin's services as dragon slayer, or what Justin called 'style master'.

Justin scurried away and in about five minutes, in the midst of post-Jim commotion and the redecoration of our suite, he produced Kevin.

Kevin took one look at me and turned to Justin. 'I will always remember this.'

I must have shown that I was ready to burst something, for Justin turned to me. 'He's happy!' he said.

'Of course I'm bloody happy, you drongo!' Kevin snapped at Justin. He turned to me. 'I am beyond ecstatic at the opportunities afforded me,' he announced, sounding constipated. And besides, I didn't like my looks rubbed in quite so much. I felt like a derelict house in front of a mad architect. Would there be anything left of me but bones, by the time Kevin was truly happy? I would have flounced away if that could have restored some dignity and I had some place to flounce to, or other resources.

'You want to be private, I can see,' Justin said, absorbed in the giant sofa being carried into the suite.

Kevin didn't hear Justin, being totally absorbed in me. His brain was busy, I could see. If he'd had a crowbar in his hand and I were that house, he would have bashed through his first wall already. I had no choice, so I led the way to my room. He closed the door behind us. My clothes now ponged more than ever as my armpits poured sweat. I was going to sit when he grunted, so I continued to stand. Finally he asked, 'I don't mean to pry, luv. But do you know your dimensions?'

Of course I didn't. He pulled a tape measure out of his pocket and offered it to me. I closed my eyes, meditated in panic for a while, and then took the plunge, because I had to jump. I gave the tape back to him and told him to take the measurements over my clothes. Then he would have what he wanted.

He was as professional in his touch as I expected him to be, writing everything down on a little pad, and even sticking his pencil behind an ear while he wielded the tape measure.

He made a number of grunts as the figures added up, enough to get a tailored wetsuit sewn with no additional fittings. At last he was satisfied, apologizing for the hassle, but adding that now that that nasty job was done, I wouldn't have to be measured again, and I could just try on clothes and enjoy myself. For someone to whom trying on clothes was worse than a trip to the dentist, his statement was funny—and I laughed.

'Don't,' he said.

I had hurt his feelings! I hastened to apologize, and explained that he should be able to understand what a pain and chore the clothes issue would be to me. An unusual frankness forced this out of me, maybe because he had been the one kneeling when my crotch-to-floor measurement had been taken.

Tight-lipped, he asked to be excused, and I gave him permission, smacking the back of my head once he was out of sight. I needed help, and had blown my chance.

A vexing situation. I went into the lounge and threw myself petulantly and experimentally into the lap of that chesterfield. Then I reached for a loquat, a bowl of which had magically appeared in the decorating flurry.

I had just spat my fifth loquat pit into a crystal bowl, when Kevin knocked on the suite door.

'Come in,' I yelled, feeling ashamed of myself, but too trapped in my own physical ugliness to grovel in front of Kevin for the sake of his ego needing to make a silk purse out of a side of bacon.

He was carrying a white tissue-wrapped package tied with lilac ribbon, and he handed it to me.

'I took the stuff out of the top,' he said, 'because you don't need it, and I'm sorry if it retains a bit of scent (here, he blushed) but I thought it could be a bit of something to wear this evening at dinner, and would maybe...'

And when I continued to look at him stupidly and irrelevantly, he stamped his foot. 'Oh, do try it on. Do. Do it for Kevin.'

Somehow, he managed to give me confidence in that tantrum, though I didn't think it was the real Kevin speaking. Maybe he could do something with this side of bacon.

He didn't do as I suggested: sit on the chesterfield to wait. He paced outside my closed bedroom door while I changed.

The package was heavy for its thickness. I unwrapped it on the bed. A top and a skirt, in diaphanous layers of what I guessed was silk chiffon, the smoky lilac of a bushfire dawn, beaded with seed pearls the colour of the moon. The pattern was teardrops.

All so delicate, yet so weighted, so rich.

I tore off my stinky rags and ran into the shower because it would have been a sin not to. After towelling myself, I tiptoed back to the bed. Why I tiptoed, I don't know.

They fitted as if made for me.

Kevin knocked, and I answered, 'Oh, Kevin.'

He knocked again, and I flung open the door.

The smell he had spoken of was the faint whiff of him. A pleasant aroma—healthy man plus sandalwood, tabac, and coriander. I knew my scents from the Higher Light, though theirs were like artificial vanilla to the scents the Restonians wore.

Superficially, Kevin didn't look at all like me. We were almost the same height, but he was curvy with a muscleman's curves, not mine.

'I did some adjustments,' he said.

The Restonia had a clothing repair service, I'd been told, but I had thought of them sending out to a wizened little tailor who was only too happy to sew a button at any hour. Kevin had to have been the needleman here. He wielded one mean needle, and worked quick as a tantrum.

The picture of Kevin as a bellydancer was too much a stretch of the imagination—and irrelevant now.

'Desirée . . . Lily,' breathed Kevin, in a reverential whisper—not reverencing me, but his genius in knowing what was right, 'you make a perfect houri . . . if you'd only stand up straight.'

He whacked me sharply between the shoulderblades, pushed his hands against my collarbones. He stood back, and tutted. 'Not good enough,' he pronounced, and marched into my bath.

He came out twirling a towel between his hands.

'You're not a kiwi bird!' *Whack* at the front of my thighs. 'Bum out!' *Whack*. 'Out more. Be proud of it . . . Yahhs. That's my girl. Give a nice curve to that back and waist. Look at yourself in profile.'

I turned obediently. Snapping towels hurt.

'See that curve? Give it more. A proper seahorse of a curve.' *Whack!* 'Then give me an "S" if you don't know seahorses.'

How was I supposed to know seahorses? But I was getting the picture—a strange picture, not contemporary.

'Ehsss!' he hissed. 'Don't forget your shoulders . . . There.' *Whack!* 'Back! Push them baaack!'

My posture lesson was painful for both of us, seeing as it had to overcome years of curling in on myself, and he wanted me at maximum unfurl. He was a martinet. I was happy he didn't have a stick, because my skin was covered in blushes by the time he was satisfied. And then I not only stood two inches taller, but had two places on my body where you could rest your mug of tea.

The pain was worth it. 'Your body was meant for another time,' Kevin said, 'But those times will come again . . . with you.' He sounded tired but elated, like a child after a party.

'Move,' he commanded. And I actually twirled!

Kevin smiled approvingly. The butterfly was opening its wings. Until he brought me down to earth.

'If only for your hair.'

14

AH, THAT ARABIAN NIGHTS romance of froth and trembling teardrops—Desirée's first garb. The low-slung diaphanous skirt that caressed my swell of thigh. The beaded bodice I spilled out of only, Kevin assured me, in the most alluring way. My below-the-waist little melon of a belly (Kevin's description) showed to its best advantage, as did my deep-as-a-pool navel (Kevin again), a crater I had previously thought of only as a cleaning nuisance.

My back now flaunted a seahorse curve.

My skin glowed. My body was so white and pink and peach that it surprised me, but it shouldn't have, since I had hidden it the whole of my adult life. My arms were a fright. I had to promise Kevin to correct that fault, being tanned from just above the elbow to my snaggle-nailed, rampant-cuticled hands, about which he lectured me again.

But enough of tan arms, broken nails, bare feet. Kevin's interest was clothes.

From his first generous lesson (he wouldn't take payment for his houri outfit), Kevin taught me that clothing can be fun, and it can make one feel bloody marvellous. Lying on my pillows reaching for Turkish delight was more delightful, when dressed right . . . popping a peeled grape into my mouth (Of course I had to order them, though only once. They are far better when you pop the skins in your mouth), the *wack wack* of air from the ceiling fan (got it installed for fun) stirred the silk to caress me, the countless little pearls, to tremble. Dressed right, I learned to move my body to its best advantage instead of its eternal shame. Freedom and joy.

But I couldn't wear my houri outfit only. Kevin had much work to do. He brought me art books, not that I needed to see what he planned, but he could not contain himself. This art he drew inspiration from for his vision of Desirée Lily was actually not art at all. Just collections of dressmaker designs, many by Worth who Kevin was madly jealous of for having lived at the right time. Kevin was a romantic, and a visionary. I giggled and he sighed over Bakst's exhibitionisms for the Ballet Russe—all bared breasts flinging and veils flying. Impractical, and not quite fitting for a famous novelist, but I was flattered.

Desirée Lily, Kevin told me, was *made* for her body. *How could your mother have known*, he asked me, *what you would be like?* He marvelled at the exact fit between my body and my name. La Belle Époque, and better yet, the ten years earlier, he told me, was my time—and the French part of it, not the American, which had those scarecrow Gibson girls with their stiff serge skirts. Kevin liked froth, and lots of it.

He taught me about ruffles, ruches, swags, bias cuts, décolletage; leg-of-mutton sleeves hugely puffed to the elbow, then tight as gloves and buttoned past the wrist. He was a stickler about skirts, because the right skirt makes the right, swaying walk—the trained skirt, which restricts the size of steps, the gored skirt that creates an elongated trumpet bell shape 'like the gently opening head of a longiflorum lily'—he adored symbolism. Jackets were his passion, unfortunate in our climate. But he persevered, begging me to wear them in training for my world tour. He made them with collars so high they exhibited my head on a plate of creamy velvet.

Kevin took me on a tour of what Justin had bought, and reintroduced me to the women in the pictures—Justin!

He brought me advertising pictures of corsets and bustles worn by beautiful women, and would exclaim, holding up a page, 'Look at you.'

Then he would make me strip and parade in front of the picture, daring it to look back at me. I didn't need a bustle or a corset or wadded tissue for my equally 'extraordinary' (according to him) breasts. It was a delight to parade with nothing on, except a pair of kid-glove boots in palest violet that came halfway up my calves and buttoned with a button hook. Kevin watched, commanded if he thought I was slouching, and when I was not, almost swooned with delight. Not a bit of passion for me, mind you. I was only the mannequin he had always wanted, his impossible dream come true.

Why did he work at the Restonia? He didn't only work at the Restonia. He had moonlighted for years sewing 'clothing for special needs', as he liked to call it, from ballgowns to day dresses—for a whole assortment of blokes. He didn't like the bitchiness of the rag trade, he said. As for me, his touch was more respectful than any doctor's, and though in his fittings and his critical assessments, he got to know my body more intimately than I had ever taken the time to, it was all for the cause of helping him to design, and often produce with his own hands, incredible creations to be worn as a canvas wears paint.

Justin and Kevin had, without even discussing it, the same vision of my colours. Not an inner vision thing as in the way of the Higher Light's many books on colour vision—'You need to identify the colour personality type of your interlocutor to understand how to use colours to influence him or her.' Kevin and Justin didn't know and weren't interested in psychology. They were aesthetes. And their different but agreeing aesthetic senses had determined that my predominant colour should be white. Kevin added other touches—lilac, violet, peach, butter yellow, ancient-mariner's-eyes blue, but their strength, according to him, lay in the spareness of their application. A lightness of touch was the secret, 'like splitches of rain'.

Of course I never told him, but Kevin had the soul of a poet.

Because I stayed in constantly, Kevin's taste for the luxurious was almost sated, but not quite. He always had room for more, and continually needed a new dress, opera cloak, negligee, chemise, ballgown, tea robe—modern only if you lived in another century, but that didn't bother him if it didn't bother me. He told me that if I wore with confidence, then my style *would* be contemporary.

He had to do a few boringly modern things for the few times I had to go outside the building and deal with the mundane outside world—the sessions concerning Jim, for instance—but even the clothes Kevin designed for these occasions made me feel almost beautiful, if I could have cut off my head. If a headless me would have been practical and socially acceptable, I would have felt wholly beautiful.

I almost forgot to tell you about the shoes. He knew a man who spoke no English but communicated perfectly. At the first appointment, Kevin and he crooned together over old shoes while Mr Hazumi held my feet. My feet were not as adorable as the rest of my body, my toes being too widely splayed to be ideal, and my heels 'cracked to buggery'—one look from Kevin made me assure them both that my feet would be disciplined immediately to be soft and smooth.

But my feet are small, thank goodness. With Mr Hazumi's considerable craft and artistry, I soon had shoes as pretty as the slippers of the lady who gave Justin heartburn, and who made me laugh. Thankfully, both Kevin and Mr Hazumi found stilettos horrible and modern and common anyway, so all my shoes were wearable, with short and curvy heels.

One day when Brett was up on his futon mountain and I was feeling fabric swatches, I noticed him easing the laces on his boots again. I couldn't remember what his feet were like, whether he had corns or ingrown nails because on the one occasion I could have noticed—that night in Kate's house when I went into his room and we discussed the contract—he gave me quite a lot to look at, and I'm afraid my eyes never did get below his midsection.

But something was wrong about the fit of Brett's boots. I didn't ask him personal questions, as he could be moody, and I didn't want to pry.

A little later, he got up and went to his room.

I took a piece of dressmaking tissue and a pin out of a cabinet, and crawled over the floor. The imprints of Brett's boots were still fresh, squashing the curls of the sheepskin rug. It was easy to lay the translucent tissue down and prick the outline.

This time I was the designer, and Mr Hazumi made up my order exactly to specifications. The toes were rounded and generous—not like Brett's clodhoppers. And the boots I designed were made of butter-soft, butter-scotch leather. They were inspired by the pictures I remembered of Puss 'n Boots.

'Puss,' I used to point, tucked halfway into bed, and my dad would say, 'And Puss fell upon him,' and here he would pretend to be Puss and drop his head to my tummy, and nibble me through my nightie, and I would pretend to be a mouse, and go 'Eee eee!' and Dad would show no mercy, as he would raise his head, bare his big yellow teeth, gather me to him in a hug, and say, 'and he ATE HIM UP!' and I would scream with pleasure, and he would kiss me on the top of my head, and tuck me into bed.

These boots, like Puss's stopped just below the knee, where the leather rolled outwards and fell in a great soft collar.

I could hardly wait but I waited a whole half day, and gave Brett the boots just after dinner.

He unwrapped them with a worried frown. When he took them out of their wrapping, his face went through—I can only call them *contortions*.

He became physically ill with a degree of speed I would have thought impossible.

I helped him to the door of his room, where he asked to be left alone.

But he turned to me first. 'Thank you,' he said, and he sounded like he meant it.

The groans and cries that I heard from his room made me go to mine, and for the first time, lock my door. That door didn't shut out noise of this sort. But about an hour later, all was quiet.

The next morning, he came to breakfast, but was odd. He asked me if I needed to talk to friends from before. Didn't anyone miss me, didn't I need to do anything from my past life?

It was already early January. I hadn't thought about my past life or anyone in it, in more than the vaguest terms for at least a month.

Gordon. He would be distraught. He had occurred to me before, and I didn't know if he would be able to get over me. I didn't want to see him now. Maybe I would give him an audience in the future.

Of my other friends, I wanted to keep as far away as possible. Especially since the tampon incident would be in everyone's mind. Simone would make sure of that. Gordon would have raging dreams of the tampon and me and Brett. But Gordon always had a cloying kinkiness to his love.

No, I told Brett. I'm fine.

And family, he asked.

'Why are you interested?'

'Part of my chaperone duties,' he said, but I don't think that's true.

I thought of Mum and Dad — of the home I left when I was seventeen. I usually rang every couple of months, and was a bit past due. It was easier ringing than writing because what was there to say? But it was hard ringing, all the same. My father wouldn't know what to say, and my mother would suck me dry of every detail of my exciting city life. I always felt choked up with Dad. He meant well. And with Mum now, I would have to invent the boringly mundane, a different challenge to the norm. And there was always the painful part of the phone call — the 'have to run, something's burning, cut off my head accidentally, gotta go to the doctor' part.

'I suppose I should ring them,' I said, feeling a lovely swatch.

Brett seemed satisfied with that and dropped the subject.

We didn't talk much at that time. Perhaps he was shy. I know I was.

Jewels.

Kevin scorned them. He said jewels were cheap. I didn't argue, though I think what he disliked was their competition.

But you might wonder about the practical stuff. Like spending millions on a purchase with a credit card. I did, too, but Justin and Brett dealt with that side of things. The company paid for all our expenses, I found out one day, when Justin casually mentioned it. On asking Brett, I learned that something that sounded as real as James Bond's cover, was the company. I hadn't worried before I learned this fact, but then it scared me. Company returns and tax department people and all that.

Brett called my worries 'piffle', which really made me panic. I assumed it was all air—that we were going to have to abscond any second, bailiffs baying at our heels. He made an I-am-piqued sound in his throat, but waved his hand and produced a computer, a model I hadn't seen, but I never knew computers well. He used it with remarkable expertise for a one-finger typist using a keyboard with all black keys. 'There,' he said, pointing to the screen. The company even had a Big Five, or is it a Big Four—multinational as auditor. A thoroughly above-board concern, with above-board trade. And he was the CEO and Chairman, and a Desirée Lily was listed as Director, newly appointed.

'Are you a believer now?' he asked.

I nodded.

He waved his hand again, and the computer disappeared. He didn't like them either.

Brett's information chilled me. I was so stressed that I demanded to know how we as *artists* could be seen to be involved with 'a Company, for godsake!'

He stepped back and regarded me. I was wearing at this moment, a Worth-inspired confection in platinum satin, its ermined-velvet train stretching out in the distance behind me.

'My dear...' Brett said.

I subsided.

He invited me to sit on the chesterfield and he settled on his mountain, where he began with a long scratch between his horns, using his long nail. When he was finished, he explained that, as I could see, Universal Imports or whatever it was called, was not only a real company, but that Justin *expected* him to buy everything through a company as all modern artists do, and that I should have known this and prepared him because Angela should have known these things, and why should he, who had not visited for quite a while, be expected to know everything about our modern age, and adjust instantly? Lucky the company existed, or he would have had to make arrangements on the spot...

My chastising lasted, mercifully, only a little longer.

Brett *had* been working hard. I felt chastened and said as such, but hoped he liked my dress.

Now, Hair.

'A disaster.'

That was what Kevin said. He asked what it was supposed to be. It didn't have a name as a style. I didn't think it looked bad until Kevin told me that bad was not the word for it. And he leaned over and retched.

He asked me what colour it was naturally. And then he felt it, and accused me of murdering it.

Mum had cut all our hair. Mine was 'impossible'. What she did to it, or maybe the way my hair grows, ensured that no matter how I wet it, it always looked like I'd slept on it funny. As soon as I got to uni I changed it to something citified, and had kept it that way ever since. In Bettawong, there were lots of people with hair like mine.

Kevin showed himself to be definitely not into what others said was cool. Kevin asked me if I valued his judgement. If I felt that he understood the soul of the butterfly.

'Do you, little butterfly, Desirée Lily? What a beautiful name! Just like you. Your mother named you well. So how could you *do* this to yourself? She must be turning in her grave! Is she dead yet? No? Well, she'd kill herself if she saw . . .'

And all this while he was feeling my hair like a medium feels the table for the spirits of the dead.

Finally, either the vision of my hair appeared unto him, or he got bored. 'Your hair is thick . . . otherwise, an unknown quantity. You will wear turbans till your hair grows out. If you touch a finger to it other than to use the treatments I give you, I'll bloody well paddywack you till your lily cheeks are purple!'

Well! That put me in my place, so I wore turbans that Kevin made till one day, he rushed out and returned with Anthony, a hairdresser friend. Kevin must have strained their friendship because he allowed not a whit of creativity. Every movement of the scissors was directed by Kevin, Anthony reduced to robotic arms. After a while, Kevin said, 'Stop.' His face filled with one of those expressions that scream *Eureka!* Something was clear as water to him. Anthony and I waited.

'A karakul hat, luvs,' Kevin said, as if then we'd hit ourselves in the noggins for being thick as two planks.

Our mouths closed as we tried not to look stupid. Kevin snorted, and explained.

The pelts of aborted karakul sheep make the best hats, with the closest waves and brightest lustre. He told us how the karakul pelts are obtained.

'They beat a pregnant ewe till it aborts. The lamb's fur only remains tight and curly for the first twenty-four hours so you have to skin it while it's still alive. And then you make your hat.'

By the time Kevin finished his explanation, all the while gazing at my hair, he was in what used to be called a 'state'. His voice, and his chest, *quivered* with passion. I thought of an image—a crowd of Greenpeaceniks coming upon the Marquis de Sade just as the Marquis spots Bo Peep with her sheep.

'Don't you see?' Kevin asked, and I suppressed a giggle.

We didn't see.

He couldn't suppress himself any longer, but turned to Anthony and chucked him a whack on the back of his head that brought tears to his tolerant friend's eyes. 'She's wearing the hat, you fool . . . and it's a beaut.'

Anthony put his hands on my shoulders and turned me so that he could see each angle. It might have been a displacement exercise. He concentrated on the haircut with a professional eye, and what he saw was what I now saw, and he smiled at Kevin in forgiveness. Kevin was an artist, Anthony just a tradesman.

What we saw was a high crown of a hat widening at the top. Its thick sides stood out from my head, and it sat deeply upon me, its rakish angle throwing a great coruscation of hair across my right brow and the top of my eye socket. At the back of my head, the hair was cut close toward my nape, where it was cut off sharply, the errant hairs on my neck plucked out.

It was a magnificent attention-getter of a hat, a Belle Époque picture hat, but with a twist—this, on a delicate, closely cropped head.

He turned to me. 'I was going to order one to be made for you, but you grew your own.'

My Face.

I suppose you wonder about that. Kevin said not to worry. That it had 'character'. Justin agreed. I didn't feel that I could ask Brett, and he didn't offer an opinion.

And do you wonder about Brett?

Except for the art bought for him, he seemed to approve the rest of the developments, or at least they didn't noticeably bother him. And though he didn't say, he should have liked my karakul look with its glossy, jet-black waves, because, except for his horns and the cock of my 'hat', we could have been wearing the pelts of twins.

15

Which brings us to Brett. How is he going in his job, you ask.

So did I.

At first, I didn't ask. We'd eat together at every meal, and he would ask about my progress, and nod and hmm, and carry on with his meal.

And we would make small talk, unsuccessfully. What do you say in small talk to the Devil? Also, he was always—I can't think of another way to put it—preoccupied—even when he was attentive.

But writing does that to you. I certainly didn't want to upset his thought process.

Sometimes he worked on his futon mountain, but mostly he kept to his room.

I never entered. I never peeked in.

And that's how it was for the first while, when I was busy affecting my transformation.

The nights were disturbing.

Howls, groans, crashes, low litanies of mumbled words—incantations? And then, commonly, silence. Or the reverse—silence in the early part of the night, to end when I was woken at dawn by the howls and groans. They sounded inhuman, and yet I remembered my dad of an evening walking out of the house and making sounds like that. We knew because all of a sudden, the dogs would start up.

I locked my door that once I told you about, the night I gave Brett the boots, when the sounds were so terrible that I ran water just to keep me company.

Brett never referred to the sounds, and I dared not.

Those howls were never made in my presence, but he was prone to *something*. His eyes would suddenly yellow in the whites, the rose-coloured red of his irises turning a muddy brown. His face would sag and tinge greeny-grey like that first evening when I thought he had motion sickness.

Sometimes I wondered—what if the taxi that had just missed Brett, had hit.

Attacks affected his balance. Once he fell from his futon mountain.

Kevin and I heard the thud while in my room for a fitting. My arms bristled with pins, so Kevin ran to help, but Brett waved away assistance.

So with this and that, I didn't say 'How's the book going?'—the best question in the world to put a writer in a rip-your-face-off mood.

I was more than content here, and in no rush. And Brett obviously needed some time to get down to it.

It would have been fun knowing how he was going, so I was sorry we couldn't talk. The plot was something that I was hungry for. I got a certain frustrated satisfaction from not knowing yet, but though I teased myself with the dubious enjoyment of delayed gratification, I was never into masochism, and would much rather have devoured the plot chapter by chapter, hot.

Was he using the 3 x 5 card technique, or did he write longhand on foolscap? Did he use loose pages or notebook, or did he type, which I sometimes thought I heard, or dictate? He never asked me or anyone else to get supplies, but with the periods of silence coming from his room when he was not in the lounge, I had to assume he spent much time out. What he did when he was out, I could only guess. I was sure he didn't stand in queues, as he could rustle up a packet of 3 x 5 cards with a wave of his hand, and without having to pollute with a plastic carry bag.

One day in late February I was stretched out on Ferdinand's portable massage table in my bedroom where Kevin was supervising my daily massage. Just as Ferdinand reached my left ankle, I broke and swallowed half a molar in a tutti-frutti frangipani fondant.

At the sudden loss and pain, Ferdinand and Kevin were all over me like a rash. Kevin got on the house phone immediately, and it was all (to downstairs) 'Miss Lily's emergency' and (to me) 'You'll love him,' and (to downstairs) 'No, right away. *Now!*'

Forty minutes later, my teeth were in the hands of the Restonia's dental surgery team led by Dr Bernard Kipple-Swan, Royal Fellow of this and that, but I was so comfortable, I fell asleep. We were downstairs in a sub-ground level at the Restonia, in its own fully equipped hospital/dental suite. Afterwards, I was taken on a tour of their completely fitted-out civil defence shelter, a level below. Their definition of essential supplies was another step in my education.

The next day, another luxurious session with 'please call me Bernard' and his equally pleasant assistants completed the molar capping, as well as some perfectionism he felt driven to perform on my front teeth. He was scheduling more for the next day when Kevin intervened.

My teeth were part of my character, Kevin said, and he didn't want Kipple-Swan getting hold of them and making them *too* perfect.

K and K-S discussed until they yelled, at which they were equally capable. When K's fists bunched, I intervened.

K had the better argument. K-S was a pedant. And a fanatic for the perfect smile. But once you thought of the subject deeply (as K obviously had), a smile you could buy had all the individuality of duty-free designer goods. So I thanked Bernard with grace, lovely man that he was, and explained to him that, in the superficially judgemental world that we live in, my writing would be bound to be judged lightweight and I wouldn't be taken seriously, if my teeth were *too* beautiful.

Kevin almost ruined my point by blurting, 'Common, common, common.'

Kipple-Swan didn't swan out. He held nothing against me, but I know he thought 'weak woman', and was just planning for that inevitable time in the future when the moon would conspire with a midnight toffee . . .

The excitement of it all surprised me, as did the disappointment, since everything was taken care of in-house. I had, in fact, no need to go out—for anything.

Those rumours about the Restonia's secrets were true. The hotel was not a simple shoebox but a warren, the defunct factories with their carefully maintained exteriors being part of the whole. Justin offered to show me around and to move Brett and me to a suite with secret access. I didn't need any secret access, and was always too busy to take Justin up on his exclusive tour offer. As for celebrities, I could only play spot-the-face by looking in the mirror. The place was quiet as a tomb. Probably quieter. I only ever came upon two 'friends'—a hag with Albert Einstein hair and an expensive handbag, in the lobby on the day of Jim's funeral; and a tall man with a bad back, a worse toupee, and a disaster of a white belt, in the lift after the Kevin and Kipple-Swan fight.

The next day I asked Justin about these friends. Justin smiled at my moniker, 'Mizz Einstein'.

'A lovely old friend,' he said, 'A retired mistress.'

'Ooh. Whose?'

Justin pursed his lips. The prude!

'About that new Lindsay,' he said.

I didn't want to talk about that new Lindsay. I wanted to know about these mysterious guests. Justin wouldn't say anything more about Ms Einstein, except that she was Hungarian and her only need was a bag of beets a week. Then he changed the subject again.

I grabbed Justin's little finger. 'Jus . . . tin?' I twisted.

'Careful!' He pulled at his finger, but I held tight. 'Who's Mister Toupee?'

He shook his head, but not at me. There was some internal angst busy here. I released his finger because this inner turmoil was far more interesting than Mystery Guest Number Two.

'Okay,' I said. 'You don't have to tell me about Mister Toupee. I've already got him down.'

'You do?'

'Film director.'

'My word! And his nationality?'

'You kidding?' I laughed. 'With that white belt, who ya'll joshing, pardner?' My cheeks warmed. I'm no impersonator.

'Ho ho ho,' Justin laughed mirthlessly. 'He's Norwegian.'

I was so shocked, I blurted, 'Is that good or bad?'

'Aussie toilet paper isn't good enough for him.'

'Crikey!'

Justin's scowled, a vanilla-blond Heathcliff. 'Where'd you see this bastard?'

'In the lift. Why?'

'They're supposed to stay in their own wing.'

'*They?*'

'It's a . . . a convention. In the Piggotts Woollens wing.'

This was bad and getting worse. From the beetledness of Justin's brow, I knew he was hoping I wouldn't ask.

'A convention of whom?' I asked, reaching out.

He shoved his hands under him—a little boy who doesn't want teacher to see his dirty fingernails. His eyes screwed shut. 'Amway millionaires.'

'Fucking shit!'

What about my reputation?

'What about me?' I demanded.

'I haven't told anyone,' he insisted. 'And I've kept most of these groups away. Telling them it's booked. Stuff like that.'

'So are any *more* of these coming through?'

He hung his head. 'Next week. I couldn't refuse. They've been here before.'

'Who, Justin?'

'They're very discrete.' He muttered something. Was it 'Effing sods'?

'Jus—'

'Coppers. Retired coppers.' He exhaled so slowly and completely that he sagged like a emptied douchebag . . . with a bow tie. 'International,' he added, poking a forefinger at his mouth and ripping its nail off down to the quick.

No wonder. I could just imagine. Perverts from Argentina.

'Periwinkle,' Justin moaned. He had forgotten I was there.

I snapped my fingers. 'A flower?'

'Brisbane. Periwinkle from Brisbane.'

'What about him?' I felt like an interrogator, my subject so broken he was putty in my hands.

'Ex-chief inspectors are the worst. They demand everything, and they're the reasons for the—' He stopped himself just as this was getting really good.

He had closed his mouth, but I could still squeeze more juice out. Besides, something didn't add up. 'I thought the Restonia was famous for the quality of its friends.'

This statement was a hypodermic jabbed straight into his vein. It produced an immediate effect.

'Oh, fickle fickle world,' he literally cried. 'Good friends are hard to find.'

I curled my lips inward, clamping them hard.

What came next was:

'Miss Lily!'

He threw himself on the floor at my feet and grasped my thighs. His eyes were wild. Not that I worried. I could take care of myself.

'Friends!' Justin cried, bitterly. 'You, Miss Lily, are above all that. You and Mister Hartshorn.'

I was astounded, and a mite insulted. The thigh grip was platonic.

However, he wasn't finished. 'Miss Lily,' he repeated, his voice a husky rasp. Perhaps its rawness stirred him, for he jerked his arms away as if I were fire.

He scrabbled to his feet, and . . . bowed! 'Oh dear oh dear,' he said, becoming more remarkable by the moment. This man wasn't Heathcliff. He was a dead ringer for that white rabbit in Alice in Wonderland. I half expected him to pull out a pocket watch, scream, 'I shall be late!' and skitter off.

Instead, he gazed plaintively at the top of my head and uttered very fast, 'You are the light of my life. I will never say it again.'

At *that*, he skittered off.

When the suite door closed, I laughed till I cried. That bow tie! How passion could move it!

Oh, the Restonia, though quiet as a tomb, was a self-contained world, all right. Justin and Kevin and Ferdinand and Serge, and outsiders like Bernard and Mr Hazumi, not to mention the trouble-free, silent and efficient maids. I don't know what you would call these maids, as they were male. They had no airs, no names that I was ever told. All such a friendly society that there was no incentive for me to visit the uncomfortable, indifferent, poorly serviced outside world.

Besides, my new persona was not made for my former pastimes, now as attractive as yesterday's baguette. The few times I did go out—all to do with the formalities around Jim's death—only made me happy to get home, back to the Restonia.

There was, however, something in the air.

16

LATE AFTERNOON. Brett was perched on his mountain, a book on his lap. I was stretched out on the chesterfield, playing with some pearls Kevin had strung for me, when Brett asked, 'Don't you read?'

'Why?'

But I thought he knew, so his question fuddled me.

'Should I?' I added.

'Do you?'

I thought I had replied. Maybe he was just confused. I dropped the pearls so I could pay attention to Brett. 'Why should I?' I asked.

'Does that mean you don't?'

He wasn't trying to annoy, so I swallowed the 'Of course not' racing up my tongue. 'There's no reason to read,' I told him. 'And I have better things to do.'

'Oh,' he said. But he sat there, not getting back to work. Instead he asked, 'Did I break into your thinking just now?'

I had been thinking something but I couldn't remember what. 'No problem,' I smiled.

'I thought you liked reading,' he said. 'Those piles of books in your room.'

His ignorance astounded me. It was hard to think of a proper reply.

'They were *work*, Brett.' I pointed to his book. 'Like you're doing now.'

When my books had burned I felt relieved—a phoenix released from the flames.

His eyes drew close together and left my face to focus inwards, to their eye-to-eye conference: *Do you understand? Not a clue. And you?* Then each looked to me.

'Reading was *work*, Brett,' I explained. 'So how could I *like* reading?'

'But they were novels, weren't they?'

'Yes? But?'

I thought, but didn't say: Get to the point!

'Work,' he repeated.

'Research,' I explained.

'Work. Research,' he repeated—a robot.

If he were anyone else, I would have knocked on his skull with my knuckles and yelled at it, 'Yodelay eee hooo!?' As this was Brett, I was at a loss to make him understand. Besides, this was too philosophical (and *booooring*) for my taste. I picked up a pile of swatches.

'Didn't you ever read for pleasure?' he queried.

At that, the silk slipped from my grip as I laughed out loud, until I saw his face.

'When we are children,' I carefully enunciated, 'if we are lucky, we are given books that delight us. But that is just a children thing. Once school starts...' But that was too much to get into now, so I cut to the moment.

'Professionals, Brett, can't *like* reading. It's like plumbers liking shit. They just plumb through it.'

He didn't say anything for a long time. I didn't feel I could get up and go, and yet I couldn't do anything where I was. I was in limbo.

He made no reply, but the answers to his questions obviously left him unfulfilled.

Finally, he climbed down from his mountain, the pile of books he was holding making him look quite academic.

'Did you ever go to school?' I asked. 'Or better yet, college...any college?'

'No.'

I should have known. 'Well, that explains it.'

The conversation ended, as they usually did, with Brett going off to his room.

I picked up my pearls and thought a bit, too. Then I flipped through some of the pattern books piled at my elbow, and then I thought of what I wanted for dinner, and then I ordered it and joked with Serge for a while, and then I had a long bath, and then I dressed for dinner, and then Brett and I had dinner together, and then it was evening.

And then Brett went to his room, and I thought of ordering a TV but couldn't bring myself to sink that low. I never learned how to work a video, and didn't want to ask. I thought of going out to see a film, but only pervs and wrinklies go to cinemas alone. I considered asking Brett along, but he might start a fire if he was bored. Then there was the prospect of going to a coffee shop and pretending to wait for someone, and in the meantime drinking alone.

By the time I knocked on Brett's door, there was silence. He must have already left. I didn't dare open the door to find out.

* * *

It was two o'clock the next day when—pedicure done, massage over, elbow-length-glove-wearing lesson adjourned and the new art hung, I woke from a doze with a raging case of ennui.

Half of me was furious at Brett, my infector. The other half of me coolly analysed the situation—diagnosis: amazement I hadn't been stricken earlier. Whatever the source, don't confuse my malaise with boredom. This was a virulent strain of been-there-done-that, what's-it-all-about, self-destructive ebola of the psyche. I couldn't even revive myself with mirrors.

But the prognosis for my future was even more alarming. I'd learnt at the Higher Light that, just as a simple cold can weaken your defences and you catch pneumonia, my agony now was leading straight to a search-for meaning crisis, which descended fast as a jumper off the Harbour Bridge to its inevitable end. Like a drowning man clutching at something on the surface (which turns out to be a shark), if I didn't get treatment *now*, I was doomed to catch *belief!*

'Brett?'

I tapped on his door. 'May I come in?'

'Please do,' he said, 'if you can.'

I turned the knob and pushed, but the door wouldn't open. Instead, there was a loud ruffling and then Brett's voice, calling, 'So sorry. Do come in.'

The door opened this time, but only enough to allow me to squeeze through. I wasn't surprised when it swung closed on its own behind me. Trying to move, I was stuck.

'Apologies again,' Brett said, ever so politely. The door opened, my skirts blew toward me, and the door clicked smoothly shut.

Brett was slouched in his usual sloppy guru stance, crosslegged—just below the ceiling. I noticed now that he had developed a scholar's hunch. Nothing I could see was holding him up. Short piles of books were scattered around him on a table made of the same stuff as his invisible seat. He looked so comfortable and the books surrounding him so ordinary in their being-read-now state, paper markers hanging out of some, others nesting, open book in open book.

The whole scene of Brett and his study materials was unmentionably mundane compared to the rest of the room. His room was as large as mine—orgy size, and simply *packed* with books, magazines, newspapers, printed matter of all sorts, including scrolls and what appeared to be cuneiform tablets. I stood on the only empty floor-space of any size. I couldn't have sat without hugging my knees to my chest. Brett's levitation put his head a foot from the ceiling, but the space between the top of the piles of reading material and his arse couldn't have been much thicker than the thickest book in the room.

He picked up an open book beside him, flicked one page and referred to something briefly, mumbled something to himself, then closed the book and let it go. It zoomed under him, flew halfway across the room, and dived below my line of sight. A pile in its vicinity rose and then settled, a little higher than it was before.

He looked down at me and waved toward a pillar of newspapers. Their edges fluttered like a zillion eyelashes. Then the whole pile disappeared. I didn't feel a whoosh but dust, powerful as snuff, pushed up my nose. I was sneezing when something shoved my knees forward, and I fell back upon soft cushions. Brett had brought my chair in—though with the tight fit, it had to have passed through walls. Small bones (?) now jabbed into my bum—the jet buttons of a chemise I'd tried on this morning. I pulled it out from under me and put it in my lap.

'What can I do for you?' Brett asked.

Do you have something to read? was no longer a relevant question.

There wasn't room to wave my arms, but I opened my hands expansively. 'Have you read all these?'

'Oh, these? Yes. But all? No.'

Did he mean *all books*?

'Don't you want me to?' he asked.

I couldn't answer immediately because my back was towards him as he spoke, as I was climbing on my chair. I turned around with care. Trained skirts and overstuffed chairs and little slippers with sharp curved heels are not the most acrobatic combination. But finally, I was up and gingerly reaching for a book, any book. Brett watched me not quite get to the book, so it removed itself from the top of the pile and put itself into my hands.

'Ta,' I thanked Brett, and it occurred to me that he possibly didn't know *ta*, it not being a bookish word. But that was his problem, as my clamber down was even more difficult than the precarious climb up.

Once again seated, I examined the book in my hands. Parchment. Not 'parchment' suitable for PAPER waste. This was real parchment. Once a sheep, always a sheep, even dead and with no fur. The skins (touching them, the thought occurred to me for the first time: why *leaves*?) in this book had been walked on by quill pens dripping gall ink, though the true art of dripping gall was developed later, satire not being a feature of the century that this book came from. I wouldn't have said it came from the Dark Ages as much as the Dull Ages. I flipped a page and saw I was wrong. Though the words had to be a bore, the people bent to fit into the decorated letters were droll indeed. This wasn't satire, but basic humour based on pain, like what sheep think to do.

I assumed it was a church book, but for all I could tell, it was *Airport*, circa 1200. I couldn't recognize a single word, not even a 'thee', though the letters were almost readable. I was placing it under my chair when it left my hand and raced back to former position.

I pointed to the top of another stack and lifted my eyebrows to Brett. He moved a finger, and the book sailed gracefully into my lap. Chaucer, first edition? I pointed to another stack. Something in squiggles. Another stack—a clay tablet. Then it was *True Tales of the Hieroglades* that didn't look true, by someone whose name wasn't believable.

I pointed to a pile in the distance, but it was as if Brett had trained in a deli. No matter how hard I pointed, what he gave me came from somewhere else.

When *Mein Kampf* dropped into my lap, in German, I'd had enough.

'Weary Dunlop!' (Dad's curse, when trying to be polite) 'You don't have to read everything, Brett.'

The pile I'd been pointing to was new books. A pile of hardbacks—specifically, I was pretty sure, the New York Times Bestseller List—and though they were close to Brett, he didn't need them close, and I couldn't reach them at all.

I threw *Mein Kampf* to the floor, smelly old thing.

Brett wafted it out and placed it carefully back on the top of its pile. Brett was either having me on, or he had seriously overreached his brief.

He needed his socks pulled up. 'You're only writing one book,' I told him. I hated to disappoint him but I waved my arms to unmistakably encompass the room. 'This looks a bit highbrow, you know.'

As usual, he didn't know, so I pointed to *Mein Kampf*.

Brett raised his eyebrows, I nodded, and the book tilted so I could see its title.

'Yes, Brett,' I said, and the book settled flat on its pile.

'You were saying?' he asked, innocently.

'You're supposed to be writing *romance*, Brett,' I said, without moving my jaws.

His expression was pure mud. Was he being dense on purpose, or was it natural? He smiled in a friendly *please explain* manner, so maybe he wasn't trying to drive me crazy.

'If you write about deep shit,' I explained, 'depressing stuff, you know...' And here I had to put a hand to my head to settle the effects of an involuntary shudder tinkling the pearls in my diadem. I couldn't afford frivolity when I needed him to concentrate.

'If you are gonna write deep shit, Brett,' I said, grabbing his eyes with mine, 'I shall have to change my name again to suit, and I'll have to change my hair again... to something awful... and get my old clothes back from the tip.'

Part of me said *This threat is stupid*. Brett wouldn't waste a hoot in hell thinking about my appearance. If I looked, and reeked, for that matter, like a fly-blown dag. If I chose that persona for immortality, then c'est la immortality! Viva la existentialism! Brett would just say, 'I wrote the book. You chose the look.' He had never made any comments other than the time when he asked me if I thought my look fit my name, and that my job was to make it fit.

So the back of my mind said to me *Don't Go Down This Track*, but the front of my mind was not listening to any wussy advice. And besides—the whole of me was shit-scared that he was racing down the hill towards Terminal Dagginess for me, not to mention the kind of fame that would mean that people would refer to me by my last name and never look at a picture of me except to confirm something, and I would have to memorize quotable sayings, and these would be quoted, along with the title of my masterpiece and a couple of phrases—but *no one would read me or want to see my image*. I would buy eternity as bibliography and pay with eternity in hell.

I felt a scream emerging. 'I didn't give my life to you for *literary* fame!'

No no no no no. I couldn't let Brett Ibsenize me. Was *Ibsen* right? Had he written novels? Does it matter? NO! And that's just the point. It *is* the point of the thing. I couldn't end up like that. And I couldn't permit that. Not when I had achieved the impossible—corporal beauty in my time.

He was pawing a book. Was he listening?

'Brett. Look at me. This is important.'

He laid the book on his lap, open.

'I don't want to be studied, Brett. I want to be loved.'

He *wasn't* listening.

It was all so spur-of-the-moment, but I had to act. In a measured tone of thoughtfulness, I asked him, 'How does A R Souse sound?'

There was no reply. He regarded *me*, on the contrary, with a measured look of thoughtfulness.

'And can I let everyone know that Brett Hartshorn is only your stage name, and you were born a mile away in the Woolloomooloo Mothers Hospital and not in a chateau, and that the closest you've been to Shichtenstein-Karslboff . . .'

Here, I ran out of inspiration, so I careered on in a different direction. '. . . and that you, my *brother*, were born "Norm Souse" and . . .'

Melodrama has always been my weakness when I am pushed to extremes. I was gesticulating now.

At which point, he tumbled from his levitation onto the uneven piles of books. They skewed and the whole piled-up mass gave, like a mountain of shale shards. I moved too late to protect myself, but my petticoats softened the blow. Brett, on the other hand continued slipping and books kept slewing, till even a Merino ram as film director would have yelled, 'Cut!'

Incredibly Brett kept going, crashing on his back as he tried to stand. On his third try, he levitated enough to cross his legs.

I was so pissed off at him, I could have choked myself laughing. But I hadn't made a sound.

He reached for a heavy volume and tenderly realigned its spine. 'Why did you come?' His voice was terrifyingly calm, and he didn't look at me. Instead, he reached for another book.

Words, unfaithful as ever, deserted me. But my options were limited, seeing as how I was jammed into my chair. He expected an answer.

'Do you have anything to read?'

And I hastened to add, 'Anything new?'

He made me wait for an answer.

Finally—looking at the book in his hand, not at me—he demanded, 'Will you read it?'

I was so relieved. 'Of course! Just please, something contemporary. I must be up-to-date, you know. I'm losing touch in here.'

If he kept up-to-date, his bestseller pile would have, at the top, the best lay-on-the-beach escapism of the year.

'Do you keep up to date?' I asked. Maybe that pile near him, was new only *relatively*. After all, in this collection, Gone With the Wind would be new.

With the Devil's provenance and his tendency to misunderstand, he needed pulling towards the present, and to be spoken to in the clearest and simplest of terms.

'*Really* up to date?' I added, to make things clear.

He smiled.

'You'll have the latest,' he assured me.

What a relief. He could be so difficult.

'Now, get...'

Ouch! My sedan chair and I were transmogrified through his door and whirled through the air to my room. He misjudged the height of the doorway, raising a bump on my brow the size of a petit four.

As I was bathing my forehead with lavender water, I heard a *whoosh*, and a thud. My reading, delivered.

My head pounded, but not too much that I wasn't pretty bloody excited. You can only look at fashion plates for a world long dead... you can only look, I tell you from experience, for so long before you want to scream with boredom. I delayed the moment of discovery by mulling over, firstly, what would go with it—my reading, that is.

> **Historical Romance**: Lavender pastilles.
> **Ethnics**: Mr Hazumi's sister's Goosy Feels. That's what he called them. Sticky little pastries. The way they shatter against my palate and melt! Dreamy!
> **Political Thriller**: Urk. A hot, overflowing dustbin. I had to trust that Brett had *some* sensitivity.
> **A Steamy Tangle of Love, Betrayal, and High Finance**: Serge's special Rocky Road with lots of violent-red cherries and hunks of homemade marshmallow caught in a cement mix of white and milk chocolate, stony with chilli-roast peanuts...

I was naked and dripping by the time I got to genre of **The Unabashedly Commercial General Novel**: Deliciously bitchy core of truth surrounded by layers of chewy speculation. There could only be one match for that: a carton of commercial, trashy, deliciously messy Violet Crumble bars.

The long shower had delayed in the most salivatory way, the Moment.

Now, swathed in a towelling robe thick as a sheepskin, I could wait no more.

Brett had outdone himself.

Racked neatly in tall, tight ranks, was every one of the latest newspapers, I think, in the world, including what looked like printouts from the internet, dammit.

'Brett!' I screamed. 'I can only read English!'

Woosh! woosh!

That gave me some room to move.

What a snide trick. Nasty little mind. 'And stick your dinner up your bum!'

I would have to forgo dinner tonight, but I reconnoitred and there were a few things I had to keep the wolf from the door.

I read in bed.

First, I had the cheesecake from my fridge. Then the stuff in my fruit bowl—rambutans and lychees. The Jordan almonds were next. At the hour when garbos were feeding trash compactors (not that I could hear the outside world), I finished off the last of a box of Pithevers Digestive Biscuits, dry.

Soon afterwards, I went to the toilet and retched, but I couldn't make myself throw up. It never happened when I *wanted* to.

At 9 am, I was still reading and had been chewing my underlip for so long that it was the shape and size of a raspberry. I was sucking on this raspberry, reading an editorial in the *Times of India*, when Brett knocked. Would I like breakfast in bed? He had the tray in his hands. No need for me to get up.

I opened the door to him and took the tray from his hands.

'We can eat together,' I said. 'Do you want to wait till I wash, or can you stand me as I am?'

He laughed. A good sign. 'As you are.'

We sat together in the lounge, me in a rumpled and grubby sheer nightie, and he, fully dressed as usual. He never looked *morning*, only varying degrees of sick and well.

Finally, even the dregs in my cup were dry. Brett had finished long ago.

'Horrible all the stuff going on,' I said. 'This is *precisely* why I *hate* reading newspapers. Always depressing shit.'

'Did you know the stuff going on?' he asked, as if I should have known.

Another circuitous conversation. 'Some stuff.'

But that didn't end it. He was waiting for more.

'It never changes.'

He sat up very straight. 'Oh, yes,' he said. 'It does!'

An ingénue! 'Who are you? Gigi in Paris?' I was too exasperated to be polite. 'People have always fought. They've always killed each other.'

The room didn't help me put my point. Gay sprays of flowers on a cashmere throw were worlds away from the stuff in the papers.

'Your world . . .' I felt I had to remind him. 'Have you forgotten it?'

He groaned.

'Do I need to remind you?' I needled him, because it was necessary in the circumstances.

He stood up and did one of his party tricks.

'You can't escape that easily!' I yelled. 'I know you can hear me!'

When he didn't reappear, I got in a final word. 'And don't forget! You got your job because of us!'

How dare he make me wallow in the shit people do to each other!

This wasn't a time to knock—and I didn't approach that door slow, either. It *banged* open, and *poof! poof! poof!* I grabbed but wasn't fast enough to get *anything*. Then there was only me, the monkish mattress, and Brett's trunk and bag. *And*—a scrap of paper. I sidled over and picked it up in the act of scratching my ankle. The paper curled in my palm and *yeow!*

Scorched.

17

Why didn't I go out? So many bookstores, so much free time, even with my appointments and eating and taking baths and sleeping. Or I could have saved my feet and just rung room service. 'The top twenty, yes. The bookstore will know. Just say that.'

I didn't want to go out. He had access to the world of books, literally. Why should I go out, and why should I have to explain anything to anyone? And besides, this was a partnership. He should do his bit.

Once Dad walked all the way home from town rather than ask someone who should have offered him a lift, to give him one. I never understood that mad streak of his, till now.

From the lounge, I punched the house phone with my unscorched hand, and told Justin and Brett to cancel my appointments.

They were most sympathetic that I was indisposed, and quite alarmed when I said no servicing for me. Mr Hartshorn would have his luncheon and dinner, but I was on a water diet, and thank you, no. No need for more water, and I would make do with yesterday's flowers, towels, the lot. Please, I don't want to be disturbed.

They understood *completely*, and sympathy poured out till I felt gluey. From their tone, this was part of the joy of serving us—the artistic temperament, you know. I wondered if they had stolen anything of ours, used tissues and the like, for selling later.

My hand hurt and my head pounded, but that was physical. The bump on my brow was Frankensteinic. What was wrong was more painful than that.

Food didn't appeal. Water, even, was too rich. I went back to my room to read.

When I opened the door, I thought the cleaners *had* been in, but it was soon clear that they hadn't.

The scattered reading material of the night before had disappeared, neatly replaced by the same assortment again—dated a year earlier.

Brett was communicating.

All day I read, and I only just touched the surface. A couple of times I had a drink from the tap. Sometime in the afternoon I took a quick shower.

No one knocked, though I heard Brett's meals being served.

I fell asleep sometime in the night, but I don't know when. When I woke, a pigeon was preening on my windowsill. The world outdoors was busy with itself.

I had slept through the transfer of yesterday's reading and the delivery of today's. These papers were dated five years earlier, which meant that instead of slick internet printouts, there were yellowed sheets, graphically ugly as only grass-roots political and Arts-Council-funded graphic productions can be. Some of today's delivery was in the English language, but not much. Instead, in Brett's handwriting, there were underlined passages, annotated and translated for my convenience, though his handwriting was anything but an easy read.

There was no time to eat, and sleep was a nuisance I tried to fend off.

The next morning, the ink was fresh. He jumped back and forth in time.

One day the delivery was an elaborate bronze trunk the size of a wombat, bearing inside on a bed of blood-stain-red leather, an accordion-pleated continuous sheet of skins sewn with sinew, bent back and forth to become an uncut book, bound between boards of gold encrusted with jewels the size of jelly frogs—a book. It was carefully scribed. In the middle of some words pieces had been cut out of the skin and replaced. Not a letter nor a punctuant could I recognize.

Beside the ancient book lay Brett's translation—a thick wad of paper pages clamped at the spine by a glue that smelt like Brett on a good day, the smell of a hot frying pan.

It was, I suppose, what we would call an epic—of some civilization lost in time (or maybe not. Brett's translation could have been off). Anyway, motivations? Things just happened. Wars just happened. People were just killed or left to starve and die, often for the sake of adventure. One person declared 'ccdor' to another. Brett noted: 'Words fail me. The closest definition of ccdor in your modern language is "filiage".' Luckily, I got the gist of ccdor without Brett's help. Anyway, the person to whom ccdor was given was most often, a right bastard. Poles were stuck up too many arses to count, and repeatedly, guests were given 'filth' to eat, or declared that they were treated to filth, and then they rampaged. The descriptions of rampage filled most of the book.

Between trying to understand why people did whatever, and finding my way through the bramble of Brett's handwriting, I never got to the 'now', if, indeed, the book ever got to the present, whenever that was.

As a factual account, come on! As a novel, it didn't work for me. Not that I had been able to put it down...

I woke with my fingers poking painfully into my eye sockets, the ancient skin 'book' somehow on the floor. Its stance was the same as a fumbled print-out from the bank. I bent to gather it up, but the thing shrunk away, pulled itself together, and settled on its bed. The trunk shut with a bang and aetherized in a huff.

The translation must have been in the trunk.

Momentarily, I felt annoyed not to have reached the end, but only momentarily. One didn't have to read more to know: in the context of a novel, the story stunk and was a bitch to comprehend. However, Brett's removal of it before I reached the conclusion put the story in yet another light—news with *no* end.

Outside, another pallid dawn that I could look at from my window, but not hear. I fell asleep and dreamt of fur-garbed garbos roaming the city, feeding trash compactors wet bucketfuls of cleaved skulls.

Full daylight, I woke to the smell of mildew. A pile, delivered right beside my bed. Such a pretty cover, so I dived in, where I went shopping in 'Royal Shops to Shop in'.

> Hand-wrought, original in design, and the work of native needlewomen in Kentucky, these useful and finely made Suzanne bags serve and serve and serve. For her, that lucky maid among the fan-waving palmettos, who would her tapestry do in all that Southern sun, there is the great hand-quilted calico bag... Lined with tan Gros de Londres, these print bags may also be used by those who, strangely enough, adore mending.

Who likes mending? The timelessness of the human condition.

> Princess Nina Toumanoff soothes your shopping-bewrinkled brain... And to prove to all you daughters of vanity that there is a Royal Road to Elegance—even though world conquerors and

> emperors have to trudge the whole way round to learning—the Grand Duchess Marie at Bergdorf Goodman's is there to talk over with you those personal harryings of chic that assail even the chicest. You know how heavenly it is to have someone of taste talk to you for two or ten minutes, or, unbelievable bliss! for half an hour, all about you. And about nothing but you!

Bliss is true!! Too bad I couldn't give this to Kevin. Prince Kevin!

> A treatment under Madam's magic hands is a tremendously exiting experience. Her charm is enormous, her touch expert beyond description and the results—well, look at her! But you must work, work, work, if you would maintain or reclaim youthful contours. Every day, faithfully and intermittently, she makes demands upon a half hour of your time, not a moment less! There can be no loafing in her scheme of things, no going stealthily to bed with neglected face.

Better for Kevin not to know. He would have agreed too painfully for me to tolerate.

Then I got caught in a short story of love and betrayal, and then I got caught in food.

> It is evident that the changing conditions of city life are bringing about a new gustatory era for New York. Even now, in some respects, you can dine better in that city, better than you can in Europe—with the reservation, always, that you cannot always have wine with your meals.

Isn't cultural stuff always the same? City always beats country. In my time in Europe, I couldn't afford more than backpackers' spaghetti, but wine with meals? Cheaper than water here. That's the only good thing I found about eating in Europe. And so much for New York. No better than here in Oz. Back in Bunwup, drinking wine was un-Australian. Only one brew was blessed to tickle the oesophagus: piss with a head on it. And why eat when there's drinking to do? Not that there was any place to go out to eat at. But some things never change, and the Anglo world doesn't do civilized alcohol well. Corkage fees in BYOs in Sydney are really outrageous, and I for one, have always refused to take a bottle to a restaurant. Why pay some gel-haired androgyne in a waistcoat to open it and poke it in my face? You're not going to say 'Corky,' for something you bought! But what if it is, and he smells it? I would have liked wine with my meals here at the Restonia, but wine in the echelons attracts sadists. I wasn't going to risk my reputation.

I dropped my eyes.

> a very delicate, almost shyly provocative sauce.

The inside of my cheeks broke out in tingles.
But in the very next para, the 'stifled soughing of saxophones' broke in—so blah de dah. Why ever write about music?
Then:

> the turban of lobster—*turban d'homard*, so called because it looks like a turban... a mousse, foam-light and pink and flavorous with the expressed juice of lobster. In the oven it had been baked in the form of a Mohammedan tarboosh, then over it had been poured a delicious sauce of fresh mushrooms, and it had been finished with a sprinkling of splinters of truffle... The St. Regis's *turban d'homard* is eminently a luncheon dish, but it must be ordered well in advance, since, to obtain the extract for the mousse, the lobster must be forced through cloth in a press, and that takes time.

Oh god! My mouth could have sunk, it was so flooded.
Shoving past dancers, I reached the raw sexual come-on of the Egyptian Room where the 'central lotus flower is as crimson as an October moon rising through smoke, while the surrounding ones are golden or mottled to alabaster in dark and passionate hues.' Cute, but it didn't make me wet. When was I last feeling sexy for anyone other than myself? I tried to think but wasn't in the mood for anything but food, food, food. But the author must have been sated, for there was no more lobster or any other mouth-waterer, and dessert was this last paragraph.

> To one occasional pilgrim at least, New York's most beautiful night street is Park Avenue... At the lower end of the Avenue

glows the great golden illuminated lantern of the Grand Central tower, a warm hearth at which all the hurrying, chilly world may warm its spiritual hands... It is all vast, Babylonic. Then, above the lantern, you become aware of a lonely red light high and far away in the darkness, like a hunters' fire on a mountain top, and with a thrill you realise the new age in which you are living. It is the light on the Zeppelin mast on the unfinished Empire State Building... you dine, under these beetling masses, amid a luxury and show such as Roman patricians never knew...

He shouldn't have ended like this. I backtracked to the title page— 'The Gourmet Trail in New York'. A contemporary theme if there ever was one. Forrest Wilson, author. Never heard of him. *Harper's Bazaar*, February 1931.

Directly underneath this magazine was a stack of news from the same period.

What a nasty trick! Did Brett know Forrest Wilson?
I went to sleep and dreamt of a luscious ad in that *Harper's* where the Hawaii Tourist Bureau says: 'Just to eat is an adventure in these tropic isles.' But now, instead of bathing-suited drinkers lounging under the palms, a little girl had crawled in, and the ad was post-modern. Green trees, blue sky, grainy, b/w insert. Actually, where did she come from? I stood under a palm drinking a pina colada, wracking my brain, till it hit me. A poor photo, not enough light—from the NY City Department of Tenements. Some article on housing. Beside her, a man in overalls trundled a cart piled high with fluffy white asbestos. Also a black-and-whiter. This blow-in I remembered. A feature on resources in *Fortune*. Perched on top of the pile of fluff sat a silk-turbaned lobster. I sucked on my drink, wondering where he came from, when he brandished an umbrella and pointed at me. 'I think you might do something better with the time,' he said, 'than waste it in asking riddles that have no answers.' A clot of coconut flew up my straw straight into my windpipe, making me cough so hard, I woke, my eyelashes sticky.

The next delivery—musty 1862. The year started with 'DREADFUL COLLIERY ACCIDENT: Loss of Two Hundred and twenty lives'.

> They went through the works, and found no living man, but a hetacomb of dead bodies...

My feet fell asleep, and I didn't notice till my ankles throbbed. I simply couldn't read more, but couldn't stop or do anything else, even eat.

> One of the wounded men prayed in the midst of his sufferings, and one of his comrades climbed down from the cage where he had been suspended, and prayed with him till the hour when death released him.

Was this story Brett's communication today? What was he trying to say? *Rage, rage, against the dying of the something or other* rang in my head. Did it ring in his?

'The agony of excitement'—that's what one paper said months later about the public's frenzy for more details of this disaster, fresh daily. I felt their agony.

> On one of the tin flasks was found, scratched in rude characters—
> — probably just at the moment the writer had discovered the full horrors of his situation— "Mercy, O God!"

At which point, though it was not yet noon, I curled into myself for sleep.

I lost track of the number of days, but they covered wars, peace, 'acts of God' and man, fashion-oriented days, and days and years when nothing made sense but death and more of it. Day after day, I read, in an agony of excitement, a feeding with no food other than the stuffing of more and more events, opinions, reactions and after-shocks, down into my bowels.

Then, Brett stopped jumping around in history, and delivered me the present, day by day.

This took up so much of my concentration that I only got out of bed to drink water, excrete, and carry more armfuls of papers to the bed. I stopped going to sleep as such. It just overtook me whenever.

A sleek boardroom. The view out the windows: sky and a skyscraper's pointyhead. I'm at a conference table with about thirty men in red robes and tall white hats that I'm sure they could unfold and use to wipe their lips—and one man who must be Chairman, partial to gold.

The door opens and a girl who must be on work experience stands uncertainly, not in, not out.

'Well, Miss Bridges,' booms the chairman.

'Mr Bosh is here,' she says, and the man who must be Bosh pushes her aside, strides towards the table, and sticks his left hand out towards the closest board member, who turns back towards the chairman without touching flesh.

'Ch'm,' the chairman clears his throat. 'You're late, but never mind. We had *hoped* to launch the campaign two months ago, but let's see what you've got.'

Bosh shrugs almost imperceptibly, but I noticed. He's smooth, he is. Dressed with stunning nonchalance, he looks great, except for those tiny, black-rimmed glasses that scream Euro Intellectual. Nevertheless, he judges his best place, and walks to it. A huge room this is. He turns his back on us (very cool), unzips a scuffed portfolio, and pulls out a large poster. No. It's a painting on canvas.

He's the Bosh with the 'c'. And that's one of his hell scenes.

He holds it up in front of him till he notices a whiteboard, bristling with bulldog clips. He clips the top of the canvas to the whiteboard, but then has to hold his arm against the bottom of the painting to keep it from rolling up. The first amateur move he's made but I don't think it matters.

The chairman speaks. 'We *gave* you the brief, both verbally and in writing, did we not.'

'Um?' Bosch is bent over, looking at his painting while still holding his arm in position. He peers closer at something on it.

'Mr Bosch. We are satisfied. Please . . . Please!'

Bosch twists his body to face the chairman. 'Would you like to look closer?'

'Mr Bosch. Was this what you have brought for the bus campaign, or is it for some other client?'

Bosch removes his arm from the painting and guides its curl upwards, leaving the clips in position.

'Buses,' he says. 'Trains, billboards. You can use it everywhere.'

'That's a crock!' the chairman yells, He whips out a stockwhip and snaps it over our heads with a rifle shot *crack*. The man's got some arm on him! and that whip! Long as an anaconda. The explosion shakes the windows, and some hats. 'Your brief,' he says to Bosch, 'was one . . . simple . . . image.' He says this so softly that everyone has to lean forward.

'One message,' he yells. 'What is this?'

A lesser man would have been cowed. The robed mob at the table slumped in its chairs. Bosch was unbowed. 'You wanted hell. I gave you hell. No one has ever gone into it so finely as I have. No one has ever reached the heights of horror as I have. That anti-smoking ad when Death comes to visit? That most recent Chainsaw Massacre? Tomato sauce! You want kids eating popcorn, laughing at your hell? Go hire a multinational. You want hell? I give you . . .'

And here he went into such detail that the chairman's mood turned from outrage, to boredom. A snore came from the table (mine?), until the whip snapped.

'Thank you,' the chairman finally said, cutting Bosch off in mid-detail. The chairman spoke to Bosch, not as a person to an artist, but as a client to an advertising agency hack. That was bad enough to wreck anyone's ego. And wrong. Dr Cleeg from Art History *loved* Bosch. He raved about the man. Humour! Metaphor! and of course, Brushwork! But Dr Cleeg didn't *know* Bosch. This man with the stupid glasses was mad as a butterfly collector. That's all these clients saw, if they saw that. No. All they saw was that he had overstepped his brief. Only one person in the room knew — Bosch wasn't lovable, but he *would be loved.*

'We seem to have had a misunderstanding, Mr Bosch,' the chairman said. 'This has cost us two months. Precious time . . . gurgled away . . . down the hourglass . . .' He fingered his stockwhip, ruminating . . . 'Gerald?'

A hat fell off.

'Gerald. I should like to have a word with you after.' And he nodded to the room.

Everyone stood but him, sitting solidly on a curiously solid chair.

Bosch zipped his portfolio with a snarl and stormed to the door. 'Don't pay me,' he spat at the chairman.

The chairman raised his hands. 'We will pay,' he intoned, magnanimity personified .'But do take that with you. And remember, less is more.'

Bosch stormed back, almost ripped the canvas from the jaws of the clips, and stopped himself in time. Instead, he tenderly handled his painting, and left.

I ran after him, scooting into the lift just as the doors closed. It was full of people and a long way down to Ground.

He took up my offer to buy him a coffee.

I was lucky about where to go. There, just where I looked to get my bearings, was my old hangout, Nostramamma's, right across the street. I led the way.

The table was sticky and the legs of the chairs and table didn't all reach the floor. This had never bothered me in the past, and I couldn't let it bug me now.

'May I look ...' I asked, pointing respectfully.

He used his sleeve to clean the table top, then spread his painting over it.

A girl passed by. A zip hanging from her jacket snagged the canvas. She turned to grab hold of whatever it was holding her up—and saw.

'Cool!'

I was aghast. Bosch was busy. His fingers worked with surgical delicacy, wriggling the canvas in the metal teeth.

'Is it for sale?' she asked.

He didn't hear, or didn't reply.

'Do you take cards?' she asked.

Finally, the painting came free—its corner now, a puppy's ear.

'Or cash? I have forty dollars on me,' she said. 'But if that's not enough ... You paint dragons, too? I love dragons.'

He leaned back in his chair. 'It's for sale,' he said, 'but not for forty.'

Her mouth made itself small. 'Look,' she said. 'In this country, we don't bargain. You want ... okay. Fifty? Take it or—'

'Don't!' I yelled, as he rolled it up.

'Thank you,' he said, shoving me aside. 'But I can't live on coffee. I need the money.'

She handed him a hundred and asked for change. He didn't have any. She took the $100 out of his hand and gave him a fifty, grabbed the rolled-up painting, tsk'd that he didn't supply a rubber band, used her hair elastic instead, and walked to a table in the corner where she threw the painting and her bag on the opposite chair.

I stood up to buy it from her, knowing what it would be worth one day. My bag, when I opened it—Mother Hubbard's cupboard.

Bosch was selling himself short, and besides, he was too obsessive. If he was stuck on wanting to paint detail, he could sell much more if he took to other subjects, like, say, food. I turned to ask him if he wanted to explore his full potential, and woke up.

One conclusion I came to: The worse things get, the more people escape into enthusiasms—and the more vulnerable to *you know what* they become. First ... food, fashion, wine, steam trains. Next stop: boredom. And next ... One easy conclusion, that.

I looked back on the sheep-stinking epic and laughed—a beach-read. Sitting up in bed surrounded by, say, ten post-(or is it post-post-?) modern-world reports, each impossibly opposite the others, I'd reach for another and the only conclusion I'd come to was a burp, biliously fresh from my cavernous insides.

When the knock came, I didn't hear it, possibly because I was both concentrating, and giddy.

Brett opened the door and stuck his head in. 'Mind if I come in?'

I dropped what I was reading beside my bed, but there was no place for him to sit. The chair was stacked with papers I'd read, and the tables, too. I crawled over and swept another mess off. But he couldn't sit there. It was filthy with newsprint.

He sat, anyway. 'When was the last time you ate?'

I tried to remember.

'And have you looked at yourself?'

The same sheer nightie that I'd put on days ago was still on me, but not so see-through now.

He walked into the water room. 'I'm running you a bath,' he called. 'What do you put in?'

After telling me that breakfast would be served in an hour, he left.

18

Something had happened to my body. My shape had deserted me. I was now jutting collarbones, jutting hipbones, a hard-edged sharecropper face. My hands, those 'plump little partridges' (Mr Hazumi's description, translated by Kevin, so who knows what Mr Hazumi was describing) were now chicken feet. The skin on my breasts and buttocks hung.

The bath didn't make me feel good. I thought I was sitting on soap bars till I discovered they were my bones. Brett had seen me in my dirty and wizened state. As for Kevin . . . I tried to think of the implications but felt too giddy, and the heat of the bath brought on a nausea attack. I threw up some water mixed with bile.

Wrapped in my robe, I padded out to meet Brett in the lounge. On the way, I noticed my bedroom. All the reading matter had disappeared. Even the racks. The only evidence of all those newspapers: coal-cellar smudges all over the formerly snowy bedclothes.

Breakfast was waiting: a coddled egg, one piece of white toast, and a cup of weak milk tea, already poured. I tasted it. Two sugars.

'Eat slowly,' he said.

It felt strange, this stuff going into my mouth.

He watched me, only picking at his meal.

'Thanks, Brett,' I smiled.

'Eat,' he said, an encouragement. Not like that time at The Troppo.

When my stomach said no to another mouthful, I stopped. Half the egg and half a piece of toast were left on the plate. The teacup was empty.

'Would you like me to get more tea?' he asked.

'No thank you.'

He cleared his throat though he didn't need to. A manner of speaking. I had to begin.

'We come from different worlds.' I ventured.

He got up and carried the table out of the suite, returning quickly to sit on the floor, leaning against his futon mountain. 'Not so different,' he said.

'Do you think I don't respect you? Is that it?'

For days, I had tried to unravel the mystery. What was he trying to communicate? Why couldn't he just come out and *say* like a normal person? On day three when I said this to myself, I laughed. Lucidity came in streaks and turned into rainbows of confusion, just when I thought everything was so clear.

'Are you trying to make me believe, Brett?'

That was the conclusion, the only conclusion that I could come to. The world now, so taken up with God.

'God's armies are everywhere, Brett. And they are more able to communicate than ever.'

He nodded.

I was right. 'But why do you want me to believe, Brett? Isn't it enough that I *accept*?'

'Do you accept evil?'

That was the point of it all! God, and evil, too. My brain was tired, and the food made me sleepy. Sleepy and relaxed to the point of taking out any snideness that would otherwise have intervened.

'Why did you pick me?'

He didn't answer.

'Do you know *anything* about me?'

'I thought I did,' he said, almost inaudibly.

Connections. Think, I told my weary brain. *Think* . . .

'Uncle Percy!' A filthy splat of memory whomped into me, leaving me grizzling hot, soiled, angry tears. The injustice of it, getting me mixed up with him.

There was something I needed, but I couldn't delay what I had to say and it wouldn't have been dignified asking Brett to conjure up a hankie. I blew my nose into my sleeve and got on with it.

'Brett, how can I accept evil, no matter how evil Percy was? Did you understand what you gave me to read? Well, maybe you haven't understood enough about us to see it, so I'll tell you. Evil isn't a thing, Brett. It's a form of fashion. God's Army this and that, each killing on opposite instructions. How many people have been killed because they supposedly work for *you*?'

Looking at him listening so seriously, I reminded him, 'You forget, do you, it seems so long ago, but I remember. You said that there are those back and forths from heaven to your place, as the fashion changes.'

He nodded—a blancmange reaction, making me more suspicious than ever.

'You're not, perchance, a moralist, are you?' I needled him. God, I *hate* moralists!

He nodded again. Was he trying to incite violence, or was he doing this in self-unawareness? So hard to tell. I had to give up speculating, and try to teach him about the world.

'In our time,' I put to him, 'how can you even run your futures market when the present is so mixed up.'

He opened his mouth.

'Excuse me, Brett, but I have to finish. This is too difficult otherwise. The thread... It isn't that I am into that Hollywood crap we had a few years ago, those "Somebody has to be a scummy hired assassin, so I might as well be it"...those shit-hot movies... Do you read Arts pages?'

Maybe not.

'Doesn't matter. What does is that this is all happening at the same time. And our communications are adding to our feelings that we are right.'

He was watching me talk. Was he listening to what I was saying? 'How much is Percy mixed up in this?'

'Who is Percy?'—his eyes wide, and innocent as a baby's—a baby with red irises. How irritating.

'You know Percy, so don't deny it.'

'I don't, my dear.'

'Let's not play games. But I will humour you, Brett, for whatever reason you have.'

Those innocent eyes stayed blank, and now to innocence was added an appearance of curiosity.

It was all too much. I hurled my plate against the wall, and its crash failed to satisfy.

Still, nothing changed on Brett's face.

'Do you accept evil?' he repeated, with the can't-be-perturbed passive aggression of a Church of Scientology sidewalk 'survey taker'.

Something was turning again inside me, and it didn't feel like food. It wanted to get out. There wasn't time to think it out. Just say it.

'Brett, it's the wrong, wrong, *wrong* question. You should have asked if I accept good. And the answer is no. Not any more. Not as anything that anyone *says*, and now I don't know, myself.'

I had always avoided news, an avoidance I had mulled over in the past days. The conclusion I had come to, had initially surprised me.

'Brett, whether we read this stuff, whether we are connected or not, doesn't matter, because we all know we're right, whoever we are. And nothing you do changes that. Brett, you must have seen this, since the first heretics way back when.'

His eyes, those baby eyes, were not where I should have been concentrating my scrutiny of whatever he would call his soul. The muscles in his neck stood out. He wanted desperately, *something*. This something had to be part of his sickness, those attacks, those weakness attacks that made him lose his balance.

'And belief?' he asked.

Brett as missionary! He wanted me to believe because it made his mission here more comfortable. His vision: I'd help on Earth, to bring order to the Otherworld in a way it hadn't known since possibly, the telegraph. Was this indeed, a recent phenomenon, and that is why this working holiday? Was I to be a tool to make some Department of Extraordinary Powers function more efficiently?

This thought was a sharp stick, stirring my entrails.

'Brett. This belief thing.' I tried to say it gently. 'It is just what's wrong. I disagree with you, and I hope you won't be offended.'

'Please go on.'—politely said.

'If people did not believe, they might act better toward each other because they wouldn't have the excuse of God telling them to commit for Him, nor heaven waiting for themselves, and hell for others.' At the end of the spurt, I laughed, embarrassed.

'If people did not believe...' he prompted. He hadn't heard anything I'd said. What a relief.

'Maybe it would be like three men in a boat, worms and pinochle.'

Whatever that meant. It just came out, a cliché. But there was something else... 'Do you know Australian fishermen?'

'Uh?' He must have been preoccupied, or thinking about the three men, for he wasn't one to grunt.

'I didn't till I visited the coast. They hang out on sandy beaches. Old blokes with bandy legs sticking out of floppy shorts. They wear knee-high socks in footy team colours, and they keep their shoes on.

The fisherman dangles the wife's nylon stocking in the shallows where waves lap the sand. In the foot of the stocking is rotting fish.'

He was listening.

'The old bloke wafts the fish in its stocking through the shallow water, and just as the waves draw back and all the little holes are exposed in the sand and they bubble and pop dry, he feels something tug at the toe of the stocking. I've never done it, but it's what they say. Anyway, he's got this pair of long-nose pliers, and he reaches down, and quick as your fingers pulling a string of spaghetti from a boiling pot—' A ghost of an expression flitted across Brett's face, so I stopped.

'Please,' he said.

'Well, the fisherman nips his pliers in between the toe and the sand, and the pliers grab hold of the snout of the worm, he yanks up those pliers in one fast long swoop, and up comes a long worm. Night crawlers, they call them. He puts it in this little case he wears at his waist, and bends over the surf again, waving that stocking. He spends half a day there, sometimes with a mate. All the hours of low tide, catching worms with fish.'

'What do they do with them?'

'I wondered, too. They sell them for beer and smokes.'

A polite that-was-interesting silence descended.

Was it not even that? Interesting, that is. Did it have meaning at all? For the first time, I doubted. Yet until that after-telling silence, it was the most profound thing I had ever seen. Never had I even mentioned it to my journal. It was too deep to talk about, until now. And now, I wished I hadn't.

Suddenly his boots were bothersome again. They took a long time to satisfy him as to the looseness of their laces.

'Do you believe, Angela?' He startled me.

'In what I just said? Well, it's true.'

'No. *Believe*.'

'As in God?'

'And me?'

About God, a grunt escaped me. How many times does one need to say something, even to a foreigner?

However, the second part of the question leaned toward me, literally. His breath stirred my hair, willing me to say *Yes*.

In my weakness, for the first time I sensed the yearning that Gordon felt every time he willed me to give in.

Of course, I should have believed. I had signed my soul away, hadn't I? And Brett transmogrified through walls with the greatest of ease, and he wore a goddamn tail.

He waited, but even in my weakness I could not give him his yes. Incoherent tears saved me from an answer.

He left, but this time slowly and diaphanously, leaving behind a faint whiff of hot bitumen.

19

Kevin was beside himself. When he saw me the next day, his first reaction was to beat me to death on the spot. After the first blow, I struck back, and that cleared his head.

I had snuck out in the morning, and when I returned, he emerged from behind a weeping fig just as I came through the door. I was wearing Bottega Bagascia—a scrap of woven butterscotch-and-tobacco leather for a top, and pedal-pushers of chocolate calf that ended somewhere near my ankle. Other than length, everything fit perfectly on my now stick-figure frame.

I had some other things that needed hemming, and after our to-do, he took them wordlessly, returning them in an hour, overlocked in puce thread.

I invited him to sit on the chesterfield, while I took a chair. He began. First, he wanted all the clothes back, though they had been paid for—and he had been paid generously, too. He had, it turned out, been busy (behind my back) arranging a show in Paris (!) with me as the model (!), hoping through the example of me, to launch himself and a revolutionary (for the 21st century) look upon the world.

No, he had not asked. No, he had assumed. Yes, he knew he presumed. No, he didn't think that he had taken unbelievably arrogant liberties. After all, he *made* me. And I 'owed' it to him. And besides, he knew 'everyone' necessary to both promote me and to promote him. Wouldn't I have liked to display myself, 'the world's most rare butterfly, in the most beautiful plumage of our time'?

Butterfly's plumage notwithstanding, he was crazy.

My stomach begged to differ. It spoke to me, agreeing with him that I would live to regret what I had done. I had, until I wasted it, the perfect launch package, it said, along with the book. That collection of extreme-retro curves, not this post-modern minimalism—was as important to my success as my book, my stomach said. My book which *would have been* one of those books with the whole back cover taken up with a picture of me. My stomach spoke loudly, rudely. An untrustworthy advisor, it had been the source of embarrassment and shame to me on many occasions, not to mention having aided in the death of one person, someone I did think of occasionally.

Kevin was speaking. He asked me to stand.

I did, smiling at him to let him know that I would let bygones be bygones. I liked Kevin. He would need to take new measurements.

Then he asked me to undress. When I refused, he asked why.

I just didn't feel like it.

'You're sagacious,' he said. An odd observation, but I could not disagree. He didn't have to bootlick, but he did have insight. My right hand fingered the hollows of my collarbones—a new delight.

Kevin had taught me so much. I had taught him, too. Acknowledgement comes hard to us all, but graciousness is a mark of style. 'Sagacious about what, oh Style Master?' I asked, returning a compliment to a genius who was already reassessing my form—and rethinking, planning his newest creations.

'About you, luv,' he chuckled unmirthfully. 'You're a flapper now. You like it?'

His face—that ugly *expression*. He wasn't talking shimmy skirts and ragtime bands. And he didn't mean 'sagacious' . . . the bastard!

He didn't need me to undress for him. He wanted me undressed, for me. He was a visionary—a cruel fanatic. He wanted me to cover myself with shame, or fat.

Sure, I now had folds where I used to have swells. I could pick my skin away from my flesh. But dieting does that to you. In a $2000 blouse that fits off the rack, what does what's underneath matter? At least I didn't have Sunday-roast skin. And so what if my buttocks sagged like Rupert Murdoch's cheeks, when they fit into Milanese leather?

'You look common,' he sneered.

'Bollocks, Kev.' His comment was spawned of jealousy. They had made it. He hadn't. Common? How many could afford so little for so much?

'Rich slut.'

'Pettyful. With a black eye.' I had punched him well.

He stormed out, but not without me hitting the back of his head with the clump of clothes he'd ruined, 'tailoring'. They hit the floor with a thud, and a heavy zip slithered.

Then it was time to order lunch. What to order?

I ran a bath instead, to think.

The water was dreamy, but feeling myself did not feel the same, and nothing buoyed. I sat on a haemorrhoid donut,. but that didn't solve the problem of my back, which felt as if I had crude wing amputations.

I got out and had a look at myself in the unsteamed, daylight-objective bedroom mirrors.

Then I ran naked into the lounge, where I picked up the mess of this morning's purchases and ran back with them to my bedroom. There, I spread them out on the bed. The hard geometry, stretch polyester, anthracite leather matched with nylon lace, mechanical rips, raked zips, and the hemlines pierced with little-girl flower cutouts (now murdered by Kevin). I splayed them all out—all of Bagascia's semi-couture (for those who are time-poor) spring-summer limited edition.

Then I walked to the wardrobe door and closed my eyes, taking at random, three things from hangers.

They were: A spring jacket in white, lilac-sprigged dimity, with a 'willy wagtail' peplum that fanned itself out behind, trailing green and pink and lilac ribbons. An evening gown of white watered satin trimmed with black karakul. It went with Mr Hazumi's elbow-length black gloves edged with the same black fur, and his little karakul mules.

I had thrown the jacket onto my chair, and threw the gown there, too, but it slid off and sat on the floor in a great pouf of skirts, leaning its frothy left shoulder against the deep chair seat.

The third thing I took off the hangers was just a little nightgown. A little moon-coloured slip of silk, with of course, a few small decorative touches.

Kevin was unavailable. No. He was really unavailable.

Justin now. Yes, Kevin was unavailable. No, Justin was afraid that Kevin was out, actually. Yes, it was unusual, and *my word*, yes, *completely* out of order, but Miss Lily, *considering* . . .

Justin's tone was just short of disrespectful, which, I learned that moment, is the most disrespectful tone of all.

I simply could not eat.

Lunch, I spent pacing, either my hunger feeding my energy, or my energy burning off my hunger.

Whatever Brett thought, he kept his thoughts to himself.

There was nothing to do. I cancelled my massage appointment with Ferdinand, the first I had scheduled since my retreat. I also cancelled: the manicurist, the pedicurist, Justin for anything for the rest of the day, and dinner for myself. I renewed my one instruction. Kevin was to report to me *immediately* upon his return.

There was nothing left to do but bother Brett.

Bloody hell! Even Brett was out.

20

I WAS JUST GIVING Brett up and wondering what to do with myself, when he tapped me on the shoulder. I won't say this frightened me. How would you feel? Some things you never get used to.

'How's your book going?' I asked. Yes, I was feeling like fighting someone—anyone.

Incredibly, he smiled. 'I thought you'd never ask. I've finished the first part.'

He disappeared and appeared a moment later. In his hands, a slim envelope. A slow writer, but beginnings are hard to do. He was offering me the scariest part, in trust.

His feet were shuffling, just as mine would be if someone read my first page. The commonality of writers!

I felt a rush of sympathy, and relief at the same time—I would never again be subjected to the torture of Waiting while Another Reads.

I opened the envelope and pulled from it the single folded sheet.

In his crabbed hand, was:

Princess Martha did not want to cook dinner tonight.

When I looked up, he had disappeared. No use yelling for him. He never came when called.

Two hours later, I was in my bedroom, suffering.

Nothing new had happened to make my day better. No one had appeared. My stomach had revolted violently. It wanted to throw things—heavy, unpleasant things—but didn't have much ammunition. It wanted to hurt, and it did.

Without a knock, he appeared, smelling like buttered toast instead of his oftentimes rankness. He radiated warmth. It is the only time I have ever seen anyone glowing with happiness.

He threw himself lengthways on my bed, crushing my toes.

'Well?' he said.

'Well...'

'Topping beginning, eh?' he said.

'Topping,' I agreed. 'But it could use some work.'

He sat up and peered at me—the pea in his tartare. 'Okay, I grant you that. But it's only the first draft.'

A groan leapt up my throat and I caught it by the tail, between my teeth, but not soon enough.

'What?' he queried, a wee bit testily.

'Not much,' I assured, cravenly. 'Not much . . . but, like . . . Martha.'

He launched himself off the bed. 'Like, as you say, what's wrong with Martha?' The disturbed air bore towards me a whiff of his odour emissions when things were not going toppingly—a smell threatening to choke me.

If only he would just crush my toes again. I had, however, no choice but to persevere.

'Nothing's wrong with Martha,' I said, dripping mellifluent, 'except that it isn't really a name for a princess.'

'Like, what is?' he spat back with a lot of bad breath, as if I had just told him what I really thought.

He was supposed to be writing the damn book. Not me!

'. . . I dunno,' I said. 'Something exotic . . .'

'Well?'

This was too much. Disaster yawned, unless I stood up for myself. 'You should know, Brett. You must know some princesses.'

And anyway . . . 'What about all your research?'

And furthermore . . . 'Why have you been surrounding yourself with books for, anyway? Can't you know what you want without the messiness of pages and dust and all that old stuff?'

He sat beside me, emanating a happy warmth.

'I like the physicality of books,' he said. 'Don't you?'

Not until he said it did I remember how comforted I felt once upon a time, having them around. But then I thought of princesses and Martha, and even that ghost of a feeling left me, quicker than mist on a summer morning.

'Princesses should have pretty and exotic names,' I told Brett. 'Gwendolyn, Xenobia, Aljazeera.'

'So "Princess Gwendolyn did not want to cook dinner tonight." Right?'

My stomach screamed out that there was not much more of this it was going to put up with. 'No. Not exactly.'

Again, he leapt from the bed, and this time he paced.

What could I say?

Then he spun suddenly and faced me, blazing a smile of victory. "Princess Gwendolyn didn't want to cook dinner tonight." Your passion for contraction. Sorry.'

The smile withered at my unspoken response. He returned to pacing, now striking his heels so violently upon the sheepskins that the wardrobe replied with a ridiculously musical tinkle and rustle of beads and feathers, making me want to strangle my clothes to shut them up.

'Princesses don't cook,' I said.

He was opening his mouth to object when I snuck in a qualifier, very gently put. 'Not earthly princesses, anyway.'

'Oh.' He stopped pacing and bent down to loosen those infernal laces. 'You mean,' he said, as he straightened, 'my first sentence is no good?'

'Not exactly.' He was taking editing better than many, but . . . 'We don't have to start there, as long as you have the rest of the story planned.'

He began to pace again, so I got up and put my hand on his arm, if only to slow him down. 'Tell me about the rest of the story.'

'That was it,' he said. 'I hadn't gotten any further.'

What have you been doing all this time? I screamed. I called him every filthy name that I ever learned, and I knew many from the shearing shed. I slammed my right knuckles into his mouth and felt the satisfaction of breaking through a slew of teeth. My fists clenched hard as coconuts, I boxed his ears so hard that blood flew. In my imagination. Only in my imagination while I stood there with my hands clawing the back of my own wizened frame, for the frustrating comfort of giving more pain to myself.

'Ah,' I said. 'What do you have planned tomorrow?'

'Work,' he answered, grimly.

Good. Maybe.

'It is only your beginning,' I smiled, meaning that I stretched my lips across my teeth.

He answered with a mirror of my facial movements.

'I'm going to bed,' he said, and went to his room, allowing us both to groan and scream to our hearts' content, which we both did. I heard him, but did he hear me?

Nothing from Kevin.

About three in the morning I woke from an exhausted doze. The only sounds were the gentle gurgles of my fridge. There was nothing to do but be depressed. There was nothing to read at all. I tossed my head on my pillow till I realized, *at all* was an exaggeration.

Sanitized Hypo-allergenic
100% White Goose Down 900+
Cruelty-free Hand-harvested in Hungary

· · ·

21

A POMPOUSLY OBSEQUIOUS Kevin rang at 6:30 in the morning, and I was gratified to deflate him with, 'No, I've been up for hours. Please do come up.'

It didn't do, however, to continue in this vein. I needed him. So when he arrived, I ushered him past the broken crockery and splatted mess of egg in the lounge, to the sanctuary of my bedroom. I offered to call down for tea, but he declined, truculently.

Kevin, Kevin. I had to do this right. He was such a Romantic.

'Kevin, I'm sorry,' I said, leaning against my bed. He hadn't sat, so I couldn't.

He turned away from me. When he turned back, of course I had to respond.

'Okay, why?' I asked, in as much of a schoolgirl voice as I could muster, and my mustering capabilities were dissipating fast.

He had attached a clothes-peg to his nose, and was brandishing his face at me only an arm's length away.

'Oooh sding.'

I turned my back on him. 'Take it off, Kev,' I warned, 'or get out.'

A *snap* sounded, so I turned around, and besides two red places on the sides of his nose and a closed-door of a face, he looked like the old Kevin.

'Begin,' I invited.

'No. You.'

Best to ignore the insurrection. 'Kevin,' I honey-toned. 'You really are most wonderful . . . No. Really!'

He sat in my chair and folded one leg over the other, so I perched on the side of my bed.

'I am sorry I was unable to maintain my weight in the press of creative pressure. But I will regain my figure again and we can have your fashion show, just as you planned.'

His lips were curving into a dangerous smirk.

'You naughty boy,' I slung in, hitting his expression smack in the middle of its superiority.

Much more of this and I would have no ammunition left. It wasn't as if I could use my proud posture to assert my position, because there was nothing left that stuck out except bones. Instead, I went to the wardrobe and opened its doors. A scream at my back tore a scream out of me. I whirled around, ready to run.

The sound was coming out of Kevin's mouth.

'Fuck, Kevin! Look what you've done.'

A golden shower I couldn't stop spangled the sheepskin and splashed my feet.

Perhaps that moved him. He marched around me and flung himself against the wardrobe door, like it was some Victorian virgin, and I ... 'Don't touch them!' he bellowed.

But they were mine. *Assert, assert.*

Shouting 'I'll have none of this from you!' I shoved him aside.

He tripped me!

'You've chipped my pelvis, you have!'

'I hope!' he growled. 'Just look down and see.'

'Enough! or leave.'

He sat in my chair instead, so I sat on the bed.

'What is this about, Kevin,' I asked, as if we were feeling reasonable.

'Not counting inconsequentials . . .' and he flicked his hand at the soggy sheepskin, 'You smell, dear Desirée.'

Although he said 'dear', he didn't murder 'Desirée'. We were getting somewhere.

'Your diet has done what they usually do,' he said, no longer attaching emotional weights to his words. 'Your body odour is quite strong now, and it will taint my beauties. We cannot allow that to happen, can we?'

I bent inwards toward my manipura chakra, and sniffed. There was no need to plumb another chakra, nor to breathe deeply.

'Your suite . . .' Kevin said.

Smelt in that light, it was a wonder that room service served on command. Brett had his moments, but I couldn't blame this noxious emanation on Brett.

Someone deserved contrition. I got down on my knees. Kevin would like that.

He did. 'It's not unique,' he allowed. 'This age . . .'

'I promise to do what you say,' I promised.

We figuratively kissed and made up, and I have to admit that my BO problem bothered me. I hoped that my former smell, whatever it was, came back quickly, so that I was no longer a social embarrassment to myself.

Kevin told me that breakfast would be at ten that morning. When I asked what it was, he evinced a residue of huffiness. 'That's for you to find out.'

I sat with Brett through a silent eight-thirty breakfast for him, after which he promptly returned to his room.

At ten sharp, I answered the door personally, not to be met with room service and a tray of some lovely fattening breakfast, but by Kevin and a tall, thin man with big hairy ears carrying a salesman's case big enough to store a dismembered child. I invited them both in, though Kevin did not introduce him.

We sat in the lounge—me, the un-introduced man, and Kevin, all in a row on the chesterfield. Kevin, still angry, I suppose, left it to me.

I inclined my head toward the man with the carpeted ears. 'Good morning,' I said. 'Miss Lily . . .' extending my hand and trying at the same time not to emit rank auras, nor to have him continue to bore his eyes into my person as he began to, the moment our eyes touched—his eyes probing intimately past the only thing that fit me, the one-size-fits-all fluffy bath robe.

'Morris K. Fishbine,' he replied, extending the tips of four long, pale fingers, and then dropping his hand to his lap before I could figure out whether I was supposed to shake it, or kiss it.

Kevin leaned out. 'Doctor Fishbine has something for you. Go for it, Morrie.'

'Morrie' reached down and opened the case at his feet. With difficulty, he pulled out several large things and dumped them on the coffee table, from where two bounded to the floor. Massive deformed jellyfish? Whatever they were, they were revolting. What had I promised?

'Yuck, Kev! I couldn't eat one of those for dinner, let alone brekkie.'

His eyes glinted.

I got up, ready to run and lock myself into my room. 'No forcefeeding!'

'Sit,' he commanded, which was too dangerous. Instead, I settled for grabbing a rubber futon and holding it up as a shield between me and them.

'Doctor Fishbine will show you, Miss Lily. Doctor Fishbine?'

Doctor Fishbine had been amused, as his tolerant chuckle proved.

'Miss Lily, these are not for eating, though you could. At no harm to yourself, I might add.' And he chuckled again at the anecdote he was already filing in his memory bank for telling to whatever he called 'friends'.

Kevin coughed and pointed to the case.

The doctor pulled out a shiny red display book, so I had no choice but to put down my shield and sit beside him. He laid the book on my lap. Then, slowly and carefully, he went through every page of his thoroughly photographed procedure of slitting through skin and muscle and fat, folding it back, and inserting blobs of various sizes into various parts of the human anatomy. Only when the last page had been open on my lap for some time and he was satisfied with my reassurances that I didn't need to revisit any pages, did he return the book to his case.

'And these?' I picked up a blob—heavy, disgustingly alive, not as slippery as it looked, but wiggly nonetheless.

'Your right breast,' Doctor Fishbine replied.

'Yikes!'

It flopped to the sheepskin with a life of its own. The rest of the collection supined in a sorority of flounce and bounced-around attitudes, none less gross than another.

The doctor was offended. It was no use my saying 'no offence'. His knees cracked as he stood up from the chesterfield. He knelt and they cracked again as he crawled on the floor picking up the pieces, and stuffing them rather viciously away.

'Thank you, Doctor Fishbine,' Kevin said, at which point I stood and repeated Kevin's phrase. You never know.

Kevin left with him, returning five minutes later.

It seemed that those abhorrences were me, what I was—what I needed to gain back... 'or what'.

The *what* was the worst. Fishbine had agreed to be party to Kevin drugging me and spiriting me off to the doctor's private clinic, where those long pale fingers would create and insert 'whatever it takes' to give me back the figure to fit the clothes Kevin had designed to fit me when my figure was at the peak of its form. Gain it again, or else.

I promised Kevin and myself that I would. *I would.* And where's breakfast?

Kevin's régime was strict, and followed strictly. He, it was, who ordered my meals, and structured my feedings and exercise so that I could gain the proper fat in the proper places. At first, it was difficult for me to keep anything down. My stomach had shrunk, but that was not the problem. The food was.

No more *Calamari Fragonzola au Carambola* (according to Serge, my most successful creation). No more frivolous cheesecake awaiting my fork. Not even a fridge in my room, to tempt me to disobey. Now everything was scientifically determined. Kevin didn't value food as food, but as feeding. Thus, his prescribed régime was chemicals with calories, and meat. Red meat.

The first meal, that breakfast, was the roughest. A steak the size of my hand, medium-burnt. The smell of cooked meat made me queasy. It had been so many years. Not in fact, since Bunwup. I could only down part of that first steak before I had to stop. Worse was the next course, a 'bodybuilding shake I formulated just for you,' he assured me, as if that excused it, 'packed with oestrogen, progesterone, prolactin, prostaglandins, phytoestrogen-derived kilojoules, *and* GF compounds ... human growth factor hormones'—in medium beige.

Kevin supervised that meal by watching me chew and swallow what I could of the meat, and going *chuck, chuck, chuck* with the shake. He seemed satisfied enough. I wasn't. I believed Kevin's threat, every last scalpel-slice of it.

Kevin assured me that if I complied, his régime would re-create for me the same body as before, since I was still young and since the weight loss had been so 'dramatically precipitous' (Kevin's new language, attempting, I think, to get beyond his body-builder vocabulary, possibly in an attempt to firmly re-establish his primacy).

I flashed an obedient smile—and hoped he was right. Time had flown, especially during my ensconcement. Here it was, already April. Kevin had planned my launch with his characteristic originality. July, when Paris is packed with visitors, but no competing shows.

Brett would be flicking his Bic by then, but he'd have to learn patience. As things stood, Kevin was a stroke of luck. Me in Paris, sashaying down the ramp (Brett should have thought of it) ... the finalé: my final twirl, and voilá—my book magically appears in my arms (Brett's contribution). Behind me, a giant screen lights up ...

Until then, I was between bodies.

* * *

Kevin, grimacing out to his fingertips, removed every scrap of my Italian designer collection for sacrifice with extreme violence. In their place, he supplied a few bathrobes in the style of my one-size-fits-all, thus both staking out his superiority and keeping me indoors.

As I didn't wish to be seen, I didn't object.

I didn't desire Justin to buy any more art, as I now knew enough and had stopped looking at what we had. As for comfort in the suite, as long as I had my water room, my bed, my chair and the chesterfield, what more could I want?

I followed Kevin's régime day after day. Really I did, though I couldn't see results.

The fear of Kevin was my greatest stimulation. Every day, I'd survey my armpit-aura and my breath, eat my steak and drink my shake-times-three, and I could tick that day off on a calendar. I couldn't do more than I did, to change my figure. I had to hope and trust, but Kevin was an expert.

I should have been lighthearted, yet I felt more and more weighted by a heavy ennui—a mixture of repletion and sleepiness and waiting-roomness—that feeling that some have made books of, exploring the tragedy—but I could only yawn, until, one day, I began to feel another sensation. A Need. The need to bother someone.

There was nothing to do. *Nothing* to do, that is, than again, to bother Brett. It was just after breakfast that I felt this bother need coming on, and it pounded its heels on the floor of my stomach. *Indulge me!*

Day after day, Brett had been quietly working in his room, so I wavered.

There was nothing to do. Nothing to read. Nothing to think about.

I fought against the bother need for what must have been a full five minutes, and then, finally, triumphed against it.

For the more I pondered what Brett was doing, the more I realized that I had more to fear from him than from Kevin himself.

Now I felt a higher Need than the basic need to bother.

What *was* Brett doing?

22

'Come in, come in!' Brett's jovial voice answered to my knock. *Well, well!*

I was turning the door knob when I heard a flurry and a *whoosh*, and then, 'Do,' from within.

The door swung easily, and there was my chair positioned for my comfort. He was again seated cross-legged near the ceiling with no visible means of support, a jumble of books and papers spread over his invisible table.

He was folding a piece of paper, so I waited. Then his left arm swung in a roundabout manner, and the folded paper flew out, navigated the room like a drunken fly, and plummeted between two mountains of books.

A paper airplane! The dear! What a deprived childhood he must have had.

'That was splendid, Brett. Why don't you try again? But you might have the wrong throwing technique.'

'Oh?' He cheered up immensely. 'What do you suggest?'

I was making the movements myself to try to figure out how to describe when his little plane swooped back into his hand, and he threw it to me perfectly.

I reached up and caught it by the tail. We both laughed with pleasure.

'Wow!' I exclaimed. 'How did you correct your throw that fast? It's inhuman!'

'You were spear-throwing,' he told me, but his initial excitement was gone. In its place was a dullness.

He was an inscrutable if there ever was one, but by now a twiddlebit tiresome. If he wasn't going to divulge, I wasn't going to dig it out of him.

There was writing on the paper, as I could feel from the texture on the back.

'Open it,' he invited, more smoothly now than a moment ago.

I opened, and read.

> When in the idyll of slow country, caught
> by coffee and remembrance of cups past

I sigh the lack of many a cup I bought
and with old clothes now hail my dear friend's face.
Then we can drown a fly, unused to go
in precious bends hid in bread's tasteless bite.
We'll weep on fresh loaves o'er date-cancelled Roe
and bone the tense of many a vanquished night.
Then you can leave as grievances slog on,
and heavily from Roe to Roe tell o'er
The sad account of Roes upon the phone
Which I do say as if not said before
    That it's the fly that winks at season's end
    If horses are enjoyed, and so Roes end.

'It's a sonnet,' he said.
I had guessed.
'You like it?'
'Well, it's very clever, Brett,' I again guessed. 'Who did it?'
'I.'

He could no longer restrain himself. He cleared a space for landing and zoomed down to lean against the back of my chair. I craned my neck to look behind me but instead, he reached over me and placed an open book in my lap. 'Read this.'

He had his finger on a poem that skewed its way crazily over the yellowed page. It said:

Poëms.

The benefit of Friendſhip.

WHen to the Seſſions of ſweet ſilent thought,
    I ſummon up remembrance of things paſt,
I ſigh the lacke of many a thing I fought,
And with old woes new waile my deare times waſte
Then can I drowne an eye (unus'd to flow)

Call me immature. Call me Philistine. I don't care. At this point, my arms were hanging helpless beside my chair, slack from laughter. Ftuff always does this to me.

'Hmm,' behind me.

Ftuffing my childishness down my throat, I put my hands back to work and turned to the book's front page.

'Poems: VVRITTEN BY WIL. SHAKE-SPEARE. Gent.'

Uh, oh. I had had my fufpishons. (Ftop that!)

'You were not invited in here to decry the great bard,' Brett intoned, earning a sharp turnaround of my head. He was, unfortunately, serious.

I read on, silently, of course:

> For precious friends hid in deaths dateleffe night,
> And weepe a frefh loves long fince canceld-credit-card woe,
> And moane th'expence of many a vanifht fight.
> Then can I greeve a greevances foregone,
> And heavily from woe to Woe tell boringly ore and ore
> The fad fashion account of fore-bemoned mone,
> VVich I new pay on a your new Visa, as it not payd before.
>> But if the while I finke on thee (deare friend)
>> All loffes are reftor'd, and forrowes end.

And onwards. And don't *you* try skipping here. I couldn't.

> Thy bofome is indeared with all hearts,'
> VVich I by lacking have fuppofed good and dead
> And there raignes Love and all Loves great acting parts,
> And all thofe friends which I thought faffely buried.
> How many a holy and obfequious croc teare

And on and bloody *on and on*, though I was ready to explode. Is it just me, or does this do it to you, too? It isn't that this is *bad*. It is just hilariously *undelectable*. It shines with not goodness as the rainbow shines on the surface of raw meat too-long-kept.

I glanced back at Brett, and he was doing what I had seen professors do—delectate. In professors, it had to be an act. In Brett . . . but first, I had to continue.

> And
> you

do
,
too
.

Just joshin'. Don't say I've got no pity. I let you off the hook, but I read the rest, and closed the book before he could find another felection.

He took it from me with a frightening reverence.

'It's the Benson,' he said.

He was still behind me, but I didn't turn to face him. Stuff him. He could come around. 'Benson what?'

He did come around, squatted and peered at me. '*The* Benson.'

The Benson, the Benson . . .

'The 1609 edition.'

Oh, god! He's—'You're a collector!'

His face showed the gloat and the guilt, immediately. 'What's wrong with collecting?'

'Outside of stealing, which you must have done with this, there's avarice, and obsession, and . . .'

I couldn't think of anything more, but 'What are you doing collecting books when you're supposed to be writing mine?'

An excuse was on his lips, but I got in first. 'And why are you writing poetry when you're supposed to be writing a novel. A romance with adventure, remember? My classic for all time?'

He smoothed the paper airplane out on my lap. 'Read it, please.'

There was no defensiveness in his tone, so I read. His poem was a take-off on the sonnet, but other than that, what?

'It's the introduction element in your book,' he said, 'to come right after the dedication.'

He was right. The book did need something classy in front, reminding me of another element I had quite forgotten. It had to be dedicated, a serious issue which produced a welling up of panic, but only temporary.

To Brett Hartshorn with Love—that would look excellent.

That settled, I examined Brett's poem. It was . . . a mess.

'Brett, uh, could I have a squizz at what you're reading?'

I must have sounded respectful enough because in a moment, my head was bashed against the ceiling, and then I was landed more softly at his invisible desk. I was supported on a nothingness that moulded itself to me but didn't present the instability problems of a waterbed.

It was evident in a second what Brett's problem was. At least, part of his problem.

An icicle ran up my spine at the sight of the bulk he was working through: a heap of leather tomes gold-stamped: '100 Best Books'.

'Brett, I appreciate your hard work,' I began. 'Catching up with the cultural stuff, remedially and now.'

He dipped his head in acknowledgement.

'But your problem is,' I said, and he cringed. He actually sunk his head between his shoulderblades, giving me a little satisfaction before I struck with, 'You're trying too hard.'

'Pshaw!' he snorted, delighted. We laughed together—he, with relief, and me, from worry.

'First of all,' I explained, 'I told you to read the one hundred best-loved books, *not* the one hundred best books.'

A blank look. I'd get to this later.

'Then, no one. No one,' I said—his attention was now all mine, all trusting, and I felt *so guru*—'No one could mix Shakespeare with chick lit and hags-in-sisterhood, and Dylan Thomas, and who else have you got here? And get away with it.'

He looked up at me with hope in his eyes. 'No one? Not even Shakespeare?'

'Not even Shakespeare,' I said with total confidence.

This was an unnatural position, and I needed closeness to get my message across. 'You can lower me.'

When I was settled in my chair again after a smoother trip, he sat on the floor in front of me.

'Just between me and you,' I said, touching a fingertip to his knee, 'Do you understand that Shakespeare thing?'

'Do you?'

'Not likely,' I laughed.

'Me neither,' he said, frowning. 'But I thought I should.'

'Don't we all.'

This reassurance produced, to my dismay, not to mention a teensy bit of wanting-to-strangle-him annoyance, that same reaction of immediate depression and dullness that had bubbled up with the paper airplane.

'Brett, you're making me dizzy with your moods.'

'What moods?' he sighed.

'What moods, you sigh?' But that was making things worse. I think I hurt his feelings. 'How sensitive *are* you,' I asked. 'Like—'

'I'm okay,' he said, ending the discussion.

But I didn't want to end it, and the way he slowly crawled through the air to his desk made me ask him a question. 'Do you know the term "hard yakka", Brett?'

He didn't, so I asked, 'Do you want to work on the book now?'

'No.' He hadn't even stopped to think.

'Are you going to work on it? The book, I mean?'

'Yes.'

'That,' I told him, 'is hard yakka. You working on it.'

He nodded. 'Thank you for explaining.' And crosslegged up there, he bent his back to work.

'Brett,' I said, 'Why don't you come down from there and let's do something else.'

'But don't you want . . .'

'No, Brett,' I smiled.

What the hell he thought he would accomplish is beyond me, but I had nothing else to do. 'I might as well help you write this book.'

He futon-mountained and I chesterfielded in the lounge.

'Why are you helping me?' he asked.

I wondered about that, too. Boredom was one reason . . .

Then I was conveniently interrupted by a knock at the door. Brett's lunch and my second dose of the day had arrived.

My steak was delicious. I had forgotten how good a good a steak *is* in those dozen meat-free years, till Kevin's régime reminded me.

The shakes were still vile. I was choking down this sludge when I noticed Brett stabbing his stiletto fingernail *stab stab stab* into his chopped meat. Something was wrong.

'Please?' I asked, now able to touch the raw stuff. I stuck my own fork into his meatball, and it stopped cold. His tartare was raw meat, all right—but microwaved, with a frozen centre!

I jumped up and banged the heel of my palm against the intercom. 'Serge!'

'When he gets his bloody arse up here, I'm gonna tear it off!' I assured a bemused Brett.

Bloody *nothing* happened.

Five minutes later, I ran down the stairs to find a strange woman at the desk. She glanced at me and raised her eyebrows. I was, of course, in my one-size-fits-all bathrobe.

She was wearing a bright red uniform suit, with a big gold label riding her right breast, reading 'Jane' and 'F.H.O.T.W.' in red and blue enamel.

'May I help you?' she asked.

'Uh.' I looked around. No one in the lobby. 'Where's Justin?'

'Mister Justin?' she asked.

'Okay, Mister Justin.'

She checked a register.

I fled—back to our suite.

23

ACCORDING TO KEVIN (who came at my third insistent *brrrring*), all kinds of things had happened during my ensconcement. The first Thing was that Justin had fallen in love. Well, I knew that. I patted Kevin's hand. Justin's tragically white-wabbit love could never be requited, but it wasn't dangerous.

But no! This 'love' had found a way—with a woman of no refinement but over-endowments in all the right places. No one knew anything about her. She was, physically, 'as extraordinary as you', Kevin said, and then he added quite unnecessarily—'were.'

Most unlikely. But Kevin wasn't interested in the Fishbinesqueness of this silicon trollop.

Worse than her falseness—this creature yearned for the lifestyle of the rich and discreet as chronicled under the sheets by Justin to her. She urged him to set aside provisions for her and him to establish a love nest.

So Justin had done just that, only to be outsmarted by the company's own finance department. Now Justin was 'languishing in chookie' (Kevin's new multicultural tongue), awaiting his trial.

At this point Kevin stopped for breath. 'I really must get back,' he said. He was extremely tense, and he sure talked fast. But he continued.

Next—oh, headache! Justin's embezzlement must have motivated the company directors to re-examine the core business, because they sold to an international hotel chain that had lusted for it.

A new regime was being established. Serge was gone (well, I knew *that*—unless the frozen meatball was his *ta ta*). An ex-McDonald's manager was running the kitchen now. And the management of the hotel was now in the experienced hands of a Pam Borghwick.

A *woman!*

Don't you just *hate* women managers!

Kevin agreed. He was practically on a leash, and had been given notice after our session this morning that he was a downstairs worker—only.

I had never known Kevin's job title. All of a sudden I felt rather protective of him. And also, a rush of gratefulness for his caring. After all,

he was endangering his job by sneaking upstairs to tell me.
'They converted my sewing room to an office.'
Sympathy.
'They're turning the underground clinic into a conferencing centre.'
Yuk, but that was a rarely-used extravagance.
'Anyway,' he shrugged, as if none of it mattered. 'I snuck up to see you now cos I gotta get my clothes out of here. Can you help?'
'Why?'
'Why help me!?' He raised his fist, unreasonably hysterical.
I caught his fist in my hand, and subdued him with no real effort. He was too depressed to fight back. 'No,' I said, 'Why do we have to get them out?'
'Because I'm getting the flick any minute. I can feel it, and Justin's antics pulled out the welcome mat from my coming back for visits to you, dear lady. And you don't know how to care for anything.'
'Why?' I felt stupid asking *why why why*, but his paranoia was forcing me.
'Because, dear Miss Lily, Borgia downstairs told all of us that no guest. And she meant *you* in particular, is to get any special treatment, anything off the á la carte, any special visits from the staff or other specialists. And in short, any more room service *at all*, until the corporation has these components of service and goods properly reassessed in a thorough and wide-ranging cost benefit analysis, which she estimates will take approximately six months.'
'Fuh! Ukh!' The toadying bitch.
His incisors gleamed in the satisfaction of my finally understanding the degree of camaraderie we shared.
'Get me something to wear,' I said, 'and I don't care how you do it.'
'Right-oh.'
'And get it up here in half an hour.'
He nodded.
'And meet us in Paris in one week. You have money?'
'Some.'
'Here.' I wrote him a cheque for what I thought was enough.
He did, too. 'Where d'you wanna meet?' he asked
Hmm . . .'At the Ritz.' (Really, how would I know?)

He was thinking hard, flexing his biceps alternately—a nervous tick. 'Somewhere else?'

'Oh?'

'Somewhere more anonymous?'

I giggled. 'You're not worried about espionage, are you?'

Sheepishly, he grinned. This was beginning to be fun.

'Prague, under the clock tower?' he suggested. 'Sunday noon?'

Much more exciting than the boring old Ritz.

I didn't know Prague, but Brett just might.

24

AFTER THAT tornado of bad news, I felt balmy relief from solving problems so easily. Until a little thought wafted into my brain with the subtlety of a piano falling on me: *What do I tell Brett? Brett, who I told zat about my launch?*

He was remarkably acquiescent.

The launch, he accepted at once. He even smiled! This was fortuitous.

When I explained how the Restonia had changed, he agreed that we should move, and was happy about Prague.

Did he know the clock tower?

Yes, he knew the clock tower.

This was obviously meant to be. My heart soared. But, back to basics. Did he need to pack?

No, he didn't need to pack.

But I did. What could I do with all my clothes? I almost called room service. Fun habits never want to die.

'Could we fit them in your trunk, Brett?' It looked way too small, but being his, it could have any amount of internal capacity.

'Sadly, no,' he said, not trying to be cryptic, but making me so curious, my palms itched.

At that point, only four minutes after Kevin left, he returned with a shirt and trousers. I pulled up the trousers, but they needed something to hold them up. He ripped off his tie, and that had to do.

'And wardrobe cases?' I asked him.

All we could come up with at such short notice was the bedclothes and the curtains. Kevin tenderly laid masterpiece on masterpiece, and tied up each bundle with an enormous bow. The shoes, he wrapped in towels first, displaying a respect for Hazumi's craft that surprised me. Everything, including my exquisite underclothing was packed. Everything except for the violet calf boots, my favourites, which were on my feet.

I would have liked to have said goodbye to Mr Hazumi, but I was ready. Brett was of course ready, so Kevin called for a taxi. At the door to our suite, he took a surprisingly emotional leave of us, till I thought he had gone on enough. I slapped him on the bum. 'Off to your dungeon, Kev.'

'Jane' was at the counter when Brett and I arrived with our bundles. She practically wept on hearing that we were leaving. 'Mizz Borghwick is not here now,' she said. 'Could you please take a seat while—'

'Fraid not,' Brett assured her.

'Plane, you see.' I reassured her.

She wasn't reassured. 'The account?'

'We'll bill you,' I said, and then remembered something. Grabbing the key, I rushed upstairs and took first, the angry parrot from the wall, and then Justin's favourite drawing of Rose.

Back at the counter I tore a page from the register and wrote: 'To Justin Abernathy'.

'Please give this to Mizz Borghwick upon her return,' I instructed Jane, handing her Rose and the note. It is debatable whether she heard. Her mouth was open but her brain had seized.

Justin didn't deserve the picture after his unfaithfulness and secrecy, but I had a soft spot for him. He had lost his ambitious sweetheart for sure, but he could have Rose as long as he could manage to keep her out of the clutches of others, in jail.

I had settled Brett in the front seat with the parrot picture, and was with some difficulty, stuffing the bundles into the back when Kevin ran out.

'I've left,' he panted. 'I'll take them.'

'They're loaded,' I said firmly, sticking out my bum to shove the last bundle in just far enough that I could sit beside it. They were *mine*, not his, but I decided to part on a generous note. 'You can borrow them when we meet again,' I said, taking hold of the door.

Rather hysterically, he sighed.

'Two days only,' I consoled him. Victory is always sweet.

'Two days,' he repeated.

He handed me an enormous tin. 'Your shake. Follow the instructions. Religiously!'

The taxi was on its way when I remembered and grabbed the front passenger's seat. 'Your trunk and bag!'

'Don't worry, my dear,' Brett said. 'They go another way.'

I wish we had.

What's the use of hanging out with the Devil if you don't get the perks? I expected Satan Class, a bit of transmogrification, our bags (okay, my bundles and his bag and trunk) jumping over the moon or however he did it—and Bob's your uncle. Before I could say *abracadabra*, I'd be testing the mattress in a luxo suite in Prague. But instead of Satan, we went Hell Class, 'for the experience', he said. Not only that, but he wanted the *whole* experience. Economy Class, laughingly called Coach, *standby*, and here it was already May the bloody first.

'Lucky' he called it, when we arrived at the international terminal to find it buzzing with news of a no-survivor plane crash somewhere over the Indian Ocean. Bonza! In no time (airport-time), Brett handed over our Australian (!) passports (!), and we had tickets. Though we carried no suitcases, my four bundles were designated 'excess baggage'—and their cost? They deserved wine with their meals. Then each was tagged PRG by a jocular attendant (ha ha), and manhandled with grace (ho ho ho) as their fabric wrappings caught in the luggage track and their bulk needed shoving through the rubber-flapped exit. But by the time our seats were organized, the bundles had disappeared.

Brett and I were free now to get excited about our new adventure, and to grump about our seats. I told him that this is part of the 'experience' for people who go Shit-arse Class, and he smiled gleefully. We had scored middle of the middle row near the back, which I was sure would not change, all the way to Prague. Did I tell you Brett's height? In feet and inches or centimetres: tall. As I boarded the first leg of the four-leg, thirty-hour journey, I smiled at the thought of it. Adventure when we landed, but in the meantime, Brett's legs would curse him all the way to Prague.

Sweet revenge came so early, my stomach effervesced. I was seated when Brett lowered himself into his own, to find that his knees jammed against the seat in front of him. I looked away. Out of the corner of my eye, I then saw Brett shrug off this discomfort. What a letdown! But only thirty seconds later when he bent over in that habitual action of his, one of his horns caught in upholstery, and I had to help him come loose. Then try as he did, he was too cramped in to lean over and adjust the laces on his boots. He didn't ask, and I didn't offer.

Then, eating, which I always thought was sort of optional with him, had, it seems, some importance as part of the 'experience'. What was he expecting? During the first so-called meal service, he turned to me. 'I'm hungry,' he said.

'Well then, eat everything they've given you,' I said.

Amazingly, he did. Watching his face was the indigestion relief I needed. So. Hah! I'd told him, 'You don't need this experience,' but he didn't listen.

But the slimebag! As soon as that first meal was collected, he climbed over his obese neighbour and walked out of my sight. At each changeover he stayed by my side, moving along and sitting in airport lounges like the rest of us sheepload of passengers, keeping his thoughts to himself. But once again boarded, he spent most of the flight out of his seat. I had never known him to go to the loo, and assumed that he was hanging around outside one but when I went exploring, I didn't find him.

Finally, on the last leg of the flight, when all the people around us were deep in darkened discomfort, he 'woke' me with a gentle tap to my knee.

'Are you awake?' he whispered.

I swallowed the first answer that came to mind.

'Your uncle Percy . . .' he said.

I sat up.

'What about Percy?'

'He didn't come to us.'

'Percy Lily?'

'And Percy Pendergast. I wasn't sure. I looked up both.'

'Impossible!'

'I didn't remember him, so I checked the records. He was never recorded.'

'But he was a monster!' Then it occurred to me. '*Great* uncle. You couldn't have looked well—'

'I am a research *expert*!'

'Okay already. But . . . Didn't you say "you decide, we abide"? Everyone knew Percy.'

Percy was before my time. Even Mum only knew him by reputation, though I got the impression that when she was a heifer, he was a bad smell, but not yet maggot-fodder. *But surely, by now . . . which just proves—*

Brett grabbed my wrist and squeezed—as only he could. A blubber came out of me. A spring under my arse sprang. At that, he let go.

'You don't believe,' he whispered, his voice a hoarse scratch. He made his fist flame-ready. A threat, but in his eyes was fright. Of what?

I draped my hand over his fist, 'Yes, Brett, of course I do.'

He looked closely at me. My wrist was already swelling and this seat was sheer torture, but I smiled—apparently convincingly.

'I can understand your confusion, my dear. What did this evil uncle Percy do?'

Do? Memories . . . *If you don't pull your socks up, you'll turn into an Uncle Percy . . . There's no redeeming him. A regular Percy, he is . . . Almost as bad that old bugger, Perce, rot his soul . . .*

Not everything needs to be said out loud to be understood. All us kids knew—it had to do with sex. And when we were young, we thought he'd put a bun in the oven of some girl living in a lonely station, which made two strikes against him. Firstly, being a man of the cloth. 'Them parsons expect hot pumpkin scones when they *visit*, though all your clobber is dust and cockatoos.' And the second strike against him was the theory of his dalliance. No one bothered about a bastard, but they did in our parts resent like blazes, any sanctimonious washing of the hands after the act. Bastards need care like anyone, or they grow up to be right bastards.

But in the last few years, I had reconsidered Percy's crime, realizing that it was worse than we kids had thought, because 1) The details were never mentioned, and 2) No matter how much we asked, Percy's seed didn't amount to anything that walked and talked, let alone dropped drunk in the dust of Bunwup. No, Percy's crime was one that had no name when I grew up, but did have now.

'Brett, I'm surprised I have to tell you. Percy was a paedophile.'

He was just going to say something when the lights went on and all around us people groaned and rubbed their faces.

I sprinted for the loo.

Did I golden-shower Prague? I don't know. But the seatbelt light went on just before I flushed.

25

I WAS READY to kill Brett.

Kevin would kill me.

How could they lose four enormous bundles? It took professionalism.

Brett was useless. *He* didn't know where they were, though his own stuff would pitch up at his command like a faithful dog.

I was ready to leave the baggage carousel when an old man in a uniform appeared, just like Santa Claus, with one of my bundles held in his arms, its white embroidered flowers now tyre-marked. I was going to thank him till he threw it disrespectfully on the carousel. I grabbed it and as I lifted, the torn and filthy contents fell out of the bottom. They were the bedclothes and curtains that Kevin had used for bundling *in*.

Yes, I found an office and no, I didn't lodge a claim. I wasn't dressed to intimidate. I hadn't slept or washed since I could remember. I hadn't locked my luggage. And finally, the form I was given to sign was suspicious in itself. It was probably an admission of guilt.

After my initial panic, I reconsidered. Oh well, I thought. Kevin will just have to make everything again. And now I had nothing to lug. A change is as good as a holiday, and I was looking forward to Prague. Brett knew Prague, so now I could just sit back and enjoy the ride.

He seemed disoriented in this big new airport—fair enough. So I led the way, up the escalator, at which he balked, then out to the front of Ruzyne Airport, where I looked to him. It wasn't a place to linger. Like blowflies around a sheep's tail, the place was a crowd of touts, each working individually to pick off individual tourists, while pickpockets milled amongst the confusion, doing a great business.

'Do you know of a place to go?' Brett asked.

'But you said you knew Prague!'

Why this made me think of the tin of oestrogen shake, I don't know. But then it was that I remembered putting it in an overhead compartment on the plane in Sydney.

Now Brett was looking to me to lead us toward shelter and comfort. I was clueless, and this mob made me want to run back into the airport.

'Would you like these gentlemen to help?' he asked, kicking backwards. I heard a satisfying yelp, but that only exacerbated the problem.

Brett was depending on me, and I wasn't up to this. We had to choose one of these parasites to help us, and hope for the best. At that point, I broke into an ugly hawking sob.

'Come, my dear,' he said, the only good thing I'd heard since when was it? It felt like years, yet was just over a day, by earthly hours.

He put his hand on my shoulder . . . and we were somewhere else.

Cold! How cold? The snot in my nose was gelato! Strong arms held me—Brett's. His teeth chattered in my ear. 'Antarctica?' I guessed, knowing already (the fuckwit!). I opened my eyes, dreading . . .

In spite of the cold, he blushed! No wonder. We hovered in a freezer room between shelves stacked with cartons marked **McDonald's**. All that 100% beef made me ravenously hungry, but first we had to get out of here.

'You're lost, aren't you?' I asked sympathetically.

'This was a castle when—'

'Hey,' I grinned. 'No worries, mate. Can you get us out of here?'

'I don't know where—'

'Can you let me down at least?'

He lowered us. There was a big red button by the door. *Open sesame!* We walked out into the blessedly hot and breakfast-hassled kitchen.

I grabbed at a burger on the grill, but it was too hot. I heard a curse behind me, but we were already on our way to the happy side of McDonald's, and out.

We strolled down the street and hadn't gone a block when a girl who should have been in high school—or maybe she was already a model—rushed up to Brett. 'Please,' she said, handing him a pen. She turned her back and pointed to her pink backpack.

I giggled. 'She thinks you're somebody, Mister Clueless.'

He didn't understand. 'What do I do?'

'I be singer,' she said to Brett.

'Well, Ell Oh Ell,' I laughed. 'Sign your name, Brett.'

He signed slowly, ending with a surprising flourish of the *n*'s tail.

She took off the pack and held it to her chest. 'Kiss?' Presumptuously, she leaned forward, lifted her face and puckered up. Her eyes closed!

This was getting tiresome pretty awfully fast, and he just stood there. 'Ooooh,' some inanity giggled.

'Brett blossom,' I whispered in his ear. 'Come on.' Looping my arm through his, I stepped forward, accidentally touching her shoulder.

'You!' she of the pink backpack screeched, pointing to me and turning an innocent pronoun into a curse. And she followed that up with a finger sign that has no innocent meaning anywhere.

Two can play at that game. Instead, I tossed her my best catwalk smile, took a firmer grip on Brett, and strode—past her and through what had become a crowd.

He *was* tremendously spunky in a *someone* way. With us linked arm-in-arm, perhaps my slept-in men's wear and necktie-belt would be the next cool look for girls.

A funny situation, though our over-all situation wasn't. He was clearly disoriented, and I didn't know Prague. Kevin did, but we wouldn't meet him for another—I checked my watch—twenty-eight hours. It would have been nice to stop and think, but now that was out of the question. We walked.

Brett frowned at a Dunkin' Donuts, yet nodded at a towered gateway. I had confidence in him. This city was known for old stuff.

He stopped at a medieval house-front. The doors were shut but that had never stopped him in the past. What did was the sign at the door, or rather, some glossy photos and a press clipping stuck behind glass.

> Gargantuan medieval banqueting served by buxom Hell's Angels in a cavernous remake of the set of *Monty Python and the Holy Grail*. Tankards of ale slapped down in front of you until you scream, 'When!' and indulge your Ivanhoe fantasies. Book early or take a battering ram.

'Such a nice house once,' he sighed. 'My dear . . .'

Patting his hand, I let him know that I forgave him. And truly, this has always been my experience with travel guides. I remembered Bali, when I ripped pages out of my *Lonely Planet* and jumped on them, wishing they were heads...

But we couldn't roam. I needed food, shelter, rest. And the aimless crowds of this tourist city were oppressing my sense of space. I took over the navigation completely now, and led till we reached a square with a Grand Hotel.

'Go get us a suite,' I told Brett, resting my hands on my hips. There was no place to sit.

He returned faster than I expected. He hadn't made it past the doorman. The fool!

'Stay!' I commanded. I'd have to brash this out myself.

I ran towards that doorman, then veered so I could watch.

He was a shoe man. No man went past him who didn't have wimpy, shined leather shoes. A simple problem, easily solved.

'... so we just have to find you a shoe store,' I explained, tugging Brett's arm.

'No,' he answered. 'I'm not changing.'

Oh, this was too much trouble for one morning!

Then some idiot jogged my shoulder, and suddenly Brett whirled away from me.

'Merdat!'—a bravura falsetto.

'Hovno!'—the deep, close voice of Brett. He held his arms out in front of him. Between them dangled a skinny, shit-smelling pimpleface. Brett had him by the ears, one of which was shish-kabobbed by Brett's stiletto fingernail.

A wad of money fell from the boy's fingers. I picked it up.

'Hrvo crampit glukskon,' (or something like that) said Brett, one word at a time, into the boy's face.

'Flsttrrukchtrch ch ch ch,' he answered, all bluster gone.

'What?' I asked.

'I told him to take us home, and... uych vrno bumpit!' (or something like that) he said to the boy, shaking him.

'Hey, that's rude,' I said. 'Speak English.'

'I no home,' the boy said.

I believed him. So, apparently, did Brett. He dropped the boy, who crawled and then ran, holding his bloody ear.

We had drawn a crowd. Someone clapped. And then a woman in a Sydney Olympics T-shirt walked brazenly up and took Brett's hand.

'Thank you,' she said. 'If more men would do that, this place would be a great city for us single women.'

'You're most welcome,' Brett smiled—the Boofhead!

'Brett blossom...' I reminded him, as I led him away. 'We must concentrate our mind.'

My soft violet boots weren't meant for walking, but that's just what they'd done for the last couple hours, on cobblestones. We reached the entrance to an alley and I steered us into it. We were blessedly alone.

'Try again,' I urged, and closed my eyes.

Much better! If you don't mind mothballs, the place was perfect.

It had been a manor house and was now a museum, closed for repairs till October. Judging from the dusty floors, no one had been here for some time.

Brett landed me squarely on the manor's biggest bed, which was dressed for visuals. However, it was easy-peasy to go through the back rooms, where lots of stuff never saw the light of day. In no time, I had a Princess-and-the-Pea bed without the pea, and I didn't even have to pinch myself to know that this was real. After I made the bed up, I remembered to check with Brett that he didn't want it. No, he didn't he said. There was another small bed in the room, and I had thought that would be his answer.

And lo! Medieval luxury with modern convenience. Tucked away beside the office, a lovely little shower and toilet, towels and lily-of-the-valley soap.

Although I was starving, the shower beckoned more.

Ahhhh. The waterfall shower pounded me till I was limp as a noodle. The fairy-tale bed beckoned.

'I'll just have a little nap,' I announced, climbed up into my cuddly tower, and passed out.

'Wakey, wakey!'

Brett's voice broke through a delicious dream. I was swaying down the catwalk in my lilac-sprigged trained skirt, my hips rolling as if my pelvic joints were oiled, my movements made more fluid by the gaze of a thousand eyes.

The interruption was unwelcome.

'My dear,' Brett's voice insisted. 'Ten minutes to meeting with your Kevin.'

'Shit!' I panicked. I was trapped in featherbedding. The more I struggled to get out of it, the deeper I sunk.

'Well then. If you're worried, we'll rush.' A hand clamped hard over my forehead.

I felt an elevator's pull, and then I was landed horizontally, with only a small bump of my head, on cobbles.

'You can open your eyes now,' he said, and as I did so, he added, 'You'd better!'

He pulled me up, and just as I was getting to my feet, he pushed me away from him so hard that I fell against the kerb and tore a gash in my hand. Just behind me, a car sped past.

I looked around and saw Brett, running a hand over his head. 'You used to be able hear horses coming!'

Nothing like having a guide from another eon.

At least he knew the way to the clock tower.

The crowd was so thick with camera-toting tourists, pickpockets and trinket sellers, that I wondered how Kevin would find us. It was a brilliant place for us to meet, as no one would notice us. If no one noticed Brett, that is.

Brett liked the clock, I was surprised to see. He said at one point when my attention waned at the saints and Death procession, 'Wait for the rooster.'

Indeed, the clock on the tower was just a kitschy cuckoo timepiece, until the rooster crowed.

The show ended, and the crowd broke up. 'How did you know about the rooster?' I asked.

Brett puffed out his chest, rubbed his nails against his shirt and smiled, a set of movements I had only seen in vintage movies.

Had he made a deal with the maker, I wondered, till I remembered the angry parrot. I had left it in the airport in Sydney.

I bit the back of my hand in a rush of anger at myself, and loss.

'Where's your Kevin?'

It was now half past noon.

We waited for another hour, and then wandered away. International flights!

Anyway, I *had* to eat. I led us by smell to a place where we shared a table with two men in Lederhosen. I pointed to what they were having, and soon I was happily bogging in. It was fatty as hell, but god, it was good. A huge sausage thick as a shearer's arm. I didn't bother with the rye bread or sauerkraut, and only sipped the beer. It was meat I wanted, and a lot of it.

Brett wasn't peckish, he said, but was happy to watch me.

He did watch, annoyingly so.

'What's up?' My mouth was full, but he could understand.
'Isn't that what you call "red meat"?'
'Mm. Wadaboudit?'
'You didn't used to eat meat.'
'No. I was a vegetarian.'
'But you ate squids and octopuses almost every day.'

When would he ever learn the fine points? I put down my fork, but cold sausage congeals. He would have to live with the mystery. Instead of trying to explain, I shrugged. He could understand that.

We walked back to our hideaway. Even though it was such a short distance and I'd slept a whole day already, I was dragging my feet by the time we got back, so went straight to bed.

The next morning, from the sounds on the street, I had slept late. Fine. I didn't want to get up.

Brett was settled as comfortably as a 1950s man-o'-the-house in a Lazy-Boy ad, but Brett was in a pre-ergonomic chair (one of those hardwood-jobbies where a griffin pokes it beak into your bum). He was reading a paperback.

'Don't you want to go out sightseeing till noon?' he asked.

Nice of him to think of what I would like to do, but I shook my head. It was such a silly reason, but it was a reason. I pulled up the covers more around my face. My stale clothes were on the floor beside the bed.

'It's elemental!' Brett exclaimed. 'Would you like to get some clothing? Is that it? And a toothbrush, and . . .'

How humanly thoughtful of him.

I craved having clean clothes again. And I craved . . . Oh, what was the use. *What a wuss* I yelled at myself, but I didn't want to listen.

Brett flew up to my bed and hovered beside me. 'You are not ugly, you know.'

That proved it! 'Oh, yes I am . . .' A snot bubble only made things worse, until he handed me a hanky. 'And now I've ruined all my job's work.'

'No you haven't, Angela.'

Angela. Desirée was dead.

'You are as beautiful as you feel.'

What had he been reading??? At least, that stupidity pulled me out of it. 'You know that is crap!' And to make sure he knew in the way he would prefer to put it: 'Balderdash!'

He wasn't insulted, but he did put a finger to my mouth. 'Listen to me. You will get your figure back in no time, if that is what makes you feel beautiful. I am sure you will. And in the meantime, I can tell you something that you might not know about yourself.'

What would *he* know!

'Have you ever looked, um, down there?'

His circumspection was so hilarious, I giggled.

'Down there?' I repeated, wide-eyed. 'Like . . .'

'And in the, uh, anterior region.'

Ah, I needed this. I'm afraid I spattered him in my helplessness. His face and his pointing were so delicately diplomatic. And it was lovely that he wasn't insulted.

'I'm laughing with you, if you could only see yourself, Brett.'

He smiled tolerantly while he waited.

'Thank you,' I said finally. 'Please forgive me. Do go on.'

He dipped his horns. 'Now, in my experience, I happen to know much about your various orifices.' And he hastened to add, 'Your, by the way, being not you personally.'

'Yes?' I could imagine. A Bosch scene in particular.

'And it has always struck me . . . since a personal gestalt (what had he been reading???) a long time ago, that no matter what state the rest of your body is in—*your* not being personal—fat or thin—two places remain the same.

I pointed down. 'This? . . . and then turned around and pointed again, keeping a straight face. 'And this?'

He nodded solemnly.

But, really, so what? It is no gestalt to know that we can still pee, fuck, and shit through the same places whether we diet or not. 'And so?'

'Do you not see?'

Well, duh, but . . .

'They, one being especially special, are the centre of your beauty, Angela. The physical side. They were, and they still are!'

An aesthete of the highest, or lowest order!

'Would you like to see?' he asked. 'I'll turn around.'

I nodded this time, enthralled.

He waved his hand and in it was a beautiful silver mirror, its carved back glinting sinuous, almost recognizable shapes.

'I'll be back,' he said, and before I could reply, he added, 'soon' and disappeared.

I examined myself from every angle. As an anti-post-feminist, I had always ignored these regions precisely because of the pressure to gaze upon them in goddess worship. Yet, what a marvel they are, this 'cunt' and 'arse' when looked at from an apolitical perspective!

I had just emerged from the shower and was wrapping myself in some mothball-reeking relic when Brett returned.

Like any tourist, he was laden with bags, and like any modern tourist, most of the names on the bags were the same as stores in the city where we came from before coming to this one to escape.

I watched as he took out the contents and laid them out on his bed, which hadn't been slept in. Clothing, and a bag. I had felt funny about Kevin's 'bag' creation—a beaded lily-shaped thing made to hang from a belt. Kevin didn't understand bags. They didn't go with his creations. But where was I? Clothing, down to a proper shoulder bag big enough to pack a cat in, not that I had anything to put into the bag, but . . . And toiletries, even down to the minty dental floss I like.

He was pleased at my exclamations, and I was amazed that everything fit. As to the styles, they were the ones in the all the big window displays. There was no full-length mirror in this room, but without seeing, I knew. What I looked like now I had regarded for most of my life as Impossible Wish Fulfilment.

Except for my hair, which needed a cut. I pointed to it. 'Brett? Do you think?'

He swirled his hands. One now held a pair of hairdressing scissors, and the other, a comb.

'Monsieur Brett!' I giggled.

One hand dropped the comb and the other hand caught underneath his hip as he crashed to the ground. His eyes turned up and foam bubbled through his lips.

I rushed around the room, and back to his side. Of medicine for him, I knew nothing. What had I done?

I put out my hand towards him, but this produced a thin scream. 'Dooon.'

Backing off, I waited, watching.

This was the worst attack yet—that I had seen.

After a few minutes, he recovered. Rather stiffly, he thanked me for my concern, and wanted to talk of anything but his health. Frankly, so did I.

It was almost noon anyway. Time to meet Kevin.

Kevin didn't come.

* * *

For dinner that night, I sniffed out a tiny hole of a place in a back street that was even better than the sausage restaurant. The meal here was steak, delightfully rare. Brett said it was horse. You could have fooled me, though the meat had a sweetness I'd never tasted in beef. He wasn't hungry—I think he moonlight ate—but he was impatient to leave after a shiny-headed crone emerged from the kitchen. Not that she did anything. She just stood in the shadows and eyed Brett, though if he had been a breadroll and the lights had suddenly gone out, I would have been alarmed.

'Perhaps her granddaughter's too shy to come herself,' I laughed.

But Brett fidgeted, so I humoured him. Besides, carrying my steak and eating it out of hand was easier than cutting it with their toothless, Sputnik-decorated knife.

That evening I was bored. The streets were loud with 'revellers', as they are called. Our room was comfortable enough, but there was nothing for me to do, unless I wanted to listen to carollers belting out 'Rule Britannia' till they chundered, or this serenade:

> *Balls to your partner,*
> *Arse against the wall.*
> *If you've never been fucked on a Saturday night,*
> *Then you've never been fucked at all...*

which lasted till liquid tinkled and glass crashed and the revellers staggered off. Of course I didn't lean out to watch, or toss them flowers or boiling oil. But the spring breeze wafted their scents up through the Romeo-and-Juliet window—and their boots weren't ballet slippers.

I found a TV in the guards' room. The chairs were hard, so I lugged the TV upstairs to our room and perched it on a convenient Dark Ages whatnot chest. I don't think I was the first to get this idea. Behind that hideous thing, a power point lurked. I climbed up to bed, carrying the remote.

A game show. Possibly Czech.

A German game show.

An Italian game show. I was just going to change channels, when this got interesting—strip poker in front of millions. She was unreal. Too unreal.

I turned off the TV.

Brett was deep into his paperback, so I climbed down for a peek.

It was in... 'Czech?'

'But of course, my dear.'

'What is it? Some Czech writer?'

'Mm.'

He was humouring me. He wasn't paying me any attention. Actually, was he really reading? He turned a page. A pose? Yes indeedy. I let him know. 'Just because you can read every language, you don't have to rub it in.'

He glanced up at me, mild as milk, and then went back to his book.

He turned another page.

Because I was one part bored, two parts exasperated, I bent the front of the book up toward me.

'Well, *quell surprise*! Barbara Cartland!'

He closed the book, but his finger was in the page he was reading. He really had been reading!

'What's wrong with Barbara Cartland?'

'Other than that she's trash? Nothing!' I laughed.

'But isn't she the best-loved author in the world?'

'Of course—'

'The queen of romance. That's what she's called, you know. Or don't you?'

'Uh—'

'Her sales are numerous as the glittering gems of morning dew. Simply awesome. Hundreds of millions. In France alone, over twenty-five million.'

A walking, talking, flying-through-the-air encyclopaedia. 'Are you quoting? How do you know that?'

'The BBC. Her obituary. You asked. But why didn't you tell me?'

'Tell me more.'

'The world's most prolific author. And according to the Guinness Book of Records . . . Do you know it, my dear?'

I curtsied, ready to smack him.

'The world's top-selling author. Which means she must be the most loved. Or am I perhaps suffering a delusion?'

My head moved back and forth, at which he happily nodded.

'Seven hundred and twenty three books,' he droned on. 'And you have to do just one. Total sales of Cartland books estimated at over one billion. Translated into practically all of your modern languages . . . You, of all people, *should know*.'

He could really rub it in, but instead of continuing, he returned to the book. Good.

I was standing in front of him wondering what to do next, when he closed it again and looked at me. 'Personally,' he said. 'I want to be loved, adored, worshipped, cosseted, and protected.'

'You?' What a strange desire for *him* to have.

'Barbara said that. I thought you might want to know. Isn't that what you want, too?'

'Of course.'

He went back to the book, and I was stuck standing there, a coat rack without a coat. 'Is it any good?'

He turned another fucking page. 'I am enjoying reading it more than any book since I began.'

'Would I like it?'

'I do not know your taste.'

'Could I try?'

'Oh, alright,' he snapped. When I was a child and was called away from my fairy tale, I was just as irritated. But me as a child and he now, had different irritation capabilities when pushed.

He waved his hand, produced a book, and threw it at me.

I climbed up to bed to read quietly.

Where had he gotten this? It was another paperback. The publisher was unusually modest, in fact, incognito. The title was innocuous enough, but the text must have been a pirate swipe off another pirated translation, maybe of lower Carpathian. I can't remember exactly, but the text went something like*: 'I, despise? Until I fit your ardent magical, I was only a player of the card, eating the fried cheese each night.'* — page after page.

I stuffed my fist in my mouth to muffle the noise.

The story was, in spite of the translation, so engrossing that at one point I forced myself to put down the book so I could call room service. This definitely deserved Serge's Rocky Road.

Reality hit with a twinge in my gut. I picked up the book again, and escaped.

The next day, we again heard the noonday rooster as my eyes surveyed the crowd—and again, no Kevin.

We waited in that stupid clock-tower square till the rooster was lucky people were watching him, or I would have thrown something to shut the blighter up.

It was a nuisance, of course, but we had to put up with the delay. But damn and blast Kevin. *Get your arse here, boy! I'm bored!*

'Standby' had been good enough for us. What was he doing? Trying to get some special lucky seat in First Class Qantas? Of him coming, I had no doubt. I was his ticket to happiness. But there was no time to waste.

He had a whole collection to make again. And even more important, I think I had lost weight. I was bony as a gnawed chicken carcass, and desperately needed an extra-powerful shake.

The next day, after our fourth fruitless wait, Brett and I were walking in that aimless way tourists do when the fun and purchasing charm of a town has been exhausted, but you can't leave yet. We were in front of a kiosk that sold international papers, and there, incredibly, under the *Orlando Sentinel*, was a *Sydney Morning Herald*. There was no chance to ask about its freshness. I was jostled from behind and harassed from ahead—choose or get out of the way. I pointed to the paper, paid, and it was folded and thrust at me with the olde-world friendliness of a machine. I stuck it under my arm and backed out from the crowd.

The cafes were full and the pavements clogged with people looking for a place to eat. I was tired and bored, and though Brett accompanied me with no complaint, he looked like he could do with a foot-up, too. We wandered into the cemetery and sat with our backs resting against a convenient stone . . . *Emanuel Porges*. At another time, names would have been interesting, but I was hungry for news from home. I unfolded the paper to page one, which screamed:

> AUSSIE TOURIST TRAGEDY Cage those Pommy louts!
> By Fiona Prith in Prague and Geoff Wyld in Sydney
>
> A tourist operator in Liverpool has been blamed as accessory to murder, after a so-called "Piss-Up Tour" got out of hand in Prague just before noon yesterday, on an otherwise lovely summer day. According to witnesses, an empty beer bottle thrown by an unnamed member of a British stag party smashed against the head of a Australian man as he was crossing a street. The blow killed him instantly.
>
> According to the Australian consulate, the man was identified as Kevin Shanahan, 35, fashion designer, of Surrey Hills, Sydney. Czech investigators revealed that this was Shanahan's first day in Prague . . .

26

FINALLY, Brett took the paper from my lap, curious, I guess, to see why I had sat like a stone frog for so long after just glancing at the paper I had been so eager to read.

I wanted to cry, but felt a scooped-out emptiness in my gut.

'Your Kevin,' he said, in a commiserating tone, and then, with curiosity, 'He loved you?'

'No.' Though Brett could have thought so, from the worship Kevin paid to the dressed-up me. 'He loved his work. I was just his mannequin.'

Suddenly, I felt how alone I was. 'No one . . .'

'You were saying, my dear?'

Now I felt stupid. I don't know what had possessed me to tell Brett, but I had begun, so I got it over fast. 'No one loves me but my parents and Gordon.'

His eyebrows jumped. 'Gordon?'

'You might have met him,' I sneered, 'if you hadn't burnt down my home.'

Oh, hell! What good was talk now? I ruffled the newspaper. 'Please, Brett. I need a space for grieving.'

He bent dutifully to the paper.

What a waste! 'Shi . . it!' I yelled. A bird's wings made a wet-sheet sound as the bird fled from dangerous me. Although it had only been innocently digging for worms, its escape was perhaps a wise decision. The more I thought, the more absolutely skin-a-cat-and-fling-it-in-your-sweet-blind-granny's-face I felt.

Why why bloody *why* had all those newspaper accounts quoted people whose lives had also gone from flower-bud lovely to turd, whined, 'I can't believe this is real.'—why?

This was real, all right. My flower-bud life, my stunning debut—zapped dead as an electrocuted fly. Brett beside me, pretending to read the paper—hadn't been writing my novel. Out of the corner of my eye, I peered at him. There was an aura of guilt about him. He'd not only not been working. He'd been enjoying himself while I was . . . and now, did he feel my pain or just wish he could slink off and find another Barbara Cartland novel?

I wanted to—

And then, from around a corner I heard sniggering laughter, a crash of glass, and a swaggering brag too indistinct to catch.

Just what I needed. Ordering, 'Stay,' I jumped up and ran toward the sounds.

They were just outside the cemetery wall—five of them. Their boots were made for kicking, but they stumbled over the cobblestones of this otherwise deserted narrow street.

One started to sing, and they all joined in. Such rich, deep voices.

Cunt, cunt, cunt.
Yer mam's a blootered cunt.
Yer brover's a chutney ferret,
what gets it up the—

One stopped, peeing a river over the steps of a brass-plaqued tourist site, some art nouveau apartment house. Wonderful! That made them only four.

I was rounding their side, sheepdog style, when one of them noticed.

He danced sideways in two clodding hops, and smiled into my face—'Eh up, choochie-face!'

He stroked a finger down my cheek.

I swung my right fist hard, straight for his swollen chunder-maker. Got him!

He doubled over, choked and hurled, choked and wheezed, sucking vomit-clodded air.

Bloody marvellous—'You beaut!' I chortled—400 decibels, straight into his earhole.

No time to drink a beer on him. Three more left.

At my back, close, a bottle smashed, not with the soprano tinkle of thrown glass, but with that special muffled hoarseness when its neck is held.

I spun around, and 'Cunt!' spattered my face, so close that I tasted him.

My head jerked back, but hit something hard. Shoulderblade?

'Got the bitch,' I heard, just by my ear. Meaty arms grabbed me around my shoulders and held me against a hard expanse of chest.

Others would have screamed, but I was too experienced for that.

I looked to my left. The arms holding me were strong, but no one expected me to slip out from under and dance sideways. My left was clear, so I stretched my leg out, but I should have looked ahead instead.

That was where the attack came. His arm swung fast. The bloke in front that I forgot about. I was wearing frail pink capri pants, not suitable for broken bottles slicing up the crotch.

His spit French-kissed me.

Then . . . a roaring in my ears as pain flamed from the centre of my beauty.

27

Some things sucked at my tear ducts. Some things were crawling up my legs. Some things were crawling into my nos—

I must have screamed, because I felt a hand take mine, and a voice tickled my ear.

'Angela, my dear.' A warm hand brushed hair off my forehead. 'Wakey Wakey.'

I turned my head to the voice, and opened my eyes. It was Brett. He was smiling at me, and had bags under his eyes and a face covered with crawling flies.

I screamed, so he clasped me to his chest. Flies were everywhere. I brushed them away from my face, and gently pushed him away. He didn't seem to mind the flies, but they were so bad that it was impossible for me to stop waving my hand in front of my face.

'Where are we?' I asked, and peeked out for myself.

He was perched and I was lying on what seemed to be a wool-classing table, about the same dimensions as my medieval bed in Prague, but the mattress here was smooth wood slats, stinking with lanolin. I looked behind Brett and, yes. This was a shearing shed. No sheep were in sight, but a clump of men and women dressed in white coats stood quietly off to one side. As with the shed at home, the walls were half-planked, up to the waist, and then open to the same hard, relentless sky. As I spat a fly away from the corner of my mouth, I tasted dust. Forever dust.

Remembering something, I raised my free hand to my body, explored, and jerked upright. No wonder I felt every slat and every fly. I was stark naked.

And those people!

'No worries, Anj,' Brett hastened to reassure me, shoving me down. 'They don't care about you.'

His conversational tone in no way excluded those people from hearing, though from their tight-packed mass, they did remind me of sheep.

'Please,' I said. Pushing his hands away, I sat up again and looked down at myself.

The body that Kevin had loved as his mannequin was back, lusher than ever. I felt my flesh all over—firm as a weather balloon.

I suddenly remembered my centre of beauty, the pain.

Brett must have been watching. In a hand flicker, he presented me with the same mirror I'd used once before.

He looked away while I examined. Aside from a faint white hairline scar running halfway up to my belly button, everything looked as it had—how long ago?

'Brett, how long has it been?'

His expression would have been adorable if it weren't hideous, the way he didn't seem to notice those flies. He smiled shyly. 'This is our anniversary.'

'Anna what?'

'In your years, allowing for time zone differentials, we met two years ago today.'

'Years!?'

'You needed a lot of work, and much recupera—'

Underneath the floor, a furious banging and barking and howling drowned his speech.

He tossed an 'Excuse,' at me, and flashed a kick against the slats of the floor.

Another assault of scratching and banging and howling shook the floor, and he waved his hand.

The trapdoors fell open under the white-coated people. They tumbled into what sounded like a pack of—what? I couldn't see down into that darkness under the shed. But I heard. I heard human screams. I heard inhuman sounds of joy. I heard what sounded like the contented chomps dogs make when they are tossed sheeptails, and I heard what sounded like kangaroos—their slow, snide three-legged slink—and I *heard more*. Amongst the screeching down below I distinctly heard mastication. This was metal sliding against metal, slicing and popping squishy stuff. It couldn't be. I used to have nightmares about these things. Kangaroos with teeth like sheep shears. They open their mouths wide, and close them on you. Their teeth—dozens of tiny shark-teeth-shaped blades—slice into you as they slide back and forth, and the kangaroo opens and closes his mouth and booms in pleasure as he bites . . . I heard these monsters now. They were just as I remembered them from when I woke screaming, at five years old.

'I've got you,' Brett murmured in my ear. And he did. His arms were around me, holding me tight. He had placed my head against his chest so that I looked away from that trapdoor, but what I now saw was the woolpress, and—my other nightmare—its base *oozed* blood.

Maybe I screamed. Surprisingly, I didn't shit. Brett held on tight, cooing into my ear. 'Nothing can hurt you,' he repeated, over and over, sweet as a turtle dove's call, till the noise below died down, and I disengaged myself, looked into his eyes and believed him.

'This isn't Prague, is it?' I asked.

We chuckled together, but I had to know.

'Why did you bring me here?'

'You would have died.'

From the examination of my scar, the cut had been a long one.

'You were bleeding, Angela.'

'Did you try getting an ambulance?'

Why had I asked? Ambulance. Treatment. Public health. I could have died waiting.

Brett full-on blushed. It was a revelation that he could. His face turned red, then green.

Then he mumbled, 'I couldn't let you go.'

He took my right hand in both of his. 'You've had the best of care, my dear.'

'Doctors?'

'We have an outstanding medical staff.'

I could just imagine.

'They were completely supervised at all times, by me.'

A giggle escaped. 'What would you do if they misbehave?'

His eyes twinkled.

'The same as I just did.'

I saw one of them falling, and the eyes were those of a fur seal pup. 'Who were those?'

'Your medical staff.'

'But they didn't look evil.'

'Who said they were?'

'All doctors, you say,' I reminded him. 'All Caligaris?'

'Don't demean yourself, my dear. One Caligari and the rest, how do you say? Shit happens?'

I was shocked. 'That's so ugly, Brett.'

'Yes. But blame has always been apportioned wrongly in the mortal world.'

I had meant the crude expression. The more I had to do with him, the more I hated modern expression.

A sigh came out of him. 'Poor blamed altruists.'

He pitied them!

'But you dumped them, regardless.'

'A kindness, Angela. Believe me.'

Not something to dwell on. A horrible thought struck me.

'So this is hell, isn't it?'

He was visibly taken aback. 'But, of course . . . Does the fact pain you?'

'Am I dead?'

'No!'

He pulled my hand toward him, in a jerk of a reaction. 'My word, no!'

'Am I alive?'

'Of course!' His red irises showed as thin red lines around huge pulsing pupils.

There was something he was holding back, as the frankness of his expression belied *something*.

'How's the book?'

'I'm not reading now,' he said, scratching that itchy place between his horns. 'I haven't the time.'

Reading? I hadn't asked him about his reading. '*My* book,' I said.

If I had stuck a cattle prod up his bum, I couldn't have gotten a quicker response. His whole body jerked.

'You never intended to write my book!'

No answer.

'What did you want with me?'

No answer.

'What did you want with me!'

Me—naked on a classing table, a-crawl with flies, the trap door just a jump away, those terror-roos sharpening their teeth. That wool-press over there, sweating blood . . . And the Devil himself holding my hand with the grip of a leach to an udder.

Suddenly, a wind blew grit into the shed. A strong wind that momentarily banished the flies from my face.

Then I heard yapping, and a mob of people came running into the shed.

'Push 'em up!' I heard. From outside the shed. And with a clatter of boots and shoes and bare feet—and screams, pushes, curses, and thuds—the group expanded to fill most of the shed's 100-sheep space. The woolpress of course disappeared behind the press of human bodies.

Who were these people? There wasn't any consistency. *They* didn't look classed. Were they just *anybodies*?

'Just a minute,' Brett sighed.

Before I could yell, trapdoors opened everywhere... and those *sounds* ...!

A prickle of chill rushed from the top of my eyebrows over the back of my head and down to the soles of my feet—an overwhelming, shiver-inducing homesickness.

This travelling companion, who I'd shared living quarters with longer than any other fellow traveller—was a stranger. A stranger who had used me, and had fattened me for *what*?

I had never believed in hell as Hell, or as Brett as a devil's Devil. He with his wizard tricks, his Victorian-era vapours. But where we were now sure wasn't Olde Sydney Towne.

And he'd had a private agenda all along.

He'd used me! And now he had some final purpose.

Knowing without asking, I asked nevertheless, 'Will I ever see Earth again?'

With insistent hands, Brett pushed me flat on the table.

He put his mouth to my ear. His mouth that had liked drinking warm blood, eating body-warm raw chopped heart.

I fought with all I could fight with. Being eaten from my ear down, held absolutely no appeal.

It was no fight, of course. He was by far, my wrestling superior.

'Angela.' The sound of the word in my ear was a rustle of dry leaves.

It was hopeless to fight, so I called upon all the bullshit from the Higher Light that I could remember in a second.

Breathe in. Breathe out. Withdraw from the self. It had never worked before.

'Do your thing,' I told him, and hoped it was fast—faster than what I had heard from below when those people had fallen to their never-never.

Good pun. Grimly, I smiled to myself. Dad would have liked the pun and approved the smile.

'Angela,' Brett interrupted, just when I was coming to grips with coping with the end.

He put his mouth around my ear entirely.

My whole body stiffened stiffer than a dead dog.

His tongue forks tickled the inside of my ear.

'Dear Angela,' whispered the Devil. 'Save me.'

28

I SNIFFED—a cautiously shallow sniff. Even with my hand waving across my face, flies clustered around my nostrils. Louder than the rancid pong of lanolin screamed the nauseating reek of asafoetida. That is the closest name I could put to this hot, dunghill stench.

Brett had pulled away from me. He stood, jaw rigid, at tin-soldier attention, emanating this repugnancy.

From his body odour and the expression in his eyes, it didn't take a genius to reckon. His very pores expressed themselves—pure, unearthly fear.

'Two always Tango,' the Devil said, after we had whispered for an hour. His smells had calmed considerably.

He was full of new clichés and gahky chumminess—had been working hard to learn language to aid his assimilation. If he got the chance.

He meant by that garbled tango thing, a backhand compliment.

We both, he had observed, reached for the impossible. I, because of a general lack of talent in the area I had wished to be talented in.

He, because of a lack of opportunity.

He told me he had yearned for many years. Many, *many* mortal years. This yearning had become the driving force of his existence.

It was not his fault that he was the Devil. At one time, he had been resigned to his position, but now it was unbearable—it was hell for him, too. Would I want to live in this? He had absolutely no control now. While I was in recuperation, for example, he had listened to many services for the dead on earth, and it was too hard to keep up with the blessed and the damned.

'Everybody's claiming, worse than a gold rush. More chaotic.'

The claim-jumping was to the point that the only solution he could put to the problem was to sink the whole gold mine. To disappear. 'To speed up the chaos that is the modern hell', as he put it.

To what end, I asked.

He shrugged.

Brett—a Trot!

His plan was fuzzy, but mine had been, too.

To Be Famous. That had been my goal, with no plan. I had wanted to be Loved as a Writer with a Book that is Loved. That was what I wanted. I never had a story to tell. The story part of my book was only a means to my end. I had a want but no plan, till Brett.

His idea for himself: He wanted to dissolve the chaos that was now this hell, spiralling fast out of control. Earth's mortal knowers and doers and condemners were now so interconnected. The damned and the blessed had turned hell into Hell for the Devil himself, who had no control, no purpose, no meaning in life any more as Master of the Underworld. He wanted to escape this hell, 'and thereby aid its spin'—his ultimate aim to do good in some vague way. An excuse I had heard from other anarchists.

At one point, he pounded his knees in exclamation. 'It can all go to the blazes.'

How could I blame him for wanting to escape. But how could he?

'What about those futures traders? What do they say?'

A bitter snort of a cackle. 'Melted. All melted.'

Hmm.

And that mother of all flies in the soup? 'And what does your Om—'

'Shhhh!'

The mouth to ear communication became intimate again. 'Don't be too loose with your words.'

I whispered into his, 'What does your Omniscient think of all this chaos?'

'He is in his firmament.'

Cryptic.

'Need I dumb it down?'

No, I did. 'He's on an ego trip?'

'How delightfully trenchant. Would you like a tour?'

'Out there?'

'I would hold you.'

'Thanks awfully,' I said, 'but I'll take your word for it.'

Escape. That was his crazy, impractical, fantastical plan.

To disappear—his goal.

His end?

He didn't know.

Did he care?

No. Not any more.

It all came down in the end, to our simple goals.

I had wanted to be loved and famed.

He had wanted quiet retirement, and now, after a taste of life, he wanted more. Retirement, with me to help him by serving as his cover and his aide de camp in the mortal world. And now that he'd learned the pleasure to be had in books, he wanted to collect and fondle his books, and read.

Why had he picked me?

Spontaneous decision.

That wasn't good enough. I forced him to say more. To *whisper* more, dammit.

'Your lack of respect for the Omniscient.'

'You didn't know that.'

'I learned.'

That earned him my most sceptical pursed-lip glance.

'I guessed, and I learned,' he corrected.

'That was not enough.'

'And your lack of respect for me.'

That was a surprise, but upon reflection, he was almost right. 'Respect is the wrong word. But you don't strike me as all that scary, or even evil.'

'See?'

'Is that the reason for your sicknesses?'

'... Partly, my dear.'

By not being terrified, I complicated matters.

His low chuckle broke into my speculation. 'No worries, mate.'

'Brett,' I said. 'Continue to talk like that, and you can press the trapdoor button for me.'

He winced. 'You don't like it?'

'I like the old fuddy-duddy you. The you who rued the omnium-gatherum of disorder, the hugger-mugger of change. The old language of yours has more...' Damned if I could think of the word.

'Resonance?'

What *hadn't* he been reading while I slept?

But back to his plan.

He had muddled along without a plan, until my accident. He had hidden me in this last peaceful corner of hell (I protested at this peacefulness, but he insisted upon its relativity). His last remaining sanctum, he called this, while flies explored his eyes. He reckoned he didn't have much time left before these shaky walls were blown down, 'as my power is diminished as this chaos grows'. That fact gave him his sense of urgency.

'And the Omniscient?' I asked, my mouth to his ear.

He switched our positions. His tongue tips tickled my ear. 'If God is on our side, who is against us?'

My laugh bounced against the boards. 'Sometimes, Brett, you're an absolute card.'

He shushed me, but smiled. 'It wasn't me, and I don't know why you laughed, though it was a breath of fresh air.'

'Who said that?'

'The Duke of Edinburgh.'

'He's known for talking without thinking. But I never knew he could be so witty.'

'Say again?'

'Was it off the cuff? Since when did he become a war protester?'

'I don't think.'

The problems with culture in translation. 'Well, what? Reading doesn't do you any good, you know, if you miss context.'

Another mob of people, most of whom looked like poor bastards, was pushed into the shed. He excused himself and processed them. These took more time. I closed my eyes, but that just opened my ears more. Soon he was back, but the sounds hadn't stopped.

'You were saying, my dear,' he prompted.

'Brett, I can understand you not understanding irony, or wit.'

'It was St Paul's Cathedral,' he said. 'A *lesson*, as you call it, in a service for those killed in the war in Iraq. Back in oh-'

'I get the idea, Brett.' This was becoming like the time with the newspapers again. 'Just stick to the comedy.'

'If God is on our side,' he breathed, 'who is against us? Your bible. Romans eight point something or other.'

Yuk!

There was one thing that this Devil in front of me, who wanted so much to be a plain old Brett— there was one thing we needed to get very, *very* straight.

I hissed so hard into his ear, my spit rebounded: 'The bible isn't *mine*.'

'Not yours *personally*—'

'Wanna know what we called it at home? Percy's pile.'

His eyebrows wiggled. 'Your uncle, the Reverend Percy Lily?'

'And as for your Omniscient, this God who's claimed by all—'

A silent puff of raw fear choked me with its stench. The only way to fight it was to ignore it.

'Disgust.' I had to stop. Breathing in caused me to cough, but I smiled and patted his hand.

The air cleared slowly, and all the while, the eerie silence—even below the shed—before what I knew would come again was so nerve-wracking that fear concentrated my mind.

'All those newspapers, Brett. They rubbed disgust for the Omniscient right into my pores.'

And something needed to be shoved up his nose—shoved so hard, it *hurt*.

'He's *your* Omniscient, Brett. And make no mistake about it.'

He felt that. Even his nostrils twitched, but he didn't answer.

'According to your perception,' I added. 'Yours, Brett. Not mine.'

He leaned forward, at the same time somehow managing to retract his neck. It was a strange position for us—me leaning forward, cross-legged on the table—he standing and bent so that his mouth could be suckered on to my ear or vice versa. Our whispers were now so low, they were barely audible. He stayed in the listening position, wanting more from me.

'You think he knows all?' I asked.

He didn't answer.

'You think you can escape?'

An evasive caul shrouded his eyes, but I had torn cauls off lambs as a child.

I yelled into the silence. 'You would be escaping this... and him... wouldn't you?'

He put his hand to my ear, but I shoved it aside.

'I have ideas!' he yelled.

But not, it seemed, for airing now.

Three more mobs arrived in quick succession. Brett dealt with the lot.

I saw their faces. I saw lots of bloody ankles, and one big bloke with his nostrils torn out. I heard language I didn't know existed, human and beast. I saw a baby in swaddling that wobble-rolled into the shed like a fumbled rugby kick. I saw a grandmother with a wooden spoon, a man with a cleaver, a man and woman who dropped together as vertical as sunshine at noon, kissing. I saw a man try to climb air.

* * *

'Will you help me?' Brett asked again.

The skin on his face—jade grey.

I sniffed, and yes, he had begun emitting again.

The bags under his eyes had aged him at least ten mortal years.

What choice was there?

I punched him in the shoulder.

'Oh, frabjous day!' When he smiled like that, he reminded me of Simone. She hadn't managed to bed him, but when he was happy, from his smells to his smiles, he was, even with the bags under his eyes, by modern mortal standards, devilishly attractive.

'Oh, that's *so much* better,' I declared. 'Now let's get going.'

He took me by the hand, but I pulled away. 'Where are we going first?'

'Sydney.'

Odd. 'I thought you were bored with Sydney.'

He bent to his laces. And yes—he wore the same outfit as ever, down to the boots that pinched. When he straightened, his face was a badly closed book. 'I have a surprise for you.'

I love surprises! 'What time is it in Sydney?'

It took him only a moment. 'Eight in the evening.'

Fine with me. But . . . 'I will not go naked into that dark night.'

Jesus-statue style, he raised both hands

'And no more commercial airlines,' I added.

His teeth gleamed. 'Methinks thee protesteth too much.'

His hands swept down and he stepped back—a perfect pantomime of laying out a sumptuous train of ermine.

29

Screeches exploded into a quiet night. The moreton bay fig trees must have been in fruit because those blessed screeches were the squabbling fruit bats of — one sniff proved it — Sydney on a summer evening.

Two bats flapped over our heads. Brett and I stood between two fig trees, each as large as a house.

I was dressed in my favourite outfit of Kevin's, white muslin spotted with violet dots. I lifted up my skirts and Brett had even remembered my violet boots.

The dress wasn't the original, nor the boots.

Brett had noticed what I liked, but he had no natural talent nor eye for detail. So the way that buttons buttoned was not quite buttoned enough. The collar didn't jut out with the same distinctive flair. The underarms pinched. He'd cut my hair, he told me, and it was almost, but not quite right.

The final effect was half haute-couture, half publicly funded.

Brett took me by the elbow and led us to the edge of the park, to the shadowed gloom of a fig tree.

Across the tarmac was the art museum.

A small crowd of people clustered at the bottom of the steps. The men wore black suits, and the women, long, unfashionable pinafores. Some carried babies in their arms, and some, balloons hanging on strings.

A Rolls drove up. The couple that emerged moved older than they looked, the woman's shoulders flashing diamante straps. They walked up the steps, into the museum.

Brett cradled my elbow under his hand in the manner of the couple ahead.

We walked up the steps but had to wait as their names were checked against a guestlist.

As they entered, the cry of 'Brett!' shrilled from within.

As we entered, a ringed hand shot up out of the crowd, a twitter rose out of the noise, and a rustle of bodies warned that at least one person was rushing toward us.

Brett waved his hand toward the approachers (there were three that I could count, homing in fast). His action was friendly but firmly dismissive. They stopped, their eyes on him and me. One of them waved, and they all put on those stage smiles for the deaf.

An all-female chamber orchestra sawed away at something tasteful. The bass player's white blouse was stained with sweat. The sound of the crowd itself made the musicians' job impossible, if music appreciation was their goal.

He guided me through the partygoers, not an easy task. There were so many, and so many hands tried to waylay him. But he didn't stop till he had led me to what must have been the exhibition's centrepiece.

He nudged people away.

I saw.

Huge, so big I had to back off — the centre of my beauty, as ripely open as a fresh fig, and about a zillion times larger than life.

Brett was examining me as I examined it.

I felt my blush. 'Who did this?'

'I,' he said. 'Would you like to see the press release?'

He handed it to me anyway, before I was ready to say yes.

LILY Retrospective: Encounters & Reflections

While ostensibly documentary, the dominant theme of Hartshorn's ouvre is oblique ambiguity. Peeling back the 'skin of reality', and eschewing the decorative of O'Keefe for what Hartshorn calls 'anatomicality', he defines the new reference, his unadorned black and whites of monumental size being what Piers Oulange has called 'the new brutality', seeming to invite the viewer to participate, or perhaps repelling from, a substantive relation between signifier and referent, while in some works, such as 'Lily 236', he navigates the intersection of . . .

'Miss Lily!'

A familiar, excessively-groomed scent enveloped me, followed by a hand on my shoulder, light as a hummingbird. 'Miss Lily,' a voice whispered.

'Justin!'

'You look marvellous, darling,' he boomed in an artificial voice, 'and a thousand congratulations on this wonderful show!' Justin was a little grey around the temples, but that just added to his sleek well-being and bonhomie. 'Your delightful Brett—'

The thing who had tempted him before, or one just like it, attached itself to him now. Despite the inauthenticity of it, I was flattered. It was, without doubt, a bountiful imitation of me.

'You promised, Justie—' it whined.

Smiling ruefully, Justin handed me a card, touched Brett's shoulder while saying cryptically, 'Later,' and allowed himself to be dragged away by his dominatrix.

I turned to Brett.

'A full restoration,' he said. 'It was someone in the company's finance department. He came unstuck a month later. Justin was out within three months of us leaving the Restonia.'

That explained part of it. I flicked the card. It didn't want to flick. It was, I think, a sliver of jade. It read:

JUSTIN ABERNATHY
Sydney   Moscow   Beijing   New York   London   Bandar Seri Begawan

And there wasn't even a phone number.

'He's really made it, hasn't he?'

'His cellmate was a financier.'

That explained some of his success. Everyone needs style help, especially jailed financiers.

'He helped me get this organized, you know.'

'Did you think of being an artist before?'

'Oh no, my dear. Aren't you pleased?'

Of his success as an artist? I admit I was a wee bit jealous. But I was also flattered. His picture was the most unusual present I had ever had. I could feel eyes on us, and my skin tingled. For the first time in my life, I felt beautiful from the inside out.

We were about to be interrupted by an unattached female.

Brett smoothly turned away and took my arm. 'You don't know, do you?'

'What?'

'It's for you. For your uncle Percy.'

'Oh, Brett. No! Don't mix this up with Percy.' I *was* having such a good time.

'But Percy—'

'Why can't you let me enjoy my surprise?' I pulled away. 'Party, Brett.'

'Your uncle was an axionymist!' he laughed.

'And some!' I hissed. 'Keep your voice down!'

'But I needed to get mixed up with Percy, as you say, or we could never have succeeded with this.'

The thought of that pervert haunting me, of everyone in the room zooming their critical faculties on me, of the axionymist info making the rounds even now, the thought of everyone viewing me with the amplified x-ray vision of an electron microscope, broke a ring of sweat out into the broderie anglaise under each of my too-tight armpits.

But Brett could be stubborn, and was always unpredictable. It was probably better to let him say whatever he thought so important. I gave him my arm.

He led me into a smaller room where people who were socially dysfunctional stood around like flies on a door.

Brett elbowed two aside and pointed to the far wall. A small framed poster featured the centre of my beauty — the same picture that Brett had rendered many times larger as the show's centrepiece. Yellowed with age, it destroyed the intimacy of Brett's huge portrait. And this wasn't exactly a Toulouse-Lautrec. It didn't look artistic to me, and it'd had a shocking life — stained with what looked like brick dust, crumpled and torn, and even after careful piecing together, missing as much of itself as a dog's ear after a fight. There was writing on the thing, but I couldn't read it from here.

He peered into my face. 'Don't you know?'

'Is this a benefit show for some NGO?'

Looking closer, and thinking of the people who go off to do good, I guessed that this was not art, but artifact. 'A health education poster for New Guineans?' I guessed. 'And what the fuck does this have to do with Percy?'

He laughed out loud and took me further around the room. The rest of the wall space was hung with small, notebook-size sketches. The art was the pictorial equivalent of the social misfits lurking in the room. I didn't want to look closer, but Brett drew me closer, till I could identify something.

'Lilies!'

'Uncle Percy's!'

'Lilies?'

'My drawings. . .' He took me back to the main exhibition. 'Go look at them up close.'

Each was just an anatomical detail of a flower, blown up a zillion-fold.

Then he took me back to the small room again, where I read that tattered poster like a half-done crossword puzzle.

'The Bachelors and Spinsters Ball, Wombo, September something . . . I can't read it. Nineteen-twenty . . .four? proceeds . . . I can't read it . . . Africa?'

'Spot on!'

Brett rubbed his hands gleefully at my deciphering. 'Percy did a bunch of these, and the day after he put them up, he was made unwelcome in the area. I couldn't get the details, but as soon as he was well enough to travel, he took the first boat out from Brisbane. Justin helped me to track down this poster.'

He leaned toward me and whispered in my ear. 'Frightfully expensive!'

'My word!'

'On my honour!' he exclaimed, hand on his heart, not realizing anything in the least. I almost laughed, but decided not to put him out of his joy.

'But,' he frowned. 'One thing I couldn't find. Where's Wombo?'

I had to think, and it took me a while . . . but then, bingo!

'A big shed on one of the back roads behind Wooronga Station.' And then I was unsure. I was always partial to names like that, but they're so many, and they all begin to sound alike—Bombo, Yatteyattah, Wagga Wagga, Nimmitabel . . .

'Aha!' cried Brett, delighted at the solving of this mystery. 'No wonder.'

'What did you call him?' I asked.

'An axionymist?'

'Yeah. What—'

'Your great-uncle, the parson Percy, the Reverend Percy Arthright Hutchinson Lily, Fellow of the Royal Society, was a world-renowned botanist, and died a mile from Kew Gardens, where he fled, having been exiled and reviled by the place and the family of his home. Most of his notebooks and specimens were lost, and most of those studies you see now have been loaned by collectors around the world. Though he had much respect from abroad, it seems that his esteem there only lessened that at home.

'Nothing changes.'

'Say what?'

'We still do that,' I explained. 'But what about his weirdness, the axi—'

'Axionymist. And don't look it up. You don't seem to have a proper word for it. He was inspired by his name, you see. Lilies. Though he expanded to all the orchids, as you can see.'

'I'll take your word for it.'

Flowers are nice in vases—but otherwise, as I could see from their studies on the walls, flowers are either boring or disconcerting.

Brett had certainly done some good digging. Maybe he could answer another question. 'Why did he become a parson?'

'I wondered, too. Nothing definitive. But it seems that was the only way he found the freedom to collect and study, and still make a living.'

'Poor Percy.'

An exile. I could understand his pain. I had missed home, too, and I was now happier than I could have reckoned possible, just to be back on Earth.

'He died respected,' Brett murmured.

But then, this exhibition was back-arsed. Reverend Lily barely appeared. 'Why are they showing you as the main attraction?'

A grunt exploded from Brett, so loud that one of the human flies that had been edging close, moved away in fright. 'I'm surprised at you, Angela.'

'Why?'

'What is gallery-worthy, in this show?'

We did another run around the walls, and the show took on new meaning. The crowd was by this time, not only looking at the pictures on the walls and trying to look as if they weren't, but there was a distinct smell of thinking-about-rooting in the air. Though Lily 1 was the most prominent and largest work, each drawing attracted its own crowd. Lily 56 was surrounded by people with a lot of hair showing. Lily 30 drew a Kama Sutra crowd. Alcohol had released some of the latent energy in the room. But Brett's 'brutal' art supplied the burning torch to what would have only been your average party-smoulder.

I looked at Brett. He was a picture of health. No attack, though this was such a human situation.

'Why aren't you sick?' I whispered in his ear.

'Frankly, my dear, I don't know. But let's not analyse.'

Someone was tapping a mike. The time of speeches was nigh.

Brett shoved a piece of paper in my hand.

'What's this?'

'Your speech.'

An appalling thought! 'Whah?'

'You, the grand-niece of the late Lily, are this show's benefactor.'

I fear that my expression was not my most attractive.

'Public speaking, Brett. To these people! This isn't my crowd. I've only seen them in magazines.'

Using my eyes to finish the sentence, I tried to get him to fully understand the horror of the situation.

He paled under my look. Uh oh. 'Fresh air?' I asked.

'Umn.'

We pressed our way through the crowd, which pressed against us. Finally we popped out and I led him down the stairs, through the little crowd of black-suited men and dowdy women who were still gathered on the pavement outside the museum—to that calm place under the fig tree across the tarmac.

The bats were still active, but less argumentative. The sounds out here were the distant buzz of the big crowd in the museum, and the low murmur of the small crowd outside.

'Aren't you pleased?' he asked, and even his horns bent forward wanting something. 'I thought you would be happy to have your uncle's honour restored. For you. It mattered to you, didn't it?'

'Oh, yes!' *A total lie.*

'Oh, yes!' I repeated, admittedly lamely. 'And your way to get him shown was brilliant.'

'It wasn't my idea. It was Justin's.'

There was something else he needed.

'Your artwork is brilliant.' I said.

'It is Justin's.'

'He did it?'

'He told me to copy those drawings of Percy's, but to make them big. People like big art.'

I didn't know what to say, but we had to get back and get this thing over with.

Punching his arm, I smiled into his face. 'A wonderful present. And thanks for the speech.'

Like hell, but the crowd was friendly, and the looks I'd gotten were a mixture of admiration and envy. The envy alone would fill my voice with confidence. I was ready to go in and face the crowd.

Brett was his happy self again as he took my elbow. 'I've practised my speech,' he said.

We hadn't taken two steps before we heard the sound of a splat. I pulled toward the sound. He pulled me back into the murk under the fig tree, put his finger to his lips, and then pointed.

I hadn't noticed the Lily Perspective banners before, since they were in the shadows on both sides of the brightly lit entrance. They were over a storey long, and featured that same flower detail Brett and Percy liked so much.

We watched as four men swung balloons, and each let go. Two balloons hit one of the banners right in the middle of its image, and the third and fourth balloons splatted with the same degree of accuracy. Now both banners had the art part as a big black splotch. A cheer went up in the crowd.

Above us, a frantic umbrella opening-and-closing announced the panic of the fruit bats taking off en masse.

The assembly wasn't put off by the bats. After a further back slap or two, they began to sing, '*Deep in my heart, I do believe, we shall overcome some day.*'

The whole group sang, and while they had no harmony, they made up for that, with earnestness. They sang the whole sentence twice, then settled down to the *we shall overcome some day* over and over, till it petered out as several of them walked out to the tarmac, looking up and down the road.

Then they all milled around for a while.

There was a small disagreement between two of the men and one woman about no one having notified the police or the press.

Someone flash-bulb popped three times, once in front of each banner, and once, standing back far enough to photograph the group with the banners in the background.

Then they left.

Brett turned to me. 'Please explain.'

Passively, I watched them walk away, but I wanted to run after them and tackle someone, and say 'Please explain,' with my knee against his throat. Then I could splotch the pavement with his head. I was still trying to figure out what to tell Brett when they turned the corner and were lost from sight, and two policemen arrived on foot.

Brett took my elbow and we strolled toward the museum.

One patrolman politely blocked our path.

'Invitation, sir?'

'Is there a problem?' an imperious voice rang out from the top of the steps.

Instinctively, I grabbed Brett's arm, ready to run.

'Everyone's waiting,' the voice rang out, and now the owner of the voice followed, jangling enough jewellery to bury someone under.

'He's the artist,' I explained to the flustered patrolman, as the curator of the exhibition tore Brett from my grasp.

They had waited for us. We were pushed through the musk and burble to a couple of chairs on the speakers' platform.

But first, the director of the art gallery spoke. I had, it seems, funded a to-be-built, permanent new exhibition space. My roles were discussed: the grand-niece to Percy Lily (never 'Reverend', his affiliation with a higher life form never mentioned) whose original drawings inspired my partner, the performance artist Brett Hartshorn, 'to take to the static'. Even though the director's intro was mostly about me, his drone almost put me and the crowd, to sleep. So I jerked in my chair when he turned to me and asked when my book was due out . . . and then he extended his hand, saying 'But she can tell us all about it. Please. Miz Desirée Lily.'

My speech was hot in my hand, but my face was hotter.

'Brevity is the soul of something or other,' I said, which got a laugh. Not that I knew at that moment what the something was, any more than I knew what name I was.

'And so, I will be brief.'

Expectant silence. I took my time looking over the admiring, but especially the envious eyes. It was lovely being someone others wished to be.

'Even briefer than you expect.' I added, and smiled. I attempted my best smile. I wouldn't have been able *not* to smile, but I think it was lopsided.

And then I left the podium, to wild applause.

Brett's speech was all art-talk, most likely brilliant—but I didn't listen any more than anyone else. Because I was facing the crowd, I was able to look at its eyes. I was happy for him that the eyes had it—everything he could have wanted, if he wanted to feel human. Admiration, but even more deliciously, envy. Of course I hoped that much of that envy had to do with me.

We left an hour later, graciously declining an after-party celebration of garlic prawns and champagne.

'Later,' Brett assured the assembled, and we walked off into the night.

He took me to a place he had found in a tourist brochure, the best luxury hotel in Sydney, it said. Five hundred rooms and a view of the Harbour Bridge. He had a suite in his name.

Looking over the toiletries, I missed the Restonia's water room. Cleopatra would have thrown a tantrum here, but I endured.

He seemed strangely down.

When I questioned him, 'A touch of the vapours?' he shook my hand off his shoulder.

'I'm going out,' he announced.

'Checking on home?'

He swung around, facing me with the anger I'd seen on a couple of occasions.

Without meaning to, I sniffed. He didn't put out a smell. He didn't even look jaundiced. But he disappeared with a puff and a bang. I went to his room, and just as I expected, his bag and his trunk were by his bed.

'Never leave home without them!' I yelled it into the empty room. 'I challenge you to a contest of clichés.'

The sound of the electric lights answered back.

I was so down, I opened the bar fridge and took out a pathetically common bottle of alcohol. I was so down, I thought about my parents. There was a little twinge of guilt that played in the back of my mind. It was late, but if I rang during the day, Dad would be out. And if I rang during the evening, he could sometimes be out, too. It was eleven o'clock, but they were always so excited to hear my voice.

After quite a few rings, Mum's voice answered.

Or rather, someone picked up the phone.

'Who's this?' I demanded.

'Angela?'

'Mum?'

'Where are you?'

'Sydney.'

'Oh.'

The phone line was clear as night during drought.

'I've got great news about Uncle Percy, Mum.'
'I didn't know how to get you, Angela.'
'Percy was an axionymist,' I chuckled.
'Oh,' she said, with no exclamation mark about it.

She was such a deflator. I was ready to hang up already. 'Aren't you gonna ask me what an axi—?'

'If you'd told us how to reach—'

Stuff her! 'Where's Dad?'

She coughed into the phone. This was a woman who never had a sick day in her life.

'Mum, if you're gonna get shirty cos I can't ring for a while, that's no incentive—'

'Angela, blossom. A tree fell on him.'

'On Dad,' she said as if I hadn't heard. 'Are you there, Angela?'

'This is precisely why I don't ring,' I snapped. 'Your histrionics. Can't you once in your life make this a normal communication? Why do you do this?'

'Angela. Listen to me. A big redgum,' she said, just like her. *With a valentine cut in the bark* I almost added, but she didn't need my prompting. She was making this up as she went along. My whole body began to vibrate, wanting to smash her for having a life so small that she would want to punish me for not coddling her for a while. I would have screamed *Get a Life* into the phone if I thought she would understand.

'Put Angus on, Mum.'

She took a big breath. A better sign. 'Remember the Griffiths' place?' she asked.

'Speak up, Mum. Or enunciate.'

'He was helping out there.'

'Who?'

'Angus, of course.'

'Well?'

'A silo accident.'

'He okay?'

'He was *buried*, Angela.'

Buried by wheat as the silo filled. These things happened, but not to Angus.

'When?' I asked.

'The month before Dad.'

Had she gone menopausal insane? I'd read about this? Poor Dad.

'So how's Dad now?' I asked, my fingers drumming on the veneer of the night table. She had about three minutes left before my patience ran out, if she refused to put Dad on.

'He left you a note, Angela. It was evening before I . . . I wouldn't have found Dad without Fly come to get me.'

'Fly?'

'His best dog, Angela.'

So hard to keep track. And the names of the hands were so often the same as the dogs.

'Who's there?' I asked.

'Me, Angela.'

'So where's Dad?'

'What's wrong with you, girl?'

My mother *never* cried. *Never!*

'Mum, it's okay' I crooned. 'I know about this. Do you want me to send you some articles or find you a doctor? It happens to lots of women—'

'Just look,' she snarled. 'Just look in the bloody obituaries!'

My gut twisted like a cut snake. She was telling the truth. I wasn't ready for this.

'Angela?' she eventually asked. 'You alright?'

'Right as rain. Mum, sorry. I thought you were . . . you know. Where's Stuart?'

My youngest brother could sing the bugs out of trees, and he was always the joker of the family. How could he let Mum get like this?

My mother blew her nose with the honk of a person who lives alone. 'In America, blossom.'

'Fuck! Fuck, sorry. What's he doing there?'

'His song *On the Land* won the Country Music Award. He's in Nashville, recording.'

The pride in him, the happiness for him, swelled her voice. He'd made it, really made it, out of there.

'We thought,' she said, calm now, 'you didn't want anything to do with us, that you'd made it, too.'

'No, Mum.'

The clear line didn't even give me the excuse of air interference.

'We love you,' she said.

'Me, too, Mum. Talk to you soon.'

I hung up, not able to take any more.

The dress pinched. And though Brett had remembered to bring his own luggage, he hadn't remembered a nightdress and slippers for me.

Or even the buttonhook I needed for these boots.

I tore off the dress and with my boots on, took a shower.

It didn't help. I couldn't stop thinking of Dad.

Wee willie winkie, run through the house. The seven little pigs, counted on my toes, with the last little pig running *aahhl the way home,* Dad's fingers galloping up my foot up my leg, tickling my tummy, then skittering all the way up to my head, and then his booming laugh joining my giggle.

Him with his arms around me, and me on his lap, and the book on my lap.

Me saying with him, and pointing to the pictures where there weren't words, 'But the little red *hen* said, "No you won't, I'm going to eat it myself!"'

The little red hen, yellow yellow butter, the man who killed seven flies at one time, and wore a special belt for doing so.

'We wouldn't do that here, would we?' he'd ask, his eyes as big as a cow's as he waited for my reply.

'No, Dad,' I'd say, very solemnly, 'because I could smoosh a dozen in an instant with my little finger.'

And I'd hold up my hand, as big as a lamb's ear.

'That's me little flykiller!' Dad would say, and he'd grab my hand and plonk it on his mouth, and kiss it.

His spit always bothered me, but I wiped off the wetness without letting him know.

My *Anderson's Fairy Tales* was from him, and *Grimm's*, and *Aesop's Fables*, and a sanitized version of *Arabian Nights*, and *Alice in Wonderland*—all from him.

Then, almost the next day: the boys I'd played with, and wrestled with, and swum with when there was any water in the creek, now sniggered at me and grabbed. The mug-of-tea teasing began. And Dad's nickname for me changed to Little Bustle, and he stopped having me on his lap, and didn't know what I would like to read, he said, as he didn't know 'young ladies' taste'.

It was his idea that I should leave, for 'a proper education, and to get out in the world', though Mum didn't need convincing. Mum did the speaking when they told me that they'd decided. Between us, two flies fought over a few grains of spilled sugar on the formica table.

That day I left, Mum was distracted. She cut her finger slicing tomatoes for a bang-up breakfast. And on the drive out to town, she snapped at Dad. Before breakfast that morning, when he went out to feed the dogs, I saw him—crying behind the water tank.

A tropical shower in Fiji. That's what the water felt like, falling on my back as I sat in the shower stall. My fingers had pruned. The boots were so sodden that when I rubbed them, the leather moved with my finger, as loose as the skin on a rat drowned in a bucket when its fur has rotted away.

I turned off the shower and pulled off the boots.

A robe hung from a hook, waiting for me. It was embroidered with the hotel's name.

30

Moaning and animalian growls woke me. Brett was back, and he was having one of his bad times. The hotel's clock/radio said 8:34.

I spoke to his bedroom door. 'Knock, knock.'

The audible pain ceased, mid-groan. 'Good morning,' Brett replied, his tone muffled by the door.

It was stupid, me talking at a door, but I didn't presume to open it. 'Can I help?'

The handle turned and he stood in front of me. Though I expected him to look sick, he was—decrepit.

I pushed him back into the room, threw back the bedclothes, and started unbuttoning his shirt.

He grabbed my hand. 'What is this about?'

'You're sick, dummy!'

He turned away. 'Never mind about me.'

What a way to wake up! My whole life wasn't worth a dog fart. 'Who the fuck else am I gonna mind about!'

I ripped at his shirt, the shirt I'd only seen off once. I put my hands to his jeans, but he took both my hands in his. 'Does it matter to you what happens to me?'

A tear ran down his cheek. I didn't know it could.

That opened up my gates. I wrapped my arms around him and cried into his chest. He smelt not like what he had when he opened the door (asafoetida and vomit), but of good clean hot iron. His chest was moderately hairy, and one of the curls tickled my nose, so much that I sneezed.

A hanky swirled. Pink silk.

'Ta,' I smiled up at him, and he smiled down at me.

'You are my hope,' he said.

We ate a room service breakfast, he wanting the same as me for the first time. The full Aussie brekkie: Two fried eggs, bacon, sausage, grilled tomato, mushrooms, lots of toast. Coffee. He'd cut off his stiletto nail.

The toast, tomato and mushrooms intrigued him, and he didn't like the coffee at all. I had never seen him consume anything other than raw meat and blood, so him tucking into the cooked stuff was almost as good as the breakfast itself, which was heavenly.

'Why didn't you eat this stuff before?' I asked, thinking how lovely it is to talk with your mouth full to someone who doesn't care.

'Adjustment problems, Angela. The process is a painful one, physically and mentally.'

And the groaning? Could I ask? 'Your nights? And those . . . sounds.'

'I must go back. You know that.'

'To check, or be checked up on?'

'Both, actually.'

'And those groans and—'

'I am sorry to have disturbed you. I have problems, Angela. Nothing I can release there. They come out here. But I will try to make sure they don't.'

'No!' That was a shock to me, how fast that came out. 'You can't. I know something about psychology.'

'I fear your university education and your Higher Light are lacking in—'

'Don't you "I fear" me, my man!'

He'd gotten under my skin, like a splinter. 'You're in transition. Big deal. Millions of trannies are, too. They cope. I bet you're worried about failing. About acceptance.'

His mouth was hanging open in a beautifully stupid way. It gave me the confidence I needed to make my final guess.

'I bet you even get outbreaks of pimples in your crotch!'

'Angela!'

I flung a piece of his toast in the air, and caught it in my mouth.

'Welcome, Brett, to the human condition!'

I'd torn his shirt. He made up a new one just like it. And then he rustled up something for me. Just something simple for going out walking, not transmogrifying. Just for buying papers at a newsagent, so we could read reviews of the show.

Brett was a lousy tailor, all glance of an eye but no talent for detail, nor a clue about construction. Everything was uncomfortably tight, or bagged in the wrong place—even, now that I noticed, his own shirt. I didn't mention any of this, because he was all little-boyish with wanting to know about the show.

'You did like it?'

'Yes, Brett.'

'Why?'

'It had wit.' That was honest. It did.

'Do you understand it?' I asked.

'What's there to understand?' He was genuinely puzzled.

It is odd, isn't it, that *fuck* and *shit* came so easily to my mouth, but the fact of an innocent flower part turned into an in-your-face double entendre, or an anti-societal pornographic work, depending on your view—I couldn't find the words, but he read my chest blush.

'Don't you find the centre of your beauty a beautiful inspiration for art? And isn't nature amazing? I never knew till your great-uncle introduced me.'

He was serious. The innocence of him.

'Oh!' He picked up a gift-wrapped package from his night table, and handed it to me.

'For you.'

I untied the ribbon and tore off the wrapping to reveal a thin, grotty thing, its pages spotted with brown—*Orchids of the Bunwup region* by P. Lily, F.R.S., etc.

'Everything came from that,' Brett said. 'Isn't it funny how orchids are called lilies.'

From the way he handled it, there was only one way to deal with this thing.

'Uncle Percy would want you to have it,' I said, holding it out.

'I will treasure it,' he breathed.

And to my amazement, he wrapped the book as best he could, tied on the ribbon, walked over and lifted back the creaking lid of that weird, winged trunk, and placed the package in.

The lid clonked shut without giving me a peek.

31

WE BOUGHT the *Herald* at a kiosk in front of the post office. The show wasn't on the arts pages. It was splashed on Page One. There was a convenient bench nearby.

Two pictures showed respectively, the defaced banners, and Brett's largest drawing (this picture spread over half the front page). The headline read 'ART SHOW BANNED AS OBSCENITY: Demands for artist to be charged with blasphemy'.

Brett was prostrate. After an initial stare at the pictures, he handed me the paper. 'Read it to me.'

'"Following the direct intervention of Communication and Arts Minister—" Oo, hoo! And *you* think you have intervention problems!'

'Just read please.'

'"... after heavy lobbying by the bible study group of Federal MPs and the Reverend Malcolm Rowd, NSW state Upper House MP and leader of the Christian Democracy Party, the management of the Art Gallery decided 'with deep regret, in the interests of the institution's future' to axe the exhibition, despite announcing a few months earlier that the Lily Retrospective would be the centrepiece of the museum's program this year." Did you get that, Brett? The centrepiece?'

'Is there more?'

I skimmed. 'You have much support. The public is on your side.'

'Who?'

'Well, the Arts Council is outraged. We are the laughing stock of the world ... You've got a lot of scientific heavies behind you ... Kew Gardens, lots of people you wouldn't know. The Wilderness Society ... Ooh, Prince Charles. If he sends a letter, can I keep it? And the Labia Lovites is holding a demo on the museum steps at two o'clock. Wanna go?'

Apparently not.

'The rest of the stuff is technical. You're not interested, are you?'

'Yes, my dear. If I'm to assimilate, I need to understand.'

'Well, it seems as if you might be able to win in the courts if you want to fight, as this falls between departments. They are quoting some statutory authority's right to ban something if, and I quote, it offends the standards of morality, decency and propriety generally accepted by reasonable adults.'

A sardonic laugh interrupted me. 'Excuse me,' he said.

'Laughing's healthy.'

'Then make me laugh.'

'Technically the standard that must be met is "discrete genital detail".'

'Hell isn't a good place to learn to be discrete,' he apologized.

'Bigger isn't always better,' I explained.

'I've always been in the larger picture.'

'Size isn't everything.'

'It seems to be, here,' he said, and pointed to his trunk. 'Nobody would ban that book, would they? Or would they?'

'Where'd you find it anyway?' I asked, narrowly catching myself before letting on what I thought of it.

'It's a library discard. I bought it at what you call Saint Vinnie's. For twenty cents.'

'Well, that just shows how hot a property you have in that trunk of yours.'

'And who says it's genital?' he asked.

'The eye of the beholder. By the way, did Percy marry?'

'No.'

'What a fascinating man.' I rustled the newspaper. 'Want to know more?'

'There's more?'

'The plot thickens. The labia thing isn't even law. It's an interpretation made by the Office of Film and Literature Classification, a government-appointed body that decides which films, books and magazines can be viewed by everyone, which by those over eighteen, and which are banned outright. If your show opens again—'

'A widdle old woman of Tyre—'

'Don't,' I laughed. 'I'm serious.'

'You're making it up!'

I lowered the paper. 'My dear Brett. I wish I had the imagination.'

'Is there more?'

'The yummiest part. It would be illegal to even advertise the exhibition anywhere in Australia, with fines of eleven thousand dollars and one year's jail for individuals, or two hundred and fifty thousand big ones, for companies that defy the ban. You could be jail-meat! And you with your lovely tail.'

He touched his crotch, a reflex action.

'Then, Section seventeen of the Victorian Summary Offences Act makes it an offence to exhibit or display an indecent or obscene word, figure or representation in a public place within the view of any person in that place.'

'What does that have to do with here? We're in a different state.'

'Nothing. But it's added weight.'

'Then, and this is the blasphemy part . . .'

I couldn't read it. I was laughing too hard.

'Oh, Flabberdeephoo!!' he cried, and grabbed at the paper, thereby ripping it in two.

'Patience is a virtue,' I continued. 'Now, the Reverend Rowd, our hard-working Upper House MP, *your* MP if you become a resident of this state, wants anyone satirizing the church to be charged with blasphemy.'

He slapped the back of the bench so hard, a flock of pigeons exploded into flight. It was a healthy explosion for us, if helpless laughter is healthy.

'If I'm convicted?' he sputtered, 'what's the sentence? . . . No!' His hand stopped me mid- mouth-open. 'Which is worse? Spending time in one of your jails, or rotting in hell for all eternity?'

'With your looks, Brett . . .'

Eventually he asked, 'Does your stomach hurt, too?'

'Mm hm.'

'A good hurt, isn't it?'

During our conference on the bench, many people had stopped for a bit to look at us—Brett, actually. A little boy now stared at Brett. The kid was so close I could have kicked him. Brett was slumped on the bench with his eyes closed, a smile on his face. A little meditation to digest the stomach-aching ways of us mortals.

The boy emptied the rest of a box of Smarties chocolates into his mouth, chewed, swallowed, and threw the box. Its edge hit Brett's mouth.

The brat knew crowds well. He stepped back to be just out of kicking range, and grinned.

Brett sat up abruptly. 'The little fiend!' he muttered, but he did nothing.

'Flick him the Bic!' I whispered.

'Say what?'

'Your flaming hand! Flick your thumb, goddamit, before his blasted mother pitches up.'

His voice was low, and it shook. 'Angela, I am not a mere conjurer!'

As my hot blood mottled my cheeks and the brat watched, entranced by the results of his experiment, Brett disappeared in a puff of stench.

No one noticed but myself and the boy.

I grinned.

He ran, screaming soundlessly toward the newsstand where his mother was just leaving, clutching her *New Idea*.

There was nothing to grin about.

Our few moments, after all our time together, when we finally clicked—fhuff!

I had hurt his feelings. Well, he hurt mine. He thought that his exhibition was for me, but didn't think of how I would feel—a nothing.

It was good to have those admiring eyes on me. But afterwards, it was Brett, the artist. Brett, Brett, Brett. No one asked me about my book. I was goggled at, but not interested in.

Three people now shared my bench, digging into their takeaway lunches. Fruit salad, falafel roll, prawn sandwich. A pigeon with one leg picked up the falling bits.

I had half a newspaper, torn lengthways.

In my bag was nothing. It was part of the clothing that Brett had supplied, but it was just a bag—just something to hold on to. Being with Brett, I hadn't needed anything in my bag.

It was anybody's guess when he would return, but the hotel was two blocks away.

32

'The Hartshorn suite.'

'Do you know which number, madam?'

'I wish you wouldn't call me madam, you little worm in a bad-fitting uniform,' I said. Actually, I didn't, but I wish I had.

'No,' I said. 'I didn't notice.'

'Well, we'll look,' he said, all warningly camp. 'And here you are, Missus Hartshorn,' he announced. 'Suite four sixty.'

I put my hand on the counter to take possession of their stupidly dumb-belled key.

'Thanks, and . . .' I corrected him. 'I'm not Missus Hartshorn.'

'Mizz,' he corrected, over-correctly.

'I'm not Mizz Hartshorn either,' I snapped, bitch to bitch, and a moment later, regretted that I hadn't bitten my tongue off. What did I care what he called me, anyway?

'I do apologize, madam. I'll just be a moment.'

He turned to a screen that faced toward him. 'Your name, madam?'

'Lily.'

'Surname, please.'

'Lily.'

'Ah, yes. And Christian name?'

'Desirée. Or Angela.'

'Um . . . hah. I'm afraid you are not registered with Mister Hartshorn.'

'Try Pendergast.'

He went *click click* on the keyboard and turned toward me.

'For our guests' protection, you understand. I'm afraid you must wait for Mister Hartshorn.'

'I came in last night with Mister blinketyblink Hartshorn!'

His delight was so blatant, his little butt wiggled. 'We respect our guests' tastes, madam,' he said, examining the pores on my nose, 'regardless . . . but you can't expect me to open the door of his suite to someone he slept with last night who is not accompanied by him now.'

We gazed at each other until I blinked.

'I'll wait,' I said, turning towards a sofa.

'Would madam like a cup of coffee or tea?' he chirruped. 'It would be our pleasure... on the house.'

Madam had a cup. It was bitter, and no one had remembered the sugar or cream or milk, or even artificial whitener. That was lunch.

For an hour, I watched the hotel lobby traffic — as interesting as an airport lounge. I watched a man read a whole, untorn *Sydney Morning Herald*. When he left, dropping it in his chair, I nonchalantly pounced.

Page One, I knew.

Page Two, local and uninteresting.

Page Three, World, unmitigated war, and more expected. Turn the page fast, so as not to fall into that abyss again.

I was in the middle of turning the page when a man sitting next to me, whose stomach rested on his thighs, accidentally on purpose jolted my elbow. I rooster-winged outwards, but he didn't move. Blazing unmistakable unfriendliness, I eye-balled him.

'Maw bad news,' he said, digging his mass deeper into the cushions. 'Hear about yestiday?'

'Nope!'

He sighed with the sound a walrus must make. A walrus that eats donuts for breakfast. 'Not inter-rested?'

'Couldn't give a shit, mister.' That should do it.

It didn't. He smiled so big, I could see his tonsils out of the corner of my eye. 'Least you not one a them wah protestahs.'

I beamed my full force of personality straight into his little blue eyes. The problem was, they were closed, and his face was in a state of rapture.

'The lawd is a man of wah,' he said, 'Exodus, chaptah fifteen, verse three.'

'There you are, Orin.' A person who was his match, but of another sex, bustled up and though she stood on my foot, I felt blessed.

'We gotta go,' she apologized to me. 'The bus.'

The sofa rose at his rising, and he waved in parting. 'Nice talkin to yuh.'

Their package-tour travel bags were printed with that fish that folks display who aren't inter-rested in fish.

Another of their group vacated a nearby chair, so in a trice, me and mah newspapah were nestled between its arms.

'Enough of the *goddamn* news,' I muttered loudly, and no one gasped. They must have all boarded.

I flicked to the Arts section.

Simone—Simone of Kate's place, Simone of the dress to suit the man, Simone of the black satin sheets loaned to Brett, with her wish to be inserted between them, and him between her legs. Simone, now taking up a good part of the arts section column space, smiled out at me. Simone—straddling a thick, black, headline:

KITCHEN'S TALES SPARK BIDDING WAR

> Australia's wildest publishing success, "Barbara" is at the centre of a bidding war involving 10 publishers.
>
> Simone Kitchen's faux diary of a serial diarist is iconoclastic, unambiguously ambitious, a tour de force. A stunningly written send-up that is part picaresque, part Bildungsroman. With the wry courage of a clear-eyed cynic, Kitchen's deadpan prose makes us squirm . . .

I was squirming, all right. When did *she* begin to write?

> Simone Kitchen's faux diaries look set to be a high point in annual releases, for years to come. Kitchen plans to give her international following one uproarious "journal" a year, delving further and further into the life and times of her unforgettable anti-heroine, "until I get bored with her", she quips.
>
> Kitchen herself is famously coy about ending the Barbara series. "Like vegemite she will! Barbara is a serial diarist!" avers her manager and now husband, wedded last month at the Isle of Jersey, Gordon Thirk.

Gordon! My Gordon! The unfaithful bastard! And that bitch!

> Barbara Heart, Kitchen's invention of Sisyphean ambition, is a character as contemporary as a boiling hot glass of latté, and as classic as Lolita herself.

My heart was pounding so loudly, I couldn't hear myself think. Putting down the paper, I composed my thoughts.

Then I ran three blocks to the nearest bookstore. On the window:

**FIFTEEN WEEKS
ON THE NEW YORK TIMES BESTSELLER LIST**

The window display was stacks of her book, the cover imitation-journal, in the style of a book meant for sequels, instantly brand-recognizable.

I ran into the store and wasn't the nicest person in the way I elbowed to the pile near the door. Grabbing a *Barbara*, I made my way to the dictionary section, where I could read in peace.

The dedication was *To Gordon, simply*

The next page had only one line, a faux disclaimer so witty that I grinned, despite myself:

The names have been changed to protect the guilty.

There was nobody near me, so I sat, the better to read.

The book was phenomenal. A completely realistic journal, the exact way that someone would write up every single day, every plan, dream, success, every bedding, longing, thought, every soggy wad of rumination. It was a masterpiece of realism, down to this scrawled snaking-around-the-margin note:

> TRY-ON NUMBER 5: James asked again if he could sleep with me. I again rejected him with gentle élan. He asked if I had saved my hair. My hair! I think if I had said yes, he would have asked for a dread as a fetish. Eeew!

Only the names had been changed.

— 33 —

AT A QUARTER TO SIX, the public address system announced store closing in fifteen minutes, and at five minutes to six, the announcement nagged to a mostly empty store, 'Please take your purchases to the checkout counters.'

So I closed the book and shoved it under the bookstand, after crumpling a fistful of its pages.

My bum was in the air as I slapped my legs to get my feet to wake up.

'That wasn't very nice,' Brett said to my bum.

'Shee-yikes!'

Though I hated him, I needed his help to get up. 'How did you find me?' I asked.

'I felt you.'

'How sensitive of you.'

'Are you hungry?' he asked, as the bookstore door closed on us.

The pavement was a tangled mess of people rushing home. It felt good to be in their way.

'The only good thing about you pissing off like that, was that brat. Congratulations on ruining someone else's life besides mine. And you ask me if I'm hungry? When I haven't eaten since the break of dawn?'

'Sorry. Where would you like to eat? I'm easy,' he smiled, all let-bygones-be-bygones.

'I didn't even have the money to buy the book I wrote. And you have ruined my life. And my book is read by millions, and loved, and destined to be a classic, in numerous languages, and not only that, but I have written many, many books. By my estimate, something like twenty-five already. *And none of them will have my name as author.* And why the fuck did you tell me that the house had gone up in smoke when everything I had there is now in the hands of the only two people who can compete with you for the greatest fucker-uppers of my WHOLE . . . FUCKING . . . LIFE!'

People turned, people moved away, people laughed. The security guard inside the bookstore opened the door and poked his head out.

Wiping my arm over my face and under my nose, I stomped off toward the hotel, or maybe the Harbour Bridge. That direction, anyway.

Brett followed, grabbing me when I stepped out into traffic.

We walked with him holding onto my elbow, and me, crying and yelling in spasms of blinding, snot-generating tears.

'Mad woman of shallot,' I mumbled, giving me a mad little giggle that broke grief's clutch.

Now, as we walked, the crowds pressed tighter, as no one avoided us. I was just a bereaved woman of means, not a casualty of the mental health system's lack of care.

We crossed the last street, and there was the harbour, as surprisingly beautiful as I had always found it, and the mysterious sea itself. We walked to the edge of the quay, and sat, dangling our legs over the water.

'You didn't set that fire, did you?'

'No, Angela. An aromatherapy candle in Simone's room started it. I only came back when everyone was running around in the house. Except you.'

'Did you do that stuff with the tampon?'

He nodded, his remorse slightly touching. His action would have looked sheepish, but for the horns.

'What about the Higher Light?' I asked.

'What about it?'

'Burned?'

'I had no need to burn it, did I?'

'None at all,' I agreed, tasting bitterness with each new realization.

'Angela . . .'

'Don't soulful look me, you bastard!'

'Angela, did you not think anything of the present I gave you?'

It was hard to think of what Brett thought of as a present. All I could bear to do is to grunt. Words would have been too hurtful.

'Didn't you like my work? The Lily Retrospective?'

My heart pumped hard at that one. Breaking. But there was no point in showing him how much it hurt.

'Brett Hartshorn. Venice Biennale, here he comes.'

'Please don't make fun of me, my dear. I have suffered a disappointment with the exhibition, too.'

My heels banged against the concrete, reminding me that my boots were soft. 'You are *made*, Brett. That was the best launch you could ever get.'

'Really?' A self-absorbed joy, something I recognized as the expression I most wanted to have myself, glowed from his face. He was *such* an innocent.

'Have you seen tomorrow's papers yet?' I asked.

He smiled back, the smile of a supplicant. 'Angela, the show was political.'

'It sure was!' I laughed.

'Not that way, my dear . . .'

His gaze was unnerving—as if I were there in front of him, but wasn't—as if I were a contact lens that he was staring at while it was lost in the grass.

'Will you help me?' he asked, and two creases at the top of his nose twitched.

What else was there for me?

Crawling back from the edge, I tugged him upright. 'Feed me, you truant from the bottomless pit.'

34

We were in tourist central, down at the quay. There was a restaurant just behind us. I ordered lasagne, and Brett followed suit. Its meatiness would have horrified me when I lived at Bettawong. Now, what I really wanted was the meat alone. Lots and lots of red—preferably seared, rare steak. Brett ate, but rather chorefully.

There's nothing like a feed when you need one. I was picking my teeth when he cleared his throat the way a person does.

'Yes, Brett?' I sighed, but only inwardly.

'He asked me how the book is going.'

'Who? Justin? He doesn't care, does he?'

Comically, Brett mouthed, 'The Omniscient.'

'Whooh! You believe that?'

'Don't you?'

'Scientifically speaking?'

'Speaking as you.'

'Speaking as'—and I sat up as tall as I could— 'Me the Great, the whole thing's a crock.'

He didn't even smile. 'Crock? What about?' He leaned toward me and stuck his elbow into cold, melted cheese, and didn't notice. 'Hell?'

It was real, all right. But the purposefulness of the supposed Him had no purpose. How could I put it so Brett would understand?

'He's Mister Chance, Brett. Random Chance.'

'He's coming,'—a stage-whisper.

This was getting weirder.

'Make sense, Brett.'

'Help me to escape.' He reached across the plates. 'Pleeeze, Angela!'

Between us, his shirtsleeves silently sucked up orange grease at a mosquito-buzz level of annoyance.

I took back my hands and stood up. 'Let's get outa here. We'll talk at the hotel.'

* * *

To my relief, the staff had changed. One can only take so much humiliation in one day.

Brett had a zillion messages waiting for him. When we got to our room, he threw them in the bin.

I made him change his shirt for another, and the one he waved into being was the same style as the last. He either liked it, or had no imagination. I didn't have a chance to ask, because he launched straight into his problems.

'So you think he wants to come here and check up on you?' I asked.

'You could put it that way.'

'Doesn't he know all?'

'He doesn't have time to.'

Ah. 'Like parents.'

'Eh?'

'They're like that, too. Pretending to be able see around corners.'

Those bootlaces of his needed adjusting again. Now I knew the pattern. While he was bent over, his words floated up. 'I never had children.' Incredibly, some biological clock tolled for him, of all . . . For a moment, his tragedy was almost funny. Only for a moment.

'My father . . .' I said. The father I hadn't seen for a dozen years. The father who I knew loved me. The father I couldn't talk to. 'My father died today.'

Brett rushed over and crouched at my knees. 'Today!'

I wanted to cry, but couldn't.

'Worse.' And doesn't having to explain make everything worse? 'It was some time ago.'

'I'm *so* sorry,' His lips and eyes twitched through several expressions—sincere and silly at the same time.

'My brother is dead too. One of them. The other is in America.'

'I don't know what to say.'

'That's all right, Brett.' I gave his head a brief scratch between the horns. 'No one ever does.'

As he continued to gaze up at me, his sympathy was no longer silly.

Two big tears splashed from my eyes onto his knee.

'How is your mother?' he asked.

'Okay, I guess.'

'Is she alone?'

'Not sure. Probably.'

'Isn't she lonely?'

'Are you asking because you wonder how we feel, or because you want to know?' I asked, and then wanted to take it back

He stood and flexed his back, turning away from me. 'Do you want anything more from Sydney?'

'... No.'

'Would you like to see the world?'

Why would I want to do that? 'Fine.'

'And then go to see your mother?'

'Hell, no!' That came out so fast, I didn't temper the thought.

'Don't you love her?'

'I guess, Brett. But I left for a reason. I *hate* living in the country. It's horrible. And you would, too.'

'I wouldn't know. But your mother ...'

'Don't worry about my mother, Brett. Didn't you ruin my life, to save yours?'

'When you put it that way, my dear—'

'It's been a long day. Days. I'm just tired.'

Appeasement had been reached. Good.

Going to the country had been forgotten. Even better.

Punching him companionably, I grinned and bounced on my bed. 'Now what's this about a world tour?'

'It's best that we move around a bit.'

'Evasion?'

'Something like that. I can call it research.'

Better to humour than to scorn. 'Does he suspect anything?'

'I don't know. He does rather think my holiday is taking a while.'

'Does he think in terms of years, too? Your years, or his years?'

'No.'

Very illuminating, but what did it matter.? The real question was: 'How do we travel?'

'Blink?'

35

I PICKED the first destination, one I had fond memories of.

On this occasion, however...

There's me, post-lunch, lying on the hard black sand of Singaraja Beach, sweat pooling between my breasts. Two beautiful Balinese girls are near me, sifting beach gravel to make cement. They've been here since morning, sifting for a while, then carrying baskets of gravel on their heads to a building site overlooking the tepid sea. Brett sits on the beach next to me, dressed insistently and interminably, even to the boots, in his Brettwear.

In this heat, the boots bother him more than usual.

My beach book was *Barbara*. It read like an airport book—nothing like that article in the *Herald* that had labelled *Barbara* 'uproarious'. Reviewers so often can't admit they cry. They have to turn every tragedy into humour, every hero into anti-hero. The success of *Barbara* showed me again the falseness of those who would be tastemakers. Just like Barbara Cartland's books, *Barbara* was accompanying millions of people to bed. As I blew my nose into the beach sand, so did millions blow theirs into manufactured tissues or fine embroidered lawn—as we cried with Barbara, yearned for Barbara, urged Barbara to victory and love, as we do all our heroes and heroines in the greatest of books—especially when we see that they, like us, have been kicked in the teeth by life.

I bought it at the little shop by the beach, the one that sold SPF 15 for us easy-to-burns, baby oil, batik sarongs, prawn crackers and dayglow-coloured sweets.

I read stretched out on the beach in my sarong. Brett sat cross-legged on a bamboo mat, reading a book he had obtained for himself. A Darwin, first edition.

'You look like a dork,' I told him, but he was oblivious to public opinion.

It wasn't only that antique book. To my surprise, he had acquiesced to my suggestion as soon as we arrived, to buy and wear an Asian-style baseball cap—the only headwear sold at that little shop. I thought it would be a good idea. Brett could blend in, and not shock the sensibilities these simple locals might have. The cap was black mesh, high in the crown, and its brim twisted like a roadkilled duck, but it hid those horns.

By our second day on the beach, it was obvious to me that the locals had seen everything and were unshockable by anything. They were not interested in me or Brett. They did their jobs, smiled gracefully all the time, and maybe hated us. Who could tell? They wouldn't. So I told him he didn't need the cap, but he didn't take it off. When I told him to dump the cap, he said he liked it.

Bali didn't satisfy me now, and the food was all pizza, and mango smoothies, and pawpaw fruit salad, and toasted cheese jaffles—or starve. They didn't even have water buffalo. And Brett was no beach bum. So we left.

After Bali, I didn't want to choose.

New York. The people were pushy, and Brett was now attached to that dumb cap, which meant that he looked as dorky on a city street as he had on a tropical beach.

He landed us in an apartment where the residents were away. Brett didn't explain anything, but the apartment was just like the house of the three bears. We slept in soft beds (or rather, I slept in a soft bed), I ate their food (fresh from their freezer), and he read their books.

'A great library,' he informed me in a somewhat scolding tone. It was an actual library with a dictionary on a stand and a giant globe, and a reading table and a giant desk and a Persian carpet to dampen the noise of a page being turned, and an upper walkway and long ladders. Its saving grace was a chesterfield.

He sat in a hard chair, a book splayed on a reading table in front of him. I was stretched out, reading my book for the third time, but that was my business.

When he again praised the collection, I responded. 'Uni ended for me years ago. I will not be told what to read.'

Happily, he didn't push.

New York was cold. It smelt of hoary diesel exhaust and artificial maple flavouring.

Barbara was in every bookstore window, and so were pictures of Simone Kitchen. I didn't read newspapers, as I would have run into her there, too, or been sucked into all the other terrible news of the world.

Brett cared for me, though. If I wanted something new to wear, I got something new. There was no point in me shopping for clothes. There was no point in me doing anything.

So I read *Barbara* in the tropical heat of the apartment, and ate steak.

It was almost my bedtime. He was hunched over the reading table in the library, making favourable and snide comments to a book. Since he had always read silently, I leaned over his shoulder to see what made him such a chatterbox. It was an oversized glossy coffee-table production, some sort of history of the Devil as depicted in art.

I unbuttoned my boots and pulled them off. 'Why isn't your tail like the pictures?'

He closed the book. 'I wondered about that, myself. Must be the reason why we have so many artists come through now, as opposed to centuries ago.'

I sat on the carpet floor and massaged the ball of my foot. 'What do you mean?'

'I haven't looked like that for nigh on a hundred of your years now, and has anyone shown my beautiful hair?'

'You mean your tail? I thought it was just like a bull's tail.'

I'd seen and combed a lot of bulls' tails. A length about a foot long of flesh-encased vertebrae covered with fur, from which a long ponytail of hair extends, ending sometimes almost at the ground, in a wavy curl.

'Want to feel?' he asked.

'Can I?'

But he had already stood and turned his back to me. He pulled down his jeans, and as I should have expected, he wore no underdaks.

I reached up and felt through the fur, to the fleshy part of the tail. Thick, bonelessly flexible as a kelp stalk, and more than a metre long, it ended as a handful-size triangulated point—a parson's nose, it was called at home, when the chook was plucked bald and that fleshy tail piece exposed itself.

Brett's thick, long ponytail hid his parson's nose. I held his tail horizontally so that the silky black hair fell away and the heart shape revealed itself in gleaming curves.

He craned his head back to look down at me, without pulling his tail from my fingers. 'Have you ever seen pictures as I am now?'

I stifled a laugh. 'No. Only the shaved version like in that book.'

He bent over and pulled his jeans partway up, his tail flowing through my fingers. In a complicated manoeuvre, he arranged his tail so that its nose rested behind his exceeding manliness. He buttoned the jeans and then bent and spread his legs, and straightened and bent back in the exactingly careful dance with a slow jerk at the end that I had seen blokes perform — blokes who had much less to be careful of.

'Do you like it this way or the other more?' he asked, going to the door.

'I don't know,' I said honestly, picking up my boots and going to the door with him.

'Neither do I,' he answered, as he ushered me out.

'Sleep well,' he said, as I opened the door to my room.

'Hope everything's well enough back . . . you know,' I said, not knowing what to say.

When my door was shut, I began to undress, but I wasn't sleepy. I had ten dollars in my bag. Though I have never liked drinking alone, I went out for coffee.

As I drank, I pondered the question: If he was beginning to develop vanity, why was he so attached to that asinine mesh cap?

The next day, it seemed, we were in Vienna. We dossed down in the State Library, where he settled in as happily as a paper mite. We slept on sofas in the library itself.

I spent two days walking in the rain.

'Are we running?' I asked.

'Mm.'

'Do you think he is watching us?'

'Don't know.'

He was hunched over another book!

'Enough is enough.' I hurled the thing. 'I'm fed up with this!'

That got his attention.

'Brett, I 'm going crazy with doing nothing. Do you have a plan?'

He tilted his head, silent movie method-acting: Listener.

I semaphored my presence with my arms, inches from his face. 'Hell-oh-oh!'

He gripped my throat with that choking smell. 'Shut up!'

His hiss was unnecessary, as I was rolling on the ground in pain.

The building rumbled.

He threw himself on me, knocking my head against the marble floor. The pain lasted through the crash of a naked marble lady smashing on top of us both.

A small, dark room, with no personality. Me on a cot.

Brett beside me, holding my hand.

Now smiling at me. 'Feel better?' he asked.

I shook my head and moved my legs. Outside of a dull headache and the general pains you would feel if you fell down a flight of stairs and were avalanched by a marble Amazon, I felt fine.

'Great, Brett.' As best I could, I smiled. 'What was that all about?'

'An earthquake.'

What a headache. But wait a minute! 'Wasn't that Vienna?'

'We were in Vienna when it happened.'

Something creepy was creeping up my brain. 'Vienna doesn't *have* earthquakes.'

'Not recently.'

'Look Brett, let's not parse the plastocene. I mean, Vienna doesn't have earthquakes in human memory.'

'Seventeen sixty-eight. I know that's not human memory.' An apology with, I was relieved to note, no sarcasm. 'But here. Let me help you up.'

'Ta.' A few hundred years ago. Not exactly earthquake-prone. 'Do you think it's a message to you?'

A hangnail of his needed to be bitten off, before 'No' came through his teeth. A practised answer.

'Maybe we better move around more,' I suggested. 'Unless . . . You ready to jump?'

'Could we move around a bit more first?'

'Sure, Brett.'

We sure did. Ten cities, ten days. I found *Barbara* in every city, in the language of the natives, and my own. I enjoyed finding and buying a copy, just as he preferred to visit libraries and antiquarian bookshops rather than take the easy route of swirling a hand and instantly obtaining any book.

It was almost hypnotic, this new life. He never told me the intended destination.

This part of the trip was something I had always fantasized about.

Going on an airplane somewhere, being packed perfectly for wherever, and not knowing till landing, where it would be. Of course, the destination would always be someplace wonderful, and the travel itself would be unreal—no lost baggage, no touts...

Brett's mode of travel had minimal problems. His luggage always arrived safely. I had none—only the bag I carried, with nothing inside except the little bit of money I asked for. If I lost the bag, another was supplied.

The motion-sickness lasted for such a small moment that it didn't matter. Oddly though, sometimes I had jet lag, depending on the distance. As for Brett, he had no problems with the travel itself. His sickness was nerves, post-trip nerves in my morning, when he came back from his nightly visits back 'there' as we referred to it.

One day Brett transported us to a palatial apartment that he said was a 'mere walk away' from the Vatican library. The important thing is that water pouted from the mouths of golden dolphins, crystal bottles of Cleopatric libations awaited my choosing, and I left a rainbowed soap ring in the chalcedon bath. On a bed fit for a queen, all red and gold and cherubim, Brett had laid out new attire. The dress and jacket and boots pulled and gapped and pinched, just as everything he made. But the clothes fit better than what I would have found by shopping.

While I was dressing, Brett suddenly walked into the still steamy bathroom and closed the door. Odd. He'd never been interested in bathrooms before. I was putting on my boots when 'Aaaaargh!' came from beyond the door, then 'Angela! Is it supposed to feel good and bad at the same time?'

Lots of things do, so 'What?'

'... Eliminating? I don't know—'

A plop... a series of little toots... and a long bugle note.

'Don't flush!' I yelled.

Eventually he came out, smiling.

'Did you wash your hands?' I asked.

'I forgot.'

While he was washing them, I examined his production. It was massive, but otherwise normal in colour, shape, texture. And the smell in this inadequately vented room was normal, too.

'And your pimples? Gone?'

'Going,' he said. 'Aren't I supposed to flush the toilet?'

'Now you can.'

He did, and with the weighty joy of a boy, he watched his shit twirl down.

Well, that apartment was fun.

The next day, we moved again.

And the next day, again.

That apartment had been a welcome interlude, but it was the only fun part of these travels with Brett. Mostly, he found us libraries where I dossed down in some corner while he read.

Actually, I don't know if he did read any more. He was acting like a paranoid looney now, forever on the move. So one day, just as he was preparing to move us again, I asked, 'Do you think he did it to us?'

'What?'

'That earthquake.'

'No,' he answered.

Something needed to be settled, and *now*. 'Doesn't he know everything, do everything? According to you.'

'Only according to you.'

'Not me!'

'No, Angela,' His hands made drunken butterfly movements, fluttering and dropping to his lap. 'I don't mean *you*.'

'Are you going back tonight?'

'You know.'

'Can you ask him a question?'

His eyelids dropped self-protectively. 'It doesn't work that way. What?'

'Ask him about the tree and the grain silo, and my family . . . Ask him, Brett!'

'Okay.'

He sat in the only chair, some plastic and chrome horror. I think we were in some sub-sub-basement room of the Library of Congress, but book tombs tend to look like book tombs the world over. I rested my back against the wall.

I was either meditating or nodding off when his voice broke the silence. 'Shit, that was close.'

'Too right,' I agreed, but there was something that riled. 'You don't have to condescend, Brett.'

His head jerked back. 'Condescend?'

'Shit. It doesn't sound nice on you.'

'I was accommodating, I thought.'

His voice said he was telling the truth, and furthermore, that I'd hurt him. Would he *never* fit in?

I reached over and touched his shoulder. '"Shit" doesn't sound worthy of you. And when you say that, it makes me want to stop saying it, too. How about neither of us says "shit"?'

He smiled at me in a sad way, acknowledging personal failure—his.

I changed the subject. 'How many dead, do you think?'

'I don't know yet. Perhaps twenty thousand people, if that's what you mean.'

'Shit!'

Shit. You know how it is. You try to stop saying a word, and then it's the only word in your vocabulary.

'Probably the same number as the Indian earthquake . . . remember?'

I didn't.

'The one in oh-one?'

Thinking back . . .'Which century?'

'Just a few years ago, my dear. Your years. You did read about it?'

The heat of my blush rose from my chest to my forehead. When the earthquake happened, I didn't bother with news. And in my frenzied period of news engorgement, those Indians in that one incident had been crushed under the weight of events.

36

'Well?' I asked.

Brett had been avoiding me all morning, and regardless of the fascinating history that he was absorbed in—something on parchment, in ancient Icelandic—he was escaping. The curve of his shoulders was a dead giveaway.

'Well?' I repeated. 'What did he say about the tree and the grain silo?'

'Do you have further reference details?'

'He didn't know sh... anything, did he?'

'He can't know everything, Angela.'

'Your omniscient? Why are we running?'

A great sigh escaped him. Or maybe it didn't escape. Maybe he wanted me to think it escaped.

I ignored it. Reykjavik's food was disgusting and I couldn't be bothered looking for a *Barbara* in their barbaric language. And this library made me sneeze. 'Brett, or should I call you—'

'No, Angela. Please. I am ready.'

'Good.' Anything was better than this aimless travelling, no one to talk to, nothing to do except read my book. 'Where do we go next?'

'Burrup? Is that right?'

'Buenos Aires?'

'No. Where you *come* from.'

'Bettawong?'

'No.'

He couldn't mean... 'Bunwup?'

'Yes. Sorry. But no. Your farm, whatever you call it. Where you grew up.'

'Wooronga Station? Where Mum lives?'

He slapped his forehead. 'That's where.'

Cold sweat ran down my back. I would rather cross a Bangkok street on foot with my eyes closed, than go back there—where I had left at seventeen, for good.

'It's going back.'

'Yes, my dear? Don't you want to?'

With all my heart, no! 'Why do you want to go there? There's no library. Not even any *streets*.'

'You don't want to go back to visit your mother?'

With all my heart, NO!

'Sure.'

The sarcasm zoomed straight past his head. He smiled, lifted his arm and I grabbed it.

'Whoa, Brett. Remember your come-on way back when?'

'Come on?'

'Don't tell me you don't. Hey little girl, wanna peesa candy? Oy, Anj baby, Wanna develop your true potential?'

'Ah.'

'Was that a wink wink, nod nod, to your own selfish desires . . . and as for me . . .'

My question dangled, partly because I couldn't think of how to end, and partly because a sob cut me off—my own.'

His strong arms gripped me at arms' length. 'Angela, my dear. I was serious . . . I was *serious* about developing your true potential.'

'And I still am,' he said, as he gazed into my eyes.

My legs felt weak. My guts, like melted chocolate.

'And love?' I whispered.

His hoarse laugh rang out—a heresy in this tomb. 'More loved than you can imagine.'

37

Flies clustered at my tear ducts like beasts at a waterhole. I blew one out of my nose and sniffed. That air, hot and acrid, was the air of my childhood—translucent, pink as face powder, and scented with eucalypt.

We'd landed halfway up a slope. Looking around the scrubby forest, I didn't see any landmark that struck me as familiar. Not that I'd ever paid any attention to them in the past, but it was disconcerting not to know which way to walk. It was useless asking Brett. I had told him as close as I could, where to go. But not having pointed Wooronga Station out on a map, it not exactly being a place of world renown, we could be anywhere.

I decided we'd walk down-slope, as I was thirsty and the forest was thick in the valley, and I could get a drink from a creek if there was one running.

My boots were not made for this kind of walking, and Brett picked his way along as if he had corns. When we were almost at the valley base, I noticed a bit of black barbed wire sticking out like a finger from a large tree, the rest of the wire having been absorbed into the tree's growth. This was once a fence, and the tree was a post. Nearby, a lemon tree as thorny as a rose proved me right because just ahead, we came upon a pile of stones, a rubble chimney, and a set of iron bedsprings, now entwined with passionfruit vine.

'This isn't our land.'

I would have known it, as we kids would have played here. We had patches of valley forest, too, but no homesteads there.

'Where is this?' he asked.

I hadn't a clue, but there was a creek running and I had a drink. The water was brown and tasted like tea. I had forgotten that.

He walked back up the slope with me, and though his feet must have been sore, he didn't complain.

When we got to the top, I saw rolling hills all around but nothing familiar, and no habitation. There was, however, a power line maybe two valleys over—and that meant a road somewhere. I led, and he followed.

Rocks that we had to climb and navigate between, twisted our ankles. Small trees the likes of which I'd never seen, bristled with brown needles, needle-sharp and just as long. Then we waded through an area of waist-high blooms of pretty yellow flowers, obscuring shiny leaves, serrated as steak knives. Candy-green vines pulled at us, and didn't break when we stumbled and fell. Flies were of three kinds: the moisture-suckers, which we waved away (Brett was chuffed when he waved and I praised the style of his Australian salute), hard biting flies (they land on the back of your neck without you feeling them, until they bite), and soft biting flies (which loved burrowing into my hair).

I led, and if he lost sight of me, he could follow my words: 'I hate the bush! I hate the bush! I hate the fuckin' bush!'

With its flies and its stinks and its dirt, and its . . . there was a tick crawling up my leg. 'And its ticks!'

I would have kicked something, except that would have hurt me more than anything.

Brett watched me politely, helping me to stand when I fell.

Always in the bush, things are farther than they appear.

By the time we got to the power line, our shadows were lurching monsters.

Brett looked to me for direction. For a few moments, I was ready to tell him to do his wafting thing, to get us to some city again, but it hurt my pride, so I didn't.

I was trying to get my bearings when, to my left, just beyond a fringe of trees, a heavy truck rumbled by.

It wasn't a busy road, but I got us a ride in twenty minutes. He was a thirty-something salesman who'd once backpacked around Europe, and was disappointed when he heard my accent. Brett just listened.

'That's where we're going,' I told him when he said he was just stopping in the next town.

'Car in service,' I explained, not caring whether he believed me or not.

'McVickers?' he asked.

And wouldn't you know it? He went out of his way to drop us at McVickers, on the other side of town.

At least that gave me my bearings. We had passed a small motel a few blocks back, so at my suggestion we walked back, and Brett checked in.

Then we walked a few blocks further, to the post office in the centre of town. Above the entrance to the post office, in big white letters were the postcode and the town's name—LYREBIRD FLATS.

We were only a few hundred kilometres south and east of where I grew up. Considering my directions and the elevation we must have travelled at (I never peeked) and the distance, our missing the mark by a few hundred kilometres and a few different terrain's worth of flora and fauna, the missing 'home' part of homecoming was a trifling affair.

Actually, Brett was the one to call Wooronga my 'home'. He didn't get the message that I had discarded Wooronga Station as 'home' when I left. I had wanted to feel 'home' about someplace ever since, but that had never happened. I had once felt that home could be Sydney, until he dashed that hope. And now that we were in this boring, comfy town, as comfortably far away from what Brett called my 'home' as I had felt in Sydney, I was happy enough.

Brett, on the other hand, was confused. He stood on the pavement, taking up valuable space, as the going-home townspeople moved around him to post their letters before the PO closed.

He was so embarrassed at his off-landing that he didn't notice his nuisance value or the *tsk*s as people avoided him. 'I'll take you tomorrow,' he promised.

That was a damper on my mood, but across the street was a pub. If it didn't have steak on the menu, I was sure they could serve up a steak and kidney pie.

I was finishing off my second pie, leaving the pastry, just going for the meat, when Brett made me choke on a piece of kidney.

'Wasn't that beautiful today,' he said. 'I never knew.'

I took a swig from my bottle. 'Just what, exactly?'

'The plants, and those beautiful birds, and those animals.'

'And the flies, and the ticks.' He had collected a whole patch of minutely small tick nymphs, some of which I picked off for him (he couldn't see them). I chuckled. As I drank my beer and he reveried, those nymphs that had escaped my fingers were most likely growing fat and grapelike as they filled up at his balls.

'A mere peccadillo of yours, my dear, this concentrating on the tiny ways we're inconvenienced by nature.'

'Nature!'

'We don't have nature, you know.' He was only half-speaking to me. 'Only people in hell. I never knew a sweet little animal, or the elephant who never forgets, or the jabberwock.'

'The jabberwock is mythical, Brett. Fiction.'

'And the majesty of those vines . . . that *strength*! The little flowers that open, the tiniest birds that sing. I never saw them, Angela. I never heard them.'

'Birds can be nice,' I allowed. 'You want to look in the pet shop?'

'Would you mind awfully, Angela . . .'

I hated the bush. I hated the bush. *I hated the bush!* But it was better than going 'home'.

However, there was another consideration—the one that had brought us here in the first place. 'What about your "he's coming, whooo whooo!"'

Maybe it was the beer, but 'he' made me laugh, and so did Brett's running from him—Brett's impending act of jumping, in which he wanted me to hold the door open or something. My beer caught in my throat as I giggled, and it spurted through my nose in a burning froth, only making me laugh more.

'We've got a little time, I'm sure,' he said.

'A little time. It's so sublime, in naaature!' My slap on Brett's back was drowned out in the five-thirty drinking crowd.

He picked at his food dreamily as I sucked the last drops from my bottle.

The next day was busy. I bought a new ute (what's money for?) so I could drive us to the forest tracks he wanted to explore. Actually, he didn't think of the tracks. I did. His idea of exploring was the trailblazing we had done together, but once is enough, and he'd had his once.

Then I got a map, thick socks and pair of bushie boots at the farm supply store.

The only things Brett wanted—and he bought a lot of them—were books about the flora and fauna of the region.

We threw his books into the cab. After I looked at the map, we took off, the empty back tray rattling. The look of us in the ute without a dog running around on the back tray, struck me as funny—as unnatural as if Brett had appeared in front of the Post Office without his jeans. A dog running back and forth on the back tray, woofing at everything that passed and everything that didn't, was a ute's natural state.

It was odd also, how automatic it was for me to change gears, listen for the sounds of the engine—to enjoy driving as much as I did, since I hadn't put my foot on a pedal since I'd left Wooronga Station.

We drove south for a while before I turned off the main road, checked the map, and drove down a dirt road, through rolling hills where paddocks stretched out on both sides of the road and cattle grazed on the short green grass.

Doing my job as tour guide, I said, 'The length of the grass now and its greenness, means there's been a bit of rain, but it's still drought here.'

'Do you have droughts where you come from?'

'Does a dog bark? Worse droughts, actually.'

'Did you ever pray for rain?'

That earned him a withering look, but a short one, as the ute slewed on a curve. Then I had to back up, because we had just missed the turnoff I planned to take.

We bumped along on what had become little more than rocks and ruts.

Grunts came out of Brett, who grinned and grimaced in rapid succession.

'Sit sideways. Hang onto the back of your seat.'

'Ta,' he grinned. 'My tail.'

Eventually I parked. He stuck two books into his shirt, and followed as I led the way along a path, my bushie boots clonking loudly, to my unaccustomed ears, on roots and rocks.

It was only meant to be a two-minute walk, but he stopped at practically everything, and flipped through pages looking for the picture that told what the thing was.

'You'll see all you want later,' I told him. 'Now, come!'

He obeyed, and if you think I should have said 'good doggy,' I didn't grow up doing that. A pat on the head was sufficient.

I led and he followed until I heard a gratifying gasp behind. Then I sat on a convenient rock while he timorously crept past and uttered a series of incoherencies.

'Don't go closer than you are,' I called. 'Or nearer to the water itself.

Just beyond him, the waterfall dropped two hundred feet to boulders that had broken off this granite cliff.

The rock he stood on had been worn smooth over millions of years by erratic, but violent water-rush. Now, the waterfall was relatively tame, the flow not taking up more than a quarter of the slick area of rock, but the drop was so great and the flow of water so much, that where the fall hit far below, a cloud billowed up.

He stood, leaning slightly over, for the longest time. Luckily, there weren't any bugs bothering either of us, and the sun was pleasant, so I didn't mind waiting.

Eventually he put his hand over his heart and declaimed into the mist that rose around him, 'The pearl of a runlet that never ceases, in stir of kingdoms, in wars, in pieces.'

'Did you write that?'

A whipbird called out *whwueeeeewuip!* though it might not have bothered, for all the attention he paid it, standing in a sort of trance.

I gathered up some gumnuts and threw them into the little pools near my feet, watching them get taken up and carried on to the next pool, and then the next, and then along the race to the inevitable oh-ver! In a hundred years, any of them could be giant trees.

My rock was warm but not hot in its bit of shade, so I shut my eyes, leaned back against a boulder backrest, and dozed.

'Furuike ya!' Brett's side was to me, and he crouched on the slick dry rock in front of a water dragon that was still as stone except for its neck, which puffed like silent bellows.

'Kawazu tobikomu, mizu no oto,' Brett whispered, which the lizard took to mean that this creature of the big shadow *did* see him, and that it was time to move, which the water dragon did at a furious pace, head high, the front of its body held off the rocks by fat fully armoured front legs.

'Did you see that?' laughed Brett as he turned to me.

His eyes shone brown and blue in the dappled light, full of sparks of brilliance caused by running water lit by the bluest of blue skies overhead. He walked to a place beside my rock and picked up a handful of leaves, flowers (already shrivelled), and strange nuts. 'Look at this,' he said, and he proceeded to teach me all about them.

'This is the fruit . . . yes, I know it doesn't look like a fruit, but it is the fruit. See where the seedpods are? of the spiny hakea. Those things you hated yesterday. Well, one of them . . .'

There were a dozen plants he had found the names for in his books, and every one of them went into his shirt pockets after showing me. 'And do you know about all the things that you call one thing, but is really something else?' His enthusiasm was so real, it was childish, and charming.

'No, Brett,' I smiled.

'I know you do, but I'll tell you anyway. There's native peach. And it's not a peach. I can't find any here, but it's supposed to be here. And native plum. But I don't think there's any here. And native cherry. No relation at all. Cupressiformis, in fact! Do you think this looks like a cherry?'

He placed into my hand, a small green berry sporting a little red bopple on top. It was cute, but not something I'd ever noticed before.

'It comes from that tree.'

A lovely weeping willow sort of tree stood modestly just a few feet away.

'It's a parasite!' he said, his eyes big.

'No!'

'Yes,' he chortled. And he launched into telling me all about how it leeches off the roots of certain eucalypts.

And then he dragged me to look at the sundews clustered in the damp places in the track. Their small beads of clear sticky insect-trapping syrup caught the sun like tears of joy.

I had planned for the waterfall to be a quick stop. Then we'd have lunch back in town and a short walk in the afternoon, maybe along the beach. Instead, I barely got him into the ute by the last gasp of day.

I was dodging the sun's glare before dusk as I drove along the dirt road, when I saw something that made me laugh.

'See that farmer there?' I said, without taking my eyes off the road.

'A farmer?'

I drove around the bend and parked where the farmer couldn't see us.

'Did you see him leaning over that hole in the bank in his paddock, and jerking away?'

'You saw all that?'

'Do you know what he was doing? You wouldn't, but you, travelling with the A-Grade Tour, will have sights explained that only locals know the mysteries of. Aren't you lucky?'

I felt pretty good, enjoying driving and the scene. That old bloke should have had a heart attack, the way he jumped away from that hole as we drove past.

'It's getting close to dark.' I explained, as if it weren't obvious. 'The wombat . . . wombat. Furry tank-shaped thing, as heavy as a pig.'

'I know wombats.'

'Oh. Oh, those books.'

'Well, yes, and also "O uommibatto. agil, giocondo, che ti sei fatto liscio e rotondo!'

'Brett, I'm an English masters, not a polyglot.'

'Sorry. Well, then you must know her brother's poem, "O how the family affections combat within this heart, and each hour flings a bomb—"'

'Do you want to tell, or learn?'

'Sorry. Learn. What was that man doing?'

He'd ruined the moment. I told him anyway. 'He's trying to kill the wombat down the hole.'

I drove on a ways.

And then, feeling as bad as I did, I couldn't leave it there. 'He's probably using phosphene. It goes off sort of like a bomb. Poison gas.'

When we were almost to town he asked, 'Why does he want to kill wombats?'

'Because they dig holes.'

'Aren't they native?'

'Yes, Brett.'

'Aren't they a protected species?'

'What have you been reading?'

'Other than these,' Brett said, 'Wildlife in the—'

'Okay,' I said. He was clearly going to list a library's worth of stuff. 'I once pulled a calf out of a wombat hole,' I said. 'Tractors turn over all the time in holes that open up over wombat tunnels. Wombats are killers, Brett.'

'Why don't people eat wombats, and not cows? Cows aren't natives, are they?'

'No, Brett.

He pointed. 'Those are kangaroos?'

'Yes, goddamit.'

'Why don't you eat those?'

'Because the animal liberationists don't want us to.'

'Why—'

'Brett. Just think about little flowers. I've gotta watch the road.'

I found a pub that had steak. So when Brett said he wasn't ready to order, I said, 'Stuff it,' and ordered for me.

The meat was tough, but it was meat.

Brett watched me cut, chew, and swallow as if he were a Martian and me, his first earthling.

'That's beef, isn't it?'

'Give that man a coconut!' I announced with my mouth full.

'From cows.'

'Yeah, Brett.'

'My tartare au jus was that, too, wasn't it?'

'Well, it wasn't whale meat,' I laughed, wanting to poke my fork into his face.

'It never occurred to me.'

'Well, what the fu—'

'All these centuries, I've lived on the damned. You.'

It might boggle your mind, but I lost my appetite right then.

'You eat all those creatures, don't you?' he asked, wagging his head toward the great outdoors.

'Us civilised folk eat only the ones we domesticate, like cows and sheep and pigs, and chickens. That's white meat.'

'All those creatures with the big eyes.'

'Most of us don't go in for the eyes.'

'Do you domesticate octopus? Wasn't that your favourite?'

'Yes it was. And no, octopuses don't tame very easily, and they're buggers getting through barbed wire. Just don't agonize, eh? Or you'll starve.'

'Do vegetables feel?'

'For gawd's sake!'

'I think I'll eat fruit that's fallen from trees, and plant the seeds. And also, I could eat vegetables that have withered on the vine.'

'And seeds that have fallen from the grasses. That's wheat.'

'Oh, really?'

'And nuts and berries, and Greenpeace banners, once they have fallen from their ramparts.'

'Does grass have leaves?'

Oh, shut up, Brett!

We bought him a bag of apples at the supermarket, and walked back to the motel.

I turned on the TV and switched channels until I found Game of the Century, something with a wheel that turned, money being held out as prizes, and people who were chosen for their competitive levels of stupidity and ugliness.

Brett sat on the bed that would have been his, had he wanted to use it. He wanted to talk, so I turned the TV up.

There was only so much of this program that I could take. But even the commercials didn't budge him.

Finally I punched the OFF button and turned to him. 'Isn't it time for you to take off?'

He sighed as Thoreau might have, or Simone and Gordon when they clicked, as the euphemism goes.

'Thank you, my dear,' Brett sighed, 'for this glorious day.'

Bedsprings creaked as he disappeared in a whiff of iron heat.

Even the electric jug waiting for me beside the little sachets of tea and instant coffee, and the four little shortbread biscuits in their cellopak, and the little jug of milk in the cheerily humming fridge, didn't lighten my mood.

I curled up in bed without taking anything off, even my boots.

Great waves of aching loneliness rose from my stomach.

Brett had bettered my education so much that I didn't dare ask where he got these words he spouted. I didn't know what was original from him. He was a sponge that soaked up everything it touched. And the problem was, it was touching everything.

The waterfall, something I had found on the map and thought would be cute and no sweat, had turned out to be a disaster.

It was beautiful, but his Victorian ravings made it impossible for me to take my mental snapshot, and drive on to the next sight. He eclipsed the small amount that I did know about the bush, by knowing so much more, immediately. And the worst part is that he fell in love with the bush in the way only possible to people who haven't grown up in it.

When I lived in Bettawong, it never bothered me when people spouted idiocies about it. We weren't in the bush together. Now, what was there for me to say, when he took only a few hours to become as obnoxious as a Jehovah's Witness?

There was no escaping the fact that the person this 'Brett' wanted to be, and had to a large degree become, was a crass enthusiast.

There was nothing left to say to him.

I got out of bed and picked up my bag and the ute keys. There was no reason to pick up the room keys or lock the door.

The engine purred on idle, but What was the use? There were only ten dollars in my bag, and where could I go? He would find me, wherever. And where would I want to go, anyway? I had nothing left to go to, and everything behind was ruination.

Sleep was my only refuge, my only escape, so I went back to the room, kicked his black bag and trunk for a bit of enjoyment—and crawled back, boots and all, into bed.

38

'Wakey Wakey!'

His hand smoothed the hair from my face, and his warm mouth kissed my forehead in the apex of my widow's peak.

I opened my eyes, and he gazed into them. He was lying on his side, but rose to a sitting position. He used both arms to turn me from my side, to my front. He positioned a pillow under my head, and then turned my face sideways, towards him.

His hot lips brushed the tip of my nose, and I smelt the rich meatiness of his breath.

His hands worked at the buttons on the back of my thin, damp chemise. As he released each seed pearl from its little fabric loop, he kissed the naked skin exposed. When he got to the deep, curved base of my back, he peeled the cloth from my back like a lychee skin from its fruit. Every cell in the powder-fine pores of my back—every cell felt the air that was stirred by him as he rose above me.

With one of his rock-hard arms, he reached underneath the fabric still clinging to me, and grasped me below, his forearm crushing one of my breasts as his hand cupped what it could of my other. My chemise came away in his other hand, and dropped somewhere soundlessly.

My long skirt was fastened in a complicated lacing, at my front. He turned me over onto my back.

'Grrrrr,' he said, as his teeth tore at the weak ribbons. His hands did the rest.

My bloomers, as translucent as bruised rose petals, trembled at the sudden movements of him, as he sat upon my calves. And in a moment, the waist-front to waist-back slit in the bloomers was open to his gaze, and his fingers.

Did I tell you he was naked? That his tail had snaked around and now ran its heart-shaped parson's nose against the curve of my swollen mouth?

That my hands rose to take hold of it, and that his stronger hands grabbed mine, and pinioned them to the bed?

That he held my hands while he lowered his body till the top of his head was lower than the centre of my beauty, and that he turned his head sideways just enough so that his left horn, slowly and gently and smoothly.

'Wakey Wakey!'

A hand shook my shoulder. *Irritating*.

'We have to leave, Angela. *A voice against my ear, urgent*. 'We have to leave!'

The room was dark. Only the green glow of the TV light and the little white numbers of the clock alarm glowed.

That irritating hand, shaking me again.

'Angela—'

I yanked myself away and turned over. 'It's bloody three o'clock in the morning, Brett. Get lost again.'

'Angela—'

'What the fuck!'

I jumped out of bed, ready to clobber him. But when I looked for his face, I saw that, even in the weird light, he already looked clobbered.

'What's wrong?' I asked, sitting on the bed and wishing I smoked.

'We have to leave, my dear.'

'Where? Why?'

I wanted to crawl back into my dream. Even now, the centre of my beauty, which Brett had so praised, was pulsing, hot and angry. If it could have cried out, the town would have woken. As it was, the only sounds accompanying our discussion were the hum of the fridge and my own erratic breath.

Brett took my hands in his. 'Angela. It's time. We must go.'

'Where, goddamit!'

'Wooronga.'

'Home? I mean—' I was so mixed up that I called it home when I didn't mean home, but then again, I didn't have a home anymore.

He looked terrible, which was oddly calming. I got up and sat in the only chair, so I could evaluate.

'Tell me,' I instructed.

'He's coming. Tomorrow.'

I didn't have to ask who *he* was. 'To check up on you?'

'And he wants to meet you.'

'Why the? Why me?'

'Why did I want to take that aeroplane flight?'

'And you told him Wooronga?'

'I thought you would be your strongest there.'

'You told him to go to Mum's place?!'

'Wasn't that—'

'No! That was not bloody right.'

A fierceness I hadn't felt before, came over me. Mum was Mum. She couldn't help who she was. She would die some day still yearning to be me, still yearning to get away from there, but she would never escape. At least she would live as she probably did now, in hope of living vicariously through me. That in itself is a kind of life.

Whatever this 'meeting' of Brett's was, I could not let it happen on her turf, where I was born.

'You can't meet at Wooronga.'

'I told him—'

'Well, you puff right back and tell him—'

'It must be near your place of origin.'

'No!'

'I have a plan—'

'Plans!'

I got up and flicked on the overhead light. His colour did not improve. He was puce.

'Angela. It's where I'll, as you say, jump.'

He began to shake like someone with the DTs. 'Please, Angela. I promise you—'

And bloody hell—he keeled over onto the floor, totally ragdoll.

I boiled the jug and made myself a cup of tea. It was the same brand I grew up with, and it all came back to me now how useful strong, milky tea is (with two sugars, of course) when you need to collect your thoughts. When the tea was finished and I was ready, I pulled and lightly pummelled the crumpled ragdoll into a sitting, though still groggy position.

'Brett, can you go back tonight, and change the plans?'

He lifted his cap to rub the side of his head. 'Why?'

'Please tell him the Bunwup Cafe, Friday, at noon.'

'Noon?'

'Noon this time, two days from now this time. And Friday noon has provenance. It makes me feel more confident.'

I smiled and punched him gently on the shoulder. 'A deal?'

'I'll try.' He sounded uncertain.

'Don't try. Do!' I yelled, but he'd already disappeared.

When the last shortbread biscuit was a distant memory, he returned, baggy-eyed but smiling victoriously.

Outside, the sky was the pink of a galah. Four thirty in the morning.

I was glad to see him. There was no point hanging around here, especially since I had made up my mind what to do. Go to Wooronga, get a good night's sleep, and—this part gave me a few laughs while I waited—achieve my full potential, and love.

Mum would be embarrassing, but then again, I wondered why I should be embarrassed about her on account of Brett.

'I'll drive,' I said, after I told him what I'd decided.

That, conveniently, agreed with his wishes. He picked up his bag and trunk, tossed them on the back tray, and we left.

Brett's head hung out the window so far he should have *woof*ed as he tried to see everything we passed. The sky blued gradually, and his cries of amazement gained in distracting power. When he made a particularly sharp sound at a cloud of white cockatoos, I reached over and turned on the radio.

Wouldn't you know it? Like I should have known, like I never shoulda left, Slim Dusty's hangdog voice intoned, *'It's lonesome away from your kindred...'*

Brett pulled his head in from lapping up the sights, but he didn't say a word, even if he did notice the way my tears gushed to the maudlin music. I cried for my life, for the lack of anything ever coming true like in the fairy tales. I cried for myself, for the death of my dreams.

Oh, sure, I drove on with him beside me, to meet something I could only define as another one of my adventures-to-be. It was better to think of them all as adventures. The adventure in the cathedral with the terrifying staircase, the adventure of the great writer, the adventure of my life being stolen...

39

WE DROVE THROUGH tall, olive-green eucalypt forest, past the occasional bloated bodies of kangaroos and wombats—night road kills tumbled to the shoulder of the road. Through one-street towns, and signposted villages of one house. We progressed ever inland, through ever drier country. Air shimmered ahead on the hot tarmac. We passed fields of young wheat, and cattle, and then mostly sheep, rocks, and short tough clumpy grasses. We left the tarred roads, and the metal tray behind us banged, Brett's bag and trunk jumping on the frypan-hot aluminium. From a far hill, looking down on us, you might not see the white cab or the glitter of its tray behind, but our wake of dust rose high before settling again, on the scurfy brush all around the gravel track. Several times we were stuck behind a mob of sheep, their little dog masters pushing them from the back and keeping them in order from the sides, a horseman in the lead.

I pointed to one scruffy little worker, never stopping in its weave from side to side across the back of the mob, her eyes locked on her charges. 'See that dog? Dad would've called her a good 'un. Red kelpie. The best. Wouldn't have a bar of your sooky border collies.'

Brett hmm'd politely, but his eyes were as locked on as the dog's.

And before I was really ready, we were bumping down a familiar road, which ended at a gate with the inevitable sign, 'PLEASE SHUT THE GATE'.

Nothing had changed. The hills had not changed their shapes. The stones were still as numerous. The sheep in the distance still looked like lice roaming the head of a grizzled gnome, a gnome with short mouldy hair, all grey-green mottled, and patches of his sunburned scalp showing through. The roof of our house still showed like a wart on the side of his head.

'This is it?'

'Yes, Brett.'

'How beautiful.'

'Yeah,' I laughed.

'I didn't mean it *that* way.'

My first instinct was to take offence, but flicking a peer at him out of the corner of my eye, I saw he didn't *mean* to be obnoxious. In fact, at that moment, I understood for the first time, tourism.

'Where does your place end?' he asked.

Ignoring the 'your place' bit, I answered. 'Not for a long ways. You can't see it.'

'Who's that?' he pointed.

The late sun backlit a hill at our side. On its ridge—the silhouette so sharp it could have been a cardboard cutout—stood a horse and rider.

'One of the hands. Can't run this place without them. Open the gate, Brett.'

'Where the hills are twice as steep and twice as rough. Where the horse's hoofs strike firelight from the flintstones every stride—'

'Brett—'

'Is this near Snowy River?'

'No, Brett. You wanna open the gate, or shall I?'

Never having wrestled a farm gate, he needed help, and a further 'Hey, where's that gate running to!' before I could drive through. While he swung the heavy thing closed and positioned it, and struggled getting the chain over the ball, I had a few moments of solitude for my own thoughts about the home I'd left forever at seventeen.

The horseman on the hill that had brought Brett to poetry was one of those scenes just made for tourists, and just as ethereal. Now, when I looked for the horseman, he had disappeared, either over the back of the ridge or lost in its shadow.

We rattled down the dirt track, and had almost arrived when Brett drew my attention to the sounds of yapping and hoof beats close behind. It was too dark for me to see them, what with looking into my own light beams ahead.

I stopped the car. We hadn't announced our coming.

In a few moments, the horse arrived by the driver's side. The rider jumped off, said *shush* to the dog, who had its own ideas about this matter (Dad would have been proud of the dog—taking its responsibilities seriously), and then there was a wide-brimmed hat with a face somewhere underneath thrust near my open window.

'Lost?' it said. 'Angela!'

'Mum.' I turned to Brett. 'This is Mum.'

He leaned over me. 'Pleased to meet you.' He thrust his hand over me, to shake hers.

She wiped her hands on her moleskins before she took his, and even so, apologized. 'Sorry for the smell. It's lambing time.'

Brett didn't know what she was talking about, and looked to me.

So did she. 'If I'd known you were coming, Angela . . .'

'No worries, Mum.' This was getting embarrassing. 'We'll meet you at the house.'

She galloped off, following by her little protector.

She was waiting for us when we arrived, and it was odd that she hadn't chained the dog. It was beside her, yapping its head off, clearly wanting to rush out to greet us one way or another. She crouched beside it, and held its collar.

'He safe?' I yelled.

'Let's see,' she called back.

'Brett, come behind, Brett,' I ordered. 'No. Leave your bags.'

He came behind obediently, and I offered my hand to the dog, who accepted me grudgingly.

'It's Fly,' Mum explained. 'He's a little spoiled now.'

'Spoiled!' The understatement of the year. 'Dad would never have—'

'It's *because* of Dad, Angela. And he'd kill for me, so don't you . . . Now, Brett is it? Just bend down. No, not over him! Get down on your haunches like me, and back away a bit. Now, give me your hand, and I'll . . .'

And to Brett's surprise and Mum's exclamation, Fly's tail wagged and his tongue darted out in a lick.

'You're in like Flynn,' said Mum.

'That means he likes you,' I explained.

'Just stand up easy,' she said, 'so the spell ain't broke.'

'His tongue meant he liked me?' Brett's question was uttered in a low, amazed warble.

Mum heard it, but didn't notice the stupidity. 'Fly says you're right by him.'

'Get your bags, Brett,' I said.

Mum opened the door (and incredibly, let Fly in), turned on the lights and probably went to the kitchen to put the kettle on.

I waited for Brett, because he had to be introduced to country ways.

'Take off your boots and leave them outside with these.' I pointed to the assortment of shoes and boots, all upside down, lined up on the verandah. 'And hang your cap on the rack inside the door. I'll take those.'

I took the trunk and bag from his arms, dumped them inside by the door, and went to get that awkward homecoming phase over as soon as possible.

Mum was messing about in the kitchen. She worked with her back to me, said she didn't need any help, and asked would I mind just Lanchoo tea, she didn't have anything fancy.

I told her that Lanchoo was just lovely (and meant it, though from her grunt, she didn't believe me), and she asked if I minded milk and white sugar, and I told her that would be great, and she opened the biscuit tin, and then banged it shut, and concentrated on the tea, and how did Brett like his, or would he perhaps prefer coffee?

And he still hadn't come into the house, so I went out to see what was wrong.

He stood just as I had left him, in his boots and with his cap on.

'What the . . . ?'

'Angela. Your mum.' He hovered over his boots. 'Would she mind terribly?'

This was stressful enough without his problems. 'You've got a thing about those bloody boots. Just wipe them well.'

'Thank you.'

'But take that thing off your head, or I'll tear it off.'

The coconut fibre mat got the drubbing of its life until I said, 'Enough.'

As he came in the door, I plucked the cap from his head. He grabbed for it, but missed. It landed on a hook on the wall, just as Mum came out of the kitchen.

'White and two is it, Brett?'

'Ta,' I said, and she ducked back into the kitchen.

He took the cap off the hook, and I snatched it again and hooked it so hard, the ball end of the hook popped through.

'Leave it!' I hissed. 'She's seen you without it. The boots are bad enough, but it would be double-rude now to put that on.'

He gave up the fight, and instead, stood waiting for instructions.

The row of hooks was as full of hats and coats and stock whips and other paraphernalia as I remembered.

The walls looked the same. On the opposite wall, show ribbons gleamed. Blue and red, with their big rosettes that had always reminded me of the roofs in Hansel and Gretel's land, from their snowdrifts of flesh-coloured bushdust. On the wall by the kitchen, just above the wall phone, a calendar from the local stock agents displayed a fine Hereford bull.

Another table smaller than I remembered stood in the place of the old formica thing, and this table was veneered wood. Newish metal and plastic chairs surrounded the table, these of a style popular in the sit-down part of Chinese take-away restaurants. There still wasn't a sofa, but there were now three sat-out easy chairs, in what had once been plush.

The desk in the far corner was piled high with papers. One of the Chinese restaurant chairs was its desk chair.

There was the same low bookcase I remembered. There were the books of my childhood: *Mother Goose*, *Grimm's Fairy Tales*, *Anderson's Fairy Tales*, *Alice in Wonderland*, higgledy-piggledy against *Diseases of Livestock* and *Toxic Weeds of Australia*. The pile of games—Snakes and Ladders, Monopoly (I always got the koala, as Dad thought I liked it best), Scrabble, draughts—looked like sedimentary rock. On top of the bookcase family photos clustered beside a drenching gun and a pair of work gloves curved as if there were hands still in them.

The light was the same overhead thing, its hanging frosted dish needing to be emptied of flies. The floor was still lino, but a newer piece.

Looking beyond the lounge to the sag of the clinkerboard walls of the hallway, I remembered a childhood nightmare—our house was really a holed ship, and we were sinking.

'Your tea,' Mum announced, bringing out three cups on saucers, on a yellowed aluminium tray.

'You sit here,' I told Brett. Mum sat at the place closest to the kitchen, and we all sipped at our tea as if it were hot, when in fact, it was almost stone cold.

'You look exotic,' Mum complimented me, and then turned to Brett. 'The furthest I've been is Cunnamulla once. Our daughter's the world traveller.'

I rolled my eyes at Brett. It was his fault. Now that she'd begun, she'd be impossible to stop.

'How's—' But my casual question curdled in my mouth as I caught the drift of her gaze. It was locked on Brett's horns. I had forgotten them in my hate for that cap and in my wish to not give Mum fuel for her fire of vicarious cosmopolitan living. But Mum's powers of imagination could never have encompassed horns.

The possibilities raced around my brain like rats in a grain bin. Would Mum have a heart attack, in terror?

She grasped my wrist. 'Remember Boofhead?' Not taking her eyes off Brett, she said, 'She wouldn't. Angela was just a teenager then, and it was just part of our boring life here. There's his ribbons.'

Brett smiled at her with a guest's politeness, not knowing a bloody thing she was talking about.

I reached over the table and touched her hand. 'I remember, Mum.'

The death of Dad, and her aloneness . . . premature senility? She was only fifty-something, but this place could turn anybody batty.

It was as if she hadn't felt my touch. 'Your horns are a sight. Just like Boofhead,' she said. 'We read here, about all this plastic surgery out in the world. And Stuart now, our son,'

She turned to me. 'Stuart's got his torn ear . . . remember his torn ear? It got restored in Nashville, for the record cover.'

'If we'd had that out here in my day . . .' she said to Brett.

'Thank you,' he smiled.

She got up from the table and pulled over a basket. I had forgotten this nervous quirk of hers. She plonked an enormous cable-knit jersey in her lap and turned to Brett, though she was already plying her needles, their wood clacking like castanets.

'They do marvellous things with plastic surgery,' she said. 'But ears. Remember Alfie Gallagher, Angela? His cousin married a Yank in the war, and anyway, his nephew came to visit only a couple years ago. We all thought he was a bit much with his tee shirts, till he gave a talk at the Bunwup Library. It's bigger now, you know. Anyway . . .' she yanked her yarn as if it were a stroppy ram. The arm she was knitting had grown at quite a clip.

'As I was saying, oh. More tea?' she asked Brett. Actually, she hadn't taken her eyes off him for a moment, though the complexity of the pattern she was knitting would have taken a computer knitter ages to program.

'No thank you,' Brett answered, his eyes big as soup plates.

'Just say when,' she smiled. 'Now, Jerry Drew, I think that was the young bloke's name. He spoke about that mouse with the ear on top.' She turned to me. 'You know that mouse, Angela?'

'I know the mouse, Mum,' I sighed.

'Well, you weren't interested in science before,' she said a trifle defensively.

'That mouse, Mum, got a lot of press.' I had read about it for the first time during my ensconcement, when the picture of it sporting a man's ear on its back like a taxi does a pizza sign, hit newspapers around the world. It was weird, but so what.

'We've got a district volunteer force,' she told Brett. 'All set to go for 'em if they make it into the district.'

She turned to me. 'Cane toads still haven't.'

'What is it about these mice?' Brett asked.

'Genetic engineering,' she said.

'Bollocks!' I couldn't help myself. 'Mum. They're for people who lose their ears. They can have a new ear. It's grown on the mouse.'

Brett's eyes went from me to Mum.

She snorted. 'That's exactly the story we read, and the stories in that scrapbook Jerry showed us from America!'

'Well Mum,' I laughed. 'What did this Jerry sell you?'

Her needles clacked extra sharply. Did I tell you that she would have spun the yarn for this bloody jersey, too? She could never just sit. 'How many people you seen with no ears, Angela?'

She didn't look at me when asking the question, so why she should look over at me now, just made my face burn more.

'And how many, Angela, who'd want no spies in their shearing shed or the sale yards, or snooping all over their property, or right in their house? No one, Angela, trying to earn a crust needs a bunch of spies around the place.'

She wasn't looking at me now. Just Brett.

'Smart boy, this Jerry. Told us something he got from Abraham Lincoln, and that man knew government. "You can kill some of the mice all of the time, but you . . ."'

'Can't kill all of the mice all of the time,' Brett smiled.

'Too right!' she exclaimed.

'And how do they report?' he asked.

'Nanotransmitters. Programmed to transmit straight to the tax office, the Lands Board. My word! Wherever they tell them. And, no offence, Angela, but some jumped-up Bettawong bureaucrat telling us—'

This was too much. 'Codswallop!' I yelled.

Mum and Brett regarded me politely. This made everything much, *much* worse.

'Mum,' I said. 'I know more than you do about these new mice. It was *one* mouse. Only one mouse's picture that went around the world. And it was a *hoax*, Mum. It was a plastic ear. Glued on that mouse, and it *fell right off* after that picture was taken.'

Mum's face fell. Brett looked at his hands.

'Well, I guess we're pretty isolated out here,' she said. 'And you in the city—'

'And another thing,' I said, as this contrition of hers was a new slap in my face. 'That's typical of these big-city plastic surgery miracles.'

'Oh,' she said, taking up her knitting again, and looking at Brett. 'I shouldn't have been so . . . things just fall off?'

'Yeah, Mum,' I said. 'All the time.'

'I guess progress is never what it's cracked up to be. Doesn't seem to be any better than your false eyelashes. Remember—'

'More tea?' I asked Brett.

'Angela once cut the eyelids off—'

'Mum!'

'What, Angela. Do you want tea?'

'No, Mum.'

'Well then. Angela once—'

'Tea, Brett?' I asked, getting up.

'Strewth, Angela!' Mum plonked her knitting on the table. 'I can't afford you to burn out another element. Two sugars is it, Brett. And white?'

We all had another cup of tea.

Fly settled at Brett's feet, to which Fly formed a curious attachment. He followed Brett as Brett went to the toilet

'Down the hall, first door on your right. Don't flush if you only pee,' I yelled, to Mum's mortification.

Mum didn't make a mention of the boots, though she did blink.

The dog followed Brett back to the table, and settled again at Brett's feet.

We sat together at the table tapping our nails against the empty teacups for a few minutes, with the dog being a welcome distraction, as he moaned in a sort of ecstasy.

'How long you here for?' Mum asked.

'Only a couple days,' I said before Brett could reply.

'She wanted to see you after hearing about her dad and brother,' Brett said, pipping me at the post yet again. I could have screamed—but couldn't.

'That reminds me,' said Mum.

She moved her chair back with a clumsy scrape on the lino, and went to the desk. She opened the top drawer, took out an envelope, and dropped it off on the table in front of me. She was halfway down the hall already as she said, 'I'll make up your room.'

The envelope was plain and un-addressed—just a holder for its contents. It was not gummed down, so I opened it and took out what it held. A dirty, torn receipt almost two years old from the local farm coop for a pair of work gloves. I turned over the receipt, and in the flesh-pink of local, soft stone was a scrawl, partly torn through the paper:

Little Blossom
Sorry I hurt your feelings.
Im sorry.
I loved you
Dad

40

I NEARLY BROKE my ankle getting down the veranda steps in the dark in my stocking feet, but the water tank was just behind the house.

Where Dad used to stand and cry, not knowing that anyone knew, I cried.

That was *such* a mean thing for her to do. It was that thought that enabled me to make my way back to the house quickly, and dry-eyed.

Voices were coming from Mum and Dad's room, and then Brett and Mum came back into the lounge.

'I've made up my room for you,' she explained to me. 'And sorry, but don't turn the hot tap on at the bathtub. I'll fix it tomorrow.'

She came over and kissed me on the forehead. 'I'm sorry, but it's past my bedtime. Nightie night.'

'And pleasant dreams,' I said, reverting to five-year-oldness.

She slapped her thigh for the dog to go with her. 'The lights,' she said.

'Yeah, Mum.'

They entered one of the bedrooms, and she closed the door.

I walked down the hall to my bedroom and opened the door. My bed was still there, tipped up against the wall to make room for junk—a broken concrete sink, a box of firewood, those old metal and plastic chairs I remembered, the old formica table . . .

Brett was in the lounge, looking at the family photos.

'Isn't it your fly time?'

He nodded.

'Well, then do it,' I said. 'And Brett,'

'Yes?'

'Friday. That's it.'

'Yes, my dear.'

He dawdled, so I turned off the light and went down the hall, had a quick pee into a toilet bowl already yellow with lots of it, didn't brush my teeth, and entered my parents' room and shut the door with a decisive click.

The room stunk of mothballs. On the bed was the counterpane that had been a wedding gift from Mum's aunt. Quilted eucalypt-green satin, the centre was decorated with a red and peach dahlia worked in ruched taffeta. Dad hated the thing, so it had lived in a tea crate along with Mum's wedding dress, which had also been her mum's wedding dress.

I stripped the counterpane off the bed and took it to my bedroom. Then I thought of the dust, so I carried it back to my parents' room, laid it across the foot of the bed, and opened the window all the way. The sheets reminded me of fine lawn, they were so thin. No wedding gifts that she could pull out for that part of the guest arrangements.

In one way, it was nice of her to assume, and in another way, I was angry she had presumed. This was the only double bed in the house, and the only room big enough for more than one single bed.

Brett's little black bag and his trunk had been neatly placed against the wall, and from the shiny state of the floor there, it looked as if Mum had swept a pile of dirty clothes away just where Brett's things sat now.

I took off my clothes and got into bed naked. Brett had forgotten to leave me a nightie.

I lay awake listening. Fly's claws scratched floorboards as he hunted for a flea. Outdoors, a fretful wind whinged, carrying with it the deep, neurotic where-are-you's of ewes, a horse's raspberry, the castanetting clapper of some local frogs that only clap after there has been some rain.

I woke to the gunshot pops of the tin roof announcing a summer day.

Brett was at the table tucking into a breakfast of Weet-Bix and milk.

Mum was in the kitchen. She immediately asked what I wanted, and was ready to make 'anything I have, but . . .'

'One toast is all,' I said, grabbing a piece of bread before she could.

She wouldn't let me make my own tea, but did the same thing as the night before, our three cups on saucers being carried out by her. An upside-down mug gathered dust on the drainboard.

It seemed as if they were both looking to me for the lead, but I had to find out something first.

'How are you managing?'

'Fine,' she said.

'No. What I mean is, who's running it? Why're you running around? Where's the hands?'

'The Trevithick boys. You remember them?'

'Of course.' Geoff and Des Trevithick, our neighbours—and also, being the same age as Angus and Stuart—my childhood playmates and teenage tormenters.

'They've bought the stock now.'

'Oh, good idea.'

'Glad you think so,' she said.

'But what you doing helping them?'

'I like to, Angela. And I may not have forever to do it.'

That took me aback. It was unlike her. 'You're healthy, aren't you?'

She was, if anything, tougher-looking than ever. No taller than me, she looked nothing like me otherwise. A wiry woman with long white lines radiating out from the edges of her eyes, where the hard brown leather of her face shadowed its creases.

'Aren't you healthy?' I repeated. 'What's this doomsday stuff?'

'Nothing doomsday about it,' she snorted. 'We're talking. They may take over the place. It mayn't work out, is all. Me staying on.'

'Wow!'

I picked up my cup to have a sip, but it was dry.

'You, too,' she said, flicking at a fly.

'Me, what?'

'Stuart's been at me to sell.'

'Don't you want to? You could finally . . . Have you had an assessment?'

Brett coughed.

'Excuse me,' I said to Mum, and turned to Brett.

'If your mother needs help,' he mumbled. 'I'd like to—'

'Her mother needs no help, but thank you for your concern,' Mum said, not unkindly.

'She's got the ears of a bat,' I said to Brett, knowing she wouldn't feel prickly about that.

'But Mum, you don't sound happy. What's Wooronga worth these days? You *have* gotten a proper assessment, haven't you? I mean . . . don't worry about Brett. He won't say anything to anyone. But what, a million and a half?'

'A little more.'

'So you're laughing! Even if Stuart hits you up for a few quid, you can go to Venice and Rome and London and New York, and drink good coffee and eat veal scaloppini for the rest of your life!'

I turned to Brett. 'She's made! And she doesn't know it!'

She suddenly grew taller as her spine went rigid. A muscle twitched in her cheek.

'They'll take the dog, Mum!'

A tombstone in Siberia was a cheerier sight. And more alive. I racked my brains to think what the hell was *bothering* her.

'Is it the horse? Or—'

'Angela,' she said, her jaws still clamped. 'What made you think I ever wanted to leave? To go see those places. That I want your food?'

I was speechless.

'I was born in this house. On that bed you slept on last night. I *love* this land. Those sheep aren't mine any more, but that doesn't mean I don't feel my most alive, out there.'

She flung her arm out so violently that her cup spun around, tinkling inanely against the saucer.

'But every one of our phone calls! And you sent me away.'

'Angela. From the time you were five years old, you told us in every way that you wanted to leave. We tried, Dad and I, to help you follow your dreams. I was *supporting* you, Angela. I was trying to be a mum. You've always needed an uncommon degree of listening to.'

Brett had the intelligence to imitate that Siberian tombstone in silence and movement.

There was no way I could escape this, except with a lucky bolt of lightning.

Finally, she patted my hand. 'I'm happy for your happy life, but I don't want it.'

'Her dad worshipped her,' she said to Brett.

She pushed her chair away from the table and put on a let's-change-the-subject face. 'What you folks want to do today? I just have to phone the boys about some wethers needing moving, and then I can . . . or you came wanting time to yourselves? Did you want something, Angela?'

'No, Mum.' I wanted to be able to breathe somewhere away from here, without my throat constricting.

'I think I'll drive into town,' I announced. 'Brett, you want to explore here?'

'Could I?' he asked—a little boy asking whether it is really true that he has been offered a whole birthday cake to eat.

'You know how to ride?' Mum asked him.

'No,' I said.

'No problem,' she said to him.

'I'll be back tonight,' I said.

The door slammed louder than I had meant, which made it worse now that I had to go back in to ask Brett for money.

He reached into his back pocket and pulled out a wad.

'Be ready for that meeting tomorrow,' I said, as I looked the money over before I left this time, to make sure it was for the right country.

The radio kept me company till I realized that *On the Land*, 'Stuart Pendergast's award-winning single' played with the monotony of a refrain on the only two stations that I could get. Then I drove to the sound of rain squalls and the regular squeak of the left windscreen wiper. Mostly I drove to the sound of myself crying.

I had planned to avoid Bunwup, in case I met anyone who recognized me, but by eleven o'clock I found myself in front of its library. It was open for another hour, so I went in. No one recognized me, though I recognized one of the librarians, now gone fright-wig-white. When I searched in Fiction K, and then looked up *Barbara*, I had expected it to be gone from the shelf, but I was shocked to find it wasn't in the collection. I shouldn't have been shocked. The only newish books in the place were used Barbara Cartlands.

There was a small bookstore open across the street. *Barbara* was not in the window, and I didn't want to browse, so I asked the sole person in the shop (a retired teacher?).

'We couldn't sell that here,' she answered automatically. But then she looked closer at me, and then out the window, her glasses rising on her nose as her head scanned the unbustle of the centre of town. Finally, she turned to me. 'You *are* from a bus tour?'

Mid-afternoon, I stopped at a petrol station, filled up and bought a bag of Minties. Once parked on a patch of oil-blackened gravel off to the side, I regretted my choice, as each toffee had to be unscrewed from its paper wrapper. Throwing the bag on the floor, I kicked the engine back to work.

Through squall and sunburnt sky I went, through my own sometimes blinding tears, and once, almost through my life when I left the road altogether while speeding round a gravelled bend.

All too soon it was time to drive back, and this needed some attention to map and route, which took my mind away for a while.

Before I was really ready, it was 7 pm and I was back at the front gate of Wooronga Station.

41

As soon as I got in the door, Brett was all over me like a rash. 'A thousand thousand thank you's. You have given me such joy!'

His hands, grasping my shoulders, hurt in pleasant ways. He held me at arms' length so we could look into each other's eyes. In the capricious end-of-day light dancing in through the windows, his irises were of many colours.

His joy in seeing me was unmistakable. Suddenly, I, too, felt a spurt of joy, and intense eagerness for tomorrow.

Behind him, though, Mum sat at the far side of the table, facing us and trying not to. I pulled away from Brett. 'Not in front of Mum.'

'Oh.' His hands came away from my shoulders instantly, and he bounced back to the table. Picking up a jam jar with a spray of insignificant white flowers, he presented it to me. 'We picked these for you, Angela!'

Two empty mugs sat on the table, and Uncle Percy's book.

'Tea, Angela?' Mum asked, getting out of her chair.

'Yes, please.'

'Brett says you like steak.'

'Just a cuppa. A mug,' I corrected, embarrassed. 'I've eaten,' I lied. I didn't want her cooking for me. Nor did I want to know what Brett had eaten.

'You didn't tell me he's a naturalist,' Mum called from the kitchen, as the kettle sang.

'And an artist,' I yelled.

Brett blushed. He reached up to his cheek, feeling it. 'You have a beautiful place here, Angela.'

'Thank you,' I said.

'Do you like the flowers?' he asked, strangely shy.

'Yes, Brett,' I smiled.

'You don't really,' he said, and then smacked himself on the head. 'I forgot.'

He reached back to the top of the bookcase and picked up a magnifying glass. 'Look at them now.'

They were lovely up close. And they had a freckling of lilac spots.

He picked up Percy's book. 'They're here. Would you like to see?'

Before I could say anything, he had opened to the page—the one that he'd done the big illustration of.

'It's the spotted lily, Angela. Not like all those other spotted lilies abroad. According to your uncle, uh, great-uncle, this is only to be found on Wooronga. And as you know, it isn't even a lily. It's an orchid.'

He was so excited, his words came out in jerks. 'And Angela. He only found it twice before they made him leave. Twice, Angela! Think of the portent!'

Mum came out just at that moment, like a servant does who's been listening at the keyhole but has to emerge some time.

Brett hadn't finished. He smiled at her, and then turned to me.

'For us!' he whispered.

I drank my tea while they pored over a collection of botanical specimens spread out on a torn sheet on the floor, comparing them with pictures in books that Mum took from the shelf. Then they took the plants off to the kitchen, where I heard them arranging the stuff on racks to dry in Mum's warm oven.

'We didn't get in so long ago ourselves,' she said when they came back to the lounge. 'Glorious day, wasn't it?'

Meanwhile, Fly was acting weirder as the evening wore on, moaning around Brett's feet.

When Brett sat at the table again, he reached down in his usual way, easing his laces.

'Ah,' said Brett, in the way he always did at that action.

'Wrrrooof!' said Fly, who went ballistic, sniffing around Brett's ankles, running to Mum, going back to Brett and circling, and then, because of the level of deafness in the room, leaping on Mum's lap and snapping a huge *woof* a hair's breadth from her nose.

'That's it!' snapped Mum.

She got up so fast, her chair fell over. 'Goodoh, boy,' she said to Fly. 'I'm ashamed of you, Angela. Don't you notice anything?'

She clomped off to the kitchen, and I heard the door open and close to the outside, as she went to a little outhouse and came back.

She came in carrying buckets and a towel and a big plastic basin.

Brett rushed up to her. 'I'll take that,' he said.

'You'll do no such thing,' she said. 'Sit in that bloody chair.'

Fly agreed, happily herding Brett into one of the easy chairs.

Mum reached for his boots. 'You taking 'em off, or do I?'

'No!' he screamed—already too late.

With a mammoth pair of scissors and one snip each, she'd expertly sliced through the back of each boot, and whipped it off.

Brett's hands covered his face.

Mum rocked back on her heels.

Then she literally jumped to her feet and rushed to the desk, where she yanked on the bottom drawer. It stuck as it always had. 'C'mon, yur blighter!' she growled, and punched up from below. She pulled again and the heavy drawer came smooth as pleeze. At that, she grabbed it out and dumped it upside down on the floor—where she sat, throwing legal documents, a paper punch, a dog collar, and empty boxes out of her way. Under all that, she found what she wanted and rushed back to Brett. He still had his hands over his eyes, and was making sounds like the death moan of a fly against a window.

She grabbed one of his legs and plonked it on the thing in her hand.

'Look,' she commanded.

The plaster cast fit Brett as if he had stepped into the very mud that the cast had been made in.

Brett looked, stunned.

'Sure as eggs,' she said, matter-of-factly, and put the cast on the floor. 'You don't remember us doing this, do you, Angela?'

I did. Boofhead was a yearling then, and had just won at Wagga.

Mum got up and opened every window and the door, and threw some books onto the desk to keep the papers safe from wind gusts.

Even so, the smell was powerful—diarrhoea mixed with Limburgh cheese.

'How could you let him get this way?' Mum asked, not looking at me. 'How do you ignore your friends like this? Sorry, Brett. I don't have a good smeller.'

I wanted to leave the room, but couldn't.

'Just treat him, Mum.'

'I am, Angela.' But first, she reached over and patted Fly on the head. He had settled by the basin, where he supervised Mum.

She mixed blue powder into water.

'I would normally cut,' she told Brett, 'But I don't know how those doctors did this. And I could hurt you. Now dunk them both in for a good soak.'

Brett had stopped moaning. He did as he was told, watching Mum's every move.

'Have you gone the whole way?' she asked, sitting back on her haunches.

Brett was at a loss to answer.

'You've got a tail, haven't you?'

He nodded, incredulous.

She smiled. 'That's only proper. Angela wouldn't remember Boofhead's tail but—'

'I do,' I interjected.

'Foot rot's a terrible thing,' Mum said. 'Fly always picks it out. They must have been beautiful when they were first done, but now .. Never mind. You have this long? And why the blazes did you shove those boots on? No wonder you didn't take them off. A crowbar couldn't have shifted them.'

She clucked for a while more as she knelt beside the basin. Then, 'Up,' she instructed, as she lifted one of Brett's legs, and he lifted the other out of the water. She shoved the basin away and picked up the towel beside her, placing it in her lap. Then she lowered the hoof to her lap, and carefully dried it. Gingerly, she lowered it to the floor. Then she did the same to the other hoof. 'Can you get off the chair and lay on your tum,' she asked, 'or you need help?'

'No,' Brett said, going down on all fours.

She dragged the cushion off his chair, and some dried peas of venerable age bounced onto the lino. The cushion thudded to the floor. 'Put your head on that' she instructed.

When he was settled on his stomach, she took up position, sitting on the back of his thighs.

'Stay there,' she ordered, jumping up and going to the desk, where she found some reading specs under a pile of papers.

Settling herself on Brett again, she picked up one of his hooves and inspected its underside, running her forefinger between its cleft. Suddenly, it jerked in her hand.

'Stuhh-die!' she commanded, clamping his calf between her thighs. 'Right?'

'Sorry,'

'It'll hurt,' she said, and set to digging away the stinky stuff with the delicate touch of a watchmaker, but the speed of a dog eating dinner.

Whether it hurt or not, I can't say. He lowered his head to the cushion, and let her do what she would.

Finally, she blew into and all around each hoof, till each was clean. 'You mind Stockholm Tar?'

His neck muscles stood out as he craned backwards. 'Should I?'

'Use it for everything. Tree wounds, sheep. Love the smell of it. Don't you?'

All this time, she had been working with the odd glance over her shoulder at his face on the pillow. Now she held up the jar of molasses-thick tar. With her other hand still holding one hoof against her stomach, she twisted her torso and stretched, to get the jar closer to his nose.

'Mum!' I jumped up to take it to him, but he was already craning his neck, so I had to sit down again.

He sniffed, and then breathed in audibly. 'It smells familiar.'

It should have. It resembled his own scent when he was happy.

She tarred, and then bandaged each hoof in white gauze. 'This breathes,' she assured him, 'You're done.'

She got up off him. He turned onto his back. She replaced the cushion on the chair and helped him to climb back onto it.

All in all, this had taken almost an hour. I offered to clean up, but she demurred. 'It's easier for me than to tell you how.'

I stayed in my chair at the table while Brett sat where he had been put. He held his legs parallel to the floor.

'Put your hooves down,' said Mum, wiping her tarry hands on a piece of torn sheet. 'It won't hurt.'

He looked stuck in position.

'What's wrong?' I asked.

Mum took his arm. 'You feel unbalanced, don't you?'

He nodded.

'How long you had those bloody boots on?'

'I don't know.'

'Well, they're Fly's now.'

And it was true. Half of Brett's left boot was already in Fly's stomach, and the way those jaws were moving, there'd be no boots for Fly, for brekkie.

'A cuppa before bed?' Mum asked.

'Ta,' said Brett, smiling at me.

'I'll help,' I said, and went with her to the kitchen before she could say no.

'Thanks for helping, but he's a very private person,' I said, somehow needing to say it rather than having everything at her level of recrimination.

'I understand, Angela. Sorry I got hot under the collar. I was red-faced, you know . . . making such a silly mistake when you came.'

'No problem, Mum.' This was better than the feral atmosphere back there, and Mum was Mum. Since there were only a small number of hours left that I'd have to put up with her, it was better that they be civil ones.

'I shouldn't have jumped to conclusions,' she said.

'That's fine, Mum. I told you, no worries.'

'Especially since he's too old for you.'

I repressed a strong desire to scream. She'd think of me as *nightie night* age, or was it seventeen? for the rest of her life. I read that somewhere. Your image jells in someone's mind, and you are forever young, as the rest of the world grows older. She didn't look any different to me, either.

'Anyway . . .' She stuck out her elbows to pour. 'I made up your room.'

'Again?'

'No, girl!'

A sound that I remembered now came out from between her teeth. 'That's what I was trying to say,' she said. 'I didn't know you weren't a couple, and that poor Brett would have to spend the night outdoors. I made up your room for you, and Brett can sleep in mine. I'm bedding down in Stuart's.'

'That was a lot of work, Mum.'

'How often do you visit, Angela? It's nothing.'

42

We had our cups of tea and Mum took her leave. She'd fixed the hot tap, and sounds of the shower travelled down the hall.

I told Brett about the sleeping arrangements. 'You better make your bed look like you've slept in it,' I instructed.

He nodded.

'You're going out tonight, aren't you?'

'I have to,' he said.

'Are you prepared?'

'I'm still preparing. Angela . . .'

'Night, Brett.' I got up from the table.

'Angela . . .'

'*What*, Brett.' This was no place to discuss anything, particularly why he hadn't trusted me enough to let me know about his feet. I wanted to go to my room, if I couldn't leave this house yet, to nurse my hurt.

'Do you think I'm ugly?' he asked.

'For god's sake!'

'Meaning?'

'Brett. You make me so *angry*.'

'But—'

'You're gorgeous. Can you walk?'

'Yes.'

'Well, get the fuck ready for tomorrow.'

'Yes, Angela.'

He got up from the table and began walking down the hall.

I ran after him and grabbed. 'I'm sorry, Brett. This is difficult here for me. Tomorrow is D-Day?'

'D-Day?'

'Aangela, save me. Pleeeze!' I mocked.

'Yes, Angela,' he smiled.

'Well, kiss me,' I said, putting my arms around his waist.

'Nightie night,' Mum called from the hallway.

'Nightie night,' I yelled, my face lifted to Brett's, confusing him so much that he broke away, embarrassed.

The moment was lost, but this house was not exactly conducive to romance.

'Till tomorrow, Brett.'

'Yes, Angela.'

'Remember to muss the bed.'

My old room had been cleared of everything except my bed and a little night table — the same I grew up with. I got into bed naked. I had forgotten to tell him, and he had forgotten to remember.

Tomorrow is the nother day I whispered to myself — Dad's saying on the eve of momentous occasions.

My head ached abominably. My spit stunk. My armpits smelt like decaying mice. And the only good thing was that now I was awake. My nightmare of a life — awake — was better than the nightmares I had just woken from, whatever they must have been. My mattress was wet — a mixture of fear and the sweat of day. What were the dreams about? I hadn't a clue, but it was already 10 am.

I jumped out of bed and had to put my clothes on to go down the hall, to the shower. Luckily, no one was there. The only soap was Sunlight, stinking of sheep, but even that was better than my own body odour.

After my shower I went to find Brett, but he wasn't about. If he delayed much longer, we'd be late.

I sat on the sagging wood of the top step, calling out occasionally, a great way to increase one's headache and general bonhomie.

Just when I was ready to cry, he rushed up from behind the house.

'Good morning!' he called.

I rattled the keys in my hand. 'We're gonna be late.'

Mum came out the front door. 'Good morning,' Angela. Have a good meeting.'

'Thanks, Mum. Come *on*, Brett!'

'Should I wear gumboots?' he asked.

His hooves were still covered with bandages. He seemed to have no problem walking but he looked pretty weird — so much plant matter sticking out from the gauze that they could have been Yeti feet in camouflage.

'Up to you,' I said, and jumped in the ute. 'But get your bloody arse into gear!'

As he fit first one pair and then another onto his hooves, finally finding the right bowl of porridge, I gunned the engine and counted the hours till this period of my life would be over, and the new chapter would begin.

I was just pulling out when I remembered something. 'Don't touch anything!' Leaving the engine running, it only took a second until I was back, tossing a real hat into his lap. 'Brush off the dust before you put it on.'

'Is this right?'

I glanced at him as I sped down the gravel track, and grunted.

Funny, I thought, how here I was, on the cusp of my life's fulfilment, and here he was, if anything, more devastatingly handsome than ever — and all I felt was a mighty irritation, a barbed-wire ball of anger.

I took the risk of looking at him for a longer moment — my companion, my life, my ticket to the future, there in the seat beside me. And *funny*, I thought, *how I much I really want at this moment, to smack him in the kisser.*

43

I PARKED in front of the Bunwup Cafe, which was empty, though there was a line of utes with dogs on their trays in front of the pub down the street.

Brett and I chose a round table in the middle of the unlit room. It was ten minutes to noon. The place smelt good. The lingering reek of broiled fat from breakfast made my mouth water. There was even a scent of geraniums from the collection of potted plants on the other side of the room, displayed on shelves low to the old, wavery board floor, on which the marks of recent broom sweeping showed through the forever-drizzle of talcum-fine dust. The business looked sadly ambitious. The smell of breakfast could have been the owner's own.

'Ready?' I asked.

'You didn't bring my bag, did you?'

'You didn't ask!'

I glared at Brett.

He gazed at me, and shrugged.

Three minutes late, still with no new customers, our appointment walked in.

Brett stood.

'This is Angela Pendergast,' he said, and the one he called The Omniscient strode over and said, as I had supposed he would, 'I know,' and didn't offer his hand, so I didn't stick out mine, either.

As soon as I clapped eyes on him, I wanted to laugh. He was the spitting image of what I had expected. In fact, he reminded me of a guy I saw briefly when I was a child. William Wheels was his name, if I remember rightly. He was at the Bunwup Agricultural Fair, in the middle of demonstrating how to run a sheep shearing power plant by natural muscle power, when he clutched his chest and toppled slowly off the seat of the converted Malvern Star (three gears). What I remember the most was how he fell, catching one long toenail in the pedal. The nail was so thick that I heard his foot break, but the nail didn't tear itself across. It was curved and yellow like a parrot's beak. When I asked Dad about it, he clucked with disapproval. 'Vegetarian,' he said, and though I wanted to stay and watch, he dragged me away.

I dropped my eyes to the Omniscient's toes peeking through their sandals. They were coated with grime. Otherwise, he could have been William Wheels twenty years on. Bushy beard, low-slung pot belly, stained flannel shirt. His shirt was open, and the V tattled the tale. That raw red flesh of the wattled neck and upper chest showed that the Omniscient was a meat eater of considerable appetite. From the ruddiness and roughness of his skin, he ate so much meat that a butcher would have been loath to hire him, for worry of too much meat loss from this bloke snacking from the display.

He chose my seat so I moved over and sat with my back to the window. There was a moment of silence, which I thought I should fill.

'Shall we look at the choice?' I asked brightly, picking a menu out from between the HP Sauce and the salt and pepper shakers, and handed it to Him. The other menus had slid out over the table, so Brett took one and I took another. We each examined ours.

The menu was surprisingly ambitious. Steak and eggs, steak and chips, steak and veg and chips (frozen carrots and peas, heated up, if the usual is what that meant), mixed grill (all that plus a fried egg, grilled sausage, a 'lamb' chop, grilled tomato, and a grilled pineapple slice, and perhaps a sliver of lettuce and a piece of beet root), and for puds, the obligatory ice cream. The surprising newcomers were 'homemade soup of the day' and 'homemade pudding of the day'. The attached note read: 'Pumpkin Soup' and 'Lemon Pie'.

I'd just finished reading 'Pie' when a woman in an apron printed with cherries and cockatoos arrived like a gust of wind. She smiled as if all her Christmases had come at once. I craved the mixed grill, but felt inhibited.

Brett ordered first, choosing the pumpkin soup and the lemon pie. I said, 'I'll have the same,' and Omni grunted. 'He'll have the same,' I explained. She took our orders with such delight that I wanted to order seconds all round. She asked what we would like to drink and *when*, which astounded me. I took the plunge and ordered coffee, lifted my brows, and said, 'Three all round.'

Then she asked when we would like what to be served, a consideration that almost tipped me out of my chair.

Her heels echoed as she made herself scarce.

We began to talk of this and that, in the desultory manner everyone does when there is an uncomfortable area of discussion that must be traversed, held up by small talk.

'I heard about your book,' Omni said to me and then turned, asking, 'When do you expect to finish?' at which point Brett said, 'Quite soon.'

The Omniscient played with the screw top on the HP Sauce, squeezing the plastic container till a bead of congealed sauce popped out of the nozzle onto his beard.

He wiped his beard with one hand and put the sauce back in the centre of the table. I noticed that he didn't screw the top down again, which meant that the sauce was going to dry up and do the same thing to someone else. I screwed the top back into place.

Brett coughed.

Seven minutes later, our food arrived with a flourish. There was a doily under each of the bowls of pumpkin soup. I crunched on two seeds in the lemon pie. At another time, I would have licked my plate. The coffee must have been the most expensive instant available in Bunwup.

Brett looked to have enjoyed his as much as I, though our guest only picked at his food, and finally shoved it away.

He fidgeted like someone who hates babies and is in charge of the hospital's incubator wing, and furthermore, is dying for a smoke.

Brett sat as if his powers of thought had been lost, or petrified.

I didn't know what to say, so I began with something inane.

'Too bad about all those people who died in the earthquake in Turkey.'

No one said anything.

The Omniscient explored his nose with a parrot-beak fingernail.

He found something after a while, which stretched out for quite a ways before it swung, slapping against his finger like a piece of cooked spaghetti.

He ate it.

'I always wanted to ask,' I asked. 'Why did you kill my father?'

I'd clearly interrupted him. 'Who's your father?'

'And my brother?'

'Who?' He was done with his homemade lunch, and now looked toward Brett, who shrugged and looked to me.

'Leave him out of it,' I said to Omni. 'Was it your sense of humour to stuff my brother's cry for help, with wheat?'

'Who?'

'Angus Fabre Pendergast, born Bunwup . . .'—automatic-memory-repeat, suddenly interrupted. 'But why are you asking me? Don't you know everything, plan everything, give us all our best chance in life, for us to screw up as we will?'

'Barring accidents and incidents,' He squeezed a hefty pimple in his beard, and inspected its contents.

That disfiguring blush I sometimes get rose up my face. 'But you make the accidents and incidents. Don't you!?'

He burped.

I sang into his face, 'He knows when you are sleeping. He knows when you're awake.'

His chuckle was rich with nastiness. 'Santa Claus, my dear... Angela? Now, I hear—'

'You don't give a fuck about any of us, *do you*?'

'What do you mean?'

I whispered, so I wouldn't yell. 'What about Bhopal? Why are they suing... what was the name of that company? when they should be suing you?'

He jutted out his beard. 'It was their fault.'

'What's an accident?'

'Their fault,' he repeated, like a bloody *cockatoo*. 'Aren't they being sued?'

'Exxon Valdez,' Brett said under his breath.

I pointed to the Omniscient. 'Exxon Valdez!'

'What about it? No one was killed there,' he said, taking a toothpick from a little holder shaped like a cane toad.

He didn't care. 'No *people*,' I said, accidentally sticking my elbow into my coffee cup.

He snickered. He actually snickered.

'Think of the penguins!' I said.

Brett threw me a startled glance. Well, I had never cared before, but that wasn't relevant now.

'Too far south,' said the fat slob. 'Think again.'

I couldn't for the life of me remember. 'Well, a helluvalot of something was killed.'

'Women!' he laughed, and rolled his eyes at Brett.

Brett's paper serviette must have slipped off his lap, for he bent his head under the table.

I kicked out when he pulled at my leg. There was *nothing* like 'Women' to get me riled. I was just opening my mouth, when Brett bit my leg.

'Here. I'll help you,' I announced helpfully, and ducked my head underneath.

'What the! Ouch!'

When our heads were both uncomfortably upside down and close, Brett took his mouth off my leg. 'Careful,' he whispered.

It was *way* too late for that. 'Frankly,' I laughed. 'I don't give a damn.'

And I banged my head on the table's underside on the way out from under, which didn't add any sugar to my coffee, so to speak.

I was ready, as the saying goes where I escaped from, *to chock a brown dog*. For a whole couple of seconds, I fought against the idea, and lost the fight.

Across the table, Brett stared at me. No. More than that. He actually pleaded with me with his eyes. They begged me, from the depths of their great dilated blackness, not to upset this slob at our table. I reached across and patted his hand.

'Sorry Brett, but this bastard...'

Kicking back my chair, I stood so close to the one called Him that his neck jerked backwards like a chook's.

An incoherent growl came from somewhere in my throat.

'Yes, you!' I pointed. 'I'd like to kick you so far, you'll be picking stardust outa your apricots.'

He goggled.

Didn't matter to me. I was off. 'Or how bout to Bullamanka, where they, uh, once boiled a preacher to soften their boot leather...'

His mouth opened wide as a snoring drunk, which only inspired me more.

'... and they're still as ropeable as, uh...' Watching his expression, I lost my track. But ways of speaking were coming back. 'They're still as ropeable as a...'

I lost my track again, and almost lost my stride, but one long drink of a look at the sum total of Himness in that chair, compared to his reputation, and I felt restored.

'There's not enough milk of kindness to be squeezed from you,' I yelled, 'to soften the foreskin of a *windchapped blowfly*!'

The toothpick stub fell out of the fat slob's fingers.

Brett picked another one out of the holder and offered it, only to have his hand slapped away—by both of us.

'Go on,' said the fat slob.

He didn't need to. I wasn't finished yet. 'Why, you're no better than a poke in the eye with a burnt stick. You're omniscient as a broken radar screen.'

He was laughing so loud that I had to yell.

I was *hopping* now. Hopping with both feet.

The woman with the cherried apron bustled up from the back, crooked her head at our little nativity scene, and must have judged that I was in control, for she flashed me a thumbs-up and rushed to the front door, swung the OPEN sign to CLOSED, and scuttled back to the nether regions.

I was feeling that same drunkenness I once felt just after I drank half a bottle of vodka—the same feeling I felt fifteen minutes before I was sick for the rest of the night.

A hand gripped my arm.

'Go to buggery, Brett.' I shrugged, keeping my eye-to-eye with his Omniscient One. 'This is my fight.'

The grip tightened, and Brett's hot breath wetted my ear. 'Angela!'

'Later, Brett!'

I tried to jump away, but he held me in place. He tightened his grip so much that I remembered the time he did that long ago, and cried out.

'I wondered when,' the fat slob said. He looked at Brett as if Brett had barely passed an exam. 'She's your responsibility, *Brett*,' he sneered.

'Yes, Master,' the Devil said, and bowed respectfully. But he let go of my arm.

I ran to the other side of the fat slob. 'No, Master!' I sneered at him. 'You're not *my* master.'

'Angela!'

'Later, Brett!'

I kept my eyes on the slimebag, and didn't look away.

'Mister Merciful,' I sneered.

'Life wasn't meant to be easy,' he tossed back.

That did it.

'You're not even original!' I screamed. 'You're nothing!'

I could have sworn he was taller than me.

'Nothing!' I repeated.

He was definitely shorter.

'Nothing!' I shouted.

His head didn't reach the top of the chair.

'Nothing, nothing, nothing, nothing, nothing, nothing, nothing, nothing.... nothing! NOTHING ... NUH ... *THING!*'

He was now the size of a bloated tick. And he couldn't even run. He was riveted by my eyes, until I ended that with my sole.

'Nothing!'
Even the splat he made was unimpressive.

In a moment, I was wrapped in Brett's arms, and he smacked great kisses against my forehead.

'Dead!' he laughed. 'Calloo! Callay!'

The floorboards groaned at the pounding of gumboots as he danced around the room in a jig of a thousand influences.

'You did it, Angela! *You did it! You killed The Omniscient!*'

I had to sit. 'Did you want me to?'

'Of course!'

'How did you think I could?'

'Your potential, Angela. Your potential!'

He pranced over and touched my head with a finger, then pranced away.

'That was it?'

'It's beginning.'

'And you?' I had forgotten about him.

'On the way.'

'What is that supposed to mean?'

But his back was to me and his steps were so loud and fast, he didn't hear me.

I sat there and watched him.

This was THE EVENT that was to CHANGE EVERYTHING.

Why did I feel embarrassed to be in the same room with him? He reminded me powerfully, all of a sudden, of an old woman who used to sing in the centre of Sydney during lunch hour. She wore a green tutu and sang with her ear to a conch shell, laughing with the joy of living, though she slept on the street. Another homeless person.

Needing to break the mood, I opened the door to the back and called, 'Yoohoo! Ta for the privacy! Our business meeting is over! Could we have some—'

She rushed to the door, and was delighted that our business meeting had gone well, and even more delighted when I asked for seconds on the lemon pie.

It was all too easy. I ate and thought.

He ate and smiled.

'What did you want your bag for?' I finally asked.

'I thought you could push him into it.'

'And then what?'

'I didn't know. It all depended on you.'

'And now all my dreams are coming true. And yours.'

'Mm,' he said, missing the irony.

'Why don't I feel it?'

'You should be beginning to, but there is more to come.'

He smiled with a smile that could melt glaciers, in normal conditions.

'Ready, my dear?'

'Ready,' I said, wondering.

44

I DROVE the scenic route back to Wooronga Station, which would take the rest of the afternoon. This gave me time to ask questions in a place where we wouldn't be disturbed.

I left him to his happiness for a while, as I needed to collect my thoughts.

On a long, straight stretch of tarred road, I began. 'Why did he look like that?'

'Who?'

'Don't owl me.'

'He is what you make him. You never valued him,. You disparaged his appearance, so—'

'Whoah!'

I pulled over on the verge.

'You mean I killed *my* Omniscient? Me, who never believed in a *Him* in the first place?'

'Why yes. Of course!'

'You . . . stupid!'

I opened the door and slammed it behind me, and began to walk. He rushed up behind me.

'What?'

I rounded on him. 'You idiot! I didn't kill anything. There's still your whole system up there, or down there, or wherever the fuck you come from. I don't care. I feel exactly the same as before, and you're a goddamn *fake*.'

'Angela!'

'Don't—'

I began to run, and he ran after me. A ball of paper sailed over my head.

'Pick it up!' he yelled.

I would have had to climb through a barbed wire fence if I ran any further.

I opened the ball. Every bit of both sides was covered in Brett's crabby hand. The ground was stones or tussocks. I bent a tussock, and sat to read:

Oyah! Oyah!

People of the world, Hear me.
He whom you call by many names is Dead.
His Kingdom that you have for many of your years,
lived and killed for, is No More.
I shall repeat, because it is often so that you do not Listen.
Pay attention Well.
He, Known by various names such as
He Whose Name Shall Not Be Uttered, and
God (by many names and faces) *is No More.*
His Firmament has been Rent Asunder. It is No More.
Ye shall not evermore be living your lives
for what comes After, for the After is
Here, and Now, to Every One of You, just as to the little Ants,
Every one of Them, upon this Earth.
From Conjuance, you were Born, so make that Conjuance: Love.
To Earth, you shall return, to nourish it. And Nothing More.
Wheels and Ladders are only that.
I have gazed into the eyes of the Alligator!
Yeah, Treat your Donkey Well, and Listen to your Dog.
Dig deeply your Wells of Love
And Remember: The Love of a Dog is still Deeper!

'Crikey! Have you?' I looked up, and couldn't see him.

His footsteps crunched the tussocks as he walked back to me. 'What?'

'Seen into the eyes of an alligator?'

'Of course not! I've only seen them in books. How about you?'

'Why did you write this?'

He squatted near me. 'Isn't it obvious?'

Nothing was obvious! I shook my head.

'Poetic license! It *sounds* better. "Yeah, though I walk through the Valley of the Shadow—"'

'Yea, not Yeah.'

'Isn't Yea a little fuddy-duddy?'

'Shut up and let me read!'

Ye shall not live to worry if you will Fry in Hell,
nor to rejoice at your Wings to Come.

> Your movements after Death will be of Worms,
> and then, of other *Things*.
> Ye shall not live to hope your enemies will Fry in Hell,
> nor to help them Hellward.
> For there is no Hell but what you make on Earth.
> And Ye shall not hold out some Future Joy
> to those who slave for You, for the Wings
> are not for your Species, during your breathing,
> nor your Afterlife, which is, I say
> Again, mere *Sustenance to Others*.
> Live well, and Love All, which includes the other Animals,
> who you so easily Scorn.

I glanced around. Brett had settled down in my shadow. He was pulling the insides out of grass stems, and chewing on the juicy flesh.

> And the Vegetables upon the earth,
> which, as with the Animals, were not put there, for You,
> but for Themselves. And
> each Lives as it needs to, and takes what it needs,
> and so You Shall, with
> Nothing More Unless.
> *Unless You Overstep.*
> For the One you call the All-Seeing is Dead.
> The One you called the Merciful, is Slayed, because He Wasn't,
> *and*
> Because too many of you Slayed Each other On His Behalf,
> and AND (I say) because you made the Evilest Construct:
> Your Hells and Heavens,
> so that so many of your kind, so undeserving,
> fried or flew, according to
> *your often SO WRONG Judgements.*
> Now, because you must Live with No Afterlife,
> Your Hell away from Home (your Earthly space,
> your Earthly lives) has been
> returned to you, as has your Heaven (open your eyes, to recognize),
> and Live,
> You Must, OR ELSE.

For Angela has Slayed the one you called the Merciful,
the Omniscient, God, etc.
And If you Disbelieve me, bitterly shall you laugh.

I wanted to laugh, too. And the thing hadn't ended yet. Brett was still engaged in his Walt Whitman imitation, bogging into more grass even as the pile of chewed ends piled up beside him. I dropped my head to read to the bitter end.

By many *Signs, shall you know the Truth*.
The signs of Angela are Everywhere. If you look.
§
The signs of this Truth will be many, and the Truth shall reign
FOREVERMORE.
For I was the Devil, the very *Satan himself*,
and now, she has made me one of You. I, who was the King of the Underworld,
and
am now a mere sojourner on the loveliness of earth.
She has Saved Me by her pity, and Slayed the Arrogant
Angela!
She will have no Servants carrying out her wishes.
She will have no Seers, interpreting her wishes. She is Angela,
and Orders you to
Love one Another, and the creatures of your World.
For I say again, THERE IS NO OTHER FOR YOU.
Oyah! Oyah!
If you Slay for Her, or Persecute in her good Name,
She will Hunt you Out, and the
Whole World shall Know.
Angela!
§

I sat so long with the paper on my knees that I forgot where I was, till a flock of gang-gangs screeched overhead. I straightened my back, but what could I say — *You write like a tourist to earth* ?

He had finished chewing and was now just watching me.

'What is this?' I asked.

'It's all around the world today.'

I was a bit slow off the mark, probably 'staring stupidly'.

'I sent it everywhere,' he explained.

'Every—'

'Almost. Five hundred and seventy-two languages. Newspapers, of course, but virtually everywhere. If you got mail—'

'And what is this supposed to do?' I asked, amazing myself with my calmness.

'It's a notice. A verse. A statement. A manifesto, if you will.'

Blood burbled in my veins. I could *feel* it running—hot lava, ready to spew.

'Politely speaking,' I kept my voice under control. 'This a *rave*. As in raving mad. Bonkers.'

He regarded me with benign tolerance.

'This is your plan?' I threw the piece of paper as far as I could. Its all-elbows crumpled mass boomeranged in a wind caprice, and hit me in the face. Which reminded me.

'And what's the eight for?'

'Resonance, Angela. Resonance.'

Soon, night would fall.

I walked back to the ute. He followed.

45

Kangaroos can kill you. The problem is, they're like starlets. Attracted to the bright lights, they stand still, staring at you till you swerve away or you hit them.

Which is just what I did, on a piece of curving road halfway back to Wooronga Station.

Not to worry. I wouldn't have bought the ute without bullbars. The roo bounced off.

I almost crashed, though, from Brett's screams.

Yelling 'It's okay!' didn't work. At the second 'Shut up!' he did.

'Aren't you going to stop?' he asked.

'It's dead, Brett, or will be soon.'

'But there might be a baby in the pouch.'

'You gonna be Mum?' I laughed. 'Grow up.'

He didn't pursue the matter, and the road took all my attention. Beside me, I heard the unmistakable snuffle and choke of grizzling.

That blood of mine could have fried chips. 'Pathetic!'

'Pardon?'

'Yes, master. Certainly, master. Three bags full, master! I've seen wethers—that's sheep with their nuts bit off—with more balls than you today. And the only one who said, "Bah, Humbug!" was me.'

The night was so dark I wouldn't have been able to see his face if I tried, but I didn't try, and anyway, the road was challenging. And frankly, I didn't give a damn.

'And another thing,' I added. 'That love of a dog crap. You smarm around that dog so much, he's gonna give you worms.'

He didn't reply, but at least he stopped that infernal grizzle.

Tomorrow is the nother day, I thought to myself.

Before dawn, I'd be up if I had to stay awake all night. As far as I was concerned, Brett had sold me his last encyclopaedia. I don't know why I didn't think of splitting long ago, but I felt a sense of strength and self-confidence that I never had before. I could get enough money out of Mum's bag to fill the tank when I needed, and by the time they were up, I'd be far, far away. The ute would sell, used, for less than I bought it for, but would still fetch enough to buy me a life.

46

A half-hour later, we got a puncture. I had to tell Brett to get out. He was both clueless as to what had happened, and knew as much about changing a tyre as I do about baking an angel food cake. He watched. In the starless night, I changed the tyre by feel. Just after dropping the flat on my foot, rain began to fall.

It rained all the way back, and the left windscreen wiper whinged *yeee chee, yee chee* the whole bloody way.

By the time I pulled up in front of the house, it was almost eleven o'clock.

The door exploded open, and a dog flew out. Brett hadn't even properly gotten out before Fly was all over him.

'Down, boy,' Mum yelled, running down the stairs.

'Me first,' she said, and wrapped her arms around Brett's neck. The night was so still that when she whispered in his ear, I distinctly heard, 'I'm a selfish bitch.'

He sighed. 'My little Dory.'

And they somehow made it into the house, though they were so wrapped around each other going up the steps, that Mum slipped. Brett swept her into his arms and clomped up the last step onto the verandah. The door had shut, so he kicked it open with his gumboot, and with the greatest of care, carried her through. Before the door slammed shut, Fly flew in.

I wasn't needed. I wasn't noticed. There was a big bowl of apples on the table, and Brett ate one, sitting in an easy chair, while Mum sat at his feet, unwrapping gauze bandage.

Dad had called her 'Dor', and that had always been good enough. Now, Brett went from 'My little Dory' to 'Adorable Dory Anthea' to 'My love' to terms he could have only found in Mills & Boon.

She called him 'love of my life', 'Brettskins', 'my beamish man', and 'heaven-sent', a term that stirred both of them to gales of laughter.

I watched. It didn't matter. They didn't notice.

'Justin called while you were away,' she said.

'I thought he might,' he said. 'Did you tell him we can't go to Venice?'

'Yeah. Though he didn't understand about a dog stopping us.'

'He's not a dog person.'

'He asked whether you would consider a quick trip by yourself,' she said.

'And what did you say?'

'I said that you'd talk to him.'

'I will, but the answer, should he lobby you again, is,' and he leaned over to kiss her on a crows foot, 'Not on your life.'

There was, at one point, a bit of excitement. She was sitting crossways on the chair, her legs over the side, her arms around him as they kissed, when one of her hands raked through his curls, and she jerked away.

A horn was in her hand. Her face was horror-stricken. 'Did it hurt?'

'Not a bit,' he said. 'Why don't you see if the other one comes off.'

It did, easy as cheese slices separating.

'Give 'em to Fly,' he suggested, and she dropped them by the chair.

'I expect the rest'll come off, too,' he murmured, before they clamped together again.

I could only watch so much.

'She's gonna give you worms,' I said, loud enough that they had to hear.

Then I went to my childhood room and shut the door on the sounds of mouths.

47

I SLEPT THROUGH dawn and much of the morning, but not a creature was stirring when I crept out the door, three hundred dollars richer.

There might have been a *woof* from inside the house as I pulled out, but I was down the road and out the gate before you could say 'bugger'.

The sun shone. Birds probably sang. I was in such a good mood that I stuck my arm out the window and banged on the rooftop to the sound of my brother's stupid song.

By the end of day, I would have enough money to leave the country.

The noon news brought the usual fright stuff. Health care is under threat, the opposition warns. A volcano blew in the Indian Ocean, somewhere called Barren Island. Death toll, a team of scientists, seven so far. One on critical list. A major portion of the Wailing Wall collapsed. Authorities are pointing fingers. There will be an investigation. House prices set to fall. A new peace initiative for Northern Ireland.

By noon, I was on a stretch of road that looked down upon the ocean. The ocean breeze caressed me, reminding me of how I needed to get my hair trimmed. I stopped for fish and chips, and took them to a picnic bench where I could see the beach below. I ate my lunch and watched two old blokes worm-fish.

I filled up with petrol and got in the car again. I drove for the pleasure of driving. The radio was lousy, but I kept it on, with its monotonous songs and its hourly news.

At two o'clock, the volcano had grown, and thousands were being evacuated in Calcutta. A scandal in America was causing titters worldwide—a television preacher caught embezzling. Housing prices set to fall.

At six o'clock, I was tired and in some decent-sized town, so when I came to a motel that looked okay, I pulled in. I could sell the car here tomorrow.

The next day dawned even prettier than the one before. I had slept beautifully, and wanted nothing more than to drive. I still had lots of cash, so I decided to sell when I had to.

This time, I drove inland again, as the roads were more fun. The radio quickly became crappy country radio, and the over-sombre ABC. 'This is the Australian Broadcasting Corporation,' it droned, sententiousness itself. But often, that was the only thing on, so I left it on that.

At the noon bulletin, I nearly crashed. 'The Angela Cult' was the top story. A bug in some Ramadan food, a tremor in Ayodhya, that scientist who was on the critical list being the eighth casualty in the initial Barren Island eruption (thousands unaccounted for now, but that was not the issue, which was 'eight'), followed by a rash of eights (including all the 8s in temperature both F and C, from Washington DC to Addis Ababa) . . . and then there was the sky raining ash in some places, and the drift of clouds in others . . . And by three o'clock, Angela had taken over the world.

I was on a deserted stretch of country, all needle-grass and kangaroos, when the sun blinded me on its way to the horizon. I pulled off the road, drove through a rotted barbed wire fence, and stopped.

That night, I listened to the radio until it stopped.

To a few billion people, I was already The Omniscient.

It was frustrating to be so isolated in the midst of such cataclysmic change. I wished I could look down upon the world, and then I was.

48

THERE ARE MANY versions of the rise of me. You might, for instance, have read the version popular in some parts, in which the first premonition came to the villagers of Cherry Hinton, from this notice posted by their Council.

> An increase in the sighting of rats by Cherry Hinton residents has been reported by Coun Dryden. Rats have now been seen around Godwin Way, where a resident says he recently saw at least three... More than 50 members and friends attended the February 12 meeting of the Holywell-cum-Needingworth Gardening Club... Tomorrow is the jumble sale at the Village Hall. Be there or be square.

The 'be square' part of it is the key, some experts say.

Then there are those who say that all was predicted in the world's ancient writings. And thinking back to my time in the Higher Light, this could well be true. For now I know: everything in my life before my Elevation was only preparation.

Oh, there are many fables of my rise, and as always, many falsenesses (such as being born in Haifa, Seoul, Mecca, Lourdes, and Irthlingborough, Norththamptonshire, and Last Chance, Colorado). There is now, however, only One Truth, and only One by Any Name. There is Only One Omniscient. And She is Me.

The hand that smooshed a dozen flies at once with my little finger, is now Incomparable.

'Her boots are wherefore de biggest'—one of your ditties—makes me laugh. When I smite, as I often must, I often smoosh too many, or miss the ones I meant. Sometimes I move mountains, and still miss. Sorry, but.

But you know the Truth, as was written for you—*Oyah!*

Of its writer, he would have died years ago—your years.

As for you—as the *Oyah!* says, love.

I feel your love, of course.

But I *am* bored.

Printed in the United States
30629LVS00002B/69